THE ARCHER'S ALLEGIANCE

THE LUMEN LEGACY SERIES
BOOK THREE

S.A. HEIDEN

To My Mom—
Thanks for being strong enough for both of us when
everything gets too heavy.

ONE

LUCY

ucy was many things, but patient wasn't one of them. She paced uneasily in her quiet bedchambers and flipped the amethyst dagger from her brother in her hands, anxiously replaying every moment of her evening tea with Laurent. Her feet took her from one side of her room to the other. She would approach the ornate wooden door that led to the rest of the castle, then turn and head to the window where she could see the village of the Northern Territories below.

Back and forth.

Back and forth.

It took every ounce of determination left within her to force herself to stay put in her room and not fly out to Laurent and demand he answer her questions.

It was rare for them to have any time at all together, and in the one moment she had with him, he hadn't been honest with her. The fact that he lied made her blood boil, but the more she thought about it, the more she considered that there had to be a reason that her husband-to-be kept the truth from her.

Laurent was not the icy, cruel Fae that others made him out to be. He was a kind and considerate male. He was worthy of his title of Lord and supported his people, didn't he? She trusted him to keep his word and protect her family and Micah from Jasper. That was why she was in the North. Lucy agreed to the marriage arrangement with Laurent solely for the fact that he promised to find Jasper DeValey. The rough handle on the dagger dug into her fingers as she clutched it tightly. He promised vengeance on the male who ruined her family.

She stopped herself in the middle of the chilly room and squeezed her eyes shut, trying to push away the harrowing memories she had avoided so diligently in the previous weeks.

Lucy's hands shook as she dug her nails into her palms, trying to take a deep breath. She felt her newly returned emerald green magic coursing through her body, trying to soothe her, but Lucy didn't want to be comforted.

Acknowledging her pain meant that it was real, and she couldn't allow herself to drown in it. Not now. Not when she had so much else to navigate.

Unfortunately for her, the sentient magic was insistent, winding around her forearms and blowing her long brown curly hair around her freckled cheeks. It swirled around her body and back to the sigil in her right palm, urging her to remember the real reason she was here.

She had made a promise under the shade of the great

tree that held the portal to The Elderwood, and her magic refused to let her forget.

As she stood in the center of her room, Lucy felt her magic tugging, like it was trying to tell her something. Lucy wasn't interested in opening her mind or heart to anyone, however, her unusual, magical companion had never led her astray. Closing her eyes, she allowed the magic in, and exhaled slowly.

In a rush, her magic vibrated through her body as the memories from mere weeks ago broke through the mental wall she had put in place. Her magic showed Lucy images she couldn't bear. Of Lucy using her magic to stop Jasper as he tried to murder Micah. It flashed the evil gleam in Jasper's eye as he used his alchemy on those she loved. But the magic also reminded her of the vengeful force within herself and how she rallied her power to take Jasper down.

Lucy's eyes squeezed tighter as her stomach flipped at the next memory. The one of her floating in the air, ready to kill Jasper herself. Then her father...

No. I can't fall apart again, she told herself, driving a different line of thought.

She forced her eyes open, breathing deeply in the empty room that felt suffocating, focusing instead on what sparked her desire for retribution, not heartache.

Jasper DeValey.

Her mind still couldn't grasp that everything happened because Jasper was also a Lumen. It didn't matter though. Jasper may have been a Lumen by blood, but he was nothing compared to Micah... Micah deserved the magic he was gifted. Jasper deserved a shallow grave and a pack of starving wolven there to pick apart his remains.

Her heart twisted at the thought of the mortal man she left behind... Micah exemplified the best of humanity, though maybe he was more than just mortal with his newfound magic. He waited patiently for her to get her life together and come back to him. He offered his heart and his love to her, never wavering. And what did she do? She left him. Again.

I had no other choice, she reminded herself for the millionth time that week.

The entire idea that Jasper DeValey was alive and here in the castle made her stomach roil. Why hadn't Laurent told her? Did she not deserve to know that her father's murderer was in the same building as her?

A shudder of sadness threatened to bring her to her knees at the thought of her father. It happened every time he crossed her mind. Grief was alive within her, running rampant with its own agenda. Some moments she could withstand it, cast it aside to deal with later, alone in her room... Other times it would overpower her, and the tears would rush down her face in a torrent even before she knew it was happening. That was just how grief worked... one moment you were fine, and the next, you weren't sure how to breathe.

Maybe that was why Laurent hadn't told her about Jasper. Had her grief been subconsciously bleeding out into the rest of her life?

It *could* have been that he didn't want to upset Lucy that Jasper was there... Or maybe Jasper had just arrived and Laurent wasn't made aware. However, both of those seemed incredibly unlikely. Besides, Lucy asked for updates at every opportunity. Laurent knew how badly she'd want to be informed, no matter how much it hurt. So why did he keep it a secret?

Perhaps he thinks I'm weak.

Lucy sheathed her dagger in her boot, turned, and sat at the foot of her bed, taking a moment to truly consider that idea. She had been walking through this castle like a damned ghost, moving from room to room to give herself something to do, but never truly having a purpose. Even her magic was subdued, barely waking until recently; maybe her magic felt her weakness and wanted to run from her as well?

Mindlessly, her thumb glided over her palm, feeling the raised brand from The Elderwood. Her life had changed so much in such a short period of time... All she had ever wanted was to carve her own path for her future, and instead she was wearing down a path in the stone tile floor of her room as she did nothing to fix her situation but pace.

She shook her head and sighed.

Think logically, Lucy.

Worst-case scenario, Laurent was hiding Jasper's presence from her with malicious intent... but that couldn't be the case.

Could it?

Lucy ran her fingers through her unruly hair in frustration, but the simple act added another crack in her already broken heart. Such a common gesture, but it was one Micah did frequently. She thought of how she'd grab his hands and steady him, helping to calm Micah when he became overwhelmed. His dark brown eyes would melt her with just a look.

Stop that, she scolded herself. *You chose to be here, and now you are. You don't get to miss the man whose heart you broke.*

Flopping onto her mattress, she stared at the silken fabric that draped across her four poster bed. It stretched so serenely across the quiet room, a pale pink that offered calm, so at odds with her frenzied mind.

How do I keep ending up here? In these hopeless situations where I can't seem to make things right.

Regardless of the many options, there was really only one choice to make here. She could no longer think about Micah and the hollow space within her. She could not fall apart at the reminder that her father was gone.

No.

Lucy had to figure out what Laurent knew—and if he was hiding something, she had to know why.

Her thoughts dragged her back to the moment she saw Jasper in his cell.

"Please, no more," he had cried. *"I have nothing else to say, and no more alchemy to give. Please, Sloan, you will drain me to my death!"*

The memory of his withered body chilled her to the bone, but his words hung heavy in her mind. What did Jasper mean? Was Laurent hurting him? Is that why Laurent had avoided answering her question?

Sitting up, she pulled her soft white blanket around her shoulders. She couldn't tell if the shivering was from the cold, exhaustion, or fear; perhaps all three.

The ancient magic swirling inside of her pushed at

her fingertips and Lucy invited it to the surface. She watched with amusement as the green mist danced from finger to finger trying to cheer her up. The sentient magic soared back and forth playfully, then stopped suddenly.

Lucy furrowed her brow, bringing her magic closer to her. A sound came from outside her door, like a shuffling of feet. She sat up, anticipating a following knock, but nothing else came. Her magic pulsed in the palm of her hand in warning. Another muffled sound made her stand in alarm.

Is someone outside my bedchambers?

Carefully keeping her magic in her right hand, she tiptoed to the door. Putting her ear to the large wooden door, Lucy heard hushed footsteps. As she opened the door slowly, she was surprised to see Roger, Laurent's trusted guard. He wasn't walking down the hall, and he wasn't summoning her for dinner—so why was he standing there?

"Can I help you?" Lucy asked through the crack of the door, keeping her magic out of sight.

Roger shifted, turning his bright smile to her. "No, Miss Lucy. Sorry if I have disturbed you." He turned from her door and continued facing the opposite wall, a longsword sheathed to his hip.

"Then why are you here?" Lucy asked bluntly. It wasn't like Roger to stand in the hall alone while she remained in her room. Roger regularly accompanied Lucy on her long walks around the castle, but he never stood by her doorway late at night.

Roger's eyes widened the smallest amount, Lucy almost missed it. "Just my rounds, Miss. Lord Sloan has asked his guards to do a few more patrols now that the soldiers are closing in on DeValey."

Lucy's eyebrow arched skeptically, knowing damn well that Jasper DeValey was locked away in the dungeons just floors beneath her feet.

"Hmm," Lucy replied, tight-lipped. "Well, thank you for your service. Good night." Then she shut the door before Roger could reply.

Appears Laurent is working hard to monitor things. Me, no doubt.

The idea made her fume. Lucy rebelled against every act of confinement her parents had placed on her; did Laurent truly think he could do the same?

What is it with males thinking females are so easily controlled?

At her thought, Lucy's magic jumped and swirled in her hand like a miniature storm. It was a power unlike anything she had ever seen. It never ceased to amaze her. Brax had told her that her magic had actualized; that Lucy was an Original.

It seemed both like a lifetime ago and within the same breath of a moment, but she was quick to avoid any reminders of that terrible day. It was her last time at the Lumen property. The last time she saw Micah. The last time she saw her father. It was when Lucy lost all sense of who she was as a Fae, as a daughter, as a lover... Everything changed.

It had to.

She took a deep breath, steadying herself. Her magic calmed and curled around her fingers in a graceful dance. Lucy had spent many nights awake, wondering where this miraculous gift had come from, why it chose her, and what it really meant to be an Original. It had never happened before—Lucy was the first.

When she learned that her magic had actualized, she was able to make the rain fall and the minerals in the ground bend to her will. The Elderwood's magic also showed her things... It allowed her to see far into the Lumen property to spot the intruders as they made their way across the land, ready to hurt The Elderwood and her family.

There hadn't been much time to learn more, especially as she came to the Northern Territory so quickly after Jasper treacherously turned on them. Once her father died and she left Micah, she shut down completely. Her life was in the capable hands of Laurent Sloan, and there was nothing left for her. She was alone, but as her magic zoomed up and down her arms playfully, she considered that maybe she was not as alone as she thought.

"What else can you do?" Lucy whispered to the bouncing green mist in her hand, a smile forming on her lips. She lifted her hand and cast a privacy charm on her room, not wanting Roger to hear her from the hall. No one in the North knew about her magic, and she had every intention of keeping it that way. For now, at least.

Since Laurent was in the business of keeping secrets from her, it seemed fair she had some of her own. It wasn't as though she planned to use this magic against anyone... It just felt good to make a decision for herself. To keep something good close to her before it could be taken away.

"You're always here helping me, aren't you?" She whispered to the bouncing mist. The simple question shook something awake inside of her.

Perhaps it wasn't The Elderwood showing her images in the distance. Maybe it was her magic? Could it be that it had been the one helping her all along? Could it help her here?

"Can you show me Jasper?" She spoke quietly, wondering if the magic could do as she asked—if it really was as sentient as she assumed. No one knew much of the magic she held within her, other than it was gifted from another time, another age—from the gods themselves.

Closing her eyes, with her arms outstretched, Lucy tried to clear her mind and allow a connection with her unusual power. With a burst of green light, a vision of her standing alone in her room appeared. She was in the same gown, the white blanket in a pile on her bed. A green mist cast a thin haze on the outskirts of the vision.

Lucy could see what her magic showed her.

Taking a deep breath to calm herself, she focused on the emerald mist. It crept under her door and slid down the hall undetected by Roger, or any other guards, meandering the castle late at night. The images passed rapidly, both blurry and clear, as she watched the realm through the lens of her magic. Doing her best to direct it to where Jasper had been, her green mist flowed quickly through the shadows, down the corridor to the left-most passage, to the off-limits section of the castle. Her heart beat quickly as she passed a servant bringing bushels of vegetables down to the cellar... No, Lucy didn't pass her. Her magic did.

With each turn, her breathing shook in trepidation. Sweat slicked down the side of her face and trickled down her back. The amount of energy this took was exhausting. Perhaps her magic *did* have limitations. Not on typical Fae spells, but on these otherworldly bits of magic she controlled—well, as much as one can control a sentient power.

She tucked that thought away for another day. Right now she had one focus: find Jasper. Her magic took her down the stairs to the dungeon and halted before a cell.

Lucy panted as though she herself had run through the castle to this spot. In truth, she remained safely tucked away in her bedchambers. She wiggled her toes to ground herself, reassuring her physical body it was not in danger. The rush caused her heart to pound with the thrill. It was working. Her magic allowed her to see whatever she wanted.

Squeezing her eyes closed tighter, she tried to focus on the image before her. All she could make out was Jasper sleeping on a filthy, thin mattress along the wall. No other Fae in sight.

He's still there.

Part of her felt relieved that her magic worked to show her what she had sought out, but another part of her twisted with disgust. She hated Jasper and wished him dead, but she still couldn't come to terms with the fact that Laurent wasn't truthful with her.

Lucy opened her eyes, amazed to see her bedchamber walls; her beautiful emerald magic still bouncing along her hands. A sudden thrill overcame her. She was able to use her power to do something completely unimaginable. Could she use it to see her family as well? Could she see Micah?

A pinch in her heart pushed that thought away, knowing the last time they spoke, Lucy had told Micah that she picked him—that she wanted to figure things out with their relationship. She never anticipated Jasper's attack and the death of her father. She never expected to go back on her word and pick Laurent instead. But it wasn't for love... her heart belonged with Micah, and that could never change.

Instead, Lucy focused on the Baum Estate. It had been weeks since Lucy saw her family and she'd do anything to hear their voices; to know they were okay.

The cold weight of the dagger in her boot made her think of Tristan and his wide smile before he tried to warn her not to come here. She thought of Gregory and Hugh in the South. Her little brothers. Her Mother.

But Wes... he was the one she wanted to see. He had taken over the family business for Central Denora all on his own. Was he okay? Was he mad at her for being forced to play messenger to Micah?

She squeezed her eyes shut once more, trying to see Wes. Lucy felt the magic reach toward him, pushing further and further from her... but it all went black. She tried again and again, but nothing showed.

Hmm... perhaps it is too far.

She sighed and fell back to her bed in exhaustion, disappointed that she couldn't reach her family. Her head throbbed and her muscles were weak. It was the first time she felt drained from using her new powers. Clearly, all magic had its limitations—even the Originals couldn't create miracles.

An ache settled deeply in her soul—a longing to no longer feel so alone. Sliding to the top of her bed, she wrapped herself in her lush blankets and rested her head. Curling into a ball, Lucy thought about her mother and brothers and the life she left behind, and prayed to all the gods who would listen that it would all be worth it in the end.

A SOFT KNOCK woke her from her restless sleep. It was not a pleasant night, but most nights weren't. Nightmares of her father's murder passed through her mind each time she closed her eyes. Lucy had to relive the moment Jasper sent a killing blow meant for her, that instead found Corvus.

Sometimes her nightmares included Wes jumping in front of the murderous magic. Other times, it was Tristan. Each night she woke up in a cold sweat, gasping for air, spending the rest of the lonely night tossing and turning.

"Miss Lucy?" Roger's voice said from the other side of her wooden door. "Lord Sloan would like to dine with you for breakfast."

Lucy bolted upright in her bed, thrown by the invitation. Laurent had been so busy these recent weeks, she couldn't remember the last time they had breakfast together. Usually, her days involved arbitrary meandering throughout the castle wings and eating meals alone or with Roger. On occasion, Laurent would carve out a moment to eat dinner with her, but not always. However, since their tea last night when Laurent had lied to her face about Jasper, she assumed he would avoid her.

Either this breakfast is a way to try to distract me from the truth, or he is finally going to tell me. Her heart trilled with equal anticipation and fear.

"Thank you, Roger," Lucy called through the door, scrambling to her feet. "Please, just give me a moment to prepare, and I will be out shortly."

After rushing around her bedchambers, she pulled her hair into a mostly tame braid down one side, and wore a pale green gown with delicate cream lace at her sleeves. Slightly flushed from her hurried state, she made it to the door, opened it, and smiled at Roger.

"Good morning, Miss Lucy," Roger greeted her, his face drawn with fatigue.

"Good morning. Were you out here all night?" Lucy asked with a surprised smile on her face. The surprise was genuine, but the smile was not. The idea of a guard at her door at every moment made her incredibly uncomfortable.

"No, Miss. Lord Sloan has stationed guards throughout the castle as a precautionary measure."

Hmm, precautions for who they deny is in the dungeon?

"I see." Lucy tightened her fist, forcing the anger bubbling inside of her to subside. She tried to remind herself to think rationally. Laurent was on her side. There had to be a reasonable explanation.

She kept her head held high and her smile glued to her face as they entered the small dining area. Laurent sat dutifully in his seat at the end of the oversized table, and Lucy greeted him with a smile as she sat.

"Lucy, you look resplendent. I've missed our quiet mornings together," Laurent said. Then he did something that he had not done in weeks. He walked over to her, took her hand, and kissed her on the cheek. "Thank you for meeting me," he whispered in her ear.

Normally, this would be a gesture that would send shivers down her spine and heat pooling in her core, but the only heat she felt was in her face as her anger and impatience grew tenfold.

Keeping her practiced smile in place, she watched as he walked back to his seat, his long silver-white hair swaying gently over his navy blue jacket. He sat and resumed his regal stature, his piercing blue eyes connecting with Lucy's.

"Thank you," she replied. "I've missed our mornings as well. While our dinners have been lovely, I've been hoping to spend more time with you."

Her heart tugged at the deception in her words. She did want to spend more time with him, but was it to enjoy his company or to discover his truths? Or could it be both?

Laurent held her gaze behind steepled fingers, deep in thought. "I will do better about allocating more time specially for you, my queen. Daily breakfasts and dinners? Maybe an adventure just for the two of us, twice a week?"

My queen, blech.

She couldn't stand the phrase anymore. Lucy appreciated the gesture of him wanting to see her, but was also bothered by the fact that he had to schedule the time to do so. She took a small sip of her tea and picked at her warm bread.

He's the leader of the entire Northern Territory. You are not his only priority.

"Yes, I would enjoy that very much."

"We could talk about the plans for the wedding, if you'd like? I know your father set the date, but if you'd like to postpone to give you time to grieve, we can do that."

Her world stood still for just a second—even her heart seemed to pause between beating.

The wedding. How could I have forgotten? Of course he wishes to continue the wedding... that was the whole point, wasn't it?

A soft nod was all Lucy could manage.

Laurent's ice-blue eyes met hers from across the table and the kindness within them forced her into action.

There's no time like now.

"I'd like to talk about more than just the wedding," Lucy said, meeting his gaze.

"What about?" Laurent asked kindly.

"About Jasper DeValey and how I know he's in your dungeons."

CHAPTER

TWO

MICAH

Slicing his axe through the air, Micah split the log into two pieces. The resounding crack tore through the trees in the otherwise silent yard. Leaning over, he grabbed one log, then the other, and tossed them over to Brax. Without even needing to look, the Vytyrian warrior caught them and piled them neatly onto the ever-growing tower of logs. Micah was already swinging to cleave another block when Brax called for a break.

"I think we have enough wood to last us at least three winters," Brax said in an annoyed huff.

"I thought you liked a good workout?" Micah asked, knowing full well that her Vytyrian magic recharged when she was exercising.

The muscles in his shoulders were screaming, but he wasn't ready to stop moving—he couldn't. He knew that if he stopped moving, he would have to face the new reality his life had become, but he was determined to ignore it for as long as possible. That was all Micah wanted to do: keep moving, one step at a time.

Physical pain was easier to manage and push away. Whatever was eating away at his soul? Well, that was harder to ignore.

He swung the axe hard into the tree stump, lodging it there for a moment to wipe the sweat from his brow with his forearm. Cutting firewood helped him to avoid his troubles, but it also reminded him of Lucy, and the fluid way she swung the axe when she was here. He should have known from that very moment that there was something special about her. Maybe things could be different. Maybe he wouldn't be in this mess.

Brax narrowed her eyes at him and leaned closer. "You and I both know I love the exercise. However, what we also both know—but for some reason won't acknowledge—is the reason we are endlessly chopping wood." She flung her arms out to her sides, gesturing at the multiple piles of logs settled around the property.

Micah took a swig of water from his worn down thermos and splashed some of it on the back of his neck. He didn't even want to look. Each pile was a reminder of the emotions he'd rather ignore.

A pile next to the house for his sadness; the never ending grief of missing his mom.

A pile near the tree line for his guilt; wishing he could have made things right with his grandad.

A pile near the fire pit for his loneliness; mourning the future he could never have now that he was stuck at this cabin.

A pile on the far side of the house for his heartbreak; a life without Lucy. It was by far the largest pile, and he couldn't stand to look at it.

"What are you trying to say?" He knew exactly what Brax meant, but he wasn't ready to have this conversation. Waiting for her response, his muscles tensed.

His dad told him that was called *flight or fight*. Micah had always had this reaction in him. When things got tough, he'd shove it all away and just wait for life to implode.

Brax looked at him with her usual fire in her eyes. However, instead of barking out a string of insults or going on a tangent about how she was right about something and how Micah was wrong, she just sighed.

"Nothing." She shook her head and looked away. "Come on, I'll make us lunch."

Micah watched her walk back into the house, and the tension in his chest slowly receded. He knew what she was going to say. Micah had been avoiding everything he was feeling and instead forced his body into staying as busy as possible in order to not think about it.

Not to think about *her*.

"You know," Micah called from behind Brax. "We make a pretty good team out here."

"Naturally. I make a superior partner in all things."

All Micah could do was laugh.

Of course, that's her answer.

Since Wes came and brought the soul shattering news that Lucy wouldn't be coming back—that she would marry Sloan after all—Brax had been a constant by his side. They completed daily chores, cooked and cleaned, talked and laughed. They had become a well-oiled machine in all things.

He was thankful for her presence... Without her, he'd

be alone at the cabin because of the curse of the guardian—he couldn't leave the property for more than a few hours at a time before death came to find him. Since he wasn't particularly ready to die, he was glad he had someone to keep him company; even if she insulted him more often than not.

Swinging the backdoor open, Brax stepped into the kitchen and immediately went to work. She grabbed a loaf of bread, some meats and cheeses, and a few condiments.

"There is much to want for in this realm, but I will say one thing..." Brax looked at Micah with a mischievous smile. "Potato chips are probably the best invention your lot could have ever invented."

Micah chuckled as he washed up by the sink. Brax had been trying to cheer Micah up for months. Some days it worked. Others it didn't. More than anything, Micah remained in a perpetual state of uncertainty.

Why did Laurent Sloan want Brax to stay now that he had Lucy?

How long would that last? Could Sloan order her away?

Why didn't Lucy come back?

Realistically, Micah knew the answer to that. Lucy thought she was helping him, keeping him safe by staying away. If only she'd return and he could tell her he'd rather suffer at the hands of death itself than be away from her.

As if she could read his mind, Brax slid a plate before him at the kitchen counter and asked the question they usually dutifully ignored.

"Still no word from her?"

He shook his head in response. They didn't need to hash out the same words over and over again. Besides, it had been almost six months for Micah, but only a month or two for Lucy. Who knew how much grief she was experiencing? And maybe... just maybe... she *wanted* Laurent, and he just had to live with that.

That she picked Laurent, and not him.

"Let's say we practice more alchemy today, huh?" Brax changed the subject with fake optimism. "You got so close to getting those darts on target the other day. I bet we could get them closer this time—even if your aim is that of an infant."

"Yeah, maybe." He took a bite of his sandwich to avoid talking. Reaching for the bag of potato chips, Brax snatched them from off the table.

"No way, Lumen." She held the bag of chips to her chest as though they were a cherished gift. Giving him a look of pure disbelief, she pointed her finger at him and scowled. "Last time we shared the bag, you ate nearly the whole thing! And I hate shopping in your awful super markets. This bag has to last, so paws off."

"You're really not going to let me have any?" Micah asked with a huff of a laugh.

"Absolutely not." Brax gripped the bag even tighter.

"Wow, we're doing this, aren't we?" Micah said, shaking his head and smiling.

"I will fight you for them—let there be no confusion."

On any other day, Micah would have laughed at her threats and let her pig out on the salty snack on her own, but today was different. His body was full of tension, the frustration with his life always prepared to spill over into anger. Thanks to his guardian curse, even going to the store to buy his own chips was a danger to him, for fuck's sake.

Maybe a fight isn't such a bad idea.

With a wry smile, he carefully stuck his hand into the front pocket of his jeans to grab the alchemy ring he had taken from Jasper when Micah had sliced his fingers off. It had been months, but Micah kept it in his pocket in case of emergencies—with everything that had happened, you just never could be sure you were completely safe.

Squeezing the ring tight in his fist, he kept his eyes on the snack in Brax's hands, noting the foil lining of the bag—the alloyed materials could give his alchemy a bit of leverage.

Activating the ring with magical intent was the part he could usually get right when he practiced alone in his room. He only needed to let his intention be clear in his mind, then he'd send a surge of focus into the ring. Once the ring warmed, it was activated.

Step one, check.

"Lumen, what are you doing?" Brax asked in frustration. She couldn't see his hand in his pocket, but it was clear he was up to something. She held a hand out in front of her, commanding him to back down. Curling her other arm around the snacks, she shouted at Micah. "These are mine, you dry pork chop! Don't make me knock your ass out."

Next, Micah recalled the words for summoning that he and Brax had found in the Lumen tome left to him by his ancestors. In a flash, he pulled his hand from his pocket, aimed it at the bag of potato chips and called it to him.

"*Vennali!*"

The bag was pulled out of Brax's iron-grip, but she refused to back down. Right before it left her fingers, she clamped down with her Fae speed and strength to claim the salty snack as her own. With a pop, the bag split into two and potato chips went flying.

It was nearly in slow motion as Micah watched Brax witness her beloved snack fall to the ground in pieces. She threw her hands out to stop it, but the chips scattered so widely, she could only catch a few. Holding the salty chips in her hands, Brax looked at them as though she wanted to cry.

Her head snapped toward Micah in a glare, but the seriousness vanished when Micah caught sight of chips stuck in her hair.

He opened his mouth to say something, but instead a low rumble of laughter came out. It was really only a chuckle, but Brax was annoyed enough that she punched him in the side, causing him to bend down on one knee. He let out a groan that was half hurt, half amusement, then he ambled down to the floor and sat.

"You dunce." Brax slid down to the ground next to him, elbowing him to get him to stop. She picked a chip off the ground and popped it into her mouth. "Next time, I'll just buy two bags," she mumbled.

"You asked for it," Micah said, taking a chip out of her hair and throwing it at her.

She caught it in her mouth and chomped down in victory.

They both chuckled, the levity bringing them back to a moment of normalcy, but the quiet won out once again.

"Let's talk about that alchemy for a second." Brax turned her body to face him, gently bringing up his use of magic. "That was your fastest attempt at that magic so far. How'd you get it to work so quickly?"

"I wanted the chips." Micah shrugged like it was obvious, and then playfully swatted her away and got up to fetch the broom. He hated talking about his failures at magic.

The reality was that he had no idea how that worked so seamlessly. It usually took at least four big attempts to get the magic to activate, and then somehow he would fuck up the spell and it'd barely work. This time from start to finish, it was less than a minute, and it did exactly as he had planned.

What made this time so different?

Part of him wanted to chalk it up to practice. He'd been working hard and things were just coming together for him. However, deep down, he had a different idea. One that was probably more likely.

The rings made it possible when his magic alone wasn't strong enough. He was never meant to have Fae magic. It was all just a fluke—some off chance that he was here when Lucy needed a guardian. The rings gave him the power he didn't have on his own, and he wouldn't admit more weakness to the strongest warrior he'd ever known.

"Just a lucky try," he lied, but nothing about it felt lucky.

THREE

LUCY

Laurent and Lucy remained in a silent stare down as he processed her revelation of Jasper's whereabouts. Lucy held her breath, but kept her head up, her magic fluttering just beneath the surface, reminding her to show no fear.

A flash of shock and anger passed over his face. "This…" Laurent began, quickly masking his features to a more stoic expression of interest and caution. "This is quite surprising… How is it you know this exactly?" He shifted in his seat, keeping his focus on Lucy.

"I saw him with my own eyes, Laurent." A moment of worry washed over her, but she would not back down. Lucy needed him to hear her as an individual—not a simpering female. "I want you to understand that I am not afraid of shocking and unsettling news." She deserved to know that her father's murderer was apprehended. It was the sole reason she was in the North. "You should have told me of his arrival."

Laurent stood from the table and walked to her. He crouched down to meet her at eye level and took her hand in his, caressing the back of her hand with his thumb. "Do you know much about Denoran politics, Lucy?" He was hesitant to speak. His voice remained calm and even, with a hint of softness, as though making the next words easier for her to hear. "Especially when it comes to prisoners?"

Lucy blinked at the topic. "Admittedly, not much. But I am not sure why you are asking me that?"

"DeValey poses a threat to the kingdom of Denora. As my prisoner, there are things I must do to gain knowledge of his crimes—things that can make it hard for a Fae to sleep at night." He withdrew his hands and grabbed Lucy's glass of water and finished it.

Lucy's stomach flipped.

Is this why he hasn't wanted to tell me? Because he's torturing Jasper?

"Lucy, I am so sorry to have offended you." Laurent took a seat next to her at the table as he slid his hand into hers once again. "It is a recent development and I wasn't sure if you would feel safe here knowing he was also in the castle." His warm fingers smoothed over the top of her hand and his brilliantly bright eyes never left hers. "He is no threat to you, but I know you've been through so much. I didn't want you to have any more fear in your beautiful heart."

At his explanation, a flutter in her mind rebounded back and forth—her magic telling her to pay close attention. She weighed his words carefully, assessing if she could truly believe him.

It was no secret that she had been through a lot, but that didn't mean she was incapable of dealing with difficult situations. Perhaps he was only trying to protect her, in the only way he knew how.

She wanted to believe him. Though, unfortunately for Lucy, she did not own the same set of truth-detecting skills that Laurent held within his magic. Lucy could not determine for sure if he was honest with her or not, but she held enough hope in her heart, so she decided to believe him. For now.

"Laurent," she began, turning in her seat to better face him. "I do not need protecting. You've asked me once before to always be honest with you, and I am. I need that in return."

A smile stretched across Laurent's perfectly pale skin, reaching from high cheekbone to high cheekbone. "You are truly a marvel." He took her face in his hand and stared at her in wonderment.

"A marvel because I have confronted you about an unsettling topic?" Lucy asked in jest.

Laughing, Laurent shook his head. "Yes, there's always that. But you harbor no ill-will toward me for keeping this from you? And you don't hold fear from DeValey?"

His eyes bored into hers, searching for answers.

Lucy knew he was fishing for lies, waiting for her to share an untruth with him. Luckily for Lucy, that magic did not work on her. Perhaps it was because of the magic that made her an Original.

"I do not fear, Jasper," she said with conviction, not needing to lie. "I am angry at the crimes he has committed. As for you... I'm hurt that you felt you could not tell me."

Her eyes searched his as she thought about the one question that would always bother her: would he have ever told her Jasper was here?

Now it was Lucy's turn to watch his reactions, trying to find a tell that may give her a clue that Laurent was keeping things from her. "You once told me we would be in a partnership—equals. Do you still feel that way?"

"I do," he said adamantly. "There is much that happens in the political realm that you may not understand. Things that may make me seem like a monster. Things I must do."

Carefully, she placed her hand on his arm to get his attention. "You can tell me," she encouraged him. As awful as it could be, Lucy supported doing whatever it took to get the information from Jasper. He deserved to be brought to justice, and she needed to understand why Jasper did what he did—why he turned on their family.

Laurent's eyes sped wildly over Lucy's features—her eyes, her hair, her mouth. He smiled again and nodded. "I can. However, there are more important things in regards to making this realm better. Things I think I'd like to show you."

Pulling her to her feet, he clasped her hand with his and guided her out of the dining area. He walked with the vigor of a child on Winter Solstice, excited to open their presents. Two guards followed in their footsteps.

Where could he be taking me?

"What about Jasper?" Lucy asked him, trying to keep up.

"There will be time for everything, my love," he replied, barely slowing a step.

Taking in her surroundings, she realized he was not walking toward the dungeon, and Lucy's heart flipped with relief. As much as she wanted answers, she realized she was not prepared to see Jasper again so soon—especially with the thoughts of torture running through her mind.

Instead, Laurent was walking with her through the corridors, past the welcoming hall, and into his private wing of the castle.

A tinge of blush seeped into her cheeks at the thought.

He wouldn't be bringing me to his bedchambers, would he?

Fortunately, Laurent pulled her into his study instead, ordering the guards to wait in the hall and for any staff within the office to leave. She watched as two female Fae took their cleaning supplies and left the room in a hurry.

"Normally they clean during breakfast and are done by the time I arrive, but this couldn't wait," he explained. Pulling open the curtains, a wall of light entered the room, illuminating the ornate statues on his floor to ceiling bookshelves and highlighting the many maps he had placed strategically throughout the room.

"You couldn't wait to show me your *office?*" Lucy asked, a skeptical grin on her face. "What does this have to do with Jasper?"

"It doesn't," he replied, his eyes alight with a zest

Lucy couldn't place. "It has everything to do with you. With us."

He stood in his office looking at her like a male starved, ready to devour her whole. His gaze felt predatory as he kept his eyes locked on hers, and Lucy wasn't sure if she loved the attention, or if it made her want to run in the opposite direction. Either way, it felt strangely good to be noticed.

With the grace only a Fae could have, Laurent rushed to her and grabbed her hips, pulling her flush against his front. A small gasp left Lucy's lips in surprise—he hadn't been this direct since their day in the woods, a day that felt a lifetime ago. His crisp scent filled the closeness, making her think of snow storms and linens. Squeezing her hips, keeping her in place, his nose trailed the inside of her neck, sending shivers wracking through her body. From his proximity, she could feel his length hardening against her thigh.

Her eyes widened at his boldness, but her center warmed with the reminder of what usually follows an act like this. She felt her cheeks blush at the thought, and looked away from the beautiful Fae in front of her. Laurent was handsome and fair and her future husband, and as much as he claimed to be hers, she wasn't his.

Laurent slid his hand up to her face and held her cheek once again, tilting her face back to his. His hungry eyes took in every inch of her and Lucy blushed more at the intimate act.

"You are breathtaking, my queen. That little smile of yours does me in every time. Did you know that?"

She shook her head, a hint of a smile still cemented in place.

If he thinks I'm going to drop the topic of Jasper just because of some pretty words, he has another thing coming.

"I want to show you everything," he whispered in her ear.

Her skin pebbled at his feather-light touch.

"But first, I cannot wait another moment to kiss you."

He captured Lucy's mouth with his own, and Lucy stilled. His tongue lingered over her lips, teasing his intent.

Lucy knew that accepting this kiss was accepting much more than a physical moment. It would be allowing part of herself to let go of Micah for good, and the mere idea felt like an arrow to her heart. But she had no other choice. She had to keep him safe. So with a deep breath in, she forced thoughts of Micah away from her, and opened her lips to him, tasting a hint of sweetness from his morning tea. He groaned into her mouth, devouring her with lips, teeth, and tongue, pulling her closer and closer to his body.

Lucy seized the chance to lose herself in him. She threw her arms around his neck and held on to him as if she were trying to hold herself together. She had been so devoid of any emotion for so long, with nothing but her grief to keep her company. Here, now, she didn't have to deal with her feelings at all. Instead, she could focus on the physical pleasure that drove her. She could just live, if only for a moment.

Walking her backwards, Laurent strode forward, never taking his lips off of hers, until Lucy's bottom hit the edge of a desk. With his Fae speed, he scooped her up and placed her on top, pulling her legs apart and standing between them. Lucy suppressed a moan at the enormous hardness that pressed at that special spot in between her legs.

Laurent raked his hands over Lucy's body. He dragged his lips to her neck down to the top of her breasts still covered by her gown. Lifting the bottom of her skirts, cool fingers slid up her legs, lingering on the tops of her soft thighs.

"My queen." Laurent growled in her ear.

The rumble of sweet nothings should have been Micah's voice. It should have been Micah's hands and lips that covered her. More than that, Lucy was sick of Laurent calling her his queen, especially when he refused to give her answers.

She didn't want to hear him speak anymore. She wanted to be consumed by this dalliance without the guilt and the shame that threatened to find her.

Capturing his mouth again, Lucy kissed him without restraint. It was desire and escape, lust and longing, truth and fiction; it was so many things, yet nothing at all. Nothing because this was the male she would live the rest of her days with, even if her heart belonged to someone else. There was no other choice, so she allowed herself a free fall into the heated desire—an attempt to feel something other than lost.

She pulled at his jacket, bringing him nearer to her as

the heat rose through her veins and he gripped her thighs tightly. Rolling her hips off the edge of the desk, she tried to get closer, wanting the friction to ease her growing need.

Laurent's hands explored her curves, gripping her round bottom firmly. Wrapping his long fingers around her hips, he obliged her demand for more as he tugged her so closely to him that if he had just freed one button of his trousers, they would be in an entirely different situation. Trails of kisses peppered her breasts and up her neck, but Lucy tilted her face away, not wanting to kiss him again.

They rocked into each other again and again, his hardness meeting her pooling core with every thrust. Laurent pulled her bottom closer to the edge of the desk and kept his pace, moving one hand to her breast. She kept her eyes shut, refusing to acknowledge who she held on to, who she was using to allow her this release. Instead, she followed the pleasure, rolling her hips as he kissed and touched her. A gasp left her lips and she saw stars, moaning through her climax. Her hands clutched his jacket and his fingers dug into her curves as her body tightened then slowly relaxed.

Panting, she opened her eyes to take in exactly what had happened. She was propped up on the side of a desk with her skirt pulled up to her waist. Laurent stood with one hand under her skirt, one hand trailing from her breast to her hip, his eyes wild, and his cheeks flushed. It wasn't a blush of embarrassment, though.

No.

It was desire.

He pulled his hands away from her and helped her to her feet, carefully fixing Lucy's stray hairs that had gone rogue during their... activity.

What in the realms has gotten into me?

"I am so sorry," Lucy apologized, looking down and straightening her dress. Embarrassment may not have found Laurent, but it certainly flooded Lucy.

Laurent grabbed her by her chin and looked into her eyes with that same heated desire. "Please do not apologize. Especially not for that," he gestured with a raised eyebrow. "Before you ask, no—it is not customary that I engage in these excitements with another. More so, I have never allowed any guests into my office." He dipped his head and looked back to Lucy with a hint of insecurity. "And I should be the one apologizing. I did not intend to take things that far, but with you, I can't seem to help myself."

Her mind flashed to Micah and betrayal sliced through her like a sword. She took a deep breath and shook her head. She was not betraying him. When she left, Lucy made it clear that she chose Laurent. Things between her and Micah were over. She made the choice to leave, and she made the choice to do this with Laurent.

Grabbing her hand, he kissed it gently. "There is an actual reason I've brought you here," he said with a wink. "I want to show you something I've shared with very few people in my life." He walked over to a wall covered by a curtain and pulled it back.

Lucy had expected to see another window looking

out into the courtyard, so she was astonished to see that behind the curtain was a large map of the Northern Territory filled with small papers tacked to different parts.

"What is all this?" Lucy asked in a hushed breath. This entire situation had thrown her. First Laurent ignores her, then he bombards her with physical affection, and now she is allowed to see his innermost private business matters? All of it had been confusing, but a hidden wall of notes was surely the most intriguing.

"These are my plans for the North" He brought Lucy a step closer to the wall to get a better look. "*Our* plans for the North," he whispered in her ear.

Letting go of his hand, Lucy walked closer to the map to read the words tacked carefully in different areas. The bottom of the map, where the village square was, had the most notes.

Food bank for those in need.

Clothing depository.

Winter Solstice gift donations.

Progressive tariffs.

"I'm not sure I understand?" Lucy admitted, turning to face Laurent. "What are all of these things?"

"The people of the North are no different from people of Central or Southern Denora. We have the same population struggles and the same groups of Fae who tackle the burdens of low income." He walked closer to the map, no longer looking at Lucy, but at his grand plans. "I wish to provide the North with an easier way of living. I've conducted the proper research and have scouted locations for a food and clothing bank, supported by our tariffs and given to those who need the support. I've even come up with a proposed tariff change to allow those who make more money to give more, and those who make less, to have to pay less."

"You're changing the tariffs?" Lucy asked in shock. "I didn't know that was even possible."

"I aim to make it possible, Lucy." He spun to face her, a lighted passion in his eyes. "We are—together."

"How?" It was the only question on Lucy's mind. Surely, this was all impossible under our current law from the King.

"Don't you remember seeing those poor families in the carriage after our first dinner together?"

Lucy's face fell. Of course she remembered it. The heart-breaking scene had been on her mind for weeks after. It was her first glimpse of the kind male Laurent was, as he hand delivered the food to those in need. She nodded, her brows furrowed.

"Wouldn't you like to actually help those people? Not look at them with sadness and wish that someone would do something—but to actually make a change and improve their lives?"

"Of course, but—"

"I know you do. It's why I have fallen for you so hard, my queen." He took her by the waist and spun her in a dance, smiling and laughing. "Together, we can do this. We will provide shelter to those in need when winter arrives. We will help Fae obtain good jobs to support their families." He held her in his arms and looked at her with a genuine smile. "*We* can make the difference."

"How will you convince the king of your ideas?" Lucy

knew King Tralont was many things, but generous to the poor was not one of them.

"Tralont and I will have a meeting and I'll explain my plan. It will all be fine. In fact, that is why I've been so busy these past few weeks since we've returned. I've been preparing."

He placed her down gently and walked over to another large map of the entire realm of Denora. Standing there, he kept his eyes focused on the castle, deep in thought, with his fingers linked around the back of his neck.

Another reminder of Micah—it made her heart hurt once more. Shoving it away with more vigor this time, she reached out and placed her hand on Laurent's shoulder.

"This is truly amazing, Laurent. I'm sure your meeting will go well. You have only the best interests of our realm at the forefront of your plan."

"Yes. Tralont should have stepped in a long time ago before the population got to such an immense size. He can be a foolish braggart, but hopefully he will see the genius of this plan. He will have to."

There was a steel to Laurent's voice that Lucy noticed when he spoke of King Tralont.

Lucy continued to analyze the map. "What's this?" Where the North's soldiers were usually stationed, there was a large "M" on the note.

"My forces are split on a few different missions at the moment. One was gone on their search for DeValey, as you know. But others are on missions to support Fae in need. In fact, there is a large group on their way to the Southern Territories soon."

"Well, I think this is all quite wonderful." She took his hand and squeezed. "Thank you for showing me."

Without taking his eyes away from the map of Denora, he replied. "I would do anything for you."

FOUR

MICAH

"Come on then, you spongey lima bean." Brax pulled Micah out of the house and into the yard after lunch.

Hesitantly, he followed, but he knew it was pointless. Micah was able to use his magic faster than he ever had before, but it wasn't from some amazing feat of power—it was all because of that fucking ring. He should have just told her, but admitting he was nearly powerless was humiliating. Besides, she was just pissed because it cost her a snack.

Stopping when she got halfway into the yard, she turned and bent her knees, crouching into a fighting stance. "You were a tough guy when it came to my property. Now bring that magic back to the surface to put to good use."

"Your *property*?" Micah balked. "They were freaking potato chips!"

"And they weren't yours," Brax replied with a vengeful smile. "Let's get this magic to work. Come on."

Mental note: don't mess with a chick and her snacks.

"Let it go, Brax. We both know that was a fluke." He dug his hands into his pockets, trying to avoid her challenge. His fingertips touched the ring and a surge of regret swept over him.

He didn't want to use the alchemical magic from Jasper—he was the one who killed Lucy's dad. He even tried killing Micah! But there was something about it that just called to him. It made him powerful when he felt helpless. Wasn't that important in this new life he lived?

"I won't be able to do it twice," he called to her. "Calm down."

"Calm down?" Brax raged. "Absolutely not. You wanted your magic to work, and you made it happen." Brax held her fists up, prepared for combat. "Now—do it again."

Micah couldn't believe she wouldn't let this go. It was a fucking bag of chips. He wasn't even sure how he did it—it was a stroke of luck. Brax just wanted to drag him out here to make him pay for the emotional burden of losing her snack.

"We both know you are holding back," Brax taunted him, taking a step forward and shoving at his shoulders.

He took his hands out of his pockets to steady himself, then pressed his lips into a thin line. "I'm not doing this," he told her seriously. Turning to walk back to the cabin, he felt another shove at his back.

Micah spun around to look at Brax, his eyes narrowed. He had no interest in fighting anymore, but she seemed dead-set. Her cropped hair swung freely in front of her eyes as her crouched body shifted left and right.

"You can't run from this." Brax kept her dark gaze steady on his, refusing to back down. "It's been an hour. Your magic should have restored just fine. Now, come on."

Micah only stared at her, meeting her glare in a standoff. The anger simmering inside of him was not toward her; it never was. Time after time he took his anger out on someone who didn't deserve it, he learned that lesson the hard way long ago. He kept trying not to do that to Brax.

"So you're not going to talk this time, huh? Fine." She lifted her foot and kicked him directly in the chest, her leather boot sending him flying backward.

With a thud, he landed on the uneven ground, grunting in frustration.

"What the fuck was that for?" He got to his feet but kept his distance from her uncalled-for violence.

What did she have to be so angry about? Fucking chips? I don't think so.

"Why are you holding back, Lumen?" Brax asked again.

When Micah refused to answer her, she came soaring toward him with giant leaps, her warrior upbringing clear as day.

Before he found his magic, she would have clocked him easily, probably even knocking him out cold. This time, he had his Fae speed to his advantage—it was the one thing that came naturally these days. Brax lifted her fist in the air and Micah spun to the left, dodging her. She crashed to the ground, her fist caked in mud.

Baring her teeth, Brax turned on her heel and came sprinting toward him again. Her fierce gaze made Micah's insides tense—he had never been the target of her rage before. With another lunge at Micah, she closed her fist, prepared to strike. Micah wasn't quick enough. Before he could manage to block it, Brax collided with his cheek, forcing him into action.

Throwing his arm up, he swatted her windpipe, knocking her off course and easing the blow. He knew even the quickest Fae still needed to breathe.

Gasping for air, Brax staggered back a few steps, her hands at her throat.

"Just drop this, Brax. I don't want to fight you!" Micah roared.

He was teetering on the edge of sanity, with each day getting worse and worse. This conversation would lead to nothing but trouble.

He couldn't do it.

He couldn't handle it.

"That's the problem here, you rotten zucchini. You aren't ready to fight for anything." Brax dropped her hands from her neck and faced Micah again. For once, she was standing still, not attacking him with every insult.

"I *am* fighting!" He took a step closer to her, pointing his finger at her. "I've knocked your ass on the ground before, and I can do it again. Isn't this what you want from me?"

"You aren't fighting *for* anything, Lumen," Brax said

with more significance in her voice, her chest heaving as she took in deep breaths of air.

Micah took a step back. Just like every other time, the urge to flee grew. He wasn't ready to talk about his feelings—it was too soon.

Why is she pushing this?

"We *need* to talk about it, Micah," she stated. She took a few slow steps closer to him and Micah tensed. "We need to talk about *her*."

There it was. The one thing he wasn't ready to talk about. There was nothing to say anymore.

He'd talk about his dead mother.

Or his grandad, who he thought had abandoned him as a child, but turned out to be the guardian of a fucking magical portal.

He'd talk about his loneliness he experienced when he was in the police force.

He'd even discuss his desperation for connection to his only remaining family, knowing he couldn't safely invite his dad here without eliminating every possible threat.

He'd talk about those things—but he couldn't talk about Lucy.

Not her.

"You can't push away every fucking problem in your life, pretending that you're fine. You're *not* fine." Brax's eyes betrayed her violent actions. She wasn't just angry, she was upset. At him.

"I'm fine," he said evenly as he turned away from her to head back into the house.

"Why are you doing this?" Brax's voice cracked with

emotion, causing Micah to stop in his tracks. "Why won't you just face what happened and deal with it?"

Sighing, his shoulders slumped.

"You keep pushing me away, Micah. Talk to me."

He turned to look at her, meeting her brown eyes full of sorrow. "Why bother?"

Brax took a step back, eyebrows furrowed at his question. "Excuse me?"

"Why bother?" He repeated. "You'll leave next." He lifted his arms to motion to the empty property. "Just like everyone else."

"I... I'm not going anywhere," Brax stuttered, searching for the words. "Why are you suggesting such things?"

"As soon as Sloan says your job here is done, you get to go home. And I'm not mad at you for it, it's just the way things go." He sighed and looked up into the clouded sky. "You will go home and be happy with your family. And I will be here. Alone. There's no point in trying to fight it."

When Brax opened her mouth to speak again, Micah held up a hand, his face drawn. "Please," he murmured. "I don't want to keep arguing. I just don't have it in me right now."

Brax pursed her lips and straightened her shoulders, shaking off her vulnerable show of emotion. With an agitated nod, she agreed to a moment of peace. She put her hands up and walked to the tree stumps around the fire pit, signaling a truce; not forever, but just for now. Without another word, she pulled logs from an oversized heap and started their nightly routine of a fire and beers before bed.

Most days, this was cathartic for Micah. They'd sit and drink and speak of nothing significant: maybe the weather, maybe the day's chores. Sometimes she'd try to pry more emotional responses from him, and most of the time he didn't mind. But if he was being honest, Micah had no interest in sitting outside and suffering through more unbearable questioning from Brax today. However, he also couldn't stand the idea of sitting alone in the quiet with his never ending thoughts.

There was no real win there.

As he watched Brax prep the fire, he realized there wasn't much of a win around for her, either. She was sent here to watch over a tree that either did absolutely fucking nothing, or acted up and tried to kill them all with shadow beasts. He was happy to have her for the killing part, but when the portal was dormant, there was nothing to do on the Lumen property.

Not only was Brax likely bored out of her mind, but she was probably counting down the days until she could go back to her family. Micah didn't blame her for that. If he had anyone to look forward to seeing again, he'd feel the same...

But that was the harsh truth about Micah's life—there was no one else to look forward to seeing anymore.

"I'll grab the drinks," he said to her, turning to walk back into the house. Stepping past the threshold of the doorway, his boot immediately crushed a crunchy chip they had somehow missed.

Micah smirked a bit at the thought of Brax's utter horror as her snack was flung through the air.

He dug his hand into his pocket to retrieve the ring once again. He had a few of them in a small box in his room—he collected them from Jasper's severed fingers for safe keeping. It ended up being a smart move on his part. Whenever he practiced his magic in private, his magic was always stronger with the use of the alchemy rings, but he couldn't figure out how or why. He wasn't intentionally keeping things from Brax, but this was something he just wanted to figure out for himself. He was tired of being the least intelligent one in every room.

There were four rings, one for each of Jasper's fat fingers. The amber colored one had never really worked for Micah—his only guess was that Jasper used all the magic from it. It was the same way when Wes and Brax took the necklace off of him after the tussle when he killed Corvus. The necklace was completely devoid of power after that.

Three of the rings were different, though—there were two ruby and one emerald. One of the ruby gems shone bright with a swirling magic within it. The other had a small bit of light, but barely sparked. The emerald ring was also bright with power—that was the one he had kept in his pocket. The green magic reminded him of Lucy.

It comforted him as much as it hurt.

On the few occasions when he used the rings to activate his magic, he noticed the magic inside of them did not wane the way they did for Jasper. He couldn't understand it, but with the rings, his magic felt immense.

Without them, his powers felt almost muted, as if they were watered down.

It's why he hated practicing his magic with Brax so much. He could do it with a murderous asshole's weapons, but he couldn't do it with the little bit of magic already inside of him.

So far, Micah had been able to manipulate rocks and dirt, but that was the extent of his power. Jasper was able to do nearly anything with his magic. What made Micah so different?

If it were up to him, he'd never use the rings—they reminded him so much of Jasper, and each memory of him caused a disgusted shudder to snake through his body.

Maybe it'd be better to just ditch the rings completely. I could live a life without magic.

With beers in hand, and sidestepping a few stray chips, he made his way to the backdoor. But before he got there, what he saw in the window made him freeze in his tracks.

A long, curling black tail made its way around a tree trunk just outside his window. An oversized paw peaked from behind the leaves.

No. It can't be.

Bright yellow eyes locked with his from amidst the trees.

There was no mistaking it.

The shadow beast was back.

CHAPTER
FIVE
LUCY

After her visit with Laurent, Lucy had spent time in her room mulling over what he had shared with her. If she were being honest with herself, it was hard to wrap her mind around it all.

Laurent had a plan for a better Denora—that in of itself felt remarkable. Could he really accomplish changing the course of Denoran tradition? Was it possible he could be the catalyst for so much more?

A faint whisper of a smile crept over her face as she remembered the way Laurent shared his positive intentions with her about their future; he always mentioned he thought of her as an equal. To consider a female as an equal in Denora was possibly the most ambitious aspect of it all. Even the situation with Jasper didn't seem to bother her as much as it originally did. Maybe he was still trying to do what was right.

Her mind buzzed with the possibilities, yet even with all of Laurent's amazing ideas, a nagging tug within her told her she was missing something beyond all of that. Something important.

So she decided to do the one thing she always did: search for answers.

Biting her lip, she contemplated where to start—this castle was still so new to her. She tried to trace her steps in her mind through the different wings of the castle and the various rooms she had explored. Lucy recalled the hall with three paths, one of them leading to the dungeons. Suddenly, her magic sent her a vision: a memory of when she first found Jasper in the dungeon. He was bloodied and disheveled, begging Laurent not to drain him of his alchemy. That he had no more to give.

Her magic rushed out of her mind, floating expectantly before her.

Alchemy to give? Why did he say give...

There was a reason she kept coming back to this moment, and Lucy needed to find Jasper and get him to explain what he meant. How did it play into everything?

Lucy considered sending her magic out through the castle on its own so that she wouldn't be spotted; however, she was nervous that exhausting herself of her magic so immensely may not be in her best interests at the moment. Luckily, the guards wouldn't think twice to see her walking in the halls during the day, since it was what she always did.

Steeling herself, she asked her magic to accompany her through the halls to the only person who could give her the knowledge she sought. Unfortunately, that person was someone she hated with all her being: Jasper.

What was even more unfortunate was that by the time she got to the dungeons, he was gone.

Out of breath from hurrying through the castle, she scanned the room in awe. There was no trace of him in the cell. It had been cleared and cleaned as though no one had been in it for years—though Lucy knew better.

Where did he take you?

Lucy looked around the dungeon corridors, trying to uncover any clues as to where Jasper went. Was he moved to another wing? A different location in Denora completely? Did Laurent kill him?

A shiver went down her spine at the thought. While she very much wanted to bring Jasper to justice, she still knew there was something missing in the grand scheme of things, and too many clues pointed to Jasper. She needed to find him and get the truth.

Perhaps that's why Jasper isn't here, she realized.

Each time she asked Laurent about Jasper, he changed the topic. And now that he knew Lucy was aware of his presence, he was moved? What was Laurent trying to hide?

As impatient magic led her through the castle on a wild goose chase, they searched for Jasper, carefully dodging the extra guards patrolling the castle. They had scoured the dungeon floor, the wait staff's quarters, and even tried to make their way into the guard's quarters, but didn't quite make it that far. Jasper was nowhere to be found.

Finding herself back in the main library with no additional leads, she called her magic back to her before anyone could question the strange green haze meandering the book stacks. It was daytime, and there were no shadows to hide in. Sighing, she took a seat in one of the oversized chairs by the windows that peered down into the market square.

Staring out into the sea of people below, Lucy thought about the change Laurent wanted to bring to his people. She could almost imagine the aiding-booths, a food stand full of meat and produce for hungry families, clothing stands for those who had worn down their jackets and trousers. Imagining the grateful Fae as they were supported by their realm made Lucy smile—really smile. Hope bloomed within her for the first time in a long time.

And Laurent wanted her to be part of it.

Her smile quickly dropped.

Well, he wanted her to be part of it, but also decided what information she could hear and when she was allowed to hear it. Just another way others tried to control her.

However, the difference they could make to the realm was more important than anything else she could have ever dreamed, and with each passing moment, she pictured herself doing those things. Finally making the changes she had always wished for in Denora. Even if Laurent had to be the one there by her side.

A fluttering sensation filled her from head to toe; actual excitement sending her to her feet. She would seek out Laurent and ask why Jasper had been moved—get him to answer the questions he kept avoiding. Then, maybe she could talk with him about more ideas for the future of Denora... Lucy knew he had always agreed with her views of female Fae, and perhaps they could work on laws for equality as well?

Walking down the halls to search for Laurent in his offices, Lucy passed a large glass display, showcasing pictures and scrolls of parchment safely tucked away behind the ornate glass.

The sight of ice-blue eyes caught her attention and made her pause.

Laurent.

The entire vitrine was dedicated to him and his accomplishments. There were medals of honor, plaques with his name engraved upon them, and flowers, magically preserved, on display. Her lips quirked into a small smile at the adoration the people of the North gave to Laurent. They truly loved and respected him.

There were three scrolls opened for others to read. One depicted his coronation when he became the ruler of the North. Another listed his heritage, going back generations from his father to his grandfather and more. But the last scroll was something that Lucy did not quite expect.

It read:

The Hero of the North

On the precipice of war, newly appointed Lord Laurent Sloan made his way across the realm to honor Denora and pay tribute to his king. On his journey, he came across the knowledge of a secret rebellion group forming to overthrow the new young King Tralont. Once childhood friends, Lord Sloan knew the importance of the power balance within the *realms, and did what any good and righteous Lord would do.*

Returning to the Northern Territories, Lord Sloan subdued the rebellion group and ensured the halt of any future rebellion in its wake. It is said he had slain over 750 of his northerners in that battle, and because of his immense power and strength, Denora remains indomitable to this day.

Lucy stilled. There were rumors about "Lord Slain" for years, and all this time, it was his protection of the realm that had cost him that horrid nickname?

As if a weight had been lifted from her shoulders, so went a few of her reservations about Laurent. This entire time she had been holding back, waiting for the other shoe to drop with him, believing deep down in her soul that an arranged marriage was the last thing in all the realms she wanted. Yet, as she learned more and more about him, there was much to respect.

Sure, she didn't always agree with him on how he handled information she wanted to know, but he had been living alone for a very long time. Maybe they just needed to work on their communication?

Maybe love doesn't need to be immediate, she thought, picturing Micah's perfect face in her mind. *Maybe love can grow with mutual understanding; with equal parts respect and intention.*

Her parents' love had been formed from a prearranged relationship. Perhaps she could find the same? And even if it wasn't love, there was always hope for friendship.

Lucy realized that this was not the life she had dreamed of, but who ever achieved their perfect life? This new journey offered her the ability to change Denoran tradition. She could help other Fae find equality and support.

There was still hope with this new path she was on, and she wouldn't keep holding herself back.

~

Lucy met Roger standing outside of the door to Laurent's study, dutifully keeping guard.

"Hello Miss Lucy," Roger said, tipping his head toward her in greeting. "Is there anything I can do for you today?"

"I'd like to speak with Lord Sloan, if he is available?" Lucy asked politely. She hoped she wouldn't get turned away, but also considered that when he spent time with her earlier, it could have been an exception, not an expectation.

"Certainly," Roger replied with a smile. "He wanted to meet with you this evening, but I am sure he won't mind a minor interruption, seeing he is not currently occupied."

He turned and opened the door for her, walking in first to announce her arrival.

"Lord Sloan. Miss Lucy is here to see you."

Laurent sat behind the desk Lucy was propped upon earlier, and seeing him there made a rush of pink appear on her cheeks.

As if he could tell exactly what she was thinking,

Laurent gave a knowing smile and stood. He came around to the front of the desk and sat exactly where she had, and waved for Roger to exit.

"My queen, to what do I owe the pleasure?" Laurent asked, his eyes raking over her body.

"I am sorry for bothering you," Lucy said, forcing her eyes to look away from his piercing gaze in order to get her question out. She was silly once and allowed a moment of physical pleasure to impede her questioning, but it wouldn't be happening again. "I wanted to ask you about the prisoner."

Laurent's demeanor changed rather suddenly, realizing it wasn't quite the social call he had hoped for. The flirtation from his eyes disappeared and instead a serious and concerned look colored his features. "What can I do for you?"

The question made Lucy stumble over her words for a moment. It wasn't *What do you want?* Or *What do you mean?* He was offering his services to her once again, putting her first, as he always had.

Her expression softened. "Jasper is no longer where he was when I... came across him. Is there a reason for that?"

What Lucy really wanted to do was ask Laurent why he was no longer in the dungeons, but perhaps that would have been a bit too brash.

Laurent smirked a bit, then nodded. "Unfortunately, he is a danger to those around him. It is for your safety, and for the safety of those who dwell within the North, that he has been relocated."

Her stomach did a strange flip.

Relocated.

"So he is alive?" A small part of her had believed Laurent had killed him, and she felt slight relief to know there was still time to find answers. Though, did she really still need them? Could she simply trust Laurent and his decisions?

"Yes, my love." Laurent walked up to her and took her hands. She hadn't noticed they had been trembling until he stilled them with his own. "You have nothing to fear. He is a crazed and dangerous male spouting strange accusations that could hurt those around us."

Strange accusations? What could be so dangerous about a male shackled in a dungeon?

"Do you not trust the guards who have him in their care?" Lucy challenged.

Where would be a safer place to keep a prisoner than a cell in a dungeon? Unless he just wanted to keep me from him.

He casually placed a stray hair back behind her ear and stroked her cheek softly. "He cannot be trusted, and I will not put my beloved in any sort of danger if I can help it."

Her eyes met Laurent's at the word.

Beloved.

He gave her a sweet kiss, then guided her to a chair. "Sit, you look quite shaken."

The truth was that she was absolutely shaken, but why? Because her father's murderer was still here? Because there were things that weren't quite adding up? Because her future husband had called her beloved? Or because the word had caused something to stir within her that she had not expected?

Shoving it all back down, she turned to Laurent and smiled. "Thank you." Trying to regain her words, she remembered what Roger had said. "Laurent? Roger mentioned you wanted to speak with me?"

"Ah, yes," he said, softly, a pinch of regret painting the air. "Your brother Wesley has contacted me."

Lucy's heart ached at the mention of her family.

"Your father's funeral is upon us. We leave for Central Denora in the morning."

CHAPTER

SIX

LUCY

The carriage bumped over the rocky landscape of the Leithe Grove as Lucy and Laurent left the Northern Territory. The ride had been mostly quiet, except for the shuffling of papers from Laurent's side of the compartment. He was busy reading through documents, his brows furrowed, deep in thought.

"I'm sorry that I must bring all of this horrid paperwork along with us," Laurent apologized again. "I fear that if I get too far behind on my plans, then the king will not hear my concerns." A look of worry etched in the lines on his forehead, the only sign that hinted his true age.

Lucy smiled and brushed away the apology. "It's fine. I understand that your work is important." Truth be told, she was more relieved than upset. She didn't have the energy to make small talk. Her mind was elsewhere. "Perhaps while you visit, you will be able to speak with the king or one of the dukes about your plans," Lucy suggested. "There will be many officials at

58

my father's... ceremony." Her voice cracked on the word.

She couldn't wrap her head around the fact that she was on her way to her father's Farewell Ceremony.

It was too much.

Pushing the thought to the side, she changed the topic. "When we get to the estate, I'm not sure how much time I'll have to spend with you. I told you it was fine for you to have remained in the North." She mindlessly toyed with the floral lace on her gown, staring out into the winding mountains surrounding their carriage.

"Nonsense," Laurent said. He slid closer to her and took her hand, calming her fidgeting. "Of course I will be with you, Lucy. You are my betrothed and I am here to support you in all things."

Normally, his doting upon her would have turned her cheeks pink and caused her stomach to flip, but everything felt too heavy.

She didn't even bother replying.

"Spend some time with your family, Lucy. I can keep myself busy. You do not need to worry about me while you have so many other important things to address."

Lucy's lips formed a tight smile. A small part of her wished he would stick around. She wasn't fully prepared to face her family, and having him there would have been the shield she needed. However, a bigger part of her appreciated that he trusted her enough that she did not need a chaperone. The stars only knew that if it were any other male in his place, they'd expect her to be followed around like a lost duck.

Well, every male but one other...

Her mind turned to Micah and the immovable trust he had in her.

The trust she destroyed when she left him in Joterra and hadn't returned... It had been months for Micah since he had seen her.

As if noticing the worry in her eyes, Laurent squeezed her hand, pulling her from her thoughts. "I will be with you any moment you need me, but I will give you the space to grieve with your family. Roger will always be nearby if I am not, and if you require anything, just let him know." His ice-blue eyes met hers with a fierce tenderness that she could hardly stand. "I will come to you. I will always come to you."

Lucy nodded again and Laurent let her hand go, turning back to his paperwork.

He may always come to me, but it isn't him that I need right now.

Her unfortunate reality was that she wasn't quite sure what she needed at all.

THE BAUM ESTATE was crowded with visitors from all over Denora and beyond. Local family and friends would arrive for the ceremony at a later time, however, there were still many guests from far away that had arrived early. A few guests would stay within the extra bedrooms of the manor, but most were settled in luxurious tents on the grounds of the estate.

There were canvas tents of all shapes and sizes, housing Fae from many different realms. Some were customers of the Baum Bowyer industry dating back to when Corvus first took over, like Matteo Lasso and Cristano Pedit, who took a few of the beige tents. Corvus's friend from childhood, Neddard Irvine, had an extravagant green tent, magicked with turrets and actual fire. He was in from Kerroz, where he maintained his mining business.

There were also more prestigious guests like Duke Renfro—the leader of the Denoran military—and his family. Even King Tralont himself would be in attendance.

Most guests were there to support Anita and her children, but there were still a handful of attendees who were there for the sole reason that Fae funerals were rare, and they didn't want to miss out on an opportunity to attend one. There would be music and food and lavish decorations.

The entire ordeal made Lucy nauseous, even if somewhere deep down she understood. Her father's death was so significant it would go down in history... The death of a strong Fae male by another Fae in his command? The scandal alone was enough. Add in the rarity of Fae death? You've got yourself the social event of the season.

But this was her family.

This was her *life*.

Choking down the lump in her throat, she continued past the grounds to the house. Everywhere she looked were faces of Fae she didn't even know. Where was her family?

Lucy wished it could just be those close to her for the

final ceremony, not a mass of strangers coming to put their nose in someone else's business. Some Fae were so fucking flawed, they would never see the issue with it; they'd never see how badly it hurt to lose the ones you love.

The problem was that most Fae thought they understood. As soon as Lucy had arrived, she couldn't turn in any direction without being bombarded by condolences for her father. But it was only a moment until those condolences turned to interrogations about the upcoming wedding.

"Where will you hold the wedding ceremony? In Central Denora I hope?"

"Who will design your gown?"

"What cake will you be serving? Will Lisette be your baker?"

To be quite honest, she hadn't thought of any of those questions. The only question she had about her wedding was, "am I really going to do it?"

Truthfully, the last few days with Laurent had changed Lucy's viewpoint about her ideas of marriage. There was a connection that she felt when she was with Laurent—a camaraderie. She knew it was partially just a physical connection, but perhaps over time it would turn into more.

He had such amazing plans for the people of Denora, and being part of that gave her something to look forward to in a future with him in the North. It wasn't entirely romantic excitement, but perhaps, with time, those feelings would grow.

Regardless, this week was not the time for that.

Laurent was busy planning his meeting with the king and Lucy just had to get through the funeral. For now, she was content to be here—in her true home.

Making her way across the garden terrace, Lucy saw her younger brothers Henry and Simon tear across the grass, laughing and playing with the other children who had come to visit.

Finally, something normal around here.

Seeing the estate booming with life made Lucy's heart warm. When she left the Baum estate for the North with Laurent months ago, it had felt so dark and dreary. Somber memories shadowed the once bright spots of her life. She wasn't sure if joy would ever return without her father's larger-than-life presence, and seeing the natural happiness of her young brothers gave her a ray of hope.

"Lucy," Henry called in a sing-song voice, darting past her. "I bet you can't catch us!"

"Wait!" Simon yelled after him. "You have to wait for us to hide!" He kept running after the children bounding through the yard.

"You forgot I am the reigning champion of seek-and-find!" Lucy called back to them. Her smile followed them as she watched the children run into the orchard and out of sight.

She rubbed her chest to ease the sharp pain of longing that struck. Seek-and-find was the same game she and Micah had played in the forest before they had fallen for one another. Or perhaps she had already fallen for him by then? There had always been something about Micah that just felt right to her... but there was no time to think about that now. She had to focus on what was in front of her.

Her family.

Grieving her father.

Then returning to the north to wed Laurent. She had to uphold her end of the deal.

There was no more time to live in the past.

With a defeated sigh, Lucy stepped through the terrace entryway and into the estate. Just on the other side of the door, Lucy saw Anita bustling around and directing Fae of all kinds. Some were delivering flowers or food, some were decorating, others were part of the cleaning staff. Anita rushed from one place to the next, making sure every detail was perfect for the most important part of this weekend. The Farewell ceremony.

Fae Farewell ceremonies were rare, as many Fae did not age and die like most mortals. The eldest Fae stayed to offer guidance and wisdom as Venerable Fae. After that, the Fae who lived to old age finished their lives with celebration as they passed from one plane of existence to the next. They didn't have Farewell Ceremonies. Instead, they simply had celebrations of life and those who passed on were usually prepared. They would carefully plan and finance the arrangements long before they were needed.

It had been centuries since the Addaxe Wars when Fae had last experienced a high death count due to violence. Since then, only those who had lived for over 500 years could speak to the unexpected passing of Fae, but Lucy was much younger than that. She, and many others, hadn't experienced a sudden Fae death in their lifetime.

Father, why did it have to be you?

She felt empty.

Corvus had been young and hearty and booming with life. It was simply unfathomable that he was... gone.

She couldn't bring herself to say the words, though the magic within her washed through her like a comforting hug. The gesture caused her eyes to sting.

Not now. I refuse to fall apart.

Thankful that her mother hadn't spotted her, Lucy took a deep breath and continued further down the hall. She knew Anita was likely having a difficult time with the funeral arrangements, and that order and precision were sure to be the only things holding her together.

Off to her right, the loud guffaw of her eldest brother, Hugh, pierced through her sadness and pulled a smile to her lips. It had been nearly a year since she heard that laugh.

Quickening her pace, she walked into the sitting room where her brothers gathered, drinking their father's favorite spirits and smoking strong cigars.

Leaning in the doorway, she took in the scene. Her three eldest brothers sat before a fireplace, lounging in deep, leather armchairs, with dragon-glass goblets in one hand and smelly cigars in the other. They all had easy smiles on their faces, their cheeks red, either from the warmth of the fire or the spirits.

"I should have known I'd find you three menaces up to no good," Lucy joked from the doorway.

"Ah, Lucella!" Gregory greeted her, walking toward

her from his seat. "Wes here has told us you've been giving him a hard time." He winked with his customary sly smile all her brothers seemed to have inherited. "Keep it up."

Lucy laughed as she pulled Gregory in for a warm embrace. Hugh stood next, giving his sister a squeeze.

"Those things smell awful," Lucy said, gesturing to the large cigars in their hands. "Why are they so massive?"

"We broke into Father's secret stash," Hugh said with a laugh. "Cigars from Kerroz—only the best of the best." He took a deep puff in and blew out a circle of smoke. "Neddard said he's got another case in his tent. We hadn't seen him in ages, but he said it was the only way we could give a fair tribute to Father."

"I see you've been working tirelessly in the South," Lucy said with mock seriousness, ignoring the mention of funeral business. "Yes, such hard work sitting around blowing smoke rings all day. I'm sure Lisette just loves that."

"For your information, Lisette loves me, flaws and all." Hugh winked at her.

"And how many flaws there are," Lucy replied snarkily with a wide grin across her face.

"Wes, I think you were right," Gregory said, with a shocked smile on his face. "Lucy's become more brazen in her old age."

"Yes, I'm a crippling old Fae." She made Wes scoot over and sat next to him, taking a sip of the spirits in his cup. With a face twisted in disgust, she quickly handed it back to him. "This also tastes old. What in all the realms is this?"

"Amartium—dragon-flamed whiskey," a familiar voice said from the doorway. "Father's favorite."

She'd know that voice anywhere.

Tristan.

Grinning from ear to ear, she turned to greet her brother, but was met with an unexpected sight. It was, indeed, Tristan standing before her, but he had changed so much. His once long hair was now trimmed short to match his soldier friends. His eyes that had always twinkled in the light now seemed dull, like a bit of his brilliance was lost. But what stood out the most was his clothing. Truly, Lucy should have seen it coming, but still it shocked her. Instead of his usual casual tunic and trousers, he wore the uniform of a soldier.

He enlisted in the Denoran military.

Her smile failed only for a second, but Lucy was sure Tristan had seen it. Putting more enthusiasm into her greeting, she walked over to him and gave him a big hug. She may not have been thrilled that her brother had a new and dangerous occupation, but she was glad to see him. More than anything, she was happy he was following his heart. He had always wanted to join the military, and their father had been against it.

I guess there was no one to hold him back any longer.

The realization put a sting in the endless ache that was her heart.

"Welcome home, little sister," he murmured in her ear.

Pulling back, she looked into Tristan's eyes and

replied, "I guess the same can be said for you." She looked over his uniform, her fingertips running down the crisp edges, the clothing noticeably brand new. "This is a recent occurrence?"

"Made it official about a week ago." As he spoke, he took a step back, straightening. He walked over to the couch and sat.

Lucy's hands dropped to her sides as she took in the change.

Tristan's entire demeanor felt different. He used to be the first to joke with his brothers, stealing their father's spirits and causing mischief. Now, he was turning down a drink from Hugh and sitting with a posture that would put Madame Paulina, their etiquette tutor, to shame.

Lucy and Wes exchanged a worried glance. While Hugh and Gregory were the eldest, Lucy, Wes, and Tristan were the closest. Tristan had always said he wanted to follow along with his friends and enlist, but this seemed different. He wasn't the happy and cheerful male, ready to follow his friends. This was something else.

"It's great to see everyone here," Wes said, changing the subject. The siblings sat in a semicircle around the fireplace—Tristan on one far end, and Gregory on the other. "I must admit, this..." His voice trailed off as he looked down at his glass. "This has been a harder transition than I ever thought possible."

Hugh and Gregory nodded, swirling the ice in their goblets. Tristan avoided eye contact and focused on the fireplace before them. The silence in the room was almost unbearable.

"We are here for you, brother," Hugh said, putting his broad hand on the edge of Wes's shoulder. "We know the business side of things will be a challenge. Don't give up. Gregory and I had each other while we figured out the business in the Southern Territory. You have..." His voice trailed off. It was clear Wes had no one. "Well, we will send a few of our finest workers to help you set up everything you need."

"Thank you," Wes said with a sad smile. "Mother keeps insisting on helping, but she needs the time to grieve and watch over Henry and Simon. I don't want to put more work on her."

"Perhaps Mother *wants* more work?" Lucy asked.

All of her brothers looked at her as though she was speaking in tongues.

"It is not insane to think that an intelligent female like our mother would like to put her mind to work instead of moping around for days on end," Lucy challenged.

Her brothers continued looking at her, then glanced at each other. Clearly they disagreed, but Lucy didn't care what they thought.

"It couldn't hurt anyone to let her help is all I'm saying," Lucy said, putting her hands in the air, deciding it wasn't time for this fight.

No. There were enough difficult things on the horizon, and they all needed to stay unified to get through the day ahead.

Lucy checked the time on the clock sitting upon the mantle and her insides twisted with dread.

"Did you speak with Marielle yet?" Lucy asked quietly, changing the topic to what really mattered.

They all nodded.

Marielle was the Venerable Fae in charge of the Farewell Ceremony. She had explained to Lucy that in normal celebrations of life; the Fae honored the dead for days on end—sometimes even weeks. However, with Corvus's untimely death, it was more appropriate for a shorter commemoration of his life, giving them the time to mourn their beloved father.

Mourning was not typical for Fae, but Lucy became more and more familiar with the uncomfortable feeling —however unwanted it was.

Her eyes darted around the room, taking in her brothers as they steeled themselves for what was to come.

A brisk rap on the door frame announced their mother, Anita's, arrival. "Here you all are," Anita said with a weak smile. Lisette, Hugh's very pregnant wife, walked into the room beside her.

Lucy stood to give them both a gentle hug.

Anita forced another smile to grace her lips as she spoke again. "I'm glad you're all together. It's time."

CHAPTER

SEVEN

LUCY

Lucy wasn't sure what she had expected, even after speaking with Marielle, but this surely wasn't it. She stood with her family along the shoreline; the wind whipping her cloak back and forth in the brisk cold. There were spells for keeping warm, but Lucy refused to use them.

Not today.

She would feel every bit of this day. She couldn't risk forgetting a single moment... Not the words that were spoken. Not the chill of the wind. Not the empty emotions that threatened to drown her as she stood before the vast sea.

Side by side, she waited with what was left of her family, dreading the ceremony that she knew would truly be a final goodbye.

The steady beat of her heart quickened and boomed in her ears, drowning out the crash of the waves and the whispers of strangers. Taking a breath in, she felt she couldn't get enough air. Again and again, she gulped down the salty, damp air, but nothing was helping. In the midst of her panic, Lucy wasn't sure where to look.

Straight ahead was the open sea, ready to take her father's physical body and swallow him whole, forcing Lucy to say goodbye forever. To her right, her older brothers stood in a firm, straight line, barely moving, giving their deepest respect to their father. To her left, her younger brothers stood with her mother, all struggling to withhold their sobs.

Each direction offered no comfort.

She risked a quick glance at her mother and regretted it immediately. Anita stood tall, her beautiful brown hair curled the way Corvus had always liked, wearing a deep purple gown to honor the one she had loved more immensely than the open sky above them. Her hazel eyes were the only thing that depicted the true emotions warring inside of her, as tears silently fell in a torrent of sorrow.

Lucy squeezed her eyes shut, tears finding their way from her eyes as well. It was all too much.

She wasn't supposed to be saying goodbye this soon.

She couldn't.

As she braced her body to turn and run, a warm hand landed on her shoulder. With a gasp, she looked up, eyes wide with mourning. Wes must have known she was ready to flee. He gave her arm a gentle squeeze—the act grounding her. "It's time," he whispered to her.

There's no running from this...

Time and time again, Lucy ran from the things that hurt her. When her father told her she couldn't be a bowyer, she hid in the orchard and did target practice until her hands were numb and her heart was full. When her tutors refused to teach her anything worth knowing, she ditched her lessons and taught herself the things she wanted to know. When her parents arranged an entire new life for Lucy, husband included, she fled to the mortal realm in a desperate attempt to change her life.

But this. There was nowhere in all the realms that she could escape to that could change this outcome... Her father was gone, and there was nothing, *nothing*, she could do to change it.

And that hurt the most.

Nodding, she stepped forward with trembling legs as she and her family moved closer to the rocky shore.

Marielle gestured for the ferry master to initiate the ceremony, using her magic to send the elderly Fae the flowers from the hundreds of guests in attendance. Each guest had whispered into the flowers, offering words of love and encouragement to help the deceased brave the next chapter—whatever that may be. It was the very last gift a Fae could offer to their loved ones. Lucy focused on her breathing as the ferry master tucked the flowers safely into the stern of the ornate boat where Corvus lay.

The vessel was beautiful—a long, narrow body with emerald and violet accents bordering the hull. Her father laid in the bed of straw, every piece tightly woven into intricate patterns. Lucy watched as each of her siblings took their next position, walking closer to the shoreline —closer to saying goodbye.

I can't do this. I can't do this.

Her breathing hitched as her eyes darted behind her, searching. King Tralont, Duke Renfro, Laurent, Roger, family, friends, customers, faces of all people surrounding her—there was nowhere to run.

She took a step back and her foot bumped into her bow. Someone had placed it there in preparation for the next part of the ceremony. Lucy knew what was to come, but she wasn't sure what was going to be worse: taking her turn or when everything was over.

"We are gathered here to honor Master Corvus Baum as he makes his way past our realm and into the realms beyond." Marielle spoke to the crowd, amplifying her voice with a magical spell. "We ask all the gods in Porvanai to watch over his passage and send him to an eternal resting place, finding peace, just as the gods do."

Lucy's breath hitched.

"When our beloved Fae cross over from our plane to the next, we must always be there to guide them," Marielle continued, turning to the Baum family. "With our arrows, we will light the way as we show Master Baum our undying love and devotion. As his family floods his spirit with their magic, Corvus will send his magic to them in return. In the highest honor a father can bestow, Corvus will leave his legacy of power within his family, allowing the Baum bloodline to continue to thrive."

The boat drifted farther and farther away from the shore as Hugh and Gregory each took a bow and arrow into their hands and prepared to go first. With unwavering strength, they drew and released their arrows, then placed a hand over their heart in their last good-bye. The arrows arched through the sky, a trail of golden magic gleaming through the air. Landing directly onto Corvus's pyre, the spelled arrow burst into flames.

A lump grew in Lucy's throat.

I can't do this.

Wes took aim next. A graceful, silver stream twinkled in the sky and landed at the edge of the straw, growing the flame.

While Tristan took aim, Lucy began to shake.

How could she be next? She would have to shoot a flaming arrow at her father's pyre, marking this as the last time she would ever see him again. Was she ready for this? Couldn't they wait any longer?

Wes looked to Lucy, motioning for her to go when he saw the blatant fear overtaking her. Hugh and Gregory took notice as well and moved to help Henry and Simon send their arrows as Wes spoke with Lucy.

"It will be alright," he whispered to her, handing Lucy her bow.

"I can't do this," Lucy whispered, shaking her head, looking at the beautiful bow in her hands. Her eyes were wide and unblinking as they glossed over with tears. "I can't. I'm not ready to say goodbye."

An immense wave of anguish consumed Lucy, making her heart an empty vessel. Breathing quickly, her shaking turned into trembling. Her magic hummed beneath the surface, trying to soothe her, but nothing worked.

Wes rolled his lips into a thin line, his eyes searching hers, clearly trying to find the right words to say, but before he could speak, Anita came up behind her.

"It's okay, Wesley," she whispered, putting her hand

on her son's cheek. She turned to Lucy. "Come, Lucella. You must go before me so I can initiate the spell."

"I—I can't," Lucy gasped, desperately trying to hold back the flood of tears. Her hand held the bow so tightly her knuckles turned stark white.

Anita just smiled at her. "My sweet girl, we both know you can. And you must. Your father deserves his final resting place with his ancestors above in the stars, and this is how he ascends. This is how Fae magic continues." She took Lucy's quaking hand and stilled it in hers, nodding at her in encouragement. "You are the strongest of us all... Your father would be so very proud of you."

Lucy squeezed her eyes tight and turned to the shoreline. Soon, the pyre would be too far away and the magic would not be returned to the bloodline. She had to make this shot so that her mother stood a chance to get her arrow to reach the far distance.

Taking a deep breath in, she closed her eyes. *I love you, Father.* She opened her eyes and took aim. *I am so sorry I couldn't stop him.*

As she released the arrow, she allowed herself to feel what she had been pushing away for so long: the fear of a life without her father, and the guilt that consumed her more and more each day.

Lucy watched as the shimmering green arrow arched high into the sky and landed gracefully on the pyre, the fire growing so large she could no longer see beneath the flames. She shuddered at the finality of the action. This was it.

This was goodbye.

Lucy turned to speak to Anita, but her mother was already in position, sending her arrow careening through the sky. Her graceful magic landed with a powerful thud.

Almost as soon as it connected, the fire on the boat grew to astonishing heights, roaring with the magic imbued within each arrow. Sparks of yellow, silver, purple, and green shot wildly from the burning straw. Then suddenly, the blaze calmed, as though the wildness of the flames left it completely. But the fire was still burning, however small it was, and it seemed to change as the water churned all around. The pyre continued to float farther and farther away from them, but from the far off distance, they could see a violet wave of power exude from the flames.

As if Corvus was sending his own arrows from the other side, a bright arch of violet light came speeding toward her family from the middle of the sea. First hitting Hugh, then Gregory, following each of her brothers in line in the same order they had sent their arrows. Wes. Tristan. Henry. Simon.

Lucy held her breath as she watched her brothers accept their father's magic, each inhaling deeply as the magic landed within their chest.

Henry and Simon cried as Anita held them tightly beside her, smiling softly at the magic finding its new home within Corvus's children.

Lucy watched, waiting for her turn, terrified of what would happen. Would it hurt? Would she get any at all? Was she deserving of his magic? It was her fault he was gone. All of this was because of her.

A shuddering sob wracked through her body, but she

pushed it back, refusing to fall apart before the crowd. She took a breath, trying to calm herself.

Then she saw it.

A purple so deep it looked black came floating on the wind to Lucy. It was nothing like the soaring violet light given to her brothers. This was smoke and shadow, mixing and dancing in the wind.

Shadow.

Lucy's eyes went wide as she realized. She risked a glance at Wes, who was standing with his mouth open wide in astonishment, along with the rest of her brothers. Short gasps came from the onlookers in the surrounding crowd.

Anita only laughed. A joyous, relieved smile filled her as glistening tears reflected off her cheeks in the fading sun in the distance.

Her father had gifted Lucy his most treasured magic—the gift of his shadows.

Lucy took a step forward to meet the dark purple shadows, her toes soaking in the Lancast Sea.

I'm here, Father.

Spreading her arms wide, the magic swirled around her gently before entering through her heart, where each Fae held their magic.

As it flooded inside of her, she thought it would feel heavy, like the added magic wouldn't fit, but it was the complete opposite. She felt lighter than she had in years, feeling the joyous reunion of magic from her family line returning to Baum blood.

It was the most whole she had ever felt.

Anita kept her eyes on Lucy, pride still shining through her tear-stained cheeks.

Lucy's heart fluttered in fear and she tore her gaze away from her mother, back to her father's pyre. What would Anita receive from Corvus now? And was there enough time? She watched as the boat swayed back and forth, getting farther away. Would his magic reach her?

Lucy turned back to her mother, worried, but Anita was only smiling quietly to herself. There was no fear in her eyes.

An eerie hush came over the crowd. Squinting in the distance, Lucy thought she could see something making its way to them. Far off, a pale purple orb of light flapped in the air, bouncing up and down as though affected by the wind.

It was nothing like the magic given to her brothers and nothing like the smoky shadows given to Lucy. No, it was small and slow and graceful in a different sort of way.

Anita grinned from ear to ear, raising her hands to meet the beautiful light. "I'm here, darling!" Anita called out to the magic as though she had expected nothing else.

As it drew closer, Lucy could see exactly what it was. A small butterfly made of lavender colored light came soaring toward Anita, flapping its wings in delight and playfully dancing around her.

Sobbing with joy, Anita held her palms out to capture the butterfly as it landed ever so gently. With two hands, she pulled it to her chest, closed her eyes, and sighed.

The magic of the butterfly entered Anita—her heart full of magic.

Another burst of flame came from the boat in the distance, and then slowed to a small, simmering fire, signaling the end of the ceremony.

It was done.

Her eyes were glued to the flames burning on the Lancast Sea.

The darkening sky played tricks on her eyes, making it harder and harder to focus her vision.

Lucy wasn't sure how much time had passed as each Fae in the crowd either silently watched the boat float away, or had walked off quietly, allowing the family these final moments in private. She continued to stare off into the wide sea, unable to pry her eyes away from her father for the last time. She could nearly hear the crackling fire still.

A heavy coat was placed on her shoulders, breaking her from her reverie. Blinking, she looked around to find that she was the last one on the shoreline. Her family was in the carriages waiting to return to the estate, and she was alone, still standing in the water, the waves lapping at her ankles.

"I'm sorry to bother you," Laurent said gently over her shoulder. "I saw you shivering and I couldn't stand by any longer."

Lucy's skin hurt from the brisk wind. She clasped her hands, realizing they were shaking. Her jaw ached. Then it registered—the sound she heard could not have been the fire, for it was too far away... it was her teeth chattering.

How long had she been standing there?

Laurent stood next to her, looking her over. Concern etched in his features, and he rubbed his hands along her arms, trying to warm her. "Are you ready to return? Or would you like to stay a little longer?"

"I would like to stay..." Lucy said, her eyes quickly returning to the sea, worried she would no longer be able to see her father.

Laurent nodded quietly, then walked away.

The sound of the horses confused her, knowing the carriages were leaving, but she wouldn't look away again. Her father was too far, and she couldn't risk losing sight of him. Not now.

Crunching footsteps on the ground behind her came closer, but she refused to turn.

"I've sent your family home," Laurent said quietly. He stood next to her, his fingers barely touching hers as he remained at her side. "We can stay as long as you'd like."

Lucy's fingers carefully reached out for Laurent's, searching for his warmth. They stood shoulder to shoulder on the water's edge until the sun was gone and Lucy couldn't see the shoreline in front of her.

As the tiny speck of light on the horizon faded, Lucy lost sight of her father for the very last time.

EIGHT

"Thank you for coming," Wes told King Tralont.

Wes had bid his farewells to his brothers and a few guests then promptly escaped to the study. He was hoping to find a moment to breathe, however, something always seemed to come up. Though, a knock on his door from the king was the very last thing he expected.

King Tralont came to offer words of sympathy and to check in on the status of the Baum Bowyer business. Wes appreciated it, but wasn't sure how to respond to the actual fucking king.

"Thank you for your kind words," he said, doing his best not to waver.

"I mean it, young Baum," King Tralont said for the second time. "Your father changed the face of our Denoran armies with his updated weaponry. Now, we are willing to give you time, but we want to ensure the quality of the bows remains constant."

Wes had already tried explaining that Hugh and Gregory had offered to send support from the South to support him in this new position, but it looked as though the king had a point he needed to get across. Wes didn't want to appear ungrateful for whatever the king offered, so he smiled and nodded enthusiastically in return.

"Duke Renfro is not far from the estate," Tralont continued. "He will come to assist you as needed. Consider him my liaison as you adjust to your new role here."

New role.

As if he had asked for it.

As if he had just gotten a cheerful promotion.

No. His father had died and now he was left to fill the shoes of a male who was greater than life itself.

Wes kept the shudder deep within him, refusing to appear weak in front of the Fae king. He nodded in a deep bow to show his gratitude and prayed he would stop talking.

He was tired—body and soul *tired.*

The Farewell Ceremony was more overwhelming than he expected, and it was draining keeping his emotions buried so deep inside of him.

He was now the face of the company business, and with Jasper betraying them all and Lucy's bowyer knowledge traveling back to the North in the morning, he was left with no one.

"I will send him within the next fortnight or so. Please, take the time to grieve and let Renfro know of anything you may need."

"Thank you, your majesty," Wes replied, his hand over his heart to show his allegiance.

When King Tralont finally left, Wes sunk into a leather chair and covered his face with his hands.

What the fuck am I going to do?

A knock on the door should have been enough to pull himself back together, but he stayed slouched in the chair, willing whoever it was to go away.

"Wes?" Lucy called from behind the closed door.

Unfortunately, younger sisters never care about things like patience or manners, so Lucy simply opened the door and strode right in.

"Are you alright?" Lucy asked, sliding into the chair across from him.

"Is there a line out there or something? I swear, one Fae exits, another enters." Wes said behind closed eyes.

"Have you seen Lisette?" she asked, changing the subject.

"Hugh and Lisette left with Gregory a little while ago."

"I can't believe we are going to have another baby in the family," Lucy smiled. "Did you see Lisette's adorable baby bump?"

"Yes, she mentioned she's traveling to the east to see her mother in the country before the baby comes. Hugh and Gregory are dropping her off there before they make their way back to the South." He released a deep sigh, already missing his brothers. "I can't imagine Hugh as a father." Wes smiled at the idea.

"Funny, they go south, and I go north..." Lucy's voice trailed off. "I'm leaving in the morning."

"I know." It was on his mind the entire day. He and Lucy had been through so much together, and when their father died, she just disappeared. Left to the North without so much as an "I'll miss you."

He understood why she did it, but it didn't make it any easier. He thought he had at least another twenty years of learning on the job before he'd be the one to take over. It was his own fault—he shouldn't have spent so much time fucking around. Now, there was no time to fix any of it.

"Is Tristan going to be okay?" Her voice was a whisper, almost like she was afraid to say it.

"He's finding himself," Wes sighed. "Not unlike yourself."

"I beg your pardon?" Lucy asked, hurt tinging the words.

"Is there a reason you are heading off to the North so soon? We could use you here at home." Someone could talk to their mother. She could help with the guests who hadn't yet left.

"This isn't my home anymore." Lucy stood up swiftly, walking over to a cabinet that held tools and polishes for bows.

The words hit like a sword to the chest.

Isn't it? Wouldn't this always be her home?

All he could do was nod. He had no more fight left in him, and from the way she lingered on the shoreline for hours after the sun had set, he wasn't sure she did either.

"Can I take a few supplies home to make a bow?" Lucy asked suddenly.

"Of course," Wes replied, smiling gently. "Everything here is yours as much as it is mine. Please, take whatever you'd like."

"I'll have Roger pick it up in the morning before we depart," Lucy said, then she walked over to her brother.

He pulled himself to stand before her, sensing her farewell. "Try out any of Father's magic yet?" Wes asked, trying to lighten the mood.

Lucy's lips quirked up into a sad smile, and Wes knew exactly how she felt. She nodded and threw her hands into the air, causing all the lights to flicker. With her hands still raised in the air, she curled them into fists, pulling the shadows from the corners of the rooms to where they stood in the center.

The effect was immediate and terrifying—the same as their father.

The shadows crept closer and closer, as though they had a nefarious mind of their own, their eerie wisps curling and clawing toward them.

Before the darkness touched them, she uncurled her fingers and pushed the shadows back to their rightful places, allowing the light to shine brightly once again.

"That will be a fun party trick," Wes teased, taking a deep breath.

Lucy took his hands in hers and squeezed them gently. "You will make Father proud and run this business better than anyone else in all the realms."

Wes's gaze pierced hers as he looked into her hazel eyes and replied, "And you will make Father proud as you find his murderer and make him pay."

The fire in her eyes was the only acknowledgment he needed.

He knew Lucy wasn't in the North just to play house —she was stronger than that.

He hoped.

THE NEXT MORNING, Wes thanked the stars for the spells to remove the lingering headache he acquired from the heavy pour of his father's amartium. He and Tristan shared the remainder of the bottle before his brother left to return to his unit. They granted him a soldier's leave to grieve, but dumped Tristan right back into the thick of his training as soon as the Farewell Ceremony was complete.

It tore at Wes, knowing Tristan was off serving Denora in the most dangerous way possible. Tristan kept telling him over and over that this was what he wanted, that this was the way to be part of the solution to Denora's problems, but Wes didn't understand any of it.

He was only thankful that their father's magic manifested in Tristan with improved strength and agility. Watching Tristan discover it as he nearly dropped a full bottle of spirits was quite amusing. It was as though Corvus knew from beyond this plane of life that Tristan would need the upper hand.

Denora had problems, sure; every place had them. But what were these problems that Tristan thought he could solve?

Wes would rather focus on the problems there in front of him. First and foremost, the silent warning given by the king himself. He was smart enough to know that the offer of Duke Renfro's services was more of a threat than a gift. It was clear: if Wes messed anything up, the king would replace him in a heartbeat.

I can't let my father down, Wes repeated to himself.

It was the only thing keeping him going. There was nothing else to say. Figuring it out was the only thing he could do to honor his father.

Walking into the study, Wes stared at the place that once seemed so familiar. Everything felt foreign now. It was one thing for the office to be his father's, but now it was his.

His desk.

His chair.

His business.

He took a deep breath to ease his flipping stomach. Sitting down at the desk, he looked around the room. He had never seen it from this angle.

"Well, here goes nothing," he said to himself. Opening the first ledger, he tried to read the contents but felt as though he was reading an unfamiliar language. It reminded him of Micah and Brax trying to read Micah's ancient tome.

He thought of them often, if he was being honest. Wes worried Lucy was making a terrible mistake in picking Sloan over Lumen, but there was nothing he could do about it. He had contemplated talking to Brax about it, but as much as the thought of her exhilarated him, she scared him a little, too.

Wes sighed and leaned back in his chair. Feeling defeated, he lifted his hands and called on his magic, forming a small ball of light.

"You give Lucella your shadows, Tristan your

strength, and comfort Mother with the beauty of a butterfly, and what do you give me?" Wes said to himself sullenly. "Light." He made a fist and doused the light, frustration filling his entire being. "Sure would have been helpful, except I already learned how to summon light when I was a child."

He slammed the ledger shut and stalked across the room, only to get there, turn around, and return to the desk. There was nowhere for him to go and nobody to whom he could turn.

"If Lucy was here, she would at least insult me while telling me the most obvious thing to do, so why can't I figure it out on my own?"

An abrupt knock pulled him from his spiral. He ran his hands through his hair, ensuring he looked presentable, and then spoke, trying to capture the same commanding tone his father used to have. "You may enter."

The visitors the previous day had been full of surprises, so he didn't even bother to guess who it could be. Though, when his mother popped her head through the door, he was glad he could at least release the facade of power he was trying to emit.

"Hello, dear," Anita spoke, smiling gently. She had changed so much within the last day. Before the Farewell Ceremony, she was like a walking shell of herself. Now, there was more light in her eyes, more color in her cheeks. "I've come to see if I could help at all?"

Wonderful, Wes thought to himself. *I'm so blatantly pathetic that my mother has come to try to pick up the pieces I can't seem to manage.*

"No need, Mother," Wes said with a forced grin, walking over to her. He kissed her on the cheek as he said, "I have everything under control. I don't see how you could help much, anyway. It's all just the business side of things."

Anita kept her face stoic and blinked, as if carefully choosing the next words to say. "Wesley, I have helped your father with much of the business for many years. I'd be happy to help you now."

He almost scoffed. At no time would Corvus Baum ever let a female in a male's business industry. He made that perfectly clear when Lucy asked to be part of the Baum Bowyers. There was no way his mother knew anything more than he did. Besides, he was at his father's beck and call for years before this, and his mother was never included in any business conversations.

"I appreciate the offer, Mother," Wes said to appease her. "Right now I must get back to work. You don't need to worry."

The smile on Anita's face faltered for a moment, but she just nodded and looked down. "Well, I am here if you need anything at all." Her eyes barely met Wes's as she turned to exit.

When the door clicked shut behind her, Wes threw a privacy charm around the office. Screaming in frustration, he let go of his last bit of restraint. He kicked the high wingback chair to the ground and threw a large jar of wood stain across the room, watching as it crashed through the window behind the desk. He shoved the desk with all of his strength and wished that something, anything could take away this empty hole within him that seemed to only have space for anger.

He walked past the desk and his pant leg got snagged on a half-open drawer. Grunting, he ripped his pants away, leaving a hole in the cloth. Reaching for the drawer, prepared to shove it shut, he wavered.

There in the center of the drawer was a bejeweled amulet, forcibly reminding him what was at stake. The amulet was the key to the beautiful, fertile land of The Elderwood that remained the backbone of the family business.

He dropped to his knees before the desk and reverently pulled the drawer open a little wider. It felt as though he was breaking a rule, going through his father's things like this... but they weren't his father's things anymore. These all belonged to Wes now.

With a shaking hand, he picked up the necklace, inspecting it closely. He recalled the first time he saw this amulet.

"This is the key to our family's legacy, Wesley," Corvus had told him when Wes was young. "With this, we are given the special opportunity to bring the most remarkable weapons to Denora to keep our people safe." His eyes had twinkled as he said it. "We have an important job that we must never take for granted."

Wes squeezed the chain in his hands and carefully placed it back inside the drawer. He closed it, pulling the desk back into position, and then righted the chair. Taking a moment to breathe, he sat, removed the privacy charm, and got back to work. His father was right. Their job was important to all of Denora, and he would do it right.

A whistle of a bird called from the broken window, making his shoulders drop yet again.

"Day one, and what do you do? Have a temper tantrum and break a fucking window," he chided himself.

The bird's whistle called again. This time it was a familiar tune from his childhood. Curious, Wes looked up at the bird, which seemed to stare at him with knowing eyes. It was a beautiful, black raven, just sitting at the window, watching him.

He had no idea what to make of it, but couldn't linger on it for long. Wes opened the ledger once more and forced himself to keep going.

He had to keep going.

CHAPTER

NINE

MICAH

"I pull the magic to me. I form my intent," Micah murmured to himself. "I feel the magic, and I take control."

It didn't matter. No matter how many times he whispered the steps to himself, the magic didn't make an appearance—not without Jasper's rings. Micah grunted in frustration, kicking the dirt on the ground, sending dust into the wind.

He was desperate to make this magic work. He kept replaying the events from when the shadow cat last appeared and how the beast nearly ripped his leg off. If it had returned, he needed a way to protect himself and The Elderwood from any more attacks.

The large metal wall that once surrounded the portal was gone. It did a remarkable job keeping the shadow creatures inside, both feline and insects. However, as time passed, the magic failed and the metal weakened, turning back into stone somehow. There hadn't been any disruptions since, so Micah assumed they were long gone. But what if they weren't? What if the beasts were ready for round two?

Brax used the river stones as a foot rest as she relaxed in the grass.

"Are you going to help me or just sit there?" Micah scowled. "If Scar returns and I can't use my magic to fight him, we're screwed."

"There's no way that shadow beast has returned," Brax said steadily from her spot where she lay in the sun. "Besides, it's been days and even you've said you haven't seen anything since."

Micah couldn't decide if Brax really believed what she said or if she just wanted Micah to believe it. Regardless, he knew what he saw, which was why he wouldn't back down.

"We need to keep working on my magic," he reminded Brax. "That's why we're out here. Not for you to sun yourself like some lizard." He stood near the edge of the shadowy tree line, keeping himself out of the midday sun as he continued his latest attempt to call for his magic.

"I'm going to pretend as though you have not spoken so that I do not have to insult you once more," she said as she waved her hand in dismissal. "Go ahead and practice. You and I both know that you aren't activating your true self, otherwise this magic would be working by now."

My true self?

Micah had had enough of her shitty attitude and the unfounded accusations that he wasn't trying hard enough. Every single day he was here on this property he was trying. He was trying to fit into this new life that was thrust upon him. It didn't even matter that he supposedly had magic. It was like giving a bear an axe and telling it to whittle a plane to fly—just because he had a tool didn't mean he knew how to wield it.

"It's such bullshit that you keep saying that," Micah said with barely confined anger.

Brax sat up with a jolt, looking him square in the eye, her kohl-lined gaze piercing straight through him. "Then tell me."

"Tell you what?" Micah snapped.

"Tell me you miss her."

Micah stilled, but the challenge in her eye was unmistakable. He knew her well enough to know she wouldn't back down, and maybe he owed it to her to be honest.

Brax had been Micah's loyal friend for the past six months. In the beginning, when Lucy had first left, there were days when he wouldn't speak at all. He couldn't. But Brax never forced anything from Micah. She let him grieve; just continued living for him, alongside him. She'd make sure he ate and dragged him outside to go for a run or to chop wood.

Every night she pulled him to the fire pit, making him sit there and listen to her, even when he had nothing to say. Some nights they sat and looked at the stars, some nights she'd tell stories of home or sing songs Micah didn't understand. But every night, a part of his heart healed, knowing that even though he felt alone, he wasn't—not really. Brax never left him. She didn't give up.

On one chilly night after a huge rainstorm, they sat around the fire and Brax told such a raunchy story about her having sex with a Kerroz ox-shifter that Micah had laughed so hard beer shot out of his nose. Since then, they were true friends, working together and getting through life, day by day.

The least he could do was be honest with the one person who didn't let him down.

"You know I do, Brax," he said with a sigh. "I miss her more than words can describe, but her being gone isn't why I'm not able to do my magic."

"You're entirely correct."

"What?" Micah was clearly lost now. "Weren't you just telling me the other day that my magic wouldn't work because I wasn't fighting for her? Wasn't there some nonsense about activating my true self?" Micah asked, exasperated with the increasingly annoying bull-shit that spewed from Brax's lips.

"I recall saying you weren't fighting for anything, you pungent turnip. You are the one entirely hung up on your life connected to Lucy Baum's, and when you realize that one has nothing to do with the other, we may finally make some progress." Brax finally stood up and dusted the dirt from her black leggings.

"Oh, so now you want to help me practice?" Micah shook his head in disbelief. He rolled his eyes and walked over to her. "Fine. Let's go."

"Time to listen." She grabbed his hand and twisted so Micah flipped over onto his back. He grunted his annoyance as he tried to catch his breath. "Look at me, don't move, and listen carefully, because I've been very patient these last few months and I'd really rather speed up this process. Got it?"

Micah's lips were a sneer, but he nodded regardless. His shoulder was screaming in pain and he wanted this over as much as she did.

"Good. One: You aren't working to your true potential because you keep closing yourself and your emotions off to the world. You must accept all of who and what you are if you expect the magic to work. Two: I say you aren't fighting for anything because you aren't. You have this vague notion in your mind that you want the bad guy squashed, but there is nothing on the line for you. You don't care what happens at the end, because you aren't thinking about the end. You aren't thinking about what you're working toward now that you don't have Lucy to fight for. But you need to come up with something you care deeply about before it gets you killed."

A stinging pain rushed down his arm as she punctuated each sentence with added force to her grip.

"Three:—" Brax's angered voice suddenly calmed, pausing for a moment as her face softened as she took in Micah. "I am sincerely sorry about what happened between you and Lucy. Lost love is the most painful of all, but you can't let it break you. You cannot let a broken heart define you."

With a gentle nod, she eased off of Micah and helped him to stand.

They stared at each other for a moment before she said, "I'll give you a minute and I'll get us some water. Then we can begin again."

Micah could only watch her walk away as he took in

everything she had said to him. He wanted to be mad; he wanted to scream that she was wrong and she had no idea how any of this felt, but that would be a lie all on its own.

The problem was, she was right—about all of it. He was absolutely closing himself off. It was what he did when things got too hard. And maybe he wasn't fighting for anything, because what the fuck was there to fight for? An empty cabin in a deserted forest?

He was no longer fighting for a future with Lucy. She left him... broke him. She built him up, healed his heart piece by piece, and then shattered it with a single stroke. She was gone, and he was an empty shell of who he once was—or maybe exactly who he had been before he met Lucy.

His eyes flickered to the tree that had started it all. The Elderwood portal was kept safely within an unsuspecting tree that looked similar to all the others; everything except for the engraving high on the trunk, about ten feet from the ground.

Careful not to step on the falling stones from the once solid metal wall, he took a step closer to look at the large engraving on the tree once more. The forest floor crunched under his boots.

They once thought it was the sigil for the Baum Bowyers, but his ancestral book had taught them it was so much more than that. The grand tree with a bow for roots and an arrow encompassing it was the symbol for the Lumen lineage. It started it all: the passageway to The Elderwood, the wood that made insurmountable weapons, a generational family business, and the source of all of his fucking problems.

It's because of this tree that I lost my family.

Grabbing the rings from his pocket, he put all four on and summoned as much power as he could, his rage guiding his intent. He wasn't sure what he was planning on doing, his emotions taking over all common sense.

He took a few steps back, feeling the magic inside of him grow. Squeezing his eyes shut tight, he felt the power surge through him. This was the power he wanted to manifest—this was the kind of magic that could make an actual difference. As he opened his eyes, two enormous spheres of red rested in his hands, his magic pooling in anticipation.

A large crack of wood sounded from the edge of the trees. Micah's eyes snapped to the sound, and there, at last, was the shadow beast, lurking in between the trees once again.

Scar.

Without a second thought, Micah hurled the magical spheres at the beast, but it dove out of the way and onto the open grass.

The back door of the cabin slammed just as his eyes met the beast's once again.

Prowling slowly on the grass, the shadow cat's two front legs reached out in front of him in a long stretch as its body transformed from solid to a shadowy mist. The last time it had done this, it seeped its way back into the portal of The Elderwood. This time though, it did something else entirely; something Micah could hardly comprehend.

Floating above the ground, the mist changed shape. First, there were two long forms...legs? The mist floated up, creating a torso, then long muscular arms. On top of that, a head. This was not the same shape as the shadow beast. The shadow dissipated completely and revealed the form of a man. Micah would have thought he was dreaming if he hadn't heard the clear thump of his foot meeting the ground.

A man with dark brown skin, golden eyes, and a scar across his face took a step closer to Micah. With a voice as deep as the ocean, the stranger spoke.

"I wish you'd stop doing that."

Micah felt his entire world spin. Was he seeing things correctly?

Brax came running over with her Vytyrian spear ready to attack, but mid-jump, the strange man waved his hand and Brax fell to the ground with a thud, her spear flinging in the other direction.

"Who are you?" Micah roared, taking a step back and trying to understand what the fuck had just happened. "What do you want?"

"Let's see," his deep voice rumbled like a purr. "You liked to call me Scar." He flourished his hand by the scar across his eye. "Clever," he retorted, though he did not seem amused.

"You were the cat?" Micah asked in disbelief.

"Cat." The man scoffed. "I am a feline shifter, yes. A *cat*? No. I am more akin to your... panthers, I believe you call them?"

Brax struggled on the ground, an unseen force still

holding her down. She grunted as she yelled. "Run, Micah!"

"Why are you here? Let her go!" Micah would not hide from this stranger and leave Brax here, unable to defend herself. It wasn't in him to abandon someone.

"I'll let her go once you listen," he said, his golden eyes shifting to watch Brax with a predatory gaze. "I do not trust her to stay still long enough to hear me, so I apologize that I must restrain her." His eyes looked purely feline, but the rest of his body was the equivalent of a warrior. He was practically seven feet tall and the width of a tree trunk —solid muscle. He wore a dark brown cloth draped over one shoulder and around his torso, coming mid-thigh.

"Then get on with it, you fucking overgrown parsnip," Brax spat.

Micah flashed a look of warning to Brax to get her to chill out, but she didn't care. Apparently Brax was afraid of exactly zero things.

"My name is Quillan. I am a sentry of what you call The Elderwood. I was summoned here by the dark magic that some evil Fae embedded inside the portal. It began to twist the insides of my realm, and I was sent here to fix the problem. I would like to first apologize for trying to kill you," he said, turning toward Micah. "Though by the sizable scar you've left upon me, I'd like to think we are now even." His beast-like eyes gazed upon Micah as though in contemplation.

Micah wasn't ready to speak, unsure what the cat-guy was getting at. He nodded, and the stranger continued.

"When you removed the tainted magic from the portal, our realm showed us that you were not the Fae at fault. Immediately it called to you as its guardian, and therefore, we standby to protect you in all battles." He gave a slight bow, keeping his eyes on Micah and Brax, clearly untrusting the duo. "There is much happening on the other side of the portal... Things you must hear for yourself."

"Why should we trust you?" Micah asked.

This all appeared too strange to be true, but then again, where did he even draw the line anymore?

"Because I could have let that Fae kill you that day, but I did not. I could have finished you myself, for that matter, and I chose not to." His golden eyes seared into Micah's. "You are The Guardian, and therefore, it is *imperative* you believe."

Micah wanted to argue, but the demanding look in Quillan's eyes told him it wasn't the best idea.

"Fine." Micah took a step forward, ready to make a deal with the strange shifter. If Quillan could bring him and Brax into The Elderwood to discuss these problems, maybe he'd get more answers. But before he could say another word, Quillan smiled, and turned into shadowy mist.

What the hell? That's it?

Micah took a step back as he watched the mist settle before him, wondering why Quillan had shifted back to leave so quickly.

Then, before Micah knew it, the magical mist dropped low and twined itself around his feet. With a swift jerk, it pulled tight as a rope, causing him to crash to the ground.

"Micah!" Brax screamed from far away.

"What's happening?!" Micah rolled to his side, trying to evade it, but the magic was far too powerful. Suddenly, he felt himself sliding along the grass. The beast was pulling him toward the portal. He dug his hands into the ground, trying to slow his trajectory. "Stop!"

The shadowy mist continued to drag him, never pausing for a moment. Micah continued to yell, thrashing his body in a desperate attempt to escape.

"Let me go!" Micah yelled, shoving his hands toward the shadows, calling upon his magic to blast it away. Nothing happened. Even the rings on his fingers had no reaction.

My magic is useless, he seethed.

As they got to the base of The Elderwood tree, the black mist lifted Micah into the air by his feet. Micah swung his body this way and that, but there was no use. He was up and over the last remnants of the stone wall and heading straight to the portal as the sigil began to glow.

"Micah!" Brax screamed, rushing toward him, the magic holding her down finally gone.

He reached his hand out to her, desperately hoping that she would get there in time. "Brax!" He screamed as he stretched his arm out as far as it could go, but it was too late. Micah was pulled into the portal, alone with the stranger who claimed to be friend, not foe.

Though Micah wasn't so sure anymore.

His mind reeled as he tried to get a handle on what was happening, but there was nothing he could fathom. Instead, his attention shifted to the portal he was passing through.

The last time he entered The Elderwood, he had felt a strange sensation of heaviness. This time, everything was different. Warmth penetrated his body, as though lightning was coursing through him. Bright colors of reds, blues, and yellows floated past him and an almost musical sound welcomed him as he stretched his arm through to the other side of the portal.

Somehow now upright, Micah stood on a bed of soft grass. Getting his bearings, he closed his eyes and shook his head. Forcing the dizziness away and tensing his body, Micah prepared to confront the man who basically kidnapped him. However, when he looked around at the beauty of the jaw-dropping Elderwood forest, he froze.

For a moment, he thought he was in a completely different place—it was not the quiet, uninhabited realm Lucy once brought him to. While Quillan stood beside him, they were not alone. Behind Quillan were at least a dozen other men and women wearing the same brown cloth draped over their bodies. They all had the same dark skin and golden eyes, eyes that stayed glued on Micah—each of them holding a large golden spear.

Micah carefully put his hands up as a gesture of nonviolence and took a deep breath of air, trying to calm his pounding heart.

"My people," Quillan announced. "I introduce you to The Guardian."

As though a wave crested over the crowd of people,

each one crossed a fist over the chest, bowed their heads, and bent down on one knee.

Micah stood in shock. Looking at Quillan for an explanation, but all the stranger did was offer a wicked smile and said, "Guardian, welcome to your people."

TEN

LUCY

*P*ull. Slide. Sand.

Pull. Slide. Sand.

The repetitive motions lulled Lucy into a settled calm as she carefully created an exquisite bow. It didn't even matter to her that she wasn't at the Baum estate, but instead in the Northern Territories once again. The drawn out motions pushed away thoughts of her father, her family, Micah, Jasper, even Laurent. There was nothing but her and the wood in her hands, creating something one of a kind.

She took a deep breath and wiped the sweat from her brow with the back of her forearm. Even with the cooler temperatures of the North, the fire in the hearth and the labor of creating the bow warmed her.

Lucy's hands were covered in sawdust, and her bedchambers would need a thorough cleaning, but she was finally done. Another remarkable weapon, made by the amazing wood from The Elderwood, creating a bow that could out-shoot any others.

This will surely—

Her thoughts faded, and her smile faltered. For a single moment, she imagined showing this beautiful weapon to her father, demanding for the eight-millionth time that she should be in charge of weapon design for the Baum Bowyers.

Then she remembered.

Her father had died.

It happened like that a lot the past few weeks. She knew for certain that her father was gone, passed on to another plane of existence, but it never stopped her from imagining, for just a moment, that he was still alive.

Holding the bow in her hands, the smooth wood grain flexed gently in her fingers. What to do with it now? She had her own bow—Laurent made sure of that when they first came to the North.

Is there anyone else in need of such a weapon?

Micah's beautiful face flashed in her mind. Her heart ached at the thought of him. She hoped he was doing well. Without the looming threat of Jasper, Micah was safe in Joterra. There would be no lurking Fae looking to steal his ancestral magic, and there would be no chance he could get involved in any other Fae incidents. There was no way for him to get hurt.

Even if she could change the course of her arrangement with Laurent, would Micah ever be safe with her? Lucy felt like a magnet to trouble, and she couldn't continue letting others get hurt on her account.

Instead, she would be right here in the North, keeping those she loved far away from her... Far away, safe and sound.

Her sacrifice of a life without Micah gave him a true chance to live. That's all that mattered anymore... She would find her own way to contentment. Lucy wasn't sure if happiness was still a possibility for her, but if the ones around her were taken care of, then that was all she could ask for.

Emerald green magic came crashing out of her hands and swirling all around her. A tug of the magic pulled at her, almost as if in question. *Who will take care of you?*

"I'm fine," she whispered to the empty room, wondering if her magic really could understand her. She stood and walked over to the window, noting the angle of the sun. The day had passed by without her noticing.

Standing and stretching, she looked around her room —a quiet space just for her. She may not have everything she had ever wanted in life, but what she had could be enough. Calling upon her magic, the green mist swirled around the room, removing any trace of sawdust or wood scraps.

It was funny to Lucy that she had once despised all acts of magic. When she was younger, she went out of her way to avoid it at all costs. Now it came to her as easily as breathing, as though it was an ingrained part of her—body, mind, and soul.

Soul.

The word strangled her heart. Was there such a thing? Did part of her father's soul come into her, gifting her new powers that allowed her to channel part of him?

She let her eyes drift close as she felt for that space within her. Shadow magic coursed over her to the dark corners of her room. Opening her eyes, she saw the room darken as the candlelight flickered out. Creeping tendrils of shadow curled toward her on the walls.

Why shadows for me, Father?

She released the magic and watched as the room lightened dramatically, returning to its otherwise normal state. A room that was given to her by someone who cared for her deeply.

Dressing for dinner, she realized exactly what she would do with her bow. She could no longer give it to her father, but there was someone near her who could appreciate its beauty. With a new determination, she picked up her tools and added a few final touches.

Looking down at the beautiful weapon in her hands, she was filled with a shade of gratitude. She wasn't sure if true happiness would ever find her again, but this hint of positivity felt close enough.

DINNER SEEMED a little more quiet than usual. Lucy wasn't sure if it was because of the time spent away during the Farewell Ceremony and that Laurent had work he needed to catch up on, or if it was something else entirely, but the silence pulled at the tension in the room.

"How are you feeling?" Laurent asked, a crease of worry on his brow.

"I am well, thank you," Lucy said politely.

"I sent someone to ask you for tea this afternoon, but I was told you did not answer... Are you upset with me?" His blue eyes met hers across the dinner table.

"Oh my," Lucy whispered in realization. She had a

privacy charm on her room to block out sounds from the village below and the noise in the hall as she worked on her bow. "I apologize. I did not hear anyone at my door."

"I see..." Laurent looked down at his plate.

"Laurent, truly," Lucy said. She stood up and walked the length of the small dining room to sit next to him. "I was feeling a bit lost, and I put my mind to a task that would soothe me. I was..." Her voice trailed off seeing the hurt in Laurent's posture.

Now is as good a time as any.

She sat and placed her hand on his. "Let me show you." Lucy smiled at Laurent, then nodded to Roger standing behind them.

Roger walked to the table with a bundle wrapped in black velvet. He handed it to Lucy, who then presented it to Laurent.

"This is for you," she said with a shy smile.

Laurent's eyes perked up, perplexed by the gift.

He carefully unwrapped the bundle on the edge of the table, his hands slowing as he got to the beautiful creation inside. His eyes glanced to the bow and then to Lucy, the slightest bit of color coming to his cheeks.

"I wanted to offer a token of gratitude," she said sincerely. "You have been nothing but supportive of me for these past few weeks, and I am sorry I have been so unsure before. You have held your end of the deal and have found Jasper DeValey. I'm ready now."

Laurent's eyes darted to hers at the proclamation.

"Ready?" Laurent asked, uncertainty quivering in his voice.

Lucy only nodded.

"You'll have to excuse me, but I would love for you to clarify exactly what you are ready for, as my heart may not be able to contain the sorrow if I assume incorrectly." He breathed out a huff of breath, trying to hide his vulnerable state.

"I am prepared to move forward with the wedding," Lucy said, thinking of the words she had practiced in her head on her walk to dinner.

There was no other answer to her future. Keeping Micah safe meant staying away. Wes had the family business under control. She would see this through—an arrangement that would benefit her in more ways than one.

Lucy could find her place here.

With him.

Laurent smiled from ear to ear, then reached over and took her hand in his and brought it to his lips, kissing her fingers gently.

Lucy wanted her heart to soar at the gesture, but she found herself empty of the passion that would periodically run through her. It took every bit of energy within her to remain smiling, not to run screaming for Micah in the other direction. She knew it was unfair, saying she was all in with Laurent while still pining for someone else, but there was no other way forward. Leaving Micah behind was the best thing she could do for him, so she would do it.

"The bow has snowflakes," Lucy said, nervously changing the subject. "I thought it would be fitting for your position here in the North."

"*Our* position," Laurent corrected her, with a tilt of his head. "It is our position now."

"What? No. You are the Lord of the North and I will just be your wife."

"If you think you are *just* anything, then you are wrong."

Lucy could only look at him in bewilderment.

He isn't saying what I think he's saying... is he?

"Lucy, what have I told you over and over since we've met?" His eyes were wild with excitement, and he took both of her hands in his and gripped them tightly. "I am looking for a true partner. You will not be a figurehead for outdated Denoran tradition, Lucy. You will be my queen. Always."

Lucy's heart *did* leap this time. Whenever she considered they would pair in an adequate union, Laurent took it another step further to prove how clearly he saw Lucy. All she could do was stare at him incredulously.

He shook his head and gave a slight chortle. "It's time," he announced to Roger, leaning forward in his chair.

Lucy looked at the surprise on Roger's face and then back to Laurent. "Time for what?"

"It's time I show you everything."

Laurent guided Lucy, hand in hand, from the dining room to his study. Roger, keeping step on the other side of Laurent, muttered urgently in his ear.

"Are you sure about this, my lord?"

"Absolutely," Laurent replied confidently.

Lucy was still uncertain about what was happening. She didn't expect a gift of a bow and an agreement to move forward with their wedding to be the cause for such activity. With Laurent clutching her hand tightly, she did her best to keep up.

Roger moved ahead to open the doors for the pair, his face stoic and emotionless.

Laurent brought Lucy to the center of the room and let go of her hand. Facing her, he put his hands on her shoulders, and when he looked deeply into her eyes, she was surprised to see him utterly beaming. "I know we have talked much about my plans for our territory," he said to her. "There is so much more I want to share with you... But first, I must know."

"What?" Lucy asked, a nervous quiet to her voice.

"What does your perfect Denora look like?"

Lucy blinked. That was definitely not the question she had been expecting.

Laurent stood before her, watching her intently. The silence of the room put Lucy on edge.

"Well, I guess," Lucy began, feeling shaken by the vehemence in his words. "I guess I'd like to see more support for our families in need. I admire the things you are doing here for the Fae of the North, and I'd like that to happen in all areas of Denora."

A maniacal smile spread across Laurent's face. "Yes. What else?"

"Um," she continued, looking around uncomfortably.

"I believe there should be a change among how male Fae look down upon females."

Laurent nodded excitedly, encouraging her to continue.

"I think there should be more freedoms for females. They deserve to make their own decisions for their future. What they would like to do with their lives." She cleared her throat. "Whom they would like to marry," she added sheepishly.

"Yes." Laurent wrapped his arms around Lucy's waist and spun her in the air. "Yes, my queen. I knew you were my perfect match ever since that day in the grove."

Lucy gasped as he swung her around once more, her hands tightening around his shoulders.

What has gotten into him?

"Laurent, I am pleased to see you are so excited about this, but I am not sure the reason."

Lucy knew something had to have happened. He was bouncing around like a young boy, not at all acting like the leader of an entire territory.

"Because, my queen, I needed to make sure." He put her on the ground and grasped her by the waist, pulling her closer to him. Turning to the map, he whispered a Fae spell. With a wave of his hand, the map shimmered as a charm was lifted. Like a rippling wave, the images on the map changed and the words rearranged.

What she saw was not a typical map of Denora with boundary lines drawn between the Northern, Central, and Southern territories. As the images melted and changed, Laurent took a step back and Lucy took a step closer to see.

Pictures started moving across the parchment, horses and beasts traveling from the North to Central Denora. Naval warships traveled far into the seas on both the East and West coasts, making a wide arch as they headed toward Southern Denora. Then, the images rushed together in a clash of those moving hordes as they finally met in the center of the map.

King Tralont's castle.

This was a battle map.

All the blood drained from Lucy's face, but she refused to make a sound. Laurent couldn't see the true terror she was feeling, she had no idea how he'd react. What if he threw her into the dungeon for disagreeing with him?

She bit her lip and took in a shallow breath, forcing her face to look interested, not terrified.

"I have plans for the North, Lucy," Laurent said in her ear, and she nearly jumped at the proximity. "But my plans do not end there. Denora needs a change, and I am planning on being that catalyst. We will support the people in need; we will truly make a difference in Denora... but first, it needs a new ruler."

Lucy swallowed the lump in her throat, begging for strength to speak without a trace of alarm.

"You wish to be Denora's new king? What of King Tralont?"

"We will kill him," he said matter-of-factly, still looking at the map. "We shall kill anyone who stands in our way."

Lucy's blood turned to ice and her stomach roiled with unease.

"And you will be my queen." He laced his arms around her waist.

Lucy stood, petrified, as Laurent's words trailed through her mind like poison. She needed to get the fuck out of the room, and fast.

"Everything has already begun. The ships here," he said, pointing to the map from over her shoulder, "have already reached the southern shores."

A breathless gasp left her lips.

"Don't worry, my love," he said, his hands moving from her midsection to her shoulders, squeezing. "They are under strict orders to just gain control of the territory. Lord Isaacs is a coward and will release his power over the land with minimal force."

My love.

Each and every word from his lips made her more ill.

Curling a hand around her midsection, she hid her derision best she could.

"Are you alright, my queen?"

The words, once a flirtatious compliment, now cast acid down her throat.

Lucy would never be his fucking queen—she was an idiot for thinking otherwise. She should have trusted her initial instinct when she first confronted him about Jasper. How could she have been so clueless?

"I'm fine," Lucy lied, thankful he couldn't read her lies the way he could for others. "This is..." she couldn't find the words. It was disgusting. Vile. "So much information at once," she supplied.

"I know it seems harsh," Laurent said, turning to her,

gazing deeply into her hazel eyes. He looked crazed with wide bloodshot eyes.

Lucy tried not to shun away from it, refusing to let him see the fear cast deep within her.

"But this is all for the best," he continued. "We will create a new Denora that is worthy of all of its citizens."

Her magic raced under her skin as though it was ready to blast out of her hands and kill the insane male before her, but she had to hold it back. If he said things were already in motion, she needed to understand all of it. Gathering the correct information here was key. She only had one focus now.

How do I stop this?

Lucy looked back at the map, studying it carefully. She would have to play into this—her stomach dropped at the thought.

Taking a step forward, she got closer to the map and out of the reach of Laurent. She couldn't stand his touch for a moment longer. "Your troops have already made it to the South to take control?"

"Yes," Laurent said seriously. She could sense his gaze watching her closely.

"Next, the North will march on the Central Territory?" It took every bit of effort for her voice to not crack. "To overtake the Kingdom?"

"Indeed." Laurent walked up to the map, pointing to the castle. "We shall take our stand and get the dukes under our thumb. Then there will be nothing else in our way." His eyes glinted with the promise of power.

"I have a question. I..."

Stop fucking talking, Lucy, she yelled at herself.

But she had never been one to stay quiet—no matter how much trouble it caused her.

"I don't understand why you want to take the throne," she admitted, pushing for him to explain. "You have so many ideas to support the people of the North. Couldn't you share those ideas with the other rulers of Denora and get them to see the benefits of your plan?"

"I've tried, Lucy," he replied with a surrendering sigh. "I've presented my ideas to them at every council meeting, but they do not agree with my views. They refuse to even consider them! The council believes that the people of Denora are happy with the current division of power, claiming that these class differences are needed for the stability of the realm."

Those words made Lucy's stomach turn. Of course, the wealthy officials would not care for those stationed below them. And it was doubtful that they would ever relinquish any of their power. But murder? There was never an excuse for murder.

"Therefore, you will take over Denora and give support to all the population?" Lucy asked, trying to understand.

"Well, not all the population." Laurent huffed a small laugh.

"Pardon?" Lucy stilled.

Here it comes.

"The population will look very different when I am done, as it should. There are too many Fae in Denora for us to have a sustainable realm where all are treated equally. By removing a portion of the population, we will have the greatest likelihood of success. We must decrease in size by a few thousand, at least." His voice trailed off, lost in thought as he gazed at the map.

He continued to ramble, but Lucy could no longer comprehend his words. He spoke of the murder of thousands as though he was discussing the weather. No remorse whatsoever.

"Sir," Roger called from the doorway. "Your meeting with the generals starts soon. Would you like me to bring Miss Lucy back to her chambers while you prepare?"

Lucy could have sobbed in relief to have the excuse to run from that room. Before Laurent could oppose, Lucy quickly turned and faced him.

"Let me allow you to get back to work," Lucy said with a painted on smile. "It is already getting late and I do not wish for you to get behind on your important work here."

Laurent looked at her, as if debating if he would allow her to leave. Something within him softened as he smiled at her. "My meeting will run very late... Can we discuss more of this in the morning, my love?"

It felt like a test.

"I look forward to it," she replied sweetly.

She had to ensure he believed in her support. He couldn't be given any hint of what she was truly feeling or what she was about to do next—it was a risk she wasn't willing to take. So, instead of running in the opposite direction, she stepped close to Laurent, pressed her lips against his cheek, and told him something he wouldn't understand until it was far too late. "Your plans are awe-inspiring, and I look forward to the outcome."

The outcome being someone killing you, you psychotic megalomaniac.

Laurent's ice-blue eyes burned with passion as she gave a slight curtsey and left the room, the smile on her face physically hurting.

It took everything in her not to run.

ELEVEN

LUCY

Lucy paced back and forth in her room, willing her mind to focus.

This can't be happening.

She replayed the conversation in her mind over and over. Had Laurent Sloan really admitted to her that he was planning treason against the king? Did he really expect her to be part of it?

The thought cast a cold sweat over her otherwise flushed body.

She was going to be sick.

Lucy believed Denora had its flaws, but to murder people in order to take over? She couldn't fathom it.

Her magic sprung to the surface, as if feeling her growing panic. It bound away from her skin and scattered around the room like a caged animal looking for an escape.

Escape. That's it.

She had to leave this place and warn others of Sloan's

plans. He had mentioned the first invasions in the South... Her heart stopped.

My brothers.

Were Hugh and Gregory in danger?

She needed to see Wes. They'd go to the King and inform him of Sloan's intentions. But what did she know, really? Were there others involved in his plan? Surely he couldn't have a large backing behind him—not with his plot to murder the king.

Could he?

The emerald magic continued to zip around the room until suddenly it stopped by the door and shimmered, as though it was beckoning her.The last time she followed her magic, it led her along the darkened corridors only to find Jasper's decrepit body, withering away in the depths of the dungeons.

Should I follow you once more?

Jasper had warned her that Sloan was not what he seemed... He said Sloan was draining him. Was Sloan siphoning Jasper's magic to empower his forces with alchemy?

It was possible—that particular magic was powerful, but rare. Unfortunately, there was no time for guessing games.

Lucy had to find out.

With careful movements, she opened the door from her bedchambers to the empty hallway beyond. Thankfully, no guard stood by her door.

Not yet.

Following the green light, Lucy tiptoed down the corridor, praying to all the gods in all the realms that she could track down the one person she never thought she'd seek out for help...

Jasper.

LUCY HELD her breath as she traversed the long corridors in the thick blanket of night. She had spent weeks getting used to the layout of the castle, and it had almost begun feeling familiar to her. But now, each shadowy corner made her stomach lurch, as though Lord Sloan would see her deceptive words and come barreling out to throw her in his dungeons at any moment.

If only she could hide.

She came to a halt.

Of course, she realized.

Looking around her to ensure she was still alone, she quickly closed her eyes and summoned her father's magnificent power over the shadows. This magic was still new to Lucy, and she wasn't entirely sure how to command it just yet, but pure force of will would have to do. She lifted her hands in the air and called the darkness to her, then squeezed her fingers into a fist and curled her arms around her.

Taking off down the passage, she wore the shadows like a blanket, making her nothing but a darkened blur out of the corner of someone's eye. It was late, and it was likely that the rest of the castle was asleep at this hour, but Lucy couldn't risk anyone seeing her. Not now.

The emerald bouncing light led her straight past the dungeons. Lucy wasn't surprised—the last time she looked for Jasper there, he had been relocated. Even Sloan himself had admitted to moving him to a more secure location.

Where was the light taking her? What would Sloan consider the safest area of his castle?

That's when it dawned on her. Her magic was leading her through the east wing; straight to Laurent Sloan's personal chambers.

The thought of being caught sneaking around his private rooms sent a healthy dose of fear straight through her. Sloan was decidedly insane. He was a manipulative liar and had planned to kill the most influential male Fae in all of Denora. Would he hesitate to kill her if he thought she was up to something that could derail his plans?

Getting caught was not an option.

Stopping in the hallway to refocus her thoughts, she hid in a small alcove under an oversized tapestry hanging near the windows. Her hands were shaking, the nerves threatening to lock all of her muscles into place until she couldn't take another step.

Her magic returned to her side, swirling gracefully around her arm, waiting for her signal to keep going, but Lucy wasn't sure how to continue forward. She was on a path to Sloan's private rooms to kidnap his prisoner and leave, preferably without him knowing. Was there any possibility she could pull it off?

Doubt swept through her mind and a veil of paranoia began to smoother her. Jerking her head left and right, she waited for the moment that Sloan would jump out and drag her away, until suddenly a golden glimmer caught her eye. Lúcy stilled. The dim candlelight caught the metallic edges of the decorative vitrine a few paces away. It was the same display that showcased Sloan's many medals and accomplishments. Her mouth turned into a sneer.

Just days ago, she had been admiring Sloan for his action to save King Tralont's reign. She was foolish. He stopped one rebellion just to start one himself.

He was exactly as the rumors had described. *Lord Slain*—only interested in his own selfish initiatives. And now she was under his thumb, too.

She squeezed her eyes shut.

Stop this, she told herself. *You are Lucella Baum, and you don't let a single fucking person in this realm or the next control you. You are powerful. You are unstoppable. You are a damn Original. Now. Get. Up.*

Opening her eyes, she shivered as pulse of her magic cascaded through her. Lucy was more powerful than any other Fae she had ever come into contact with, and she would not be bested.

This would not be the end of her.

She only had to glance at the shadows lurking in the corners of the dimly lit hallway for them to come swooping toward her, her intent clear in her mind. Lucy would take hold of her father's gift and become little more than shadow and mist as she walked through the halls.

Looking down at her hands, she saw the magic forming. Her hand was nearly transparent as a dark fog covered her, cloaking her from view. A wicked smile crept onto her face as she was reminded of the many times she had snuck into her father's office. Only this time, as if by ironic design, it was her father who gave her the power to slip through the corridors unnoticed. She felt comforted by the presence of his magic within her, shielding her from danger, as if this was Corvus's intention for her all along.

The emerald mist sprung forward, ready to lead Lucy to Jasper, but she wasn't sure if she needed it. It was as though an innate force was leading her right to him, and for once, she trusted her magic over logic.

The corridor was empty when she reached Sloan's private suite, which meant he was still in his meeting and Roger was sure to be by his side. Taking a deep breath, she dropped her shadows. Tiring herself out before she even got to Jasper was not a risk she was willing to take, and whoever watched over him would see her one way or another. Her magic would better serve her if she was focused.

Now to get in, she considered as she took in the enormous metal entryway.

Putting her hand on the door, she felt the safety charm she assumed was in place. It reminded her of the same security her father had on his office. A darkness in her rose at the thought, especially as his killer was nearly in her grasp.

"Open," she commanded the door. As soon as the words left her lips, the lock disarmed and allowed her into the space. The familiar hum of power beneath her skin was a quiet cheer of success.

Lucy took in the rooms before her. Off to the left was a bathing chamber, where she stood was a welcoming chamber with a sitting area and fireplace, and to the right were his bedchambers. That's where the prisoner would be. Her magic tugged her toward the right, confirming her suspicions.

She knew there wasn't time for a clever plan, so after a few careful steps, Lucy charged into the room, her magic vibrating under her skin.

"What are you doing?" A large guard with enormous tusks asked in surprise. He was one of three hulking ox shifters surrounding a large steel box. His brows furrowed and his face reddened with anger. "You shouldn't be in here."

He and the other guards slipped in front of the steel contraption, which stood taller than them all.

Lucy offered him a saccharine smile and continued walking toward them. Her heart was pounding, but she forced herself to proceed with a look of carefree ignorance.

"Ah, give it a rest," the other tattooed guard said with a laugh, stroking one of his tusks as one would a beard or mustache. "Clearly she's in here for a little late night comfort from Lord Sloan."

The guards laughed with him, dismissing Lucy's presence.

Typical male bullshit. I guess Sloan doesn't hire these Kerroz guards for their intelligence. Her eyes twinkled. *This should be easy.*

"Hmm..." Lucy came nearer, her eyes focused on the closest guard. "It certainly *is* late. You must be so tired."

The guard tilted his head in confusion. With her eyes on him, she heard the other guards stir, watching her.

Taking gentle, graceful steps, she placed her hands on the enormous chest of the tusked guard and smiled sweetly. Standing on her tiptoes, she rose to eye level with the guard. His head jerked back with surprise, clearly unsure of what to do. Leaning closer to him, she whispered into the guard's ear.

"Sleep."

Without looking back, she twirled away from him and faced the other guards. She lingered as their gaze swung from Lucy to over her shoulder at their friend and back to her.

A quiet thump of the guard collapsing behind her only put a greater smile on her face. Their expressions twisted from confusion and into fear as she took another step toward them.

"You, too," she said quietly to the tattooed male. "Sleep."

"What are you?" The tattooed guard ran for the exit, pushing his companion out of the way. Lucy only winked at the other guard in the room as he stood frozen in fear before her.

Another thud from the next room brought a hint of green to Lucy's eyes, which she saw in the reflection of the steel structure.

"Two down," Lucy said, watching the last guard trying to fight off the effects of his impending slumber. She casually padded over to face him, then blew a small gust of air from her lips. At last, he toppled over, crashing to the floor. "Three."

A wave of satisfaction broke over her, knowing her

magic wouldn't let her down. She subdued three Kerroz guards with a simple word.

But her smile faded when she turned to the enormous steel box off to the side of the room. What she needed was inside of the towering structure. As she neared the it, it was clear what it was... Not a box, but a cage with three sides of solid metal and one side with iron bars.

Stepping around to the front, she looked through the bars and saw Jasper crouched in a corner, terror contorting his face.

"L-L-Lucy?" He stammered, his stringy hair covering his face smeared with dirt. The fear in his voice turned into amazement, perhaps relief, as his bulging eyes took her in. "You've come here to save me?"

"Absolutely not," Lucy spat.

Whatever relief she thought she would feel upon finding Jasper was gone. She didn't want to save him. Lucy hated Jasper with a passion that lit a fire deep in her soul. He killed her father.

"I'm here to ensure you get the sentencing you deserve."

For a single moment, she thought about killing him right then and there. The hatred that sparked inside of her knew it would take all of one single thought. Just one thought, and her magic would carry out the task. She could crush his windpipe. Stop his heart. Slit his throat right there in his cell.

Each idea seemed more tempting than the last, but she would never stoop so low as to become a murderer like him. She wouldn't sully her father's memory with that kind of violence.

"You're coming with me."

"You are saving me," he blubbered, scrambling to his feet. "I always knew you were the best of your family."

"Don't you dare talk about my fucking family!" Lucy roared as she stepped closer to the steel bars. "You will not speak unless I ask you a direct question. Do you understand?"

"I cannot believe it, just wait until—" Jasper continued to spout more nonsense, but Lucy held up her hand and snapped her fingers once. Immediately, the sound ceased. There was no more noise coming from Jasper's lips after that. He opened and closed his mouth like a fish gulping air, but he made no sound.

Lucy gave him another smile, but he would have been foolish to take it for anything other than ruthlessness. "You will be coming with me, but I am not here to save you. I'd just rather be the one to dole out your punishment."

She needed to ask him more about Sloan and his plans, but getting out of here in one piece was top priority, and they were running out of time.

Lucy waved her hand and the door to the cell swung open, allowing her to step through. Jasper gasped and jumped back, falling over himself and crawling backward to get away from her.

With a simple point of her finger, vines sprung from out of nowhere and twined themselves around Jasper's hands, keeping them in place.

"Come. We're leaving." Lucy started to walk, then

paused realizing she hadn't quite finished her plans after this point.

Getting out of the castle without running into Sloan or Roger was imperative, but how? Taking a moment, she called upon her Original magic, hoping to get a glimpse of where they were so they could find a safe passage out. Her emerald magic filled her mind's eye, but Lucy wasn't able to find Sloan anywhere. Perhaps she was drained after sending the guards into a deep slumber.

Jasper was glaring at her, his eyes bulging with the need to speak.

"What is it?" Lucy snapped, impatience waning on her.

"The boundary line." Jasper's eyes widened in amazement when he heard the sound of his voice, then he quickly went on. "There's a large boundary line that does not allow any magic to pass, not even Lord Sloan can conjure. It lasts for the length of the bridge—it acts as a defensive protection from those beyond the castle. We need to get past the boundary line and then you can use your magic to free us."

Lucy thought back to her travels when she first reached the Northern Territories... Sloan had brought them in the carriage until he crossed the bridge to the guard's outpost, only then was he able to bring them into the castle using his magic to travel instantly.

"Time to go," Lucy announced. Jasper tried to open his mouth to argue, but no sound came out.

Lucy smiled to herself.

She was finally able to shut him up.

Gripping his collar, she shoved him in front of her. "Lead the way."

LUCY KEPT HER SHADOWS CLOSE, cloaking her and Jasper as they traveled through the castle. Each noise made her startle. At any moment, Sloan would return to his rooms to find slumbering guards and a missing prisoner. They had to get to the bridge as fast as they could before he caught wind of what had happened. It was only a matter of time.

Shuddering to a stop, Jasper turned and looked at her, sweat covering his pale skin.

"What is it?" Lucy asked him, knowing he couldn't speak until she allowed it.

"This is the door to the exit, but the guard, Mairlor, is on the other side."

Lucy remembered the tusked sentinel guard in his icy outpost—another Kerroz shifter.

"My magic will work from here. I'll make him sleep, then we make a run for it across the bridge."

Jasper opened and closed his mouth again, trying to speak but failing.

"Speak," Lucy commanded, rolling her eyes in frustration.

"Your magic will fail on the bridge. Your powers won't work again until we pass completely."

Lucy nodded in understanding. "You will keep up. If you fall behind and get us caught, he will do much worse to you than I ever could, and you and I both know it. Do you understand?" Lucy wanted to bring Jasper to justice, but she wouldn't get caught on his behalf.

Jasper was asked a direct question, so he could have replied, but instead he nodded his head quickly. They both knew the reality of the situation, and while Lucy was no fan of his, Jasper was better off with her than Sloan.

Turning back to the door, Lucy closed her eyes and focused her magic on the guard at the outpost. Forcing the command for the guard to sleep, Lucy hoped it would last long enough to get them across the bridge.

Nudging the door open slowly, Lucy winced as it creaked, the sound echoing across the large castle foyer. Peeking her head out, she saw the guard asleep at his post.

"Now," she told Jasper, shoving him out the doors. "Run."

Together, they sprinted across the icy bridge, careful not to fall into the deep chasm below. Over and over, Lucy thought to herself that she would fix this, fix all of it, as long as she could get away.

She would go to her mother and be the daughter she needed her to be.

She would help Wes with the Baum Bowyer business.

She would return to Micah and make things right.

They were halfway across the bridge when Lucy begged the stars for extra time to get away before they were found.

But as history would have it, Lucy's timing was never quite that lucky.

"Stop!" Lord Sloan's yells echoed from the doorway of the castle.

Her stomach dropped.

"Keep running!" She ordered Jasper. "He has no magic on this part of the bridge. We need to outrun him!"

Lucy's Fae speed made her quick, but Jasper was old and weak, especially after being imprisoned. He couldn't keep up with her, and as she pulled him along, Sloan was gaining on them.

Just a little further, she thought to herself, seeing the end of the bridge. They were almost there.

"Come on!" She screamed, pulling at his arm to urge him on; but it was no use.

Lord Sloan crashed into them, knocking Jasper to the ground. Lucy lost her grip on Jasper as Sloan grabbed her shoulder and spun her to face him. His hands clutched her, his fingernails digging into her shoulders. She tried to pull away, but his undoubtable strength kept her from breaking free.

"What is the meaning of this?" Sloan growled.

"What do you think?"

"Lucy, come back inside." Sloan's voice was cold and detached, as though he was holding on to his last bit of restraint.

"I'm not going with you. You're a monster!" Lucy bellowed. Her voice echoed through the icy mountains and reverberated from the cavern below. "I can't let you do this."

"So you side with the weak Fae who murdered your father?" He seethed, his ice-blue eyes momentarily shooting to Jasper. "You and I are united!" He shook her body, pulling her closer. "You belong with me!"

"I belong to no one," Lucy said through clenched teeth as she stood tall.

"I forbid you from leaving here," Sloan said, his teeth grinding as he spat the words, leaning close to her face.

"You do not control me," Lucy said. Looking her nose down at him, she added, "no one controls me."

"All of Denora controls you, Lucy! That's the problem!" His fingers dug into the sides of her arms, bruising her. "Together we can be more."

Lucy shoved his chest with both hands and snarled, "Get off!"

With a derisive laugh, he just held on to her tighter, yanking her to his chest.

"Oh, Lucy," he crooned, his nose in her hair and his words like acid to her ears. "It didn't have to be like this. But you will learn, I am the more powerful Fae here."

And with those words, Lucy remembered what Brax had said about her powers.

She was an Original—the rules of Fae magic did not apply to her.

Gasping for air beneath his unrelenting grip, Lucy screamed, shoving him away with all her might. With a shimmering blast of emerald light, Sloan flew backwards, landing on his back in the middle of the bridge. The bridge that didn't allow magic.

Lucy's chest heaved with panting breaths, and her eyes darted back to Jasper, making sure he was still nearby. She couldn't let Sloan have him.

Sloan's gaze darted to Lucy as she stood before him

in the bitter wind. He scrambled to his feet. "How?" Sloan demanded in disbelieving rage.

"You will not use Jasper for his alchemy any longer. He will be punished for his crimes, and then we are coming for you." Lucy felt her magic coursing through her body. Her hair twisted wildly in a gust of warm air that seemed to surround only her. The green mist swirled around her, prepared to protect her. "You no longer have access to his alchemy."

She reached out to get Jasper back on his feet when Lord Sloan began laughing—a slow, sinister taunt.

"I don't know how you were able to hide this from me, but I will figure it out. I will figure *you* out." His eyes landed on her grip on Jasper, and his deranged glare flew to her once more. "You think this will stop me?" His maniacal laughter continued as he stood up. Walking toward her, his sneer turned rabid. "There are others with alchemy I can use to get what I need. You can't save everyone."

Other alchemists?

Lucy's blood turned to lava as she registered the threat.

He meant Micah.

"You're going to want to take that back," Lucy snarled.

"Where do you think you'll be able to run where I can't catch you?" Lord Sloan asked arrogantly. "Once we get past that boundary line, my magic will reappear and I will return you to where you belong."

"You're delusional," Lucy snapped.

"I am your future king, and soon you will see you are my fucking queen! Mine!"

Enough of this.

She wouldn't waste another second on this madness.

Grabbing the back of Jasper's collar, she changed course and pulled him toward Lord Sloan.

Sloan's eyes brightened with delight as Jasper's bulged in fear.

"Yes. Let us return him to his cell and get back to where we were." He held out his hand for Jasper. "I am very interested to hear more about your... magic."

Lucy stopped short, just far enough to stay out of his grasp.

"I just wanted to make sure you hear me clearly," Lucy said with a venom she never knew she held. "I will *never* be yours."

Lord Sloan lunged at Lucy to seize her. With a blink of an eye, Lucy and Jasper were gone and Sloan swung his arms in the empty space in front of him.

Sloan hollered, swinging his head back and forth wildly, looking for them.

Lucy reappeared behind him, then whispered into his ear. "You're going to lose."

Before Sloan could turn around once more, Lucy and Jasper were gone again.

The only thing Lucy heard as her magic took her and Jasper away from the North was Lord Sloan's screams as they echoed through his icy domain.

CHAPTER

TWELVE

MICAH

This was more than anything Micah had ever expected. The last, and only, time he and Lucy were here, The Elderwood was vacant. Trees and plants in every direction, but no life—not even an insect in sight. Now this? Not only animals roaming the land and birds soaring through the skies, but people—real people!

And they were still on their knees, bowing to him.

"Uh," Micah started, hesitantly. "Please, there's no need." He waved his hands for them to stand, awkwardly sidestepping and looking to Quillan for an explanation. As expected, he ignored Micah.

However, Quillan didn't ignore the people before him as they looked to him for answers. Nodding his head, Quillan motioned for them to rise.

Micah remained silent, hoping for someone to talk— to explain what was happening here. But instead, they all looked at him expectantly.

Well, fuck.

"Hello," he said, clearing his throat. "I'm Micah."

Each of the people lifted their spears into the air and drove them to the ground in unison, creating a loud thud. Their faces remained stoic, eyes never leaving his.

Micah just blinked.

"Thank you all for welcoming The Guardian with such passion," Quillan said to the group.

That was passion, huh?

"I must bring our honored guest to the grand counsel. Remember, we are here to listen to all concerns. Please find your advisor and share whatever burdens your heart. We will be working toward a better future for the lives of all."

Concerns? Burdens? What has been happening here?

"Come with me, Guardian," Quillan said to him quietly. "We have much to discuss."

WALKING through The Elderwood was an experience like no other. The trees were magnificent, each one a different color. Seeing the typical green and red trees was fine, but a bright blue tree? It seemed impossible.

He wondered if it was anything like Lucy's realm of Denora. However, from the way the leaves glittered in the breeze, he wasn't sure if there was another place like this anywhere in creation.

As they traversed down the long stone path that led them down the side of the hill, Micah took in all he could about this place. The waterfalls off in the distance were still breathtaking, with the most clear blue water he had ever seen. The strange moons in the sky still took up much of the expansive horizon before them. Everything looked perfect.

What could possibly be going wrong here?

Suddenly, he paused, an eerie sensation creeping through his blood. From what he remembered, the forest was not all sunshine and rainbows, though. The last time he was here, there was one place that sent a shiver down his spine. Remembering the darkness that dwelled at the edge of the forest, he turned to the west to see it.

His blood ran cold.

There it was. The forest that seemed cast in eternal shadow—so at odds with the rest of the realm. Blood red leaves blooming from black branches fluttered ominously in the wind.

His stomach dropped.

Why am I really here?

Could Quillan have lied to him about peace? Was this some terrible ruse to get him here and hurt him?

"What is the matter?" Quillan asked, seeing Micah tense and worried on the path beside him.

Micah stopped in his tracks. "I'm not going with you to some evil forest for you to kill me. I won't let you." He took a step back, preparing his body for a fight, and calling on the magic deep within him.

The smile on Quillan's face faltered. "If I wanted to kill you, I would have done so already," he replied, completely unamused. "You *do* realize you have done much worse to me than I've done to you. Correct?" A blazing fire lived behind those amber eyes.

"Then why are you taking me into a cursed forest?" Micah demanded.

"We aren't going there," he said, looking over to the dark red leaves. "We are meeting somewhere else. Everything will be explained in the counsel. Now, please, move your feet so we can get there and I no longer have to listen to your incessant mumbling." Quillan turned and continued to walk toward the forest.

Everything inside of Micah's brain told him to run. It was idiotic of him to be following a stranger who once had gouged a hole in his leg with his teeth.

Didn't he know anything about following random strangers?

Yet, something within him urged him to keep walking, to find out what Quillan urgently needed him to know.

There must have been a reason he was still alive.

So Micah continued, somehow knowing this visit would change his life forever; whether it'd be for better or worse, he wasn't sure.

BY THE TIME they came upon the building, Micah's heart was beating out of his chest. It wasn't for lack of exercise —something about this place just felt different, almost as if the air itself was thinner.

The monumental structure before him would have taken his breath away if he wasn't already having such a difficult time breathing. It stood at least two stories high, with a large golden dome for its roof, its surface reflected the bright afternoon sun that peeked between the canopy of leaves. There were large windows, from the floor all the way to its vaulted ceiling, which only added to the brightness of the room. The walls were a pale pearl color that shimmered in the sun, even with the structure nestled into the shadow of the looming trees.

"This is our counsel building, The Dome. The advisors come here to meet as needed when trouble arises... Unfortunately, that has been frequent as of late. Hopefully, with your arrival, that will change."

Micah could only nod, still taking in this new place. Still wondering if he was welcome there or not.

Quillan opened the wide, ornate doors and led Micah inside.

The interior was as beautiful as its exterior. Large windows scaling the length of the walls opened at the top to let the greenery of the forest trail inside. A filtered light gave a pearlescent glow to the walls, accenting the clinging dark green ivy. Small ornate fountains were placed throughout the building, giving off gentle and relaxing sounds of the forest. It was as though the inside was as wild as the rest of The Elderwood—as though nature came first, and the people came last.

A clearing throat brought Micah back to his reality. Standing in the middle of the otherworldly room, he took in what he assumed was the grand counsel. Around a large oval table, made entirely of wood, three men sat watching him intently.

"Sit, Guardian," Quillan told him gently. "You're going to want to sit."

Micah nodded and took a seat at the far end of the table made for eight, seating only four.

He felt completely out of place.

The three strangers smiled at him gently, all wearing the same style of clothing worn by Quillan and the others. Brown fabric draped around their muscular bodies; and while the fabric was simple, they sat with the poise and importance of royalty. Each man looked to be in their late thirties or early forties, but knowing the Fae, they were likely much older than that.

That is… if they were Fae.

"We know you have many questions," the first spoke. "My name is Fergh. I am the lead advisor for the biosphere here. I ensure the safety of our plants and wildlife —as we have many." He outstretched his hands to the plant life all around them. The soft lines around his eyes crinkled as he attempted a show of kindness, though barely a smile appeared on his freckled face.

"I am Rowan," the man across from him said next. He had long braids pulled back with a strip of leather. "I speak for the safety of our people."

Safety, he scoffed in his mind. He was tired of always being the last to know what was going on, and he wasn't going to sit around and make idle chatter.

Before the third man could speak, Micah cut him off. "What am I doing here? First, I'm attacked by this dude as a cat, and then I get dragged here and no one will tell me why."

Rowan looked to the third man who had not been introduced, but all he did was nod, his steepled fingers hiding a small smile on his face.

"We apologize for Quillan's… abrasive manner upon your first meeting," Rowan said, looking at Quillan with judgment.

Quillan remained standing beside the table, smiling.

Jackass.

"As he was *supposed* to tell you," Rowan continued, "there was a dark magic that affected our realm. Our understanding is that a Fae male put something tainted within the base of the tree that holds the portal here. It caused the magic within our realm to suffer."

"Trees were withering," Fergh said with distress. "The animals were in hiding and even the morning birds did not sing the songs of a new day." Fergh took a deep breath, steadying his shaking hands. "The magic that lives within our people is tied to our land. With the magic in the plants suffering, it started a chain reaction of devastation. That is... until you removed the tainted magic."

"We are truly grateful for your interference with the immoral Fae. We hope he has been brought to justice." Rowan's face was the picture of sincerity.

Micah's stomach curdled at the thought. He hadn't heard from anyone, and he wasn't sure what came of Jasper.

"So you've brought me here to thank me?" Micah asked, still not seeing what they wanted from him.

The three men looked at one another seriously, then back at Micah. "Indeed, we wanted to thank you. However, there is more. We are in need of your assistance." Fergh shifted in his seat, almost uncomfortable to admit they needed help.

"Since the magic in the land was affected, our seers have been ill. We did not have the ability to see into our future for the weeks that our magic was harmed," Rowan said, glancing back at the third man uneasily.

"Seers?" Micah asked, sitting forward in his seat.

"Yes," Rowan replied solemnly. "Now that the dark magic has been lifted, we have been able to see what is to come." His eyes widened in fear as his voice dropped to a near whisper. "Another Fae is on their way here to disrupt the prosperity of our land."

"What do you mean?" Micah asked, not understanding the threat. "You were all here in secret for who knows how long. Can't you go back to acting like you were never here?"

"Perhaps," Fergh replied. "Unfortunately, the Fae who threatens our future doesn't want anything to do with us. They want the magic of our land—the magic we cannot give-up. It doesn't matter if we hide or not."

Micah nodded, thoughtfully. "How did you do that, anyway? Make it seem as though there was no life here?"

This time, the third man spoke. "We have a special magic that allows us to change things as needed. When visitors come through the portal, namely the Baums, a magic spell allows them to see only what they have come for—the wood of our trees." He smiled and crossed his hands on the table, his fingers adorned in rings of all colors. "We have allowed the Baum and Lumen families to enter our realm to gather the wood they require because they take only what they need and never take in excess. It is what holds the balance."

"So can't you do this to whoever this bad guy is?" Micah asked, still not seeing the issue.

"No," the third man said with severity. "The seers

have all agreed. He will come to take the wood—all the wood. He will level our realm until it is nothing but piles of dirt, siphoning every ounce of magic within."

Micah felt the gravity of that. Another entitled jerk coming and expecting to take whatever he wants, no matter the repercussions.

"Well, how can I help?" Micah asked. "I don't have the same kind of magic you guys do." It had been less than a year since he learned magic existed, and he had only recently discovered he had magic of his own. What use was he?

"You're a Lumen," the third man said with pride. "We have every faith in you that you will continue to protect the portal." He turned and nodded at Quillan, then looked back to Micah with his deep brown eyes. "We shall help you."

Micah turned to see what was happening. As Quillan stepped closer, he held in his hands a large bundle wrapped in a thin cloth.

"This is for you, Guardian," Quillan said with reverence. "We have heard of your alchemy and have provided you with the tools you need to be successful."

He pulled the cloth off to reveal a large axe with a wooden handle. The axe blade gleamed in the light of the room. Embedded in the knob at the top was a beautiful red jewel.

"The metal is a mix of iron and steel. The wood is crafted from one of our most cherished trees in our realm —it is harvested for only the most revered weapons we must create." Quillan turned the axe handle toward Micah, offering the weapon to him. "The red sunstone can be imbued with your power to utilize your magic and alchemy as one."

Micah looked around the room in amazement. It was a gorgeous weapon, but how did they know about the alchemy? His stomach turned with unease. Grasping the axe, he noted the way the sunstone glittered in the light. The handle was smooth and the blade was heavy, yet it was perfectly balanced.

The third man rose from his seat at the table and walked over to Micah slowly. "May I?" He extended his hand to the weapon.

Micah could only nod, still at a loss for words.

Turning the axe over, the stranger displayed the other side of the handle. At the shoulder, where the wood and metal met, was a deep engraving.

Micah stilled.

It was the same sigil Lucy had on her amulet that allowed her entry into The Elderwood.

"If you ever need to come here, you now have the ability to do so." The man smiled at Micah, as if he knew something Micah did not.

And that didn't surprise Micah at all.

THIRTEEN

LUCY

"Come on. You've given me enough trouble as it is. Stop slowing me down," Lucy bristled as she dragged Jasper the final steps to the Baum manor.

It was an exhausting journey with multiple stops along the way. Her Original magic was beyond powerful, but even that had its limits. She could jump miles at a time, but each use of her power drained her. When they finally arrived in Central Denora, she couldn't so much as cast light to guide their way, let alone jump through space and time once more. Instead, Lucy had to grip Jasper by his damned collar and drag him through the Nilban Woods, a small part of her hoping some wolven would come looking for a snack.

The entire time they trudged to the estate, Lucy had one thing circling her mind: how was she going to tell her mother that her brothers were in danger?

Could Anita handle another horrific incident at the hands of someone they were supposed to trust?

And what if, somehow, she misunderstood, and they

weren't in danger? What if Lucy put fear and worry into her mother's heart for no reason? Was it worth the risk?

Over and over, she battled with herself internally as she battered Jasper, tugging him along as his feet reluctantly took one step in front of the other.

At the sound of their struggle, a few of the estate staff came peering through doors and windows. Normally, Lucy would have preferred not to be seen. For this occasion, however, time was of the essence.

A gardener came around the curve of the walkway, hands full of tools. Upon seeing Lucy and her captive, he froze, unsure what to do.

Frustrated from hauling Jasper halfway across the damned realm, she huffed out a request. "Please, go get my brother."

The gardener's eyes widened as they took in Jasper's disheveled appearance and vines tethering his hands. The male dropped all of his tools and took off running for Wesley.

He'll know what to do. He has to, she hoped.

"Lucy?" Anita's voice spoke quietly from behind them.

Lucy turned to see her mother holding a bushel of roses from her garden. They fell to the ground in a flourish as Anita rushed to Lucy and embraced her in a hug.

"What are you doing here?" Anita asked Lucy, scanning her body and taking in her messy hair and the dirt peppering her clothes. "What happened to—" she began, but stopped as soon as she saw the Fae male standing behind Lucy.

With narrowed eyes, Anita made a beeline for Jasper. "You."

That's all Lucy heard as her mother tightened her hand into a fist, pulled her arm back, and punched Jasper so hard, he collapsed right at the terrace entrance.

Anita stood over his unconscious body, panting as she kept her focus on the monster who terrorized her family and murdered her husband.

Lucy's eyes burned at the pain her mother had to endure by his presence, but she forced a smile instead. "I wish I would have thought to do that."

Before either could say another word, Wes was at the door, standing with a look of pure astonishment.

To be fair, it was quite a sight to stumble upon.

Lucy covered in dirt, Jasper knocked out cold, and his mother with reddened knuckles.

LUCY WAITED as Wes stared at her in wide-eyed silence, apparently taking in everything she had just told him. She couldn't blame him, though. If someone would have told her that Laurent Sloan was in cahoots with Jasper, using him for his alchemy, and had plans to overthrow the entire Denoran kingdom, she'd probably be in shock, too.

"So, what do we do now?" Wes asked. His voice sounded small. Scared. It was so at odds with how Lucy had always viewed him and a wave of hopelessness crashed over her...

She had raced Jasper here, hoping Wes would have

some answers—at the very least a plan. She was so tired of running from one place to the next, and she couldn't keep doing it by herself.

Wes sat slumped behind his father's desk in a chair that seemed much too big for him. It was as though he was a child playing as an adult. It had been only a couple of days since she had seen him last, and already he looked more tired.

Jasper lay unconscious on the floor in front of them, his legs sprawled at odd angles after they'd dropped him there. With his head pinned against the front of the desk, they could at least see when he woke up.

Anita, however, stood in rapt attention, taking it all in. She did not shudder with fear, nor did she balk at the bastard at their feet. She kept a keen awareness, her mind contemplating... calculating. That surprised Lucy the most, if she were being honest.

Since when did Mother become so determined?

"It is obvious what we do, son," Anita said to him, pulling Lucy from her musing. She turned to face Lucy, her eyes blazing with resolve. "We must stop him, at any cost."

Lucy nodded in agreement, knowing in her heart it was the only course of action.

"But first," Anita began, scowling as she spun toward the unconscious lump on the floor. "It's time to wake *him* up and hear it from him."

She pointed her magic at Jasper and soft curls of gold mist formed chains, which wrapped themselves around him, lifting him and plopping him unceremoniously into a chair. Then, with a snap of her fingers, the magic walloped Jasper in the face, waking him up.

Lucy snorted at the brash behavior of her mother.

She approved entirely.

Jasper gasped and his eyes bulged as he woke. He opened his mouth to speak, but didn't make a sound. His mouth bobbed open and shut like a fish out of water.

"Oh," Lucy said, remembering. "You can speak freely now."

Jasper stretched his mouth wide and screamed in their faces. It was a long, drawn out yell that was completely unintelligible. His face turned a ruddy red and his eyes bugged out wider than ever as he kept at it, his voice cracking at the end. When he was done, he heaved in a deep breath and eyed the Baums with oily hatred.

With a sneering face that could sour milk, he glared at Lucy. "Do you know how horrific it is to be stuck with you, yet unable to speak?"

"Do you know how horrific it is to hear you speak?" Lucy spat back.

"Enough of this," Anita announced, taking a step closer to Jasper. "I need to hear it from you." Her shoulders were pulled back as she looked down her nose at him, the venom in her gaze something that seemed to chill the room.

Wes stood and walked to the front of the desk, watching Jasper with menacing intent.

Lucy angled herself to be closer to her mother, prepared to protect her from the horrid Fae at any cost.

All three Baums were ready to strike at the very hint of magic. Lucy wasn't sure who wanted his death more.

"What do you want me to do? *Apologize?*" Jasper scoffed. "I clearly never meant for things to go this far, but I'm not sorry for what happened. I'm only sorry that I ended up here, on the *losing* side."

"Silence," Lucy said, unwilling to hear him spout any more wretched words.

Jasper scowled. He tried to speak, but nothing came out.

Lucy smirked at him before turning away, facing her mother and brother once more. Seeing their expressions brought a whole new level of pain to the next words out of her mouth, but they deserved to know the truth. "I think Hugh and Gregory may be in danger."

"Why?" Wes asked, his brow furrowing with concern.

Anita gasped softly, covering her mouth with her delicate fingers.

Secrets won't bring back the dead, nor will they save the living... no matter how badly they hurt.

Taking a deep breath, Lucy continued.

"Sloan mentioned his soldiers were on different missions in the South, and when I got a good look at his map, it appeared that this was step one of his plan. He's sending his ships south, but directing them to stay far away from the coast to stay unseen. When they arrive in the Southern Territory, it will be a surprise as they dock. They will try to take over the land, then it's only time until they work their way toward Central Denora." Lucy looked at her mother, and then Wes. "If Sloan is prepared to kill, then his soldiers are, too. We need to find a way to warn them—we need to give the South a chance to fight back."

Wes swayed on his feet. Anita quickly pushed her magic to the chair behind him, bringing it closer, as he fell into the seat.

"What is it, Wes?" Anita asked him in alarm.

Wes looked at his mother, his face pale and a shallow devastation clear in his eyes. "I have been trying to call my brothers since they left... There has been no answer." His voice trailed off into a whisper.

Any shred of hope that Lucy had been holding on to was clipped—it felt as though her heart plummeted straight through her body and to the bottom of the rocky Lancast Sea.

"Then they have already arrived," Anita said matter-of-factly. She straightened and walked to the window, her hands clasped in concentration.

"We must get to them." Wes lowered his face into his hands and shook his head. His voice was barely a mumble. "We need to save them."

Lucy never expected things would end up moving so quickly. They went from planning to inform her brothers about potential trouble to saving them from the terror that is Laurent Sloan?

She thought they had time... Months... weeks at least. But this? They were down to days! There was no time left to plan. They had to move *now*. "I need to get to Micah, too," Lucy whispered.

At that, all three Fae in the room looked at her,

including Jasper, who had stopped struggling long enough to hear her next words.

"Why would you involve him in this?" Wes asked, lifting his head to look at her.

"Sloan told me he needed an alchemist... Not Jasper in particular," she said, her eyes darting to Jasper just as he sighed in relief. "Just someone who can form the magic he needs." Her eyes moved to Wes's, who was looking at her in harrowing understanding. "He's the last alchemist that we know of... We need to warn him."

I need to keep my promise to keep him safe.

The sigil burned into her hand tingled with recognition of the promise she made at the base of The Elderwood portal.

In a flurry, Wes stood. He had always been a male of action, prepared to do what was necessary. "I will come with you." He rushed to the desk to grab his coat and looked down at the papers and ledgers sprawled on the desk. His face flared in realization. "I-" He bit his lip, trying to form the words. Desolately, he dropped his coat back into the chair. "I have to stay here." He placed his two hands on the side of the desk and dropped his head in defeat.

"What? Why?" Lucy asked. Why wouldn't he support her in this? Didn't he care about what happened to Micah?

"King Tralont graced me with a visit and warned me that if I didn't keep the business moving as Father had, he would replace me with someone else."

"He can't do that!" Lucy demanded. "This is *our* family business!"

"There is a simple way to solve this," Anita said, waving her hands at her children, shooing them away as she walked to the desk. "I will stay here and run the business. Wes, you will go with your sister to warn Micah. We will throw Jasper into the cellar and lock the doors. Our staff will be under strict orders to not let him out." Standing before the desk, she whipped her head to Jasper with a ferocious glare. "Though not one soul here would ever consider freeing a leech like you."

"Mother, you can't be serious," Wes said with a half-smile on his face.

"Denoran tradition has always said that the eldest male will lead the family, but I am telling you now it is *me*." There was a fire in Anita's eyes that Lucy had never seen before, but it cast warmth within her heart to see it now. "I was helping your father run this business while you were in diapers, and well before. I will do what is needed while you do the same."

Wes stood in shock at Anita's resolute declaration.

"You need to help your sister set this right before there is no family business to attend to. Go with Lucy. Fix this." Anita's determined countenance left no room for argument.

Wes nodded, then looked at his sister. "Let me prepare and we can leave."

Lucy watched as he approached their mother, a curiosity in his eyes mixed with love and concern. He kissed Anita on the cheek and headed to the door.

Lucy couldn't help the grin that spread across her face. Her mother was finally coming into the powerful magic she had within her. She was no longer being stifled... but what had changed?

With quick steps, Anita crossed the study to the hallway doors and opened them wide to call for Thomas, the head of the estate staff.

"Put this lout down in the root cellar with the rest of the vermin." Anita cast the golden chains across to Thomas as the male stood tall, eyeing Jasper with equal amounts of hatred and loathing. "No windows. No sunlight. No escape. Do you understand?"

"Yes, Madame. I will ensure no one is privy to his whereabouts and no one will stumble across him," Thomas replied.

"It will be as though he doesn't exist," Anita said dismissively, then turned away as Thomas led Jasper from the room to his next prison.

The room was quiet for a moment, like the calm before a storm. "You can say it, you know," Anita said to her, seeing Lucy's inquisitive gaze. "Nothing's ever stopped you from speaking freely before." There was a hint of mischief in Anita's eyes, but despondency, too.

"Why now?" Lucy asked plainly, a tinge of sadness coloring her words. "You've always held your magic back, always played the role of doting housewife... What changed?"

"Nothing. Everything. You name it," her mother sighed.

"This is about the magic, isn't it?" Lucy asked. "The butterfly?"

"Your father's magic? Yes, partially. But, this is more."

Anita turned away, walking back to the windows, as though she couldn't face Lucy.

"More?"

"What you've said has stuck with me, Lucella." Anita looked down at her hands, then closed her eyes. "I know my magic is wonderful and powerful, and I know that I've kept it closed off for many years." She lifted her head, turned, and gazed into Lucy's eyes. "Your father and I had a wonderful partnership. There was kindness and respect, but most of all, there was love." Her hazel eyes lightened at the memory and a smile played on Anita's lips. "I owe it to Corvus to be my own person now. I cannot hide behind another male just to ensure that the Denoran ways are upheld, and I should have seen that before. I should have listened to you, Lucy."

"Mother, I didn't mean it like that."

"You did, but you were right." Anita said, her expression soft. Walking up to her daughter, Anita held Lucy's cheeks in her hands. "You are brave and kind and true... just like your father. It has been an honor watching you grow up to turn into this remarkable female."

It was hard to keep eye contact with her mother as tears threatened to fall.

"I will not shy away from my power," Anita promised her. "I will not let this family crumble under Denoran tradition while we fight tirelessly to save it. You and Wes go and save your Micah." She dropped her hands and walked over to the wing-backed chair behind the desk. With shoulders back and a fierce determination in her gaze, she sat, and Lucy could have sworn the chair was made for her and her alone.

She was the epitome of elegance and power, and if anyone tried to challenge her, they would surely fail.

"You and I will talk more when you return," Anita said to her. "But Lucy?"

Lucy stood, waiting for her mother to speak.

"Make him regret it."

CHAPTER
FOURTEEN
MICAH

With axe in hand, Micah stepped through the portal to return home. It felt strange being alone there, knowing he had a way to travel back and forth through the realms without anyone else needing to guide him.

Without Lucy.

It should have made him feel strong—independent. Instead, it made him feel lonely.

Returning played out exactly as he assumed it would. Brax was left pacing in front of the tree and proceeded to curse at him when he stepped onto the Lumen property.

"What the fuck was that?" Brax cried. Then she fell into a battle position, ready to fight Quillan, assuming he'd be stepping through next. Her eyes were wild as she surveyed the portal, seeing it close as the rippling bark turned to solid form once more. "Where is he?"

Micah stilled at a loss for words, staring over Brax's shoulder as she berated him about utilizing his magic and not getting captured by cats, but he could barely focus on her. While he expected Brax's volatile reaction, there was something he certainly did not expect.

In the middle of the yard, from seemingly out of nowhere, stood the one thing that could both shatter his heart and mend it completely.

Lucy.

Everything inside of him screamed for Lucy—her embrace, her touch, her scent. Why was she here? Was she hurt? His eyes darted over her perfectly curved body.

Is this a dream? Did I hit my head?

She wore a midnight blue tunic synched with a thin leather strap, black leggings, and a pair of boots. Her long brown hair fell in waves over her shoulders. She looked exactly as he remembered—utterly breathtaking.

He took a step toward her, and a hint of regret shone from her eyes.

Micah paused, remembering his new place in her life. Lucy was marrying Sloan.

She left me.

He couldn't figure out why she was there. It was likely she was just there to enter The Elderwood to get supplies to make another bow. Maybe she was taking over that part of the family business. Maybe there was something else with the business that she needed to discuss. Maybe she had a message from Sloan.

His mind was reeling. But at the root of it, it didn't matter why she was there... All that mattered was that she was.

It was really her.

Unblinking, he walked around the screeching

Vytyrian warrior toward Lucy. Steeling himself for what was sure to be more heartbreak, he smiled at her.

"Lumen, what is your problem?" Brax began, but stopped as she turned.

"Hi," Lucy said sheepishly. "We need to talk to you."

"We?" Brax asked.

That's when Micah heard it: retching in the bushes.

Wes stood up and walked over, his skin pale and clammy. "Let's just say Lucy's fancy magic is not as fancy in practice." He wiped his mouth unceremoniously.

The little bit of hope he was holding on to left Micah completely. If Wes was here, then he doubted she was there to speak about where their relationship stood... but then again, Micah didn't know the answer to that, either.

What did he expect from Lucy, anyway? For her to run into his arms and apologize for leaving him high and dry with no explanation? To say sorry about telling Micah she chose him, and then changing her mind as soon as things got hard? Perhaps she was there to invite him to her fucking wedding.

Damn. Nothing she could say could fix this... Could it?

Brax just sighed in annoyance. "Well, let's go inside then, shall we? Instead of standing out here staring at one another like a bunch of moldy potatoes?"

"Potatoes?" Micah asked, looking at Brax, the random insult pulling him back to reality.

"Yes, you nitwit. They have eyes?" Brax just stared at him dully.

Wes snorted and threw his arm around Brax. "You know, I think I've missed you."

Brax recoiled, pushing his arm off of her. "Please

continue to do so." Then she walked ahead of him into the house, swaying her hips a bit more prominently as she went.

Micah's gaze turned back to Lucy, and he offered her a weak smile, tipping his head toward the house to invite her in. She was there because she needed him, and that had to be enough for now.

They walked in, side by side, without saying a word to one another.

"Let me get this straight," Wes said to Micah as they all sat in the kitchen. "The shadow beast was a male shifter. There are actual real living beings within The Elderwood, and they gave you some magical fucking axe to wield as their guardian and savior?"

"Actually, that about sums it up," Micah replied.

Brax just crunched on her salty potato chips sullenly, listening to what she had missed. "It's not fair," she mumbled. "I should have been dragged over, too."

Micah laughed at her. "You wanted to be dragged into a portal by a beast?"

"I mean, when you say it that way, Lumen, it sounds even better." She winked coyly in his direction.

Micah snorted and stole one of her chips, earning him a glare from Brax once again.

"It's good to see you two getting on so well," Wes replied, eyeing them both curiously.

Lucy hadn't spoke since she first arrived. It made Micah uneasy.

"Well, when you're stuck with someone for nearly six months, they grow on you," Brax said with a saccharine smile.

Micah didn't know what to say. It was true. They had no other choice but to figure things out together. Thankfully, Brax was the perfect person to have stayed with him.

The more Micah thought about it, he realized fate had thrown them together, and somehow, they just worked. She was his best friend. He didn't know the last time he'd had a best friend, but the thought warmed the frozen parts inside him. He looked over at Brax and let out a breathy laugh as she chomped down on more chips. He doubted he could ever tell her what she meant to him, but he meant it all the same.

No longer willing to keep the tension at bay, he finally asked the question they were tiptoeing around. "What are you doing here?" His eyes landed on Lucy this time. He needed *her* to be the one to say it—to say anything.

"There have been some... developments. All of them bad." Lucy looked at Brax in apology. "There are a few things I have to say, and I don't think you are going to like them."

"There are many things you've done that we didn't like, Baum," Brax replied with ire in her tone. "May as well spit it out and add it to the list."

Micah gave her a warning glance, imploring her to calm down.

Brax returned the look as if to say, *you can't make me.*

With a sigh, Lucy began her tale. It definitely wasn't

anything Micah had expected, and with the way Brax put her beloved snack to the side, he didn't think she expected it either.

At the end of her explanation, the room was dead silent. Wes looked as though he had seen a ghost, the pallor of his skin dull in the light.

Brax, however, was seething. With her eyes narrowed on Lucy and her teeth clenched, her jaw twitched. She shifted in her chair to lean toward Lucy, her motions stiff, as though she was restraining herself from doing something brash. "You're wrong," Brax stated, pointing an accusatory finger at Lucy and refusing to believe what she shared. "Lord Sloan is not the Fae whom you describe."

"I have been wrong about a lot of things," Lucy said bleakly, sending a quick glance toward Micah. "But I am not wrong about this." She shook her head and stood her ground.

As much as Micah was thrown by it all, he believed Lucy. He wasn't sure if it was his loyalty to her, his hatred for Sloan, or for the circumstances of the situation, but he believed her. .

"I'm going for a walk," Brax declared, storming out of the room. The slam of the door on her way out seemed to echo in the silence.

Wes let out a long huff of breath. "Well, that was awkward."

Lucy and Micah just looked at him in disbelief.

"Yeah, all of this is a bit awkward," Micah replied with a touch of irritability.

Wes put his hands up in surrender and walked out of

the kitchen toward the sitting room, plopping down on the couch with his hands over his face.

"Can we go for a walk?" Lucy asked Micah gently. "I've missed this place, and I.... I was hoping we could talk?"

Micah knew this was coming. May as well go outside in case his magic wanted to lash out like it did every other time he was upset. At least he wouldn't break any furniture. "Sure."

His footsteps always happened to lead him to the tree house near the back of the cabin, but today he wanted to avoid it. It had been his safe haven whenever he needed to think things through, and if Lucy had something else bad to share with him, he wasn't sure if he'd ever be able to sit there among the trees in peace again.

Their path took them the long way around the property, but Micah knew it well by now. It was the same path he took on his daily runs; it was flat and serene. However, he had a feeling this conversation would be anything but calm.

"So," Micah said awkwardly. "Seems like trouble in paradise."

Lucy looked at him with furrowed brows. "There was never any romance there, Micah. You know that."

"Do I?" He challenged. "Because it seems to me that *we* were ready to move things forward with what we were, and instead you took the coward's way out."

"The *coward's* way?" Lucy stopped dead in her tracks, her voice rising in disbelief. "I agreed to an *arrangement* because it would benefit the cause of finding my father's murderer. I agreed to a *deal* because I knew it would keep you out of harm's way."

"Harm's way? You think I'm doing fine right now, Lucy?" His voice rose with every word.

"You're in one piece, aren't you?"

"No!" His jaw dropped at the realization that she had no idea what she had done to him. "No, I'm not in one piece, Lu. I'm fucking broken."

Micah took a step away from her, and then a step toward her, reaching out to touch her face and then thinking better of it, dropping his hand. He didn't know how to deal with this—how to talk to her and be there with her when she wasn't his.

"All I wanted was you. Us," he said in a near whisper. "But you chose him."

"I didn't choose him for love, I chose him for revenge."

"How'd that turn out for you?" Micah scoffed. He turned away from her, not wanting to talk anymore.

There was nothing that could fix this.

"I never stopped thinking about you," she admitted softly. "It was only you, but I couldn't be selfish. Finding Jasper would keep you safe. Sloan promised me he'd find him. I had to go. I had to keep you safe."

"Seems like promises aren't really your thing then, huh?" Micah replied, venom dripping from every word. He stormed away from her, no longer able to keep his resentment in.

"Please!" Lucy cried, stopping Micah in his tracks. "I want us to be better again. Can we please just..." but the words died on her lips.

Turning, Micah finished them for her. "Just forget this happened? Just pick up where we left off?" He took steps toward her, his temper fading in the shadow of her sorrow. "I wish we could, but we both know we can't."

Lucy's tears streamed down her face, her hazel eyes glinting in the afternoon sun. "I'm so sorry."

"I know, sweetheart," he said, wiping the tears from her cheeks. He wanted to hate her.

He wanted to find the reason for all of his outrage and leave it there, allowing it to grow and rot into something else entirely... but he knew he couldn't. Micah was mad, but he wasn't an idiot. He couldn't turn away from all of this.

"Unfortunately, it seems like we have bigger things to deal with right now," Micah told her. "We should probably work on that first."

Lucy nodded, turning her gaze downcast.

The gesture shattered the tiny pieces left of his broken heart. It didn't matter how angry he was, he never wanted to be the one to hurt Lucy. She could run him over with a fucking truck and he'd still be there, ready to love her.

He was a fool.

However, one way or another, their lives were twined together, entangled with The Elderwood and his alchemy. Alchemy that apparently Sloan was on the search for. Micah needed to figure out how to survive being around Lucy without letting his ruptured heart get in the way.

Micah lifted her chin with a finger, forcing her to look at him. "I'd like us to be friends again, if that's okay with you." His eyes seared into hers, looking deeply for the love that was once there, and now lost. "I don't think I can keep up with the whiplash that's been forced between us. But we were always a great team," he said, with a crooked little smile. "So let's be *that* as we bring down Sloan and make him fucking pay. What do you think?"

Smiling back at him, Lucy nodded again. "I think that's a good plan."

Rubbing his thumb over her cheek, Micah let go of her chin and they continued on their silent walk around the property. He knew it wasn't the best plan, and it was only temporary, but there was no other choice.

One thing was for sure, though—together they would crush Sloan, and that would probably make him feel a little bit better.

FIFTEEN

LUCY

The walk through the wooded area of the Lumen property brought so many memories back to Lucy. Each creek held a memory of her and Abe splashing in the water and each leaf shimmering in the trees reminded her of the games they would play on the early summer mornings when she would come to visit with her father. Her heart stung at the memory of two important figures, both stolen from her by the same male.

Jasper may not have killed Abe by his hand, but he played a significant role in it nonetheless.

He's going to pay for this, Lucy seethed.

Her anger bubbled up inside of her once again, clashing with her sorrow, and threatening to drown her in self pity.

Lucy's emotions were a wreck. She was walking in a beautiful forest with the man she loved who refused to love her back, planning to kill the male she was betrothed to. She was even hiding her father's murderer in her family root cellar! All the while, she was surrounded with memories of those who had died, leaving her alone in this wasteland of a reality. The juxtaposition was laughable.

What a fucking mess.

She scoffed at the thought, causing Micah to look over at her.

"You alright?"

"I just keep thinking about how awful all of this is," she admitted. "I miss my father. I miss Abe. I keep making awful choices thinking they're good ones, and now I feel stuck."

"I get it," he said, shoving his hands in his pockets as they made the turn toward the cabin.

She still couldn't get used to how different it was with its modernized look. It wouldn't have suited Abe, but it seemed to be the right fit for Micah.

Lucy glanced over at the portal to The Elderwood, longing in her eyes.

"What I wouldn't give to go back in time," she joked. "I'd go into The Elderwood to experience the pure beauty of creation, not a care in all the realms." It used to be her safe space, a place of beauty and calm.

"I don't think it'd be as quiet as you remember" Micah said, a small laugh in his voice. "Would you like to see it again?"

Her eyes brightened instantly. "The Elderwood?"

He smiled in return. "Yeah. You've got your fancy hand thing to get us there. I'll take you to see The Elderwood at its finest."

"Do we have time?" Lucy asked, looking back at the cabin for any sign of Wes or Brax.

"We won't be long. Besides, if Sloan is on his way through the realms destroying everything, maybe you want to see a bit more of what you're fighting for."

Tentatively, he held out his hand to her, and her heart soared with relief. She smiled at him, and with his hand warming hers, they walked through the portal to The Elderwood.

Lucy should have realized that when she came through to the other side, it would be different—Micah had warned her of such things. However, she evidently did not understand how different, because when she saw a fawn bending down to munch on a patch of grass, she squealed in delight.

Gasping, she scared the small deer away, but she kept her eyes trained on it as it bound down the hill. As the deer crashed into the forest below, it startled a flock of birds from the trees. The birds soared through the sky above her, wings of all different sizes and colors. Her gaze followed them as they landed one by one near the small lake at the base of the mountains.

She nearly fell to her knees as she watched the wild rabbits scamper off at their arrival. Animals of all sized drank from the clear water of the lake; wild horses cantered in the sandy shore, turtles lazed on warm rocks, and large fish jumped in and out of the water.

"I can't believe this is the same place," she murmured to Micah, who stood close by her. In all the times she had visited, she had never seen this side of The Elderwood—what had caused this change?

"I know." The warmth of Micah at her back comforted her. "Let's go for a walk. There are a few people I'd like you to meet."

"People..." She could barely form the word, so astounded by the change.

Smiling, he guided her down the path to a group working around a garden.

Lucy's heart thumped nervously as they neared, a million thoughts running through her head.

Have they always seen me here? Do they even want me here?

The group stopped what they were doing as Micah approached, and in unison, they bowed their heads in deep reverence, placing a fist over their chest.

Lucy could only blink, stunned by the act.

"It's wonderful to see everyone again," Micah said, bending, trying to get them to look him in the eye. "This is my... friend," Micah stated awkwardly, "Lucy Baum."

They all stood upright, and Lucy gave a quick wave as she laughed nervously.

"Some of you may know her from her visits here in the past."

They looked at her and nodded, showing no sign of emotion, their amber eyes trained on her.

"She is here to help keep you safe," Micah said seriously, earning their attention. "Lucy Baum is a fierce warrior and fights for the good of your people. She has always admired your home, and I wanted her to see the people who took such great care of the realm; those who allowed her to enter."

"I am eternally grateful," Lucy said, nodding her appreciation.

As one, they lifted their staffs and pounded them on the ground.

Lucy jumped back a little in surprise, but Micah just chuckled.

"I think it's a good sign," he joked under his breath. "Come on, let's keep walking."

They waved their goodbyes to the group and walked toward a grove of bright orange and magenta trees.

"Friend?" Lucy asked him, her eyes dragging over his muscular form. "Is that what we are?"

"I'd like us to be," he replied, his eyes meeting hers. "Friendship is important in any kind of relationship. Right?" He slid his hand through his hair.

Lucy smiled at the familiarity of the move, his stress getting the best of him. "Yes. I haven't had a real friend since Abe." She sighed. "He would have loved this place so much, I just know it."

Micah's lips quirked up in a smile. "I agree."

Lucy paused under the shade of a bright pink tree and sat beneath it on a bed of grass, her eyes burning at the idea of Abe here—happy and healthy. She pushed the thought away and tried to relax, laying back on the soft earth. Tucking her hands under her head, she looked into the canopy above her, watching as the sunlight trickled in between the leaves. Small birds and bugs fluttered this way and that. To think, she once thought she was alone here when the entire realm was booming with life.

She patted the ground next to her. "Come on down," she joked.

Micah laid down beside her, assuming the same position. Their elbows touched slightly, and a burst of electricity shot through her. She missed his touch. She missed his lips; his broad shoulders as they embraced her.

Sighing, she let go of those desires. There was nothing to be done about that now. Not here. Not after all this time.

The birds chirped above them in the trees. She watched as they bounced from branch to branch.

"It feels nice here," Micah whispered, breaking their silence.

"It does. I wish I could just lie here and allow things to slow down." She propped herself up on one elbow, looking over to Micah. "But we can't slow down. Not yet. We need to stop Sloan."

Micah sat up and put his elbows on his knees. "I know." He glanced over at her, as though he was about to say something, but then closed his mouth and turned the other way.

"What is it?" Lucy asked.

"It's just... I think that's our problem," he began to explain, still having a hard time looking at her. "We rush into everything, don't we?" He offered her a half smile, filled with more sadness than joy. "We rushed into a fake friendship built on lies. We rushed into me becoming the guardian. We rushed into thinking we could build a life together while we were realms apart. And now this. We keep rushing all over without ever slowing down. Without allowing ourselves to feel."

His words seemed to pierce straight into her.

Did she force him into these roles he didn't want?

Lucy sat up straight, tucking her feet underneath herself, as anxiety pooled in the pit of her stomach. "Do you regret becoming the guardian?"

"No," he said quickly, reaching out his hands to her and stopping short.

Each time he did that, Lucy's heart stung.

"I'm glad I became the guardian. I know how important it is, and I'm happy to have taken the role. It's just... everything has been so quick. I just wish we could get to a normal pace and do things the right way."

"What do you mean?" Lucy asked, confused by what he meant.

"Never mind. Come on," he said, changing the topic and brushing the dirt off his legs as he stood. "We have a lot to take care of if we want to stop that asshole."

She didn't want to leave, not after being here for such a short period of time, but she knew he was right. Nodding, Lucy followed him back to the portal so they could pick up where they left off. They needed to make a plan to accomplish the one thing that mattered above all others: take down Sloan.

"THESE ARE the rings that Jasper left behind," Micah said, holding out four rings shimmering with jewels encased in gold. He placed them down on the living room table as they sat on the leather couch. "At first I just kept them in a drawer, afraid to look at them, but the more I thought about it, I realized I could probably use them."

"Why did you want to use them?" Lucy asked, taken aback. These were the same rings Jasper used to hurt The Elderwood... to kill her father.

"Because my magic isn't coming to me the way that it comes to you," he said, a bit of bite in his words. "I was able to use the book to figure out how to imbue some of my magic into them. It's not much, but every bit helps. Then I learned I could also garner some of my strength from the gems themselves. Come on." He grabbed a ring and led her out the front door to the forest's edge.

It was hard for Lucy to watch the man she cared for wear the rings. It made her nauseous if she was being honest. But she knew Micah must have been on to something, because when he slipped the ring on, it glowed a bright red, his magic responding immediately.

He levitated a branch over his head, his outstretched arm guiding it back and forth through the air. "With the ring the magic comes quicker, and I don't tire myself as easily."

Lucy watched as the red mist that gripped the branch flickered in and out, almost like lightning. The branch trembled in the air and Micah's magic failed him.

He jumped out of the way as the branch came crashing down. "Unfortunately, I'm still not great at making the magic work for me. Some days are better than others, but..."

"Most days are shit?" Wes offered.

Lucy nearly jumped.

Where did he come from?

"Yeah," Micah admitted, running his hand over his face. "Brax has been trying to help me, and I think we are getting there. It's just taking time." He looked around in confusion. "Speaking of Brax, you still haven't seen her?"

"You mean when you two just left me at the cabin and went frolicking in The Elderwood without me?" He threw his hands up in the air. "What is it with people just forgetting I'm around?"

Lucy scrunched up her face in guilt. "Sorry."

"Well, the answer is no, I haven't seen her." He paused, then cocked his head toward the trees, his brow furrowed.

Lucy heard it, too.

Something was rushing toward them from the forest.

Wes and Lucy shifted in front of Micah, readying themselves for a fight. Lucy pulled her magic to the surface, the green orbs curling around her arms. Wes's silvery magic was like a whip in his hand as he whispered the words to summon the magical weapon.

From the trees, out crashed Brax, looking windblown and grief stricken.

With a deep breath, Lucy stood up from her defensive position, but she didn't let her guard down. While Brax was not an unwelcome guest, something was still not right. Lucy's green magic slithered around her, ready to strike.

"What's wrong?" Micah called, running to her.

"I'm sorry," Brax said weakly. She placed her hands on her knees to catch her breath.

"What happened?" Wes demanded.

Brax stood and shook her head in hesitation. "I didn't believe you," she said, looking at Lucy. "I couldn't believe you. Lord Sloan has been nothing but good to me—to *all* who work for him..." her voice trailed off.

"What happened?" Lucy asked again, fear filling her.

"I contacted him."

Lucy's heart dropped.

"I used a bespelled mirror to reach him, to see if what you said was true. I asked him what else he wanted me to do here, or if there were other places I could be of use. Maybe he could use me in other missions, maybe in the South."

"No," Lucy's mouth popped open. "You may as well have just come out and shouted that we were here."

Fuck.

"I know. I'm sorry," Brax said, her eyes set with a quiet determination. "He asked me about you—about you both," she said, looking at Lucy and Micah. "I tried to tell him something to steer him astray, but I think he knew I was lying. He knew. He knew!" She roared. "I don't know how."

"What else did he say?" Lucy demanded, grabbing Brax by her shoulders.

The next words out of her mouth would navigate their course of action, and she had to know what he knew.

Brax's eyes were full of fire as she spoke. "He's on his way to Central Denora... He's making his way to the Baum estate."

My family.

Lucy's eyes widened in alarm, and she looked at Micah.

He gave her a swift nod, knowing she had to leave.

She grabbed Wes's hand and squeezed, holding him tight.

"Ah, not again," Wes moaned.

Within the span of a blink, they disappeared from Joterra and landed in her room back in Denora.

SIXTEEN

LUCY

Lucy quickly threw a privacy charm over Wes as he landed, sputtering and keeled over in her bedchambers. She didn't have time to wait for him to master himself before finding their mother. With Sloan's power to travel with just a thought, he may as well already be here.

Lucy thought back to when he transported her from the woods into his carriage, how she sat in his lap and imagined a life with him. The very memory that once gave her butterflies now appalled her.

Manipulating her magic to split the privacy charm, she left a bubble around Wes to allow him to regain his composure, and tightened one around her body as she ran to the door.

"Stay here until you're steady," she told Wes over her shoulder as she made it to the hall. "Then come find us immediately. I don't know how long it'll take Sloan to get here."

All Wes could do was throw a hand in the air as his

head bobbed between his knees, trying to ease the contents of his stomach.

Lucy ran down the stairs, hoping to discover her mother alone so she could prepare her for Sloan's arrival. Magic swirled beneath her skin, her panic rising with every breath as she raced around the estate. Where could she be? The gardens? Her study? Lucy sent a silent prayer up to the stars to ask for guidance and protection. It was one thing to go against Sloan on her own; it was something else entirely to have her family at risk.

Green light sprung from her hands and flew ahead of her erratically, leaving a trail of light in its wake as Lucy followed quickly behind it. She had no idea what she would walk into, but with her magic so frazzled, she could only assume it wouldn't be good. Perhaps her magic knew something Lucy did not?

Stretching her Fae senses throughout the estate as she searched for her mother, she reinforced the shields around her, hoping it would be enough.

"Oh, yes!" Anita said, her voice coming from the parlor. "They should be back soon."

Is he here already?

"I don't mind waiting for my betrothed," Sloan's voice replied, a touch of coldness seeping over the words.

Lucy ran faster, keeping her privacy charm tight to her body so he wouldn't hear her approach.

"Yes, we are all so excited about the wedding! How are your people in the North taking to the news?" Anita continued making small talk.

Lucy's stomach churned. Sloan had a special magic and could always tell when someone was lying to him.

What would he do to Anita when he realized she was spouting off nothing but falsities?

She couldn't let herself find out.

Racing to the doorway, she paused, fixing her hair and blouse from her quick travel, and dropped the magical shield.

"Mother," Lucy said, cheeks flushed from her rush. "I'm glad to see you. Wes wanted to discuss some business with you upstairs."

Anita's eyes flared in relief at the sight of Lucy. "No problem, dear. Lord Sloan and I were just talking about the wedding and how you had some wedding day jitters." Anita smiled at Lord Sloan and feigned an airy laugh.

Laurent Sloan just stood there and smiled at Lucy, a smile so cold and dark she wondered how he could force the gesture at all. He nodded in agreement with Anita, his sneer made proof he believed none of what she said.

"I told him you just needed some motherly bonding to prepare you for the big day." Anita said it with such ease, Lucy was shocked at the seamlessness of her lie.

"Mother, get upstairs, please." There was no more time to pretend, and the command came out more forcefully than she intended. Lucy kept eye contact with Sloan, refusing to let her mother get involved in whatever was about to unfold. She couldn't risk her getting hurt.

Losing one parent at the hands of this monster was enough.

Sloan put a hand on Anita's arm to stop her, his fingers curling around her wrist.

At Anita's gasp, Lucy's eyes tinged with green. "Don't touch my mother," Lucy barked as she felt the wave of magic spring to her fingers. All pretenses of civility were far gone.

Lord Sloan just smiled, placing his very best mask of kindness on his face, slowly tightening his grip on Anita. "No need to worry, my beloved. We—"

But Lucy cut him off. "I know why you're here. And you and I both know everything my mother said was a lie. Now let her go before you fucking regret it."

Sloan must have read the steel in her eyes, because for the briefest second, he released Anita, allowing Lucy to rush forward with her Fae speed and pull her out of his reach.

"There's really no reason for this, Lucella," Sloan said each word carefully. Though something just under the surface of those ice-blue eyes was filled with allure. "It's time to come home now. We can discuss your... unusual departure in private."

"This is my home, and I have nothing to say to you." She took a step back, trying to get Anita to the hallway exit.

"On the contrary," Sloan replied, his lip curling. "I think we'd have much to discuss for our future."

"You want to hurt people," Lucy said, the sheer disgust in her voice evident. "I can't let you do this."

"Now, now. Let us not get ahead of ourselves," he said dismissively. "Return to me, and all will be forgiven." He held out his hand to her, expecting her to take it.

"You're fucking delusional if you think I would ever stand by you," Lucy hissed through clenched teeth.

"You will!" Lord Sloan snarled, his face twisting with violence as his temper flared.

Lucy took another step back, holding her mother behind her and away from his outburst.

I need to get her out of here. Where's Wes? Panic bubbled in her chest.

He straightened his shoulders, trying to regain his composure. "You and I will do this, and you will be by my side every step of the way. You and that *magic* of yours." He took an angered step forward as though he would grab her, but then thought better of it.

His words turned Lucy's wrath molten. The magic in her body swarmed through her hands and curled around her and Anita in a protective stance, prepared to oppose Laurent Sloan. "Never."

The one word was enough to tip Sloan into a fury. "You will be mine," he roared as he cast a blue rope of ice toward her.

Anita stepped in with a graceful swish of her hand, shifting Lucy to the side and sending Sloan's magical ice ropes into the wall with a deafening crash.

Anita spun her arms in front of her in a circular motion, creating a vortex of ribbons in a shimmering gold. Then, she pushed forward with two open palms, blasting a powerful force of magic directly into Sloan. He barreled across the room and hit the wall with a clatter.

"Don't you ever attempt to hurt my daughter again," she said with a deadly edge to her voice.

Lord Sloan pushed himself up from the ground and narrowed his eyes in hatred at the two Baum females. His usually perfect hair was in disarray, tangled strands of white covering his revenge-filled eyes. With a grunt, he threw his hand out, sending shards of ice careening toward them. Lucy's arms dashed up to protect her mother and herself, but Anita got there first, turning his icy magic into nothing but gentle flakes of snow.

Laurent Sloan screamed as he sent burst after burst of magic toward them. Each time, Anita's unyielding power met his, dismantling his spells, blow for blow. Sloan released a deranged bellow as he pressed on.

Lucy watched in stunned silence as Anita's powerful magic bested the great Lord of the North, not one hair out of place. Lucy cast a shield to keep her and her mother safe from any more icy attacks. Wonder and pride raced through her at her mother's remarkable skill.

"You are going to regret this," he hissed at Lucy, capturing her attention. "You are supposed to be by my side as we make Denora better. We are meant to be together! But instead you want to do... what, exactly? Thwart my plans so you can play house with some weak little mortal?" He scoffed, then spat at the floor. "I will get my hands on his alchemy and your magic. You are *mine!*"

Anita's arms shot in the air, and glass from the windows crashed to the floor around them. Vines came pouring in from the outside garden, slithering in front of Anita and Lucy like snakes. Anita's fierce gaze remained on Sloan as she controlled her magic, her fingers curling into tight fists. Swooping toward Sloan, the vines tried to bind him, but he cast blades of ice, cutting them down.

Lucy dug her heels into the ground, strengthening her shields, her body humming with power.

"I can't hold him," Anita said, her voice trembling as she attempted to continue the attack. "But we can block him, don't let down your shield!" Steadily, the vines retreated from Sloan and instead began to weave together in front of them.

"You can hide now," he shouted over the din, "but you *will* come crawling back to me! What we have is real! You belong with me!"

Sloan threw darts of ice at the wall, but Anita's magic wove the vines into an impenetrable blockade. Channeling more power into the shield, Lucy focused all of her anger on keeping Sloan away from her mother. A gust of wind lifted her into the air, a green haze tinting the shield she formed. With her hair flying wildly, her magic raised her higher and higher until she could see above the wall of vines, Sloan still screaming through the chaos.

Anita's magic grew tenfold, matching his rage. "If you'd like to die today, I invite you to stay where you are." Her words promised violence and Lucy couldn't have loved her mother more in that moment. Anita continued to build her magic until the vines were a towering wall of protection. Then she slammed her hand on the vines, causing a dark, gray wall of swirling magic to build.

The magic vibrated loudly, unlike anything she'd ever experienced before. With gusts of smoke, the magic billowed around the vines. As each second passed, the wall of misty magic seemed more solid than smoke, slowly blocking Sloan into a corner and cutting him from Anita's view. But from her height, Lucy could see the wall rippling, turning into something else entirely. The vines melted together, forming a solid gray wall.

"This is just the beginning," Sloan said with darkening promise, and before Lucy could even blink, he disappeared. She waited, looking for his reappearance, but it never came. Taking a deep breath, Lucy floated back down to the floor.

Anita stood at the ready, breathing heavily, her hands pressing against that shadowy magic that stood tall and strong in the face of their enemy. Her eyes were scrunched together and her brow was furrowed in concentration as she worked tirelessly to keep this blockade before them, keeping her daughter safe.

Lucy gently placed a hand on her mother's shoulder, and Anita startled—the only proof she was nervous at all.

"It's okay, Mother. He's gone... for now," Lucy whispered, calming her.

Sighing, her shoulders slumped, and she released the giant wall of magic she had built to protect her daughter. In an instant, it turned back into smoke and began to dissipate.

"What was that?" Lucy asked, marveling at the enormity of the magical wall her mother had produced. The solid form changed back into vines and they fell to a heap on the floor.

"When I felt as though there was a chance that Sloan could break through my wall of vines, I called on your father's magic. I wasn't expecting it to, but... it appeared as stone, transforming my vines into something unyielding."

Lucy's dark shadows swirled with recognition.

"An immovable force field," Lucy said, warmth coursing through her.

"Leave it to Corvus to be stubborn as a rock in both life and death," Anita said dryly.

Lucy looked at her mother incredulously and burst into a fit of laughter.

"If he was one thing, he was consistent." She chuckled along with her. Then Anita looked over at her daughter, a serious expression appearing on her face. "Seems like we have a lot to talk about... Follow me."

CHAPTER
SEVENTEEN
ANITA

The halls were quiet as they walked side by side from the foyer to the gardens. Anita always felt most like herself when she was outside, and today was just the same. She needed the comfort of her garden if she were to have this conversation with Lucy.

"What happened while you were away?" Anita asked Lucy softly, worried her questioning would scare her daughter away like it usually did.

"We saw Micah and Brax," Lucy began. "We warned them about what was to come." Her voice trailed off, as if she was unsure of what to say next. "I know you don't approve, but I just needed to make sure he was safe."

Anita stopped on the stone walkway to the back gardens, reaching out for Lucy's arm to face her. "What do you mean you know I don't approve?" She furrowed her brow, but Lucy just stared at her, unfazed.

"I'm well aware you don't want me paired with a mortal," Lucy said, pulling away from her mother and continuing her walk down the path.

Anita kept her pace with Lucy, contemplating how to share what she knew. "From my understanding, he is no longer mortal. Is he not?"

Lucy whipped her head to look at her mother. "What do you know?"

Anita rolled her eyes but offered a soft smile. "Do you really think I don't know what goes on around here?"

Lucy said nothing, which was typical for their conversations.

With a deep sigh, Anita continued through the gardens, making their way to the east side of the large maze of foliage. She kept her hands clasped in front of her as she always did, and the sway of her large skirt shifted in the breeze. Long moments passed until she finally arrived at the section with the butterfly bushes—her favorite. The memory made her smile.

"Do you know why I love this place so much?" Anita asked Lucy, changing the subject. "The butterflies come here to lay their eggs and start the next cycle of their lives." She ran her hands through the leaves of the soft green bushes. "They eat the leaves of the plants to give nutrition to their bodies, lay their eggs in the safety of this little garden, then the caterpillars come out in beautiful shades of greens and blues and pinks, only for them to once again wrap themselves in their silk, hiding away from the rest of creation."

Lucy said nothing, watching Anita with questions clear upon her face. She also looked as though she was ready to walk away, like she usually did when it came to the two of them. But Anita couldn't let her do that today. There was too much that needed to be said.

"They stay that way in their little silk wrapping for days, did you know that?" Anita continued, walking through the garden and smelling the beautiful violet flowers that were planted in ornamental pots. "Inside, they turn to goo. No more caterpillar. Not yet a butterfly. They become something else completely—something in between. And when they emerge?" A smile lit her face as she focused on the memory.

"Why are you giving me a lesson on insects?" Lucy asked from the other side of the square in her usual sassy tone Anita had come to love. It often reminded her how powerful Lucy was—something she could never forget.

"Your father and I used to sit right there on that bench for hours, watching the butterflies." Anita pointed to the wood and stone seating just behind Lucy.

"You're telling me Father sat around and watched bugs with you?" Lucy said in disbelief, her cocked eyebrow slightly hidden by her voluminous, unruly curls. "He must have hated it."

"It was *his* idea," Anita countered with a fiery challenge in her eye. "There was something about the in-between that always made him take pause. It took a lot to slow that male down, but for some reason, the butterflies did..." Anita drifted off, deep into remembrance. "Once, we were picnicking right here, drinking wine and snacking on cheese and bread until late in the day." She grinned, happy to share this memory with someone for the very first time. "We let time get away from us, and found ourselves sitting in the dark under the stars." A giggle escaped her lips, and she put a hand up to her mouth to soften the sound.

Lucy looked on with curiosity in her gaze, a faint, begrudging smile playing on her lips at her mother's story.

"We didn't think butterflies came out of their silk wrappings so late at night; but there was one. Just once. I don't think I've ever seen anything like it, and your father said the same. The butterfly was bright purple; so bright it nearly glowed in the dark. Have you ever seen such a thing?"

Lucy shook her head slightly, but Anita continued on, wrapped in the memory.

"Your father took his magic," she said, lifting her hand to act out what Corvus did. "And he blew on the tips of his fingers ever so gently, allowing the smallest bits of light to pepper the sky above us, like a shimmering mist that floated through the air." She threw her hand in the air, the way she remembered Corvus had, wishing she could repeat the same beautiful magic he once created.

It was quiet for a moment. Anita tried to reel in the wave of sadness that was threatening to crash over her. She needed to speak to Lucy about him. She needed to stop shying away from the memories that stung because they healed her as much as they hurt.

"Like this?" Lucy whispered, then she lifted her hand high in the air. With a wave of her fingers, tiny orbs of light floated all around them.

Anita's broken heart soared. "Very much like that." She smiled through watery eyes, looking at the daughter she was beyond proud of. "You know what happened next?"

Lucy shook her head again.

"The butterfly floated around us for the next few hours, just shimmering its violet light around the beautiful glittering sky your father created for us. He..." She took a deep breath, calming her shaky words. "He told me the gods must have sent him that violet butterfly, and I believed him." Anita walked closer to Lucy and held her hand. "That same month, we found out we were pregnant with you. And when you were born, we knew you'd be the most amazing thing to ever happen to us."

Lucy's smile faltered as she bowed her head, no longer able to look at her mother.

"You have other children." Lucy's words were a mumble. "You cannot truly think I believe that a butterfly made you change your entire way of thinking simply because I was born."

"You're right—we have many children, and all of them change us in different ways. Hugh and Gregory taught us to be patient and loving parents. Wes and Tristan taught us how to be strong, how to guide each of you and mold you. Henry and Simon taught us to bring a little fun back into our lives. And you, Lucella..."

How do I tell her that she changed my world?

"Do you know what your name means? They are two Fae words for *light* and *warrior*."

Tilting her head, Lucy looked back up to her mother with tears filling her eyes.

"I did not give birth to you for you to fall to the whims of society. I gave you life so you can fight for the things you want. To build the life you want for yourself. Lucy, you were that in-between... We knew you'd be more than a female Fae in the Denoran courts. We knew you'd be more than just our daughter. You'd become *more*."

"You can't honestly say that," Lucy said, tears full of hurt and pain slipping down her cheeks. "You were so quick to throw me into my endless schooling with my tutors, never listening that I did not want to go. Father would never let me join the family business, saying I was simply a female who would never be able to be worthy of such a position. And then, when I upset everyone, I was married off to the first Lord who had enough money and space to handle my temper. Don't tell me you paved the way for me to be who I am today —you've stifled me!" Her words came clipped and full of emotion.

Anita knew this conversation was coming. She had been dreading it for the last hundred years, if she was being honest with herself.

"Lucy, whose idea was it to teach you how to make a bow?" Anita asked quietly, never taking her eyes off Lucy. "Who encouraged Wes to take you with him to Joterra?"

Lucy stared at her, surprised by the turn of questions. "Well, I... When I..." But she never finished her sentence.

"I told your father you were ready to learn the trade because you were a natural, it was evident from the first time you picked up a bow. I saw you getting restless and I told Wes to take you, to show you the ropes. I knew you needed the adventure. You needed more than what Denora has to offer."

Anita watched as Lucy's eyes widened at the admission.

Keep going, Anita, she told herself. *Help her see the beauty and strength that lives within her.*

"And darling, of course everyone hates their classes. Do you think I was overjoyed to sit around and learn how to do needlework when I could very simply create beauty with a flourish of my hand?"

Anita turned and paced before Lucy, the nerves within her body getting the best of her. She had always hoped Lucy would put it together herself one day. Anita never wanted to take ownership of anything that helped mold Lucy—she was her mother, she always did the best she could. Even if Lucy didn't see it.

She turned once again to look at Lucy, who was standing there, dumbstruck.

"This marriage to Laurent Sloan was supported by me because I knew you would be your own person, no matter what. No male can change you, Lucella Baum. You are a force to be reckoned with, and I'm sorry I didn't see how badly you wanted out of the arrangement to begin with. You've always been... opinionated, but this time I should have listened. I thought with time you'd see we weren't against you at all."

Slumping into the bench behind her, Lucy's face went slack. "I don't understand... I've been so upset with you... with Father... and this whole time—what? This whole time I've been screaming from the tops of my lungs that this wasn't what I wanted and now, now when everything is too fucking late, I find out that it was all for nothing?"

"What was all for nothing?"

"Being so mad at Father!" Lucy yelled. "I've run from

him, put so much distance between us that it was never able to be mended. I ruined everything and now he's... he's dead. He's dead because of me!" The words crashed through the garden like a rushing torrent.

Anita hurried to Lucy, holding her by her shoulders and forcing her to look her in the eye. "It was *never* your fault for your father's end. That responsibility lies solely with the cretin holed up in the cellar waiting for his judgment." Her eyes burned with pain.

Looking up at her mother, Lucy's face crumbled. "If I had just listened, this never would have happened."

"We raised you to follow your heart, Lucy. We—"

"I didn't do that either!" Lucy sobbed, cutting her mother off. "I'm heartbroken. I chose Laurent over Micah all because of a fucking vendetta and now I'm left with nothing! Nothing but anger and pain." The sobs wracked through her body and Anita held her through it all.

"You are strong, Lucella Baum," Anita told her, fiercely determined to get her daughter to listen. "There is so much riding on the next few days as we navigate this new reality Lord Sloan wishes to force upon us, but it is our destiny to stop him. I feel it in my bones." She felt the presence of her husband deep within her, encouraging her on. Tugging Lucy's chin up to look at her, their hazel eyes mirrored one another. "You will overcome this. Your life has not ended, and if my instincts are correct, you and Micah Lumen will have time to work this all out."

Lucy nodded through the tears, wiping them away with the back of her hand. "I don't know how we are going to get through this."

"Together," Wes said, coming out from behind one of the larger bushes. "We will get through this together."

Anita startled. She didn't hear him approach—perhaps she was too distracted by their conversation.

"Dry your eyes, my love," Anita told Lucy. "There is time to figure this all out. We will put one foot in front of the other and we won't give up. Do you understand me?"

Lucy took a deep breath and looked at Anita, her eyes shining a pale green.

"Lucy, are you okay?" Wes asked her. "Your eyes are glowing again. That only happens when you get lost in your magic."

Anita smiled, pulling Lucy's chin up to look her in those beautiful eyes more closely. "You will glow. You will get lost in your magic. And you will take down anyone who has ever doubted you. You are Lucella Baum, and you were born to become something more."

Lucy nodded at her, with an unshakable resolve settling in her gaze.

"I will go to the King," Wes stated. "I'll try to convince him to stop Sloan before it's too late. Perhaps we can intervene before he's even begun."

Anita nodded her agreement, proud to see Wes finding his footing in his new position. She knew he had more inside of him than he had ever dreamed, but it would take time for him to find it... and she would do whatever it took to make sure he had the time to do so.

"I need to go to the South," Lucy said, turning to Wes. "I must see our brothers and make sure they are safe. I'll figure out what's happening there and report back. Then, hopefully the king will do something to step in and stop this madness."

Wes gave her a determined nod, and Anita just watched in adoration at the beautiful souls she had raised. They were good, noble, and honorable Fae.

Corvus would be so proud of them all.

CHAPTER

EIGHTEEN

MICAH

With another swing of his axe, the blade came rushing down toward the tree trunk, expertly heaving it into two pieces. The same maneuver as always, but now with his gift from The Elderwood. The sunstone in the hilt of the handle glowed with other-worldly radiance, and in the light, Micah thought it looked exactly like his own magic.

"How do you feel?" Brax asked him for the tenth time.

"I'm fine," he replied. "Stop asking after every damn swing."

Micah was still frustrated with Brax for contacting Sloan, and as much as he was trying to get past it, the action felt like a betrayal. The second she contacted him, it put Lucy in danger. In that moment, Brax was careless, but she was his best friend. She'd never do something to hurt him—not intentionally.

Stretching his shoulders, he cracked his neck to calm himself down and recenter. It had been two days since

Lucy had to run home, and the tension of not knowing if she was alright coiled around him like a snake. He wouldn't be able to take a deep breath again until he knew she was okay. He prayed she got there in time before anything bad happened. There was nothing else he could do except hope it went well and wait, impatiently, to hear from her.

That was his life lately. Rushing from one bad thing to the next—a time bomb just ticking away like a big fucking joke.

"I ask after every swing, you caved in cantaloupe, because I need to know when your magic wanes." Brax jumped down from where she was standing on the tree stumps and walked over to him. "So far you've swung thirty-seven times, and the magic has sliced through the wood like it was carving warm butter. That is not your strength alone—that is your magic."

Micah turned to look at her, his face clouded with doubt.

It couldn't have been thirty-seven times. I'm not tired at all.

"Hmm, strange, isn't it?" Brax said with a grin curving up her lips. "You're powerful and are using your magic without weakening in the slightest."

"It must be the gemstone," Micah said, looking at the red tinted jewel. He wondered how something so small could have such a powerful effect.

"That is my thinking as well," Brax replied.

"Then why did my magic drain when I used the rings from Jasper?" Micah asked. "It's all alchemy, isn't it?"

"Pfft," Brax sounded. "Just as there are varying

powers of magic, there are varying elements to strengthen your alchemy or weaken it."

"And now you're the expert on alchemy magic?" Micah said blandly.

"No," she replied sweetly. "I'm simply smarter than you. Which isn't saying much."

Micah rolled his eyes and swung the axe again. He cleaved another piece of wood, this time focusing on his magic. Tuning in on each swing, he tried to sense it. The problem was, he didn't know what he was looking for.

He never quite found the well of power inside of him, but he also didn't feel tired at all. Instead, he felt refreshed. Re-energized.

"I think Jasper never mastered alchemy," she said as she watched him line up for another strike. "There must be some gemstones that are more apt to taking and holding power for your alchemy than others. His rings would wear thin after as much as two uses."

"So either he sucked at alchemy, or he picked the wrong stones?" Micah asked, swinging again.

That makes forty.

"Perhaps both," Brax said matter-of-factly. "He's an imbecile."

"This magic *does* feel different," he admitted at last. He wanted to stay mad at Brax, but that wasn't fair. He had more than his fair share of shitty situations, and Brax always helped him through it. She had proven over and over that she was a loyal friend. Sometimes friends just fuck up. Casting the remaining annoyance away, he looked at her. "I just wish I understood it better."

"Your alchemy powers the gem, which activates the

magic within the axe. It is a weapon specially made for you to wield without tiring." Her eyes shimmered with interest. "It is a wonder to behold." Her head snapped to Micah again, and her voice turned stern. "You better learn to use it correctly."

"Yeah, yeah," he waved her off. "I'm working on it."

"Try using the axe for something *other* than chopping wood," Brax suggested. "This is a ridiculous amount of logs to store for no reason."

Looking around at the piles and piles of wood around them, Micah replied, "Good point."

"Go over there, where we won't be crushed by an avalanche of logs, and try to harness your magic to do things you've done before. Call over an item. Or perhaps try to raise the stones as weapons as you once did in front of Wes?"

Micah walked over to the open area and recalled the day she had mentioned. Lucy had been there with him, and together they had pulled the metals from the ground, turning them to gold. It was the day he learned she was more than Fae.

Or maybe not Fae at all.

That part he still didn't understand.

With his axe in both hands, he squeezed the handle tight and looked at the stones on the ground at his feet. He aimed all of his intent at them, ordering them to raise up and form a large boulder.

But nothing happened.

He looked at Brax and shrugged his shoulders.

"Try again, you wrinkled prune."

"That insult doesn't make sense. Prunes are already

wrinkly."

Brax just stared pointedly at him, directing him back to his task.

With a roll of his eyes, he focused back on the rocks. He saw them just sitting there and had no idea how he'd get them to move.

Closing his eyes, he tried to picture it all in his head. The stones lifting one by one, the pieces grouping together to form a large ball, just like the one that he aimed at Wes. He remembered how tired he was that day, and he prayed that this time when he made the magic work, he would have any energy left over to continue practicing.

To his shock, when he opened his eyes to perform the magic, the massive boulder was already there in front of him, hovering in the air.

"Trying to throw another boulder at me, Lumen? I thought we were past that," Wes said from the edge of the forest.

Instantly, Micah dropped the rock pile and it landed with a loud thud.

"Where did you come from? I didn't even hear you come up." Micah looked around, hoping he had brought someone with him.

"Yes, explain Baum." Brax's eyes were wild with caution. "How did I not sense you before your arrival? Have you learned to travel the way your sister does?"

"Thankfully, no," he blanched. "I hate that form of travel. Give me my own two feet any day."

"Then how?" Brax grated, her eyes narrowing with suspicion.

"It isn't nefarious, calm down. My father blessed me with the gift of light," Wes said with a mischievous smile, producing a ball of gleaming light in the palm of his hand. "But my father was full of secrets, and this light does more than brighten spaces."

He tossed the ball into the air before him, and the small light crashed into his chest, encompassing Wes and making him glow. For all of one second, he was illuminated by the strange magic before it faded away, leaving Wes looking exactly the same as before.

"What does it do?" Brax asked curiously.

Wes jumped up and down, clapped his hands, and stomped his feet. Not one sound was heard. It was as though he wasn't there at all.

Waving his hand over his body, he dismissed the spell so he could explain. "It allows for lightness on my feet as well. It has proven to be useful to sneak up on people unsuspectingly."

"Why are you trying to sneak up on us?" Brax asked accusingly.

"Relax. That was just practice," he said with a sigh. His usual charm seemed muted, like he couldn't find the energy to be himself.

A cool shiver went through Micah's body at the thought of Wes needing to use that magic to sneak around.

"Practice for what?" Micah asked.

With a weary glance, Wes explained. "Lord Sloan's visit was less than pleasant."

"Is Lucy okay?" Micah asked, panic rising in his chest.

"Yes, she's fine," he clipped.

"Why are you here, then?" Brax asked, trying to get to the point.

"From the sound of it, Sloan's plans are already unfolding in the South, and I've come to ask you to ally with us against him if he rises in Central Denora." The somber expression in his eyes filled Micah with dread.

They are already expecting the worst.

"You know we are on your side, but what can we do?" Micah asked. "I'm stuck here, remember?"

"Yes, but Brax has many allies who just so happen to be undefeated warriors." Wes lifted a brow at Brax, imploring her to consider.

"You want my people to fight against Lord Sloan?" Brax asked, incredulous.

"Most definitely," Wes said, thrown by the question. "We must stop him by any means."

"There has to be a misunderstanding here. He would never hurt others for power." Brax took a step away from them, clearly choosing sides.

Micah shook his head, crestfallen. "I know he's done a lot for you, but you really don't think there's any truth to what they've been telling us?"

"No. I don't." Brax crossed her arms, staring daggers at them.

"Listen, you called Sloan and gave away Lucy's position," Micah countered. "And you felt awful about that, didn't you?"

Micah couldn't understand why she would feel so bad about betraying them just days ago, yet she still believed that he wasn't exactly how Lucy had described.

"I am sorry for betraying your trust before by calling Lord Sloan. However, he has a right to be upset that his bride-to-be was here with her ex-lover." Each word out of her mouth had more bite than the last.

"That isn't fair and you know it," Micah said softly.

"Well, I—" Brax began, but Wes cut her off.

"He came to my house and tried to take Lucy," Wes snapped. "He cast battle magic upon my mother in our own home. You cannot tell me that unhinged Fae is anything beyond a power hungry psychopath."

"He did what?" Micah snarled.

"Sloan put his hands on my mother and attempted to bind Lucy with his ice ropes and whisk her away back to the North." The anger in the air was palpable and Wes's eyes were anything but calm.

"Is she okay?" Micah asked, barely able to restrain himself.

If Sloan hurt one piece of hair from her perfect head, I'll take my axe and scalp the mother fucker.

"Thankfully, yes," Wes said, looking at Micah now. "She and my mother didn't let him get away with a stunt like that." His gaze narrowed and flicked to Brax. "But clearly Brax would have been willing to."

"Of course I don't want anyone to get hurt!" Brax shouted. "Maybe it was an accident? Maybe he just lost his temper because Lucella Baum is an infuriating Fae."

Her eyes darted to the left, then the right, but never landed on Micah. He knew Brax was avoiding looking into the eyes of her friend and admitting she was worried about something beyond her control.

"What ties you to him so deeply that you cannot see him for who he is?" Wes asked her.

But Micah knew.

Micah knew that Laurent Sloan was her ticket back to her family. Brax relied on him to earn the money she needed to retire and spend the rest of her days with her family—her sisters. Any threat to that plan was not acceptable.

But could she really just ignore the flashing signs before her? Could she not see him for the monster he was? Or did she see it and choose to ignore it, because that was what would benefit her?

"He's marching on the South, Brax," Micah said with measured strength in his voice. "He plans to take over and become Denora's next king."

"Maybe Denora needs a new king," she spat back.

An exasperated sigh left Wes, and as he opened his mouth to counter her argument, but Micah simply held up his hand, stopping him.

"I want to show you something, Brax," he said, the calm tenor in his voice still present.

I hope this fucking works, he said to himself.

Taking a few steps back, Micah held onto his axe with two hands. Gripping it by the handle, he lifted it high into the air and squeezed his eyes shut tight. Slowly, he swung it in a wide circle in front of him, skimming the ground and soaring above his head. Feeling the magic coming to his fingertips, he began to swing faster and faster.

Then, as the axe got to the top once more, he paused, and opened his eyes. Just as he had hoped, the magic was there before him, a large wall of glowing red magic.

"What is this?" Brax asked him, anger still there, but fading.

"My magic," he said softly, the words gentle as though he was afraid he'd scare her away. "Can you see it?" His words were shaky as he tried to hold the magic in place.

"See what?" Brax asked, looking at him, her weight shifting from foot to foot.

"Come closer," Micah told her. "Stand next to me." Sweat trickled down his neck, pooling on his back.

Taking slow strides to him, she glanced between Micah and Wes, unsure of what Micah wanted. Then, as she stood there with Micah, his magic did exactly what he had hoped.

"It's our reflection," she stated, looking at the glimmering magic. The red wall shimmered in and out with silver, creating a mirror.

"Yes," Micah said, as though it explained everything. "It's us. It's you and me in my magic." He looked at her reflection, speaking to her—his best friend. "You were the one who taught me how to use my magic. You showed me how to rein it, how to nurture it, and how to understand it. Without you, this would not have been possible." He said the next words slowly and with the utmost sincerity. "Without you, there would be no me."

"That's nonsense," she scoffed, trying to walk away.

Micah reached out to stop her, still holding the axe in the air with one hand. "Wait. I mean it, look—look closely."

He couldn't have her walk away just yet. He was lucky his magic worked for him the first time, there were no promises he'd find a way to make it work again.

She paused, giving a warning glare to Micah, but when her gaze found the wall of magic, her eyes widened, and she gasped in surprise.

There in the reflection, it was not just Micah and Brax as they stood. Instead, there was a set of moving images... Memories of them together.

Sparring in the shade of the trees.

Fighting over the bag of potato chips.

Laughing side by side as they chopped wood.

Smiling shoulder to shoulder under the stars.

"It's us." Brax's voice caught and she tried to clear it. "How?" Her glossy eyes looked to Micah's as he dropped the axe and the reflective magic disappeared.

Taking deep, heaving breaths, he rested his hands on his knees; the magic taking more out of him than he thought it would. "I channeled all of my power into reminding myself, reminding *you*." Standing up straight, he looked her in the eye, refusing to let her walk away and choose the wrong side without him knowing how important she was to him. "You're my best friend, Brax, and I can't do this without you."

"It... It doesn't make him what Lucy says he is," she whispered, yet something in her tone told Micah that her conviction was failing. Doubt crept through her words.

"Believe it or don't," Wes said crossly. "It will not change the course of our future. And for your sake, and mine, I hope you figure that out."

CHAPTER

NINETEEN

BRAX

Brax's bedroom in the Lumen cabin was simple: a soft bed with rich earthy colors, a large brown leather chair near the window, and a simple wooden dresser near the door. The room was otherwise empty of her belongings since she didn't take many personal items with her on assignment. She always kept with her a few changes of clothes, her weapons, a picture of her family, a looking glass for communications, and a gift from Laurent Sloan.

"Where is it?" She cursed under her breath as she tore through the drawers of her dresser.

I know I left it here at home. Did I put it in the...

The simple phrase stopped her, catching her off guard, unable to finish her thought.

Home.

She called the Lumen cabin her home.

But that was what it had become... hadn't it? A place she yearned for at the end of each long day; a place to rest her head at night and feel safe.

Somewhere she belonged.

She dropped into the leather chair in front of the window and gazed out, chewing on her lip. It had been years since she truly felt as though she belonged somewhere. There were the years at home as she grew up in Vytyr, but since she had gone out on missions, Vytyr felt more and more like a memory of days long past. Not her future.

Brax couldn't stop thinking about what Micah had shown her—their friendship on display before them within his unique magic. He showed her everything they had been through: the laughter, the anger, the moments of peace. Their connection was something that people wished for all their lives—a true friendship.

It was worth fighting for, wasn't it?

She gulped down air, the weight of her decision before her making it hard to breathe.

Even Wes had been right, though she'd never admit it in a million years. She could be 20,000 years old and still refuse to ever concede to that shriveled up fig. Whatever she felt about the situation was irrelevant; all that mattered was the truth. She needed to figure out what was really happening one way or another—so she would, with the help of Lord Sloan himself.

Shooting to her feet, she grabbed the leather satchel off the edge of her bed. Reaching her hand down to the very bottom, she found what she was looking for with a sigh of relief.

Lord Sloan had given her two complete doses of traveling powder, for emergency use only. When he first gave it to her, so many years ago, he told her it could be used to get her anywhere she needed to travel. The enchantment was written on a tiny piece of parchment and the bespelled powder was in two separate vials in a small drawstring bag. One dose to get her to her destination, and another to bring her back.

She never thought she'd use it—that was, until today. She desperately needed to find answers to the questions that plagued her mind. Micah was busy with learning how to wield his axe, and she knew she could leave without his marshmallow brain noticing. He'd probably understand if she had explained, but for whatever reason, each time she tried to voice her emotions, the words wouldn't come.

Brax couldn't come to terms with the betrayal of the male she revered more than any other.

What *was* Lord Sloan truly planning? It couldn't be what the Baums assumed, nor what Micah interpreted it to be. What was the real truth?

She couldn't ask him outright. The last conversation they had through the looking glass did not turn out the way she had expected, and she didn't want anyone else to get hurt. Besides, going behind Micah's back to speak to Lord Sloan had unexpected repercussions, and she couldn't imagine dishonoring their friendship again.

Her heart raced at her plan, but her mind was set, because more than anything, she had to choose a side. She needed to know if the accusations around Lord Sloan hurting others were true.

They simply couldn't be.

Laurent Sloan was a mighty and fair lord, with enough power that he need not hunger for any others.

Baum had to be wrong about him. There had to be a misunderstanding that she could set straight.

There was no other option.

She tucked one vial of traveling powder deep in her pocket and palmed the other. She'd make it to the South and uncover the truth, once and for all.

THE THREE TERRITORIES of Denora were recognized for different things. The North was known for its steadfast cold as the icy mountain range kept the borders protected. The North contributed to the realm by mining all the ore for weapons and tools, but otherwise the Northerners kept to themselves.

Central Denora was where the wealthy officials lived with their families, serving King Tralont and his kingdom. Most businesses were run through the center of Denora. Lavish dinners, elegant clothing, and snobby Fae seemed to be the highlight of the capital, and Brax did her best to avoid it.

The South, however, was very different, indeed. The streets were always filled with working-class Fae peddling their wares or walking down the main road to and from their jobs. The docks kept many of the Fae employed with fishing and ship maintenance, but more than anything, it was a welcoming place for the masses to gather and celebrate life.

That's what Brax loved the most about it—each day people were truly living in Southern Denora, working by day, and revelling by night.

Merchant Lane was her very favorite, for once the sun set, each of the street vendors would close up their shops and they would all meet at the local ale houses. There, they'd sing the songs of great wars past or drunkenly brawl over the last turkey leg like complete oafs.

She loved it.

However, arriving in Southern Denora with the traveling powder Lord Sloan gave her was very different this time around... and the incredible change took the breath right from her lungs.

Brax took a step forward on the cobblestone road, the sun nearly set as shadows crept from the corners of the buildings. There should have been workers and customers and people on the streets, but Merchant Lane was abandoned. The shops were left unattended—their wares still in the stalls, as though they had left suddenly, unable to properly care for the root of their livelihoods. Brax glanced around the lane to the large buildings that surrounded it... not even a flicker of a candle in the window of a home gave so much as a hint to where the Fae were.

The eerie silence pressed down upon her as she slowly tread down the vacant lane, looking into each window and door, holding her breath in hopes of finding someone, anyone, who could explain what was going on.

These Fae relied on their shops to provide for their families... they would not just leave things behind that they valued so deeply.

Where are they?

She stretched her Fae hearing as far as she could, and all she met was muffled silence. Not a stray cat searching for food in garbage. Not a child giving their mother a hard time about going to bed. Not a laugh, or a cough, or a clang of dishes from the alehouses. There was no sign of life anywhere, not even the faint whisper of voices carrying on the breeze.

Merchant Lane was empty. Not a single sound.

Quickening her pace, she rushed down the street toward Town Square. There must be answers somewhere, and the officials in town would know something.

Her heart pounded in her chest, a mix of anxiety and fear, because she knew deep down that whatever caused the lane to be abandoned could not be good. Turning the corner in a sprint, she slid to a stop and fell to the ground, her arms and legs scrambling to back up as she stared in horror at the tapestry of devastation that lay before her.

Everywhere she looked was utter chaos. Flames flicked in and out of the windows of burning homes. Fae were huddled and crying, mouths open mid-wail. Soldiers were stalking down the square, forcing magical bindings on the helpless Fae they dragged behind them.

But not one single sound or smell met her.

A ward.

A powerful, menacing ward, blocking out all sounds and smells from those beyond it.

Scurrying to the shadows of a building, she watched the scene surrounding her. Panicking Fae tried to fight against the soldiers, but were beaten down to submission. The chilling sight of their faces contorted in anguish, yet still in utter silence, made Brax's skin crawl.

She took one slow step forward, and then another,

until she felt the magical barrier at her fingertips, a weak vibration that caused her hand to snap back to her chest. Looking closely, she saw the shimmer in the air, pulsing ever so gently. Placing her hand up to it, it went through seamlessly.

It allows movement between sides...

There were many different kinds of wards that could spellbind an entire area as this. Some focused solely on sounds, and apparently others on smell. There were few which could act as a physical barrier, stopping anything from traversing between sides. Brax was thankful that this one allowed her passage—she only prayed it wouldn't sound an alarm that could give away her position.

As she stepped through, desolation ravaged her ears.

"Please, someone help us!" Fae mothers cried for their children.

"Get back in line," a soldier screamed, pushing a Fae male to the ground next to a group of others.

The fire in the buildings roared behind them all, the cracks and booms of the blazing embers sounding in the distance. The smell of smoke made her cough and gag as it crashed into her.

Rushing to an overturned wagon, she hid as she worked to control her breathing. The desperate cries for help from the Fae tore at her heart.

Becoming a Vytyrian warrior was an honor given to only those of purest spirit and intention. They did not hurt the weak and defenseless, and they only represented the divisions of their choice. Brax had fought in dozens of battles in her many years of life, killing numerous Fae in the process, but each moment of bloodshed had been for the betterment of the realm. She chose the sides she fought on to ensure the safety of those who would otherwise be left unprotected.

But this? What was the reason for such violence?

Keeping low, she crept to the edge of the overturned wagon to better analyze her battle grounds. She spied a group of Fae locked in a magical barrier. A shimmering rope penned them together like livestock.

Her eyes scanned the crowd on the border of Town Square; there were at least a dozen groups detained by these magical enclosures. The clusters of Fae were separated; some had only males and the others had females and children. The smoke and ash made them all look filthy in their worn clothes—clearly the working-class Fae that made these businesses successful. As the light from the fire flickered nearby, she saw it was not only ash that covered their skin, but blood as well.

Her heart sank. Did these Fae commit any crimes? Surely a child cannot be held accountable for the actions of the mature Fae here. Why were they being included in this horrific round up? Staying close to the shadows, she continued on, looking for clarity.

Brax dodged several soldiers as she slipped from one hiding spot to another, carefully staying out of sight. Finding a row of hedges at the edge of a property, she hid, staying low to get her eyes on the center of the disorder.

In the middle of Town Square, the Fae in the holding pens looked different. They were clearly more wealthy, wearing fine fabrics adorned with jewels. That didn't seem to give them any upper hand though, as they were equally bruised and bloodied as the rest of the detained Fae.

Watching closely, she waited until the soldier watching the nearest pen turned and walked away to another group of prisoners.

Prisoners. Her stomach wound tight at the thought. *Could Laurent have done this?*

She raced to the enclosure and questioned them in a hushed whisper. "Why are you all trapped here? What are your crimes?"

An elderly Fae with long gray hair looked around nervously, ensuring the soldiers were nowhere in sight before he spoke. "We have no crimes," he said with fervor. "The soldiers came here and rounded us up during our dinners. Some of us were putting our children to bed, for goodness' sake. Now we are here in the middle of this filthy fucking street, being pushed around like cattle."

"Who is in charge? What do they want?" Brax asked, urging them to answer before anyone came back.

A younger Fae male leaned over to whisper to her. "The Lord of the North," he said.

Brax's veins turned to lead.

"They informed us that we have no choice but to follow him and his rule, otherwise they will imprison us," the young Fae male spat. "He's giving us no option at all. If we don't follow him, he will kill us."

"Those who have already defected have been collected about four blocks from here," the older Fae said. "They are to be tried first. I think he wants them to change their mind and support his side."

"His side for what?" Brax snapped.

The two male Fae glanced at one another, and then back to Brax.

"War."

As if the ground rushed up to meet her, Brax's head spun. She forced herself to kneel, putting a hand on the ashen dirt to steady herself.

Lucy was right.

They were all right.

Lord Sloan is doing this.

"Get out of here," snapped the elder Fae. "They're coming!"

With a quick breath in, she ran for cover as two soldiers took count of their prisoners before them. Brax reeled as she listened from a shadowy alcove.

"What are we supposed to do with all of them?" The soldier asked his companion.

"I have no clue," the other replied, looking down at the Fae. "But we aren't bringing them all back to the North, so I assume nothing good."

The first soldier sneered, then spat on the prisoners. "About time you elitist pricks get what's coming to you. Not so strong and powerful now without all those riches, huh?"

The second soldier just laughed. "King Sloan will rectify all of this."

King Sloan.

Her blood, which was once frozen with dread, turned to molten rage.

A sneer worthy of the most vicious Vytyrian warrior graced her face as she took in the enemy around her. There were too many soldiers for her to kill and still get away, but luckily, like most flaccid zucchini, these males all underestimated females. And that was precisely where she would focus her energy—on the females and children who were forgotten and left off to the side, unwatched.

She ran to them without a second thought. There was no way in this life or the next that she would stand by as innocents were hurt due to a male on a power trip.

As she got to the group, the females bristled, unsure of what she was doing there. Silently, Brax analyzed the magic containing them. From the way it was flickering, it looked as though it was weak spell work, but she wasn't able to perform Denoran magic. She'd have to find a way around it.

"I am going to help you get out of here," Brax whispered to a group of females nearest her. "It may take me a moment because I do not know the spell, but I *will* get you out." The determination in her eyes mirrored that of the young females before her. Brax touched the magical bindings keeping the Fae within the pen. A crushing wave of despair overtook her—she had no idea how to dismantle the charm.

"There's nowhere for us to go!" hissed an older Fae female with long white hair, her face colored with fear. "Get away before you make things worse!"

"It is a tether charm," one of the younger prisoners told her, shuffling closer to the edge. She had violet, wavy hair and brown eyes so dark they reflected the flames from the buildings all around them. "I can break it, but half of these old hags are too afraid to get caught. Every time I get close, they push me away." She shot an angry look at the Fae huddled behind her. "I only stopped because I don't want to draw any more attention to us."

Brax nodded in understanding, looking at the beautiful Fae before her. Beneath the soot and grime from the chaos all around them was the strength of a warrior. Behind her, she held tight to two young Fae children. Brax understood why she stopped; keeping the children from being noticed was imperative.

"I told them we needed to get the fuck out of here before it's too late, and all they said was to wait for them to let us go home." The young female stepped closer to Brax, drawing her attention back to her. "Be frank. What are their plans for us?"

"You won't be going home today," Brax said. "I'm sorry." Her eyes glanced around the group: females of all ages, each with a bit of fire in their eyes. "But you do not need to die here at the hands of males who care nothing for you. Save yourselves and your children from these monsters."

"What do we do next, then? Huh? Do you have an answer for that?" The older Fae scowled.

"You live," Brax said in anger. "You get up, you leave here, and you live to see another day. You fight for a future for your children. Now stop your ridiculous complaining so I can find a way to release you."

"I can do it," the younger Fae told her. She rushed

over and called to her magic and a beautiful pink mist gracefully swooped around the spell.

"You are very powerful," Brax said to her knowingly. "What is your name?"

"I am Ruthani," she replied as she worked to pick apart the spell like a knotted string. Thread by thread, she worked until the spell collapsed completely.

The females shared in a silent cheer and clasped hands as they rushed to leave their holding place. Brax stepped to the side to give them room to escape, pointing toward an empty lane for them to run.

"Please," Brax implored, stopping Ruthani as she followed the others. "Tell me how you did that so I can release the others."

"You mean to free us all?" Ruthani asked, suspicion in her eyes as she held the young children close to her. "Why?"

"Because I will not sit idly by and watch innocent Fae suffer because they happened to be in the wrong place at the wrong time," Brax retorted. The ice in her voice meant for Sloan crept out with each word. She couldn't believe he did this.

Ruthani nodded, casting a furtive glance behind her at the young children hiding behind her skirts, then meeting Brax's eyes once more. "If you can be quick and help me keep my siblings safe, I will help you unlock the spells on as many pens as I am able."

Brax opened her mouth to refuse, to insist she flee to safety instead, but a blood-curdling scream cut her off. Gripping Ruthani and her siblings, they ran to the row of hedges to hide. In the center of Town Square, a female was held by the back of her long braid of hair to watch as a group of four male Fae fell to their knees in pain.

"King Sloan will accept nothing other than greatness," the soldier's voice boomed across the cobblestone square. "Let this be a lesson for all."

Then, with a flick of his hand, the female screamed again as the heads of each male fell to the ground.

The Fae all around Town Square took in a collective gasp at the blatant violence, but Ruthani made not a single sound, only moving to cover the eyes of her two young siblings.

"You will not deny my help," she whispered to Brax. "We will get these innocent Fae out."

Brax looked over at Ruthani, and took in the grim line of her mouth and the mettle in her eyes that refused to back down. She had no other choice than to agree, knowing she needed the help to get this done quickly.

"Then when we are done, Sloan is next," Ruthani said, staring into Brax's eyes with the spirit of a Vytyrian.

Brax could only nod, the promise of his demise more than enough to fuel them on.

TWENTY

LUCY

Running through the blazing streets of Southern Denora was not what Lucy expected when she arrived, but she had little choice in the matter. She traveled directly to the Baum Bowyer office to speak to her brothers, but instead of finding Hugh and Gregory, she was met with an abandoned building in the midst of a nightmare.

Smoke towered high in the sky and the screams of Fae carried in the distance. Buildings were on fire and the streets were empty, save for a few Fae soldiers clad in navy blue uniforms which blended with the quickly darkening sky. Upon each shoulder was a silver mountain.

The uniforms of the North.

Lucy froze.

Sloan is here.

A scream pierced through the air and Lucy's emerald magic coursed through her body, ready to be used. There was no time to hesitate. Lucy shook off her nerves and focused on that scream, letting it propel her into action.

If there are Fae in trouble, I must help.

Staying tucked into the shadowy corners with the help of her father's gift, she followed the sounds of screaming toward Town Square. Along the way, she crossed paths with more soldiers. Lucy was able to keep out of their sight, but each terrified step toward the cacophony made her heart race in her chest.

She couldn't force herself to accept that this horrific landscape was the Southern Territory. What was once a joyous and bustling town had been razed to the ground; everywhere she looked were upturned wagons, homes on fire, and businesses left abandoned. The notion that her brothers were here somewhere in this chaotic madness of fire, ash, and ruin was unbearable.

Sprinting from one street to the other, she followed the commotion, only to be shocked once again when she ran headfirst into none other than Brax.

Pulling her shadows away from her, Lucy revealed herself and was met with an equally surprised expression from the Vytyrian warrior.

With her quick reflexes, Brax held an arm out to stop the Fae next to her—a beautiful female with purple hair, holding the hands of two children.

"What are you doing here?" Lucy asked her breathlessly.

Is she secretly supporting Sloan? Did she bring Micah here?

"I... I didn't know," Brax said, shaking her head slightly. Her mouth hung open, still in shock, Lucy assumed. "I came here to be sure. I needed to know the truth. I would have never..."

But Brax didn't need to say anything. Lucy understood completely. She, too, had been completely brainwashed by Sloan's *good intentions*. He was a manipulative liar, and apparently quite good at it.

"I'm sorry I didn't believe you," Brax said, her lips pursing with anger as her eyes welled with an emotion seeped in devastation. However, not one tear fell from the warrior's eyes; her hardened exterior locked in place.

Lucy just nodded. There was nothing else to say, was there? Not about the past.

Now it was time to make things right.

"We are freeing the females and children," Brax said, gesturing to the female beside her, catching on to Lucy's line of thinking in the presence of her silence.

Lucy glanced at the small children at their side. "Take them to my mother," Lucy said pointedly. "She will have the means to care for them and keep them safe."

Brax nodded.

"We need to save as many as possible. This is going to get ugly. Do you have a way to get them away safely?" Lucy looked around, a pit forming in her stomach at the destruction of such precious life.

"I do," Brax replied. "What are you doing here?"

"I need to find my brothers. They weren't at the offices or their homes. We need to understand what happened, and I..." The words turned to ash in her mouth.

I can't lose anyone else.

She wanted to say the words, but she couldn't.

Perhaps Brax understood, because she didn't push the matter.

"They are likely in Merchant Square along with the other nobles," the violet-haired Fae said.

"Lucy," Brax began. "Do not hesitate. Do whatever you need to do."

"When you are done, go straight to Micah," Lucy ordered. "Keep him safe. And... here." Lucy handed her the amethyst dagger she had tucked in her boot for safe keeping. "Stay out of sight and free as many as you can."

A sharp nod from Brax, and she was off with her companions to the next group of females. However, Lucy went on in a different direction.

Toward the fire.

Toward the screaming.

Right into the heart of chaos.

EMERALD MAGIC SPUN around Lucy's arms, preparing to defend her. Without knowing what to expect here, she was thankful for the extra protection.

In the large open area the town normally used for their bustling Merchant Square, were now six enormous wooden platforms erected in a large circle. In the center was another smaller stage, big enough for only three others. A Fae commander stood in the middle of the stage, peering over the edge to the ground below, giving orders to the soldiers standing on the street.

Lucy's eyes scanned the crowds. Each large platform held Fae of nobility or money—all of them male.

Brax was right to think the males would underestimate the females here, not worrying about them until later. She needed to buy Brax more time to get the innocent Fae out, but what of these males grouped together in these clusters? How would she get them free?

Reaching down deep into her magic, she asked it to shield her from prying eyes. She needed more than her father's shadows. If she were to be seen here with Sloan around, there was no telling how he would react.

Feeling a cool sensation rush over her, her shadows and an ancient magic covered her from head to toe, masking her from the surrounding Fae. Looking down at her hand, all she saw was shadow and mist. Knowing she was well hidden, she rushed closer to the crowd to scan for her brothers.

Where are you? Where are you? She thought to herself, using her Fae eyesight to see as far as she could, hoping to find them.

For once the stars listened, because as she inspected the second wooden platform she found her two brothers, kneeling but not shackled.

They were alive.

Relief washed through her so fiercely tears threatened to burst from her at the very sight. She hadn't realized how much she dreaded not finding them. If anything had happened to them, she wasn't sure if she'd ever come back from it.

In a blink, she appeared on the ground next to their stand. Still shrouded from view in her father's shadows, she stepped close enough to see them from below. With a whisper on the wind, she called over to her brothers.

Shoulder to shoulder, they heard her at the same moment. First, their eyes were set on the platform before them, and then their heads whipped up in unison, searching for her.

Letting her magic fade from her face, Lucy waited for them to find her.

Locking their gaze with Lucy, their eyes bulged in terror. With soot covered faces, they shook their heads in silent warning, pleading for her to go.

Lucy steeled herself for it, knowing they were only trying to keep her safe, but she'd never leave them. Ever.

She shook her head in anger, refusing to let them push her away. She was here and she could help. Surely they couldn't be so stubborn as to refuse her assistance in the midst of all of this?

Hugh tilted his head up to get her attention, then gave a pointed glance behind her to another stall of Fae. It was difficult to see with soldiers everywhere.

She looked back to Hugh, making a show of not understanding what he wanted her to see.

His eyes filled with sorrow as his shoulders slumped. He whispered the words, willing them to her ears. "Tristan."

Her mouth popped open in shock.

Tristan is here? Was he captured?

She swung her head back, searching for the bright eyes that had always been so full of humor and joy.

When she finally spotted him, she couldn't contain the gasp that left her lips. The shock rocked her entire body.

Tristan was there. The light in his eyes was dimmed

by the devastating reality around them, but it was him nonetheless... But not as a Fae prisoner. Tristan was wearing a navy blue uniform.

He was a soldier in Lord Sloan's army.

No. No, it can't be.

Her head jerked back toward Hugh and Gregory, the misery searing through them. All Gregory could do was nod.

"Save him," Hugh whispered to her once again, his magic meeting hers with a heaviness that nearly brought her to her knees.

Her eyes gleamed with tears, but she refused to cry. There was nothing she could do but continue to fight, even if it meant dragging Tristan home kicking and screaming.

She would make him see.

Nodding, she turned toward Tristan and in a blink was hidden in the shadows near him. The soldiers continued to mill about, talking quietly among one another. Some of them were clearly drunk as they took swig after swig from a dark brown jug.

Tristan's eyes, though... They weren't rejoicing. They were terrified.

Lucy's insides twisted, not knowing how to get to him safely. Her magic must have felt her worry though, because it snaked its way along the dirt and debris, crawling over to Tristan, creeping up his leg like a vine.

Lucy sent a tendril of shadow in its wake, keeping it hidden from view.

When he felt it, he jumped with a start, but at the recognition of the emerald green mist just barely visible around his ankle, his gaze popped up. He scanned the crowd, looking for the source as Lucy dropped her shadows. When his eyes finally found hers, they swam with regret.

He opened his mouth to speak, but shut it quickly. Glancing around him, he walked to her, his eyes wide with fear. His face was completely panic-stricken.

"Where?" He whispered in a daze. "Where did you come from? Why are you here?" His eyes searched her, darting around her face and her body, likely ensuring she wasn't hurt.

"I heard about the invasion. I had to make sure our brothers were safe," Lucy said, putting her hand on her brother's arm, calming him. "Why are you here? Are you... are you with Sloan?"

The words hurt as they came out. She couldn't see any other reason for him being here, but she prayed she was wrong all the same.

His head hung down in shame. "It wasn't supposed to be like this," he said dejectedly. He tried to raise his head to look at her, but couldn't bring himself to do it. "I *am* here as his soldier,"

"What was it supposed to be like?" Lucy bit back, sounding harsher than she intended.

He took a deep breath and looked her in the eyes, shaking his head solemnly. "He told us he would create a new Denora. He spoke of equality among the classes; equality for females. He told us he wanted to make a home Denorans would be proud of, and we all agreed." He inhaled deeply, as though the words were too hard to voice. "But when we got here, it was clear there were some soldiers who knew more—knew the plans they didn't share with everyone."

He looked around at the Fae soldiers among them, and Lucy took stock as well.

"The soldiers with the large mountain and star patch on their uniforms? They are his generals," Tristan explained. "When we got here, they divided us all and sent us to gather people in Town Square. They made it sound like we'd scare them a little, make them realize the error in their views. But then, they started shackling those who rebelled with this magic I've never seen before."

"What kind of magic?" Lucy asked, trying to scan the Fae prisoners to see what he meant.

Tristan pointed to a group of Fae nobility down the street. "Their wrists are shackled with what looks like normal metal, but alongside it there are gemstones that glow." He ran a hand through his hair. "I've never seen anything like it," he admitted. "When they... when they started hurting people, I tried to help some of them. I tried to free them." His eyes looked to Lucy's in panic. "The shackles don't respond to my magic at all. Like it's something else entirely."

Alchemy, Lucy realized. *He's found a way to use it in his rebellion.*

"We must get out of here, Tristan," Lucy said firmly. "Come with me."

Tristan nodded and followed her, the relief visible on his face.

"We will tell our brothers. I will take you home and come back for them."

"Perhaps not," an icy voice drawled behind her.

A shiver swept over her skin as she took in the voice of the male she'd been wary to avoid. Spinning, she eyed him with disgust.

There stood Lord Laurent Sloan. His fine navy uniform bejeweled with blue and white gems reflecting the orange and red fire beyond. His stark white hair that so often wafted in the breeze was secured in place by a large, ornate crown he had fitted on his head. That, too, covered in glowing gemstones.

More alchemy, Lucy realized with a scowl.

"As lovely as it is to see you, my beloved Lucella," Lord Sloan said with oily affect, "you were not invited here. But I'd be happy to escort you to a more appropriate location." The threat that loomed behind those words was clear.

"I will not be going with you anywhere," Lucy snarled.

"Oh, I think I have something that will change your mind," he laughed.

Lucy grabbed onto Tristan's arm at the same time that Sloan grabbed hers. She tried to transport them out of there, to blink and return to home, but her magic did not respond.

"Don't fucking touch me," she spat, pushing his arm off of her. She took a step back, shaken by her magic failing.

Sloan laughed again and put his hand out toward her and Tristan. Tristan stepped in front of Lucy, trying to protect her from whatever it was Sloan was about to do.

A bright blue glow lit from one of Sloan's fingers, and he covered Tristan in the sapphire haze.

Realizing too late what he was doing, Lucy tried to tug Tristan out of the way, but there was no use. It was as though his body was covered in a thick shield that her magic could not touch.

She gripped his arm tightly, but the shield around him zapped her in response.

"What did you do to him? Let him go!" Lucy yelled at Sloan, but all he did was stand there with a satisfied smile on his face, grinning from ear to ear.

"Is it hard to accept I know something you do not?" Lord Sloan chided. His eyes bored into Lucy's—the glare sending spears of ice down into her gut.

"Which is what, exactly?" She took a step closer to Tristan, preparing to force her magic into whatever shield Sloan tried to wield against him so she could transport them far, far away from here.

"That my alchemy is stronger than your... *unique* magic," he whispered to her. "By the way," he said, bending closer to her, speaking directly into her ear. "I can't wait to peel you apart, layer by layer, and learn how that magic of yours works."

Lucy blanched, tilting her head away from him and grabbed Tristan by the back of the neck, ignoring the shocks of pain radiating through her from Sloan's alchemical shield.

Release him, she commanded her magic.

But nothing happened.

She stood there, blinking. Her magic had only ever failed her once before, when her heart was torn and she didn't know what to do. But this? She knew exactly what she was doing. There was not a sliver of doubt in her mind, yet her magic could not break the spell.

"Release him," she said aloud, compelling her magic to work, shouting her command into the universe.

Alas, the blue, shimmering shield remained on Tristan.

"He will be coming with me," Sloan said. He waved his hand and Tristan walked toward him, his eyes bearing the only emotional response.

Fear.

"You can't do this!" Lucy roared, her magic forming at her fingertips, preparing to unleash on Sloan and his entire fucking army.

"I can and I will, Lucella. However," Sloan drawled, watching Lucy closely. "I'd be willing to form a trade." His disdainful laugh drained the warmth from her body.

"A trade?"

"Yes," he said simply. "But before then, here's something to remember me by."

He lifted his hand to a nearby soldier and gave a firm nod. The soldier saluted in return and turned to the group of Fae he was patrolling. Reaching into the penned area, he grabbed a male by his hair and lifted him into the air.

Lucy's breath stilled.

The soldier unsheathed his longsword and swiftly beheaded the Fae right there on the platform, his blood covering the others surrounding him.

Shrieks of terror unleashed around Town Square.

Then the soldier lifted the next Fae male and beheaded him all the same. Then another.

And another.

Lucy couldn't pull her gaze away from the horrific act. Sloan's soldiers murdered the helpless Fae in cold blood.

How? How could anyone be so cruel?

Her eyes narrowed to slits as she swiveled her head to Sloan, her magic roaring through her veins. He was watching her with a smile on his face. Summoning her magic to build, she prepared to blast Sloan away into dust.

"If you leave now, I will allow your brothers to live." Sloan's words cut through her like a knife.

Her breath faltered and her magic paused.

My brothers.

"I'll see you in a week, my beloved," he crooned.

With a hand on Tristan's shoulder, Lord Sloan and Tristan vanished from sight.

Lucy released the air trapped inside of her lungs and fell to her knees. The sound of soldiers yelling and Fae prisoners crying rose and fell from behind her.

The rumors were true... They were murdering Fae.

And Lord Laurent Sloan captured three of her brothers.

TWENTY-ONE

WES

When Wes took his position as head of the Baum Bowyers, he never imagined most of his time would consist of sitting around and worrying.

Since his father's death, patrons of the business were giving the family time to grieve. As much as that would have bothered Corvus, Wes didn't mind a bit. The family had more than enough money to carry them the next few months, perhaps the next few years, if he played his cards right. He was in no hurry to feign a hectic work schedule while there was so much else to concern himself with. However, while the rest of his family was working tirelessly, he wasn't doing much of anything.

Anita was forever bustling around the house, watching over his younger brothers and ensuring the safety charms were active. Lucy was off visiting the South to find Hugh and Gregory and bring them home safely.

And what am I doing? He mused. *I sit and stare at a fucking desk.*

There was nothing for him to do until Lucy returned with news, but the inaction was getting the best of him.

As soon as Lucy returned, they could go to the king and request his support. Wes just hoped they would get to King Tralont before he sent any of his delegates to take over the Bowyer business.

I have time. It's been days, not weeks. The king wouldn't even know production had slowed.

A sharp knock on the door pulled Wes from his spiraling thoughts, and he straightened his desk to suggest he was working.

"You may enter," he called, assuming it was his mother or their house steward, Bernard, who took excellent care of the manor.

Wide wooden doors swung open and Bernard stepped through.

"You can place the food at the coffee table, Bernard. I am not quite hungry yet." Wes's mother was sending Bernard with food roughly five times a day, in hopes he would keep his energy up. It was kind, but he wished she would let it go.

"Today is a bit different, sir," Bernard said, the aged smile lines on his face creasing. "A female is here demanding to speak with you. She has... well. Perhaps it's best you come see for yourself." He took a step back and raised his eyebrows, inviting him to follow.

With a tilt of his head, Wes stood carefully and followed Bernard to the front of the estate.

"At least we can say your mother's wards are working," Bernard chuckled lightheartedly. The quiet padding of his leather shoes echoed in the empty manor. "This stranger kept trying to take a step into the courtyard, but Madame Baum's magic held." A glimmer of pride crept from his eyes. "And for some reason, this Fae kept insulting me with names of arbitrary vegetables."

Wes took a surprised breath in and rushed to the door, seeing the Fae at the end of the cobblestone path.

"You better let me in, you rancid rutabaga!" Brax yelled from the other side of the courtyard. "We have to talk."

"What was so surprising about her arrival?" Wes asked Bernard as he quickly dissolved the wards to allow Brax to enter.

"It wasn't her so much as it was the rest of them, sir," Bernard replied.

"The rest?" Wes asked, looking over at Bernard.

Bernard only pointed to the trees beyond the path, redirecting Wes's gaze.

There, slowly leaving the tree line, was a group of at least fifty Fae, all females and children, covered in soot and ash.

Dropping his hands to his sides to stare in disbelief, Brax took it as a cue that she was safe to enter. "About time," she snarled, stepping up to the pathway. She got about a third of the way down before she turned and beckoned for the others to follow her. "Come," she said, her voice gentle. "You'll be safe here."

The softness in her words sent an unfamiliar jolt of warmth through Wes.

A female with violet hair stepped forward first, a look of determination clear upon her face. Behind her, a small group of children followed. Then more Fae joined the queue until they were all walking to the manor.

Wes walked out to meet Brax, confusion marking every inch of his face. "Who are these people, Brax? Why are you here?" His eyes danced over her skin, noting the ash and dirt covering her, but no injuries. A breath of relief left him at her safety.

She looked so different from the last time they were together. Her cropped hair was windblown and in disarray, the kohl that lined her eyes smudged and blended with the soot covering her face. But more than that, her eyes were wide... not in fear, so much as in concern.

"I went to the South," she said solemnly, her chest rising and falling with the deep breath she took as she spoke.

Wes opened his mouth to ask about his family's safety.

About Lucy. Hugh. Gregory. But no words could form. If she looked this poorly, then clearly things were not alright in the South, just as they had feared.

"I saw Lucy as I was freeing the females and children," she said to him, glancing over his shoulder as Anita walked through the doors. "She said they would be safe here with you, Madame Baum."

Wes's mother put a hand up to her face in shock at the sight before her, but quickly turned to Bernard and started giving him orders to prepare the rooms for guests.

"Absolutely," she said with a wide smile, then went to take the hands of some of the terrified Fae to welcome them into their home. "I think some warm tea and fresh bread and jam are in order, don't you?" Anita smiled at a young girl who immediately took her hand and gave her a toothy grin.

One by one, they followed Anita into the manor as Brax and Wes remained outside, ensuring no stragglers were left behind.

The female with the violet hair lingered at Brax's side as well, looking over Wes with distrust.

"Wes, this is Ruthani," Brax said, smiling gently at the stranger. "She helped me to free all the Fae here. She is a hero."

Ruthani looked to Brax with skepticism and shock. "No. I am no hero. I only helped."

"You did what I could not, and it is because of your willingness to stay that we saved those people."

Seeing these two females, covered in ash and despair, brought Wes back to the moment Lucy returned from Joterra after fighting off Jasper's goons when they set the fire.

These were Fae running from a monster and finding their way to safety. But more than that, they were warriors, rebelling against evil, and refusing to let the innocent suffer in their wake.

"Let's go inside," Brax said to Wes. "We have much to discuss."

By the time Brax finished her tale, the room was deathly silent. Anita was sitting with her hand permanently over her mouth in shock and Wes was slumped on the couch next to Brax in utter disbelief.

"*King Sloan?*" Wes repeated. "How can he get away with this?"

"He won't," Brax replied sharply. "Not if we have anything to do with it."

"What are we supposed to do?" The panic in Wes's voice crept in, and he took a swig of amartium to try to hide it.

"We gather anyone willing to fight against him," Brax said matter-of-factly.

"What about Lucy?" Anita asked quietly. "Was she able to get anyone out?"

"I'm not sure," Brax said, looking at her hands. "Ruthani and I were busy freeing those you see here, but the female clusters were much farther away from the males. They wanted to keep the males front and center. I'm not sure how much luck Lucy would have had in rescuing anyone."

"The Fae I spoke with were very guarded," Anita replied, confirming the terrifying conditions of the South. "Many are worried about their husbands and sons."

"And rightfully so," Brax replied. "It was... horrific." She shook her head in disgust.

"If we are going to go against Sloan, we will need to know more about his plans," Anita said decidedly. "Wes, bring Brax to the vermin in the cellar. See what you can get out of him."

"Vermin?" Brax asked, looking from Anita to Wes for an explanation.

"Ah, yes. We have Sloan's loyal follower in the root cellar," Wes said. "Jasper DeValey."

"You have that withered fungus *here* and you didn't tell me? What are we waiting for?" Brax jumped to her feet with a fiendish smile and strode to the door.

The right side of his lips quirked up into a smile as Wes walked behind her.

This is sure to be entertaining.

"What's so funny, Baum?" Brax asked, stopping in the hallway to let him lead the way.

"Honestly?" He paused next to her. Crossing his arms in front of his chest, he smiled and shrugged. "I can't wait to see you call him strange names and beat him up a little."

"Hmm, that's interesting, coming from you," Brax replied, smiling back and beginning to turn back down the corridor.

Reaching out, he gently took hold of her arm, slowing her to a stop.

Brax turned to look at him, questions lighting her eyes.

"You're sure you're alright?" Wes asked her quietly, carefully wiping the soot from her cheek with his thumb.

She bit her lip and leaned into his touch ever so gently, Wes almost missed it. "I will be." Her eyes burned with the intensity of that truth and the words behind it that she did not say.

Wes nodded in understanding. No one was alright, not anymore. No one would be until Sloan was stopped and the people were safe.

And they would stop Sloan by any means necessary.

Dropping his hand, he tilted his head to the right, leading her down the hallway to the cellar stairwell. Milton stood at the top of the stairs, acting as guard for Jasper's makeshift cell.

Milton gave a quick nod and let Wes and Brax down the stairs.

The heaviness of the entire situation weighed heavily on Wes, and Jasper played a major role in all of it. His mind was reeling with what could have happened to Brax in the South; with Lucy and her wellbeing. However, his smile returned when he listened as Brax called to Jasper, knowing what came next was sure to cheer him up.

"Jasperrrr," she sang. "You have visitors."

Wes's chuckle just grew stronger at the sound of Jasper's whimper, and he wondered if it was a bad thing to laugh at Jasper's demise or a good thing that he was smiling this much at all.

"What do you want from me?!" Jasper shouted between gasps of air.

Brax kicked him again, a wicked grin on her face. "Nothing yet." She spun to look at Wes. "This is making me feel a lot better."

Wes thought watching someone beat the living daylights out of someone would bother him, but it was putting him in a pretty decent mood himself.

"Good," he replied. "Though we should ask him what

we came down here for. My mother is probably wondering where we are."

"Oh, fine," she sighed and rolled her eyes. After another swift kick to the gut, she placed her foot on his side and rolled him over. Crouching down, she touched his arm to spread her magic through his body. "Here. I'm not healing you completely, but I need you to stay alive long enough to be of use to us."

Jasper mumbled more insults, but they were promptly ignored.

"Listen, you curdled fish," Brax spat.

Wes tilted his head in confusion from the nonsensical insult.

"How do we stop Sloan's alchemy?" Brax balanced her arms on her knees, staying low to hear Jasper's response.

"You don't," Jasper responded with a maniacal laugh, spitting blood on the cellar floor. "First step, the South, and then he will move to the king."

"Obviously, there must be a way to combat the alchemy. Don't play dull with us," Wes scolded.

"And you think I'll tell you?" Jasper's laughter grew. "The more stones he has, the more powerful he will become. He will kill you all! He—"

Before he could finish his sentence, Brax knocked him out with a hit to the side of his head.

"We barely got anything out of him," Wes said, looking at Brax with annoyance.

"We know he's an idiot, we know Sloan has more stones, and we know Jasper doesn't have the answers." Brax gave him a pointed look.

"And how do we know this?" Wes asked her. "You didn't give him much of a chance to talk."

"First of all, he told us things we already know, as if he was so special to know about them at all," she replied. "Additionally, he says there is no way to stop the alchemy, and Jasper is a fool who thinks his own alchemy is unstoppable."

"Right," Wes said, still confused. "But that doesn't help us."

"Sure it does," Brax said, smiling brightly. "Jasper is currently in this root cellar surviving on what looks to be raw potatoes, and he has no alchemy powering him."

"That's because we didn't let him have his gems," Wes replied, still not seeing what Brax was getting at.

"Exactly," she said, bopping Wes on the nose with her finger and turning for the exit. "Without the gems, he is nothing."

"That should have been obvious," Wes murmured.

"Yes, you're right, but bloodying him sure made me feel better."

Wes couldn't help but smile as he followed her sashaying hips up the stairs.

Whatever Brax is, she sure is something.

After Brax said her goodbyes to Ruthani and the other Fae, and gave her thanks to Anita, Wes offered to accompany her through the Nilban Woods to the portal that would return her to Joterra.

"I am completely capable of making the walk alone, Baum," Brax replied with a distinct tinge of vexation.

"Believe me, I have more worries for myself on the return trip than you going anywhere alone," he laughed.

"Then why the suggestion of a chaperone?"

Brax and Wes walked slowly, her speed clearly proving she was not upset about his company at all. If she had wanted to, she could have sped off through the trees to the portal before Wes could ever have the chance of catching up.

"You are the first thing that has made me smile in quite some time, and maybe I'm just not ready to let that go just yet," he said quietly.

The ground was littered with damp earth and fallen branches, so each footstep they took was muted. The wind rustled through the trees; the leaves shaking ever so slightly in its dance.

Brax turned to look at him and smiled brightly. "Well, I *am* breathtaking, so your cheerful attitude is to be expected when I grace your presence." Her hair fell from behind her ear and brushed across her high cheekbone.

Wes laughed again. "You are definitely that."

Wes questioned over and over if he should push her hair back behind her ear or if she would break his hand if he attempted it. Either way, his heart raced at the thought.

"There is much for you to still smile about, Baum," she said seriously.

"There is," he agreed, "but there is also..." He paused,

changing his mind. There was no point in talking about this with Brax—with anyone.

"What is it?" Brax asked, stopping them in the middle of the forest path. She placed her hand on his shoulder and forced him to face her. "You can tell me. You don't have to hide."

"I'm not hiding," he said defensively.

"You are," she countered. "There is nothing wrong with being sad—you've gone through so much in such a short period of time. It would be more strange if you were not."

"That doesn't mean I'm hiding."

"You hide because you are pretending to be something you are not. You can be broken and still be strong. You can live in the darkness and still search for the light."

The determination in her eyes forced his attention.

How could he admit he felt broken in front of this remarkable warrior?

"I'm not hiding, I'm just..." but the words never came. Because what was he?

"You're lost," she answered for him.

Wes froze at her response, his stomach sinking at the truth in them.

I am lost.

Taking a step closer to him, she placed both hands on his face and leaned closer until there was only a breath between them.

"I want to tell you something that I don't want you to forget, okay?"

All Wes could do was offer a subtle nod, the smell of

her intoxicating—like a bright winter day mixed with a dark summer night.

"No one wants you to be your father."

The words struck him like a bolt of lightning. He had definitely not expected that. And more than that, she was wrong. "That isn't true. People are relying on me to do the things he was capable of doing."

"The realm needs you to be Wesley Baum and no one else." Brax inched closer, her lips nearly grazing his. "You are different from so many others, and that is why you will do wonderfully in this new position. Allow yourself to be seen for you—stop trying to be someone else. Do the things you want to do, not what others expect of you."

He closed the space between their bodies, wrapping his hands around her taut waist, feeling the strong muscles beneath his fingers. "What if I want to kiss you?"

Before he could make a move, Brax kissed him with a fervor he would have never expected.

Her lips were soft, and her tongue teased the edge of his lips. As he opened for her, desperate to kiss her with the same enthusiasm, she pulled back.

"*I* kissed you," she said with a mischievous grin. "If you wish to kiss me, then you must figure out who you are in all of this and claim it. And when that time comes, come and claim me."

Then, she shoved him away and took off running for the portal, laughing in her exit.

Wes could have chased after her. He could have used all of his Fae speed to try to catch up to her and make her stay, even if it was just to kiss her again. But he knew she was right.

He needed to figure out what in the realms he was doing and stop waiting around for something to happen.

Instead, he needed to *make* it happen, and he would.

WES WASTED no time at all when he returned from his walk with Brax. He went straight to Bernard and requested his assistance. The very next day, as he paced in the study, his waiting was over.

"Master Baum," Bernard said, entering the study. "Your guest has arrived."

An older Fae with a formal green military uniform followed behind him.

"Hello, Young Baum," Duke Renfro said with a polite, if not forced, smile. "You called for my presence?"

CHAPTER

TWENTY-TWO

LUCY

Lucy crashed into the center of the study at the Baum estate, despair drowning her every thought.

"No..." Her voice was faint.

This can't be real. I have to go back.

"Lucy!" Anita's voice cried as she and Wes raced over to her, surprised by her unexpected entrance.

"He took him, he..." the words were a jumble as Lucy said them, over and over again.

Wes pulled her to her feet and set her in the chair in front of the fireplace. The sound of the fire crackling sent a shiver down her spine at the memory of the fires surrounding Southern Denora.

The South.

Where her brothers were held prisoner.

Where she lost Tristan.

Her teeth began chattering, the shock settling deep into her bones. It was almost a relief as it muffled the burning logs.

"He... he..." Lucy rambled again, trying to understand what had just happened. Coming to terms with what she allowed to happen.

"You're freezing," he said, rubbing his hands up and down her arms in an attempt to warm her. "What happened? Did you see our brothers?" The desperation in his voice tore at her heart.

With her head still bent down, she lifted her face only enough to make eye contact with Wes. Her heartache apparent as she very faintly nodded in answer.

"It was terrible," Lucy said, looking away again. "Sloan was there with his entire army... They..." She couldn't say the words. The nausea threatened to turn her stomach inside out.

"Darling, I understand that what you saw must have been terrible," Anita told her, holding her hand tightly. "Brax came with the others. She told us some, but she left to return to Micah... Please, Lucy. Your brothers. Are they alright?"

Lucy took a deep breath, then closed her eyes, finding the strength to share the danger her brothers were in.

Could her mother handle it?

"They rounded up every Fae from their homes and brought them to the Town Square. The females and children were placed into large tied off areas, and all the males were brought to the center of the square. They were separated on these enormous raised platforms."

Wes quietly pulled over a chair for their mother, then sat on the ground with Lucy. No one dared to ask a question, allowing Lucy to tell her story at her own pace.

"Brax was there. She was helping the females and children to escape. I sent them here knowing we could help." Lucy pulled a hand to her chest, rubbing at the pain buried deep within her. Her skin was still caked in soot and blood from the Fae she couldn't save.

Wes nodded, confirming they had arrived.

"The males—they were to pledge their fealty to *King* Sloan," she spat. The words were bitter on her tongue.

Anita scoffed at the name.

"If they don't agree, they..." she couldn't finish the thought.

Lord Sloan was an evil-hearted Fae who would stop at nothing to get what he wanted.

"Sloan's killing them?" Wes asked, quietly.

"Yes," she whispered.

A small gasp left Anita's lips. "So Hugh and Gregory... they were there? You saw them?" Anita asked quietly.

Lucy nodded. "I saw them. They were there... They know the danger they are in. I only hope they are willing to play Sloan's game before they get the chance to escape. Sloan told me to leave before he killed them, too."

Her hands shook at the thought.

She couldn't leave right away though, she didn't trust Sloan. Instead, she hid and watched as more and more soldiers rounded up Fae and imprisoned them. Lucy tried to create distractions for Brax to have the time she needed to get the innocent females and children out, so she toppled over tents and created small explosions on the other side of the square. Her anger drove her, and the destruction she made came easy. She wasn't sure if it would be enough, but she had to at least try.

Then she spent the rest of her time hiding in shadows, watching Hugh and Gregory shackled on the podium. Lucy spied on them for hours, trying to convince herself to leave them and come back with a plan, but it was nearly impossible. It wasn't until another soldier spotted her that she finally left, worried her magic would wane and she'd be stranded there.

Wes stood and began pacing the room. "They are smart, they will find a way out of it. Thank the stars Lisette left to the east instead of returning home with them."

Anita only watched Lucy, observing every movement she made, every glance, every facial expression. "What is it, Lucy?"

Lucy couldn't bring herself to say it.

"There's... something else. Isn't there?" Anita asked, her question heavy with emotion.

Lucy nodded, finally looking her mother in the eye. Tears rolled down her cheeks at her guilt. Her frowning lips quivered as she formed the words. "I found Tristan."

Wes stopped his pacing.

Anita held her breath.

"He was there with Sloan's troops, but he didn't know," Lucy said quickly, looking to her brother, her bottom lip quaking. "He had no idea. He didn't support any of it." She sniffed, trying to get a breath down. "We —We tried to leave. Hugh told me to take him and go, and I—I tried."

Anita covered her mouth.

Lucy choked down a sob, squeezing her hands into fists. Her fingernails broke skin as she buried them deeply into her palms. She needed to tell them.

"Sloan took him. His alchemy... I couldn't penetrate it. I couldn't stop him. He took Tristan, then he killed those Fae as a warning to me. I tried waiting. I tried finding a way to get them out, but there was nothing I could do. Nothing." Lucy wrapped her arms round herself, curling into a small ball, rocking back and forth as sobs overtook her.

Everything about this kept bringing her back to the moment she lost her father. Having to tell her mother that he was dead. That Lucy couldn't save him in time. Feeling so detached from reality as she replayed every moment in her head, trying to find the path where she could have saved him. Could have stopped Sloan.

Her breathing got faster and faster as her magic felt further and further away from her. Gasping, she couldn't get a breath down. She couldn't do this. Couldn't do this again. She couldn't lose another person she loved. She couldn't handle it.

"Lucy," Anita whispered. "It's okay." Putting her hands on her daughter's shoulders, she sat on the ground next to her, trying to pull her back to reality.

"How is it okay? He's gone. I let Sloan take him. Now all three of them are there with that monster. I've failed." Her voice was raw as she choked out the words between sobs.

"No, you didn't, honey," Anita said, taking her hands,

sending small swirls of magic down her skin. Her smile was soft and sad.

But why wasn't her mother angry at her? She should be angry, she should be furious that Lucy kept putting her family in danger. That she was the one responsible for this fucking mess.

She couldn't do anything right.

"Lord Sloan is a disgrace to the Fae, and no matter what you could have done, he would have tried to hurt us," Anita said assuredly. She lifted her hands to Lucy's arms, sending a spread of calm through her golden swirling magic. As she touched Lucy's hair gently, her sense of dread receded.

"What are you doing?" Lucy said in a panic.

"You were like this after Father died, too," Wes said quietly over her shoulder. "Mother needed to calm you before you hurt yourself."

Lucy could barely remember it. She remembered waking up next to Wes, but she also remembered faint moments of her mother's sad eyes watching over her carefully, combing through her hair.

"No," Lucy said, distantly. "Please, don't put me to sleep. Please."

There wasn't time for her to fall into a spiral of darkness. She needed to prepare. She needed to fight back.

"You aren't going to sleep," Anita said, pulling her hands to Lucy's shoulders again, sitting her up straight, looking her directly in the eye. "You are stronger now than you were before. You are going to take a deep breath, we are going to get up, and we are going to make a plan to take down this son of a bitch for everything he's done."

Lucy stared wide eyed at the female in front of her, as though seeing her for the first time. She nodded vigorously.

"Good," Anita said. "Come. It's time to show our true hand."

STANDING around her father's study, Lucy tried to find an inkling of hope, but came up empty. Anita sat at the desk, pulling out a paper and quill.

"We are going to write our plan down?" Wes asked her, a heavy skepticism in his words.

"We are going to be *thorough*," Anita countered. "Sloan wants a trade, you said?"

"Yes, but what?" Lucy replied. She paced in front of the desk, biting her lip as she wondered about the safety of her brothers.

"I think he is after something valuable to him." Anita's eyes were bright as she pulled out a piece of parchment and a map from the desk drawer.

"I didn't even know that was there," Wes mumbled.

"Valuable like what?" Lucy asked.

"His alchemy is nearing the end of its power, I'm sure," Anita said, pointing to the North on the map. "You said when Jasper used the magic before, it would wear out after a few uses, correct?"

Lucy nodded, feeling foolish for not thinking of it

before. "He wants to power his alchemy. He wants Jasper back."

"Possibly," Wes said, catching on. "But we can't give him up. We can't give him the source of his power against us."

"There will be no stopping him," Lucy said, a shiver coursing through her again. "We can't let him come here with Henry and Simon around."

"Yes, I've already sent word to Lord Klimek," Anita replied, writing a few notes down on the parchment, then tearing off a small piece. "They leave in the morning and will be safe in a quiet village in the east."

"What?" Wes said in shock.

"They will consider it an adventure and will be much safer away from us. Klimek has been instructed not to let us know exactly where he is, that way we do not need to lie about it. He will send a messenger bird to us as needed."

Lucy stood stunned at her mother's efficiency. It was the perfect plan to keep her youngest brothers safe.

"What about the rest of the staff?" Lucy asked.

"We will send them away," Wes responded. "They will have no idea why we are sending them away, and only a few know of Jasper in the cellar. Their honesty will keep them safe from harm."

Lucy nodded in agreement as Anita wrote another note and tore it from the parchment.

"Bernard and Milton will refuse to leave your side," Wes said thoughtfully.

"Perhaps. I will not force anyone away, but we will

highly encourage it." Anita gave a short two-note whistle and a black raven came flying through the window, perching at the desk in front of her. Anita tied the piece of parchment to the bird's claw and told it to return to Klimek. Then she whistled again, and another black bird landed on the desk. She tied the second piece of paper to its claw. "Bring it to the staff quarters. Don't miss anyone."

"Mother, why are you speaking to birds as though they understand you?" Lucy asked with uncertainty.

"Because they can," Anita said, smiling. "I think it's time I tell you the rest of my secrets. They will be handy in the days to come."

Standing abruptly, Anita waved a hand in front of her, sending glittering gold magic over her body. The golden specks first touched her hair, turning it a dark color, so black it seemed to swallow the light around them. Next, the glitter landed upon her face as her nose began to elongate. With a gasp of surprise, Lucy watched as her mother shrank before them, slowly transforming.

Lucy looked over to Wes in alarm, but by the time she looked back at her mother... she was gone. Instead, in her place, was a black raven, looking at them carefully.

Backing up a step, Lucy reached out for her brother's arm. But Wes only walked forward, smiling.

"You clever Fae," he chuckled. "I should have known it was you all these years."

Lucy looked at Wes in disbelief. "What in the realms are you talking about? What happened to Mother!"

Wes didn't seem worried at all. He whistled off a familiar tune, and the bird chirped it back.

Recognition soared through her. The raven at the

window after her trip to Joterra. A black bird following her in the trees, watching over her as a child as she traversed the forest. The dark wings that soared over the orchard where she and her brothers would practice their archery.

With a small pop, a puff of smoke filled the air, and Anita returned to her normal Fae body. She stood before her children, her hair color fading from its dark black back to its beautiful brown to match Lucy.

"It's been you all along?" Wes asked in awestruck disbelief. "Why didn't you just tell us?"

"Your father and I felt it was best to keep that one a secret," Anita winked.

"So you're a bird?" Lucy sputtered.

Anita only laughed. "No, dear. Do you remember when I showed you my magic's likeness for nature?"

Lucy nodded, remembering the night she came into her bedchambers and showed Lucy her powerful magic, making the bushes sprout amazing flowers in a heartbeat.

"I can also communicate with some of the smaller creatures of the wild. I seem to have a natural affinity for birds, and they agree to do my bidding."

"You have bird minions?" Lucy said blandly.

"No," Anita said, grinning through her words. "They are my friends. They help me when I need to send messages but can't be seen sending the message myself."

"So Father knew about this, too?" Wes asked.

"Yes." Anita smiled. "He liked for me to sit in his meetings, but since Denora is full of males who have an aversion to females, we agreed my appearance in my bird form was more useful. I'd sit in the sun of the window ledge and be an extra set of ears for your father. We were a great team for many years."

No wonder Mother kept offering her support to Wes; she knew more than him all this time.

The distant memory seemed to fade with a touch of sadness.

"Alright. Henry and Simon are going off into the woods, Hugh and Gregory are smart enough to play Sloan's game for now, Lisette is safe in the east, Tristan is a prisoner, there are a bunch of Fae females and children in our guest rooms, and our mother is a bird." Lucy's dejected summary made for a bad joke.

Anita's laugh was full and bright that time. "That about covers it," she said.

The three of them sat in silence for a moment, taking in the dire reality before them. There was so much to do.

"Wes, you ensure Milton and Bernard know of the plan and give them the option to stay or leave. They are part of this family, and I want to keep them safe, but we could still use a bit of help if they are willing." Anita gave the orders like she had been doing it for years; as though she wasn't just a silent figurehead.

She wasn't, Lucy realized. *She just played the role so damn well.*

Lucy stared in awe at her mother. So much pride ran through her at her mother's strength and power.

"I'll make sure Jasper's still alive down there. Then I will prepare the rest of the guards here at the estate and ensure our people are safe." Anita turned to Lucy, a smile of understanding filling her.

"I have to make sure Micah is safe," she said on a whisper.

"Yes, you do. Do what you must to keep him and The Elderwood safe."

And with her mother's blessing, she left, urging her soul to find the other part of her heart.

TWENTY-THREE

MICAH

"War?" Micah asked Brax for the third time.

He couldn't wrap his mind around it... A war of powerful beings who would fight one another using magic—actual fucking *magic*. Fae lives would be obliterated...

"There hasn't been this kind of division since the Addaxe Wars—and that was centuries ago. But this..." Brax shook her head in dismay and continued pacing in front of the living room windows. "This will be a complete annihilation if someone doesn't stop him soon. He now has the North *and* the South, we cannot let him take Central Denora."

The hairs on the back of Micah's neck went taut at the reality of their situation.

So much death.

Didn't Lucy say that unexpected Fae death was more or less unheard of?

"How can they stand by and let this happen?"

"Lord Sloan's powers..." Brax shuddered, unable to

continue. Placing a hand on the windowpane, she stopped her anxious walking, staring out into the world beyond the sanctuary of the cabin.

Micah watched as his friend retreated into herself, quiet and unsure for the first time since he'd known her. It left him unsettled.

Since Brax's return, the light in her had dimmed. Her bronze skin always shimmered with power, but now she seemed ashen and dull. It was as if everything in her was buried somehow.

Brax had seen so much in her extended lifetime, watching as nearly four thousand years of Fae history came and went. She had survived in numerous wars and had come out on top.

But this is what she feared?

This was what threatened to break her?

"If that's the case, then we are going to need reinforcements." Micah leaned back into the couch cushions, bringing his head to his hands, rubbing his brow for the oncoming headache he was certain to acquire. Where would they find people to help them?

"Yes, Lumen." Brax slowly sunk down into the chair across from him. "We need to call upon our allies."

He dropped his hand and sat up, looking at his friend who had been by his side since the beginning. She looked so torn, her elbows rested on her knees as she sat, lost deep in thought.

"It is time to call on the warriors of The Elderwood," she said confidently. "They would not appreciate their Guardian turning into mush—then who would watch over the portal?"

"The Elderwood?" Micah asked, dumbfounded. "Why would they fight in this battle?"

"Because you are their only line of defense from here," she pointed to the floor, "before the evil takes over there," pointing to the portal.

Micah followed her pointed finger out the window and to the forest beyond. As much as he wanted to argue, she was right. If anything happened to him here, who would protect them?

She stood up abruptly and walked toward the door. "Come on, you snack thief," she said, the hint of humor in her otherwise defeated eyes. "Grab your axe and let's go pay your friends a visit. I want to see this place for myself."

"And you're sure they are going to help?"

"No, I'm not," she admitted, the brightness in her eyes gone once again. "But that's why I'm coming with you. I will make them listen."

IN NO TIME AT ALL, Micah found himself sitting at the same large oval table in the domed room with Brax on his right and Quillan on his left. Only Fergh and Rowan came to speak with him this time, the other unnamed advisor nowhere to be found.

"We apologize for the short notice, but it was imperative that we met. There are new developments with the safety of your realm, and this couldn't wait." Micah tried to explain to the two male Fae sitting before him.

"What's the problem?" Fergh asked.

"You were right," Micah said solemnly. "Your seers were correct... There is a Fae in Denora who wishes to take over all of the realm."

"Our seers are never wrong," Rowan said seriously. "We have warned you that this would happen."

"If this Fae takes over Denora, his next stop will be to me, then to you," Micah told them, trying to tame the rattle in his voice. "And, I hate to break it to you, but if he's able to level Denora, then I don't stand a chance."

"What do you mean?" Fergh asked, his otherworldly eyes troubled.

"If he plans to come here, I won't be enough to stop him."

"But you are the Guardian," Rowan said, his voice cracking with surprise.

"I am a mortal man who acquired magic less than a year ago with zero understanding of how or why it works," Micah contested. "I wish I could say I could take this guy down, but I know I can't. Not alone."

"Guardian," Quillan's deep voice rumbled. "What is it you're asking of us?"

Micah took a deep breath. By the look on Quillan's face, it was clear he knew.

"I need you to come to Denora to fight. I need help."

"We do not fight for Denora," Rowan said, almost insulted.

Fuck, this is exactly what I worried would happen.

"Please, hear me out before you make any decisions," Micah pleaded.

Both males looked to one another and then back at Micah, and nodded. Quillan kept his stoic eyes on Micah.

Sighing, Micah told them the entire situation. He explained his magical alchemy, about how Jasper tried to kill him for the power to come here. He told them all about the Baums and how Corvus had been murdered, and how Lord Sloan now wanted to take over all of Denora, not caring how many lives he must take in the process. He explained that they were already in the Southern Territories, taking over and hurting innocents.

The shift of Rowan's chair was the only hint that they were uncomfortable at all. They stayed quiet and attentive, listening to Micah's tale.

He left out the part of Lucy promising herself to Lord Sloan.

He left out the part where his heart was torn to shreds by her choice.

"What I'm saying is that without your help, Sloan will come after my alchemy next." He cringed at the admission of weakness, but he had no other choice. "If I'm not around, it won't take much for him to turn his attention here."

"How does he know about our realm?" Fergh asked in concern.

"Because Corvus Baum made a deal with him before we realized his involvement in all of this... It's why Brax is involved." Micah turned to face Brax, her body still rigid with unease. She always had her defenses so high for strangers.

Micah realized how lonely it must be to have to be on guard all the time. To have no one around to rely on. Being the one who has to look out for others and never the other way around. He put his hand on her arm, calming her. Reminding her he had her back.

"Why are we to believe she is no longer in collusion with the Fae lord?" Rowan asked, eyeing Brax suspiciously.

"I'm here, aren't I?" She said, narrowing her eyes at the two Fae males before her. "You can either stand by his side and fight, or risk a male of evil intentions knocking at your doorstep."

"There is no reason to threaten us," Fergh said with a wave of his hand and a defeated sigh. "We will provide our resources to you. Though we will need to come together in our counsel to determine who and how many will assist."

"Really?" Micah asked in relief at the same moment Brax asked, "Why?"

"Yes," Fergh said, eyes softening as he looked at Micah. "For one, our realm holds more than its Fae and its wood… Much more that is precious to all… But also because our leader taught us to never hide from the fight that matters."

"Who is your leader?" Brax asked. "Why are they not here to have this conversation?"

The third advisor came from the doorway. Micah hadn't realized that he had been standing there. "I think this is their leader," Micah said to Brax.

Her face tensed with a shimmer of knowing. As if fighting a smile, she kept her eyes on the male.

"This is my friend Brax," he told the Fae. "Brax, this is…" He looked back at the man in realization. "Actually, I don't think I ever got your name."

"It's great to see you again," Brax said with a wry smile. She shook her head gently and gave a light laugh as she stood up and embraced the stranger in a hug.

"Wait, you know him?" Micah stood, trying to understand how that could even be possible.

"Micah, you empty walnut," Brax turned, her arm slung around the male. "Meet Alderic Lumen."

"Wait a minute," Micah murmured. He couldn't seem to stop his mind from spinning. "You're Alderic? Like. *The* Alderic Lumen?"

The Fae just continued to smile at the group. He nodded as if it was not the most reality altering thing in Micah's existence.

Micah turned from the table and walked away from the group, not trusting what would come out of his mouth next.

"Where are you going?" Brax called after him.

"I need a minute!" Micah stormed out of the room and ventured through the trees to an empty courtyard behind the domed building.

The stone court had beds of flowers nestled in the shade of the forest. There were benches made of wood scattered throughout and a large fire pit in the center. It was clearly a place for large gatherings or celebrations, but Micah was glad to find it empty now. He needed a moment to deal with another bomb of information being dropped in his lap.

Why the fuck wouldn't he have told me who he was when I first met him?

He paced, running his hand through his hair. In his other hand, he kept the axe held tight in his grip. It steadied him somehow to have this weight grounding him as his thoughts spiraled.

Alderic Lumen's been here this whole time. He could have helped me with this alchemy. He could have been around to help us fight off Jasper during all his bullshit.

Micah kicked at a rock and listened as it scattered off into the trees beyond.

"I'm not the last Lumen," he said to himself in disbelief. He had felt so alone for so long, believing he was the last of his line... and now this?

"No, you're not," a deep voice replied.

Micah spun around to see Alderic standing before him, a gentleness to his face.

"Why didn't you say something before?" Micah asked, not understanding the endless secrets of the Fae.

"When it was my turn to introduce myself, you cut me off." Alderic shrugged. "I guess it didn't seem important at the time."

"Not important?" Micah scowled. "I was mortal before your magic changed me. You're my ancient fucking ancestor and I have no idea what I'm supposed to do."

"And we've been guiding you," Alderic said casually. He picked up another rock from the ground and tossed it in his hand as though he was mulling over a grocery list.

"You sent a fucking cat to bite my leg off and left me a book in a language I can't fucking read." Micah's lips pressed into a thin line, trying to hold back his temper and failing miserably.

"In our defense, we didn't know you weren't the one hurting our realm," Alderic said with ease. "But yes, I wasn't expecting our languages to change so much over the past centuries. The mortal land is very different than our Fae realm."

Micah just looked up to the cotton-candy colored sky and shook his head. "This is too much."

A snap of branches behind him made him turn, expecting the worst yet again, but it was Brax walking up to join them. "Come on, Micah," she said softly. "It can't be that bad. Besides, now we have the opportunity to ask more questions. Right?"

Since her return from the South, she had mostly stopped insulting him. He didn't know what to make of her kindness, and if he was being honest with himself, it kind of put him on edge.

Alderic's face lit up and he extended his hand to the benches, inviting them to sit. "I've always preferred to be outdoors anyway," he said with a wink. "I'd be happy to tell you anything you'd like."

"Fine," Micah replied with a punch of attitude. He turned to Alderic Lumen; his great-great-he-didn't-know-how-many-greats-great grandfather. "How does the alchemy work?"

Brax slapped him on his arm, chiding him for his attitude. "Sit up, stop acting like a child."

As much as he wanted to fight her about it, he knew she was right. There was something innate within him that tended to push away his family. He didn't have time to act this way. What they needed more than anything else were answers and allies. Micah nodded, sat up, and looked to Alderic to continue.

"The alchemy was Sanni's most incredible discovery," Alderic said with a smile. "She was brilliant. The other mortals in her realm didn't take her intelligence seriously. They always said she had her head in the stars and needed to come back to reality." He smiled, lost deep in thought. "That's how I found her. It was late at night and she was laying in a field, completely silent. I had not figured out the time difference between Denora and Joterra yet, and as I walked through the lush landscape of the forests of Joterra back then, she was just lying there. I almost fell upon her!" He chuckled. "I remember she was so mad at me for crushing one of her gemstones with my clumsy footing. But when I convinced her I wasn't a rogue bandit and asked if she'd let me repair it with my magic, her eyes lit with fierce wonder. A bit of residual magic was trapped inside of the gem I fixed for her. It seemed to glow, even in the darkness of the night."

"You put your magic into the gemstone? That's how we get the alchemy to work?" Micah asked, trying to understand.

"Yes and no," Alderic smiled. "Sanni had no magic, so the alchemy acted within the bounds of science. Elixirs to improve health were more akin to modern medicine. Changes to rocks and minerals were chemistry. However, when magic and her alchemy united, it wove a new tapestry for magic the universe has never known."

Brax scooted forward in her seat, prepared to learn as much as possible.

Micah's head tilted as he took it all in, a question in his mind he wasn't yet ready to ask.

"Her alchemy and my magic together allowed for new magic to arise. For Sanni, my magic within the stones allowed her to cast her own spells, utilizing the alchemy in a new way. For me, using her stones amplified my powers, almost giving it a jolt of extra energy. That's why your magic is so unique." A proud smile graced his barely aged face.

"But I can't do the magic without the stones," Micah said bleakly.

"What?" Alderic had clearly not expected that reply, his smile faltering.

"When I try, my magic is next to nothing unless I have the gemstones to amplify it." Micah explained.

"No, your Lumen magic should come first, the gemstones just support you." Alderic stood and paced the small stone platform. He ran a hand through his hair and Micah noted the similarities between them.

"It's true," Brax supplied. "He was able to do some of his magic, but it has waned tremendously. Now he gets the most power from the stones."

"It's probably the fucking curse," Micah huffed under his breath to Brax. "We could have done without that one, so thanks." The bitterness in his voice was enough to make Alderic stop.

"The what?" Alderic looked at Micah, completely perplexed.

Micah stood up to come face to face with Alderic, his anger just simmering beneath the surface. "The curse," he spat. "The one you put on every Lumen descendent so that we could never leave our post."

"I don't know what you mean. What curse? Where did it come from?" His eyes were wide.

"You're the one who gave it to me," Micah snarled. "Your entire fucking family line."

"That's impossible," Alderic breathed, taking a step back. "Sanni and I put the utmost love and care into that spell. You should have received a blessing of magic, not a curse."

Brax stood slowly and put a hand on Micah to calm him. There was a look of realization in her eyes and Micah knew she had put something together that they had missed.

"When Micah went through the portal," Brax explained gently, "he was given your magic." She looked between the two Lumen males before her and a sadness painted her face. "However, before that, when he agreed to remain as guardian of The Elderwood, he and Lucy Baum completed the transference rite. Somewhere in that initial guardianship rite, there must be a mistake."

That's when it hit Micah. It wasn't the magic that caused the curse, because Abe had the same curse with no magic. It was the rite. Brax figured it out.

"The rite allows for the guardian to stay on the land and protect the portal," Brax said. "But it also ensures that the guardian can never abandon their post. If they were to ever leave, they would get very ill. With enough time away from the portal, the guardian would... die."

Alderic's face paled.

He had no idea.

"There was never meant to be a curse," Alderic said softly. His gaze jerked to Micah, his eyes wild with grief. "Surely, you must believe me. I would never wish ill upon my family—my own blood."

Micah's brows were still furrowed with anger, but he dipped his head in agreement all the same. As much as he hated the curse for killing his grandad, he believed that Alderic never intended that outcome.

Taking a quick step toward Micah, Alderic put his hand on Micah's shoulder and another across his own heart. Looking deeply into his eyes, Alderic told him, "I will do everything in my power to find a way to break this curse. I am so sorry for... for... all of it."

Micah nodded.

"How do we imbue the stones with his magic so that we can use them on the battlefield?" Brax asked.

Micah was grateful for the change of subject.

"I will tell you what I told my son," Alderic smiled. "Your magic is strengthened by alchemy, but there isn't anything special needed to imbue those stones."

"What do you mean?" Micah asked. "Jasper—another long lost Lumen—made it seem it was impossible to do without the right spell?"

"It's within you already," Alderic said. His eyes were bright in wonder. "*Everything* you need is inside of you."

"If we remove the curse, will my magic improve?" Micah asked, hopeful for an answer.

Brax smiled gently and shook her head. "I don't think so. I think the curse is tethered to the physical body and where it lies in relation to the portal. I don't think it calls to your magic at all."

"I, too, don't think it is related. But I will do everything in my power to break the curse quickly," Alderic said, his face grave. "I give you my word."

Another barrage of footsteps approaching made all three of them turn at the sound.

"Sir," Quillan said as he came around the side of the domed building. "You three are going to want to come out here. We have another visitor."

Alderic's face turned serious as he followed Quillan.

Brax and Micah could only exchange quick glances of concern as they trailed behind.

Micah's head was spinning. First, he finds out his magical ancestor is still alive. Then, he discovers his magic is supposed to be more powerful than it actually is.

What's wrong with me?

It was the one question that had been plaguing his mind this whole time. What was different about him that the magic didn't work the right way?

He could have sulked and moped over the question for hours, but what he saw before him changed his entire course of thinking.

There, in between at least four different guards, was a Fae female, full of freckles and ash and blood.

"She came through the portal and refused to tell us who she was until we told her where the Guardian was," one guard explained. "Some villagers said she was familiar, but she refused to confirm who she was or why she was here until we brought her to him."

The next words on Micah's lips were an answer to his pleas.

"Lucy Baum."

TWENTY-FOUR

LUCY

"Micah," she breathed, the tightness in her chest subsiding for the first time in hours. When she had first arrived in Joterra, there was no sign of him nor Brax anywhere, and immediately she panicked, thinking of her visit to the South and finding her brother's home empty.

Lucy had only hoped that she'd find Micah in The Elderwood. However, upon arriving, she realized she had no idea where to look, so she approached the first guard she found and demanded that he bring her to Micah; to their trusted Guardian.

"Why wouldn't you just tell them why you were here?" Brax asked, clicking her tongue in disapproval.

"Because I no longer trust blindly," Lucy said, an undercurrent of vexation lacing her tone.

Lucy was still angry at Brax for not believing her, for going behind their backs to try to prove their theory wrong. Inevitably, Brax came around to their side, but so much could have been avoided with her trust that they all thought they had from her.

Brax's eyes dropped ever so slightly at the dig, but she again raised her head to the Fae before her. "Lucy, this is Alderic Lumen."

Lucy's mouth popped open in shock.

"She is here for the same cause. Lucy Baum is a trustworthy and noble Fae." Brax nodded her approval in apology.

Alderic sighed, then turned to Micah. "I will assemble our advisors and we will discuss our next steps. Convincing our people to leave our realm may take some time." His brow furrowed with concern, but something in his posture spoke of a male with conviction.

Micah's Fae ancestor is still alive here...

"I thought Rowan and Fergh said all of you would fight?" Micah said, worry cracking through his usual solid exterior.

"Many of us will, yes." Alderic looked past them all to the realm beyond them. "But for all of us to come together to fight this evil, we will need time to prepare. Brax, I'd like you to join us for the conversations, if you don't mind."

Brax nodded and gave Micah's arm a squeeze.

"Micah, take some time with your friend. We'll summon you when our decision has been made." But before Alderic left, he leaned over and whispered something in Micah's ear. Words so quiet even Lucy's Fae hearing couldn't pick up.

For a long moment, Micah just looked at him with raised brows, clearly bemused.

Alderic clapped him on the shoulder and walked away with the slightest smile, winking at Lucy as he passed.

As the guards turned to exit, Brax followed, leaving Micah and Lucy alone in the courtyard.

Lucy had imagined she would find Micah and run into his arms. She had thought she'd wrap her hands around his neck and feel his warm embrace around her middle as it filled with butterflies at his touch.

But that was not what happened.

They stared at one another, silently taking each other in.

Micah with his axe in hand, devastation and concern in his eyes.

Lucy across from him, full of dirt and grime from her time in the South. She didn't even give herself time to clean up before she had to come to Micah.

To the one who held her heart.

But perhaps he no longer felt the same, as he stood far on the other side of the stone path, feeling like another realm away.

He took a steady step toward her, and Lucy held her breath.

"Come on, Lu," he said softly.

The nickname was like music to her ears and lead in her gut.

"Let's get you cleaned up." He took her hand and led her away from the building, past the endless trees, never looking back or speaking to her once.

She followed, sending a prayer to all the stars in the sky that she could fix what she broke.

MICAH BROUGHT her to the water's edge of a small, familiar lake. The view was stunning. At the base of the mountain, the water trickled down from the snowy tops, creating the perfect place for animals to drink. She saw the trails of deer and other smaller creatures in the brush. Some tall grasses lay just beyond them, where animals could hide. Colorful, little rocks peppered the shore line—pinks, oranges, and yellows to blend in with the sands. Though every once in a while, there were blues and purples shimmering with beauty.

The only animals she saw now were small aquatic creatures like turtles and fish as they swam freely in the clear blue water. A small waterfall cascaded into the lake towards the side of the mountain, nearly out of view from their position in the front.

It was beautiful, and Lucy was not.

Finally looking down at herself, she saw what made all the villagers pause when she arrived. She was covered in soot and blood.

Whose blood is this? She asked herself, but she didn't know—didn't want to know.

She couldn't remember. There were so many people she had helped in the South, and still so many lives taken. Shuddering, she forced the bile down, not willing to tarnish the breathtaking coast more than she already was.

Micah took the red bandana out of his back pocket and dipped it into the water.

The same bandana they had used for seek-and-find.

He kept it all this time?

She held her breath as he cleaned her, first wiping the dirt away from her hands and arms as he rinsed them at the water's edge.

Each movement reminded her of the first time they met... Her sitting on the edge of the closed toilet seat in Abe's old bathroom as Micah cleaned her wounds from her scuffle with the wolven.

So much had changed since then.

He immersed the red cloth into the water and brought it up to her face, gently wiping away the ash lined with trails of tears.

Everything is so wrong.

The back of her throat burned and her eyes began to water, but she couldn't cry. Not now. Not when Micah was dealing with enough of his own shit—Alderic Lumen was real and he was here. Clearly, that had to be so much for him. Lucy had to hold it together for Micah.

As if following her thoughts, Micah smiled at her. A soft smile, full of sadness. He dropped the bandana and scooted closer to her, rubbing his thumb across her cheek.

"You can let it go," Micah whispered tenderly.

Lucy refused to blink, for if she did, the tears would flow and would not stop.

"When it gets too heavy, you don't have to hold on to it all," Micah said again. "Let it go."

Even if she wanted to, she could no longer hold back the tears. They cascaded down her cheeks, mirroring the waterfall just beyond them.

A choked sob escaped her chest and her hands flew

up to her face to cover her mouth as she wept, her body curling into itself.

She felt broken inside, like the tears were crashing through her and ripping her to shreds. Tearing her into pieces that could never be put back together again.

Micah embraced her as she cried, pulling her closer and holding her tightly, like it was the only thing keeping her whole. And maybe it was.

"It's okay," he murmured in her ear. "I'm here. You're okay. It's okay."

"It's not okay," she sobbed. "Nothing is okay, everything is wrong. It's wrong!"

"Shh, slow down, slow down," he whispered, trying to calm her. "What happened?"

His eyes were like windows into her soul, seeing her own sorrows reflected in his perfect brown eyes.

"My brothers," she said, taking a deep breath to calm her racing pulse. "Sloan has them. Hugh and Gregory are captured in the South, and Tristan..." Her voice broke on her last brother's name. "He took Tristan and we need to get him back." Another choked sob escaped from her lips. "He said he'd return him to us for a trade."

"You don't believe him, do you?" Micah asked, tension lining his entire body. "He'll cross you the first chance he gets."

"That's the problem," Lucy said, her voice barely above a whisper. "I know I shouldn't give in. He wants Jasper. He wants his source of alchemy back... If we give him Jasper, then he has access to more magic that could kill thousands. But without Jasper, then his target is *you*." Lucy could barely get a breath down at the thought.

"That was the whole point of all of this." Her voice cracked through her tears. "I went with Sloan to keep you safe..."

She couldn't bear to face Micah. She squeezed her eyes shut tight and curled into herself again, feeling the warmth of Micah's body. Reminding her she was here with him, and that he was safe. That through all of this, she needed him to be safe.

But Tristan...

With her head on Micah's strong chest, she listened to the steady thump, thump, thump of his heart. His kind, loving, full heart.

The heart she broke.

"I don't know what to do," she whispered. "If we give him Jasper, then more people get hurt. If we don't, then we don't get Tristan back, and you become his next target."

"I can take care of myself," Micah reassured her, forcing her to open her eyes and look at him again. "But you're right. There's no easy answer here, but I know you'll figure it out." He squeezed her tight.

She sat curled in his lap and his fingers delicately stroked her arm. He leaned down to nuzzle her hair and kissed her brow so gently Lucy thought she would crumble.

They sat there in silence for a while, taking in a gifted moment of calm in a reality that appeared to never slow down.

"You're here for reinforcements?" Lucy asked, putting together what she heard from Alderic earlier.

"Trying," he responded.

"And... Alderic?" Lucy asked. "He's here?"

"Mmmhmm," he replied, clearly not interested in talking about it.

She let it drop, not wanting to pry. Micah had always had a hard time sharing those emotions, and she was not in the position to demand anything from him.

Not now.

Not anymore.

She had ruined that part of their relationship when she chose Sloan.

The realization made her nauseous. Lucy used to think of the Lord of the North and see his regal stature and his handsome features. Now when she thought of him, the image of his maniacal face as he killed those innocent Fae burned in her mind.

She shook the thought away, refusing to let such evil and hatred fill her mind in such a beautiful place.

"When I was younger, and I'd come here with Wes, I used to camp out at this waterfall," she told Micah, forcing her mind to think of something else.

Anything else.

"I never saw traces of animals. It was always just me—alone. I'd find little colored rocks on this shoreline, and I'd toss them in and make a wish."

"What did you wish for?" Micah asked, his voice deep and warm.

"I wished for a life full of adventure," she told him. "And love. Real love." She bit her lip, reining in the tears, happy to be facing away from him. "Now I have too much adventure, and I lost the only love I've ever had."

CHAPTER

TWENTY-FIVE

MICAH

With each declaration from Lucy's mouth, Micah's heart ached more and more. She had told him the last time they were together that she had picked Sloan in order to save him. It had infuriated him—the idea that she thought she was doing him a fucking favor by leaving him behind.

But with her curled in his lap, baring her soul to him about her love, all he wanted to do was kiss her. He wanted to hold her freckled cheeks in his hands and pull her pouty lips to his and make her forget all the pain that she felt.

It would take one kiss. Just one perfect kiss for him to fall right into the same patterns from before; make him fall deep and hard for her, and never let her go.

But he couldn't.

He couldn't risk falling apart again. Not right before they dove head first into battle against Sloan. A battle that needed them all thinking clearly if they wanted to succeed.

286

Micah was tired of people coming into his life just to leave again. He was tired of hurting.

But then he remembered what Alderic had whispered in his ear, and he sighed.

"Come with me. I want to show you something," Micah said to her, helping her to stand.

Lucy sniffed, her eyes puffy from crying, but otherwise mostly clean. She dipped her head and followed, slipping her hand into his.

His heart jolted with the feel of her. The rightness of her.

He pulled her along up the side of the mountain, bringing her toward the first ledge of the waterfall.

Just as he had expected, the view was magnificent. They weren't so high that it was dangerous, but high enough that they could see the water below them and groves of trees in the distance. The landscape of The Elderwood never ceased to amaze him, and from the look on Lucy's face, he knew she felt the same way.

He pulled out of her hand, feeling her reluctance to let go. He didn't want to, but he needed both hands for this. Placing his axe down, he bent over and untied his boots, throwing them to the side, away from the ledge.

Lucy's face twisted in confusion.

He pulled off his socks, then shifted out of his heavy pants, standing before her in just his shirt and boxers.

Before, the movements would have made his arousal apparent, but he had no intention of seducing Lucy right now.

"Take off your boots," he told her, smiling slightly.

She raised her eyebrow to him, but nodded and did so, throwing them with Micah's.

He reached out for her, and she stepped close to him. Once Lucy grabbed his hand, the electricity between them heightened again.

"Alderic told me something today, and I think I understand what it means." He gripped her hand tightly and took a step toward the edge of the mountain. "He said, when you're at the edge of your hope, and you aren't sure what else to do.... We don't back up and hide from it all. We jump, feet first, and have faith that what molds us today stays with us forever."

With a twinkle in his eye and a tug on her hand, he jumped with her into the water.

Lucy screamed on the way down, but not in fear. No. It was joyful laughter that he hadn't heard from her in far too long.

Splashing into the refreshing body of water was completely different than he had expected. It wasn't cold at all, but a perfect temperature. It seemed to have a natural buoyancy that pulled them to the top on its own. As they swam around the surface, Lucy's gaze met his. Her eyes were so bright, full of love and wonder.

"Just jump, huh?" She asked him with a smile. They were still near the waterfall, and the spray of the crashing water landed on her face like glitter. Lucy was completely clean now thanks to their swim. A trail of dark brown curls floated behind her.

The curve of her lips as she smiled at him was his complete undoing.

Fuck it.

He wrapped his long arm around her waist and pulled her to him, capturing her mouth with his and tasting her once again.

A breathy gasp left her as their lips and tongues collided, reacquainting themselves once again. She tasted like roses and honey and he could not get enough of her.

They kicked their feet under the water as their arms wrapped around one another in a desperate rush to get closer. Almost as if a wave pushed them, they floated under the waterfall. The crashing water above them broke their kiss as they looked around at where they landed—a small alcove behind the waterfall, just out of sight.

Micah kept his hand wrapped around Lucy's waist as he pulled her further into their hidden space, his length hardening with every lingering thought of Lucy in his hands.

Far back in the little alcove, small ledges jutted out at different intervals. His feet felt the tip of one and he was able to stand on it and stay above water. He lifted Lucy onto another one a few feet in front of him, plopping her down in a seated position before him, their faces level.

"I love you," she told him, her fingers trailing his face. The touch sent bolts of need through him.

Micah stared into her gorgeous hazel eyes, knowing in his heart how he felt but being too scared to admit it.

What if she hurt him again?

What if she finds someone else to spend the rest of her days with?

He took a deep breath.

Just jump.

"I never stopped loving you," he told her. Gently pushing his fingers into her hair, he caressed her face with his thumbs. "I'll always love you."

This time, their lips met slowly, savoring each word they announced. Lucy ran her tongue over Micah's lower lip, and he opened his mouth to her. Lucy's moan had him pulling her closer, her chest pressing against him.

"I want to feel you, all of you," she breathed in between her kisses.

A small echo over the watery alcove repeated her words in his ears.

She tugged at the bottom of his shirt and he complied, pulling it over his head and throwing it to the back of the alcove and out of the water.

Lucy's tunic floated around her midsection, lifting just enough for his hands to find her bare stomach. His fingers trailed her skin, exploring the silky smoothness of her body, wishing he could see all of her.

Reading the desire in his eyes, she smiled as she removed her top. Micah held his breath as he looked at her, sitting before him in just her lacy undergarment and a pair of thin leggings.

Taking it as an invitation, he wasted no time burying his face in her neck. As she panted with arousal, he never stopped kissing her, worshiping her. His hands traveled to her breasts, squeezing them as she moaned breathlessly. As his kisses traveled lower, he pulled her lace down and captured her breast in his mouth, flicking her pink bud with his tongue.

"Micah," she cried out, pulling him closer. Begging for more.

He scrambled for her leggings, trying to pull them down and failing in the buoyancy of the water.

Lucy put two hands behind her back and removed her lacy garment, uncovering the most perfect breasts Micah had ever seen, but before he could bury his face between those perfect curves, she jumped down to the ledge he was standing on.

Swinging her arms around his neck, she pressed her bare chest to his and kissed him. Again, it was slow, and he moved with her as she turned them so he had his back to the ledge. She pulled his boxers down just to his thighs and palmed what was hidden there, sending a shudder of pleasure straight through Micah.

"Sit," she told him between kisses, and Micah obeyed, feeling the hardness of her nipples as he rocked himself back onto the ledge.

Lucy took a step back and shimmied out of her leggings, making herself completely bare to Micah. Then, with her Fae grace, she climbed up onto Micah's lap and wrapped her arms around him.

He was trembling. Shaking uncontrollably.

"Are you okay?" She whispered to him, their bodies pressed close to one another.

"I'm scared," he told her. His eyes gazing deeply into hers—the only person he had ever fallen in love with.

"We don't have to do this if you don't want to," she said, pulling back with surprise and barely concealed hurt.

"No," Micah said, holding her in place. "I'm not

scared of this—of us. Not anymore." He closed his eyes and pressed his forehead to hers.

"Then what?" Lucy wrapped her hands around his neck, her fingers playing with the hair at the base of his neck.

"I'm afraid of losing you, Lu," he told her, the rushing water outside their alcove hiding the quake in his voice. "I'm afraid of what tomorrow brings. But even if we were to die tomorrow, I'd never regret loving you. Choosing you."

Micah knew the risks of love when he couldn't even leave his post as guardian, but the rest of his family knew the risks too, and they took it. They never missed out on a chance for love. For family.

"I choose you, too." Lucy pulled his face to hers and kissed him with a passion that told him she was just as scared of tomorrow as he was. Her chest pushed against him and his hands found the firm roundness of her bottom. Caressing her from hips to breasts, he felt Lucy move, lowering herself down onto him.

They stayed in the cave for what felt like an eternity, hoping the sounds of the crashing waters would hide their cries as they came together, again and again, leaving no room for regret.

TWENTY-SIX

LUCY

Lucy wasn't sure if it was the buoyant magic within the lake or finally letting go of the worry and strain after missing Micah so badly, but she felt as though there was a lightness to her.

Hand in hand, they left their watery alcove, hearts united as one. Lucy took the time to squeeze out some of the water from her hair and tame it into a braid while Micah retrieved his axe, the rest of his clothes, and her boots.

As she watched him in the distance, a realization came to her. She would do anything in her power to keep him safe, would do anything at all to protect him. Anything except leave him again.

Her heart was his.

"Got them," Micah said, walking over, holding her boots up. The smile on his face was lighter now, too.

"Thanks," she replied as she put them on.

Micah took a deep breath in and looked back at their hidden spot behind the waterfall. "So what do you think the chances are they already made up their mind but decided not to interrupt us?" His face pinched in embarrassment.

Lucy laughed. Her first real, honest laugh since her father had died. "I'd have to say it's pretty likely. They're Fae—good hearing, remember?"

"Oh, yeah," he said, the tiniest bit of blush covering his cheeks.

Smiling, Lucy pulled him into another kiss. "It's fine. Let's go find Alderic and hear their decision."

LOCATING Alderic was the simple part. He was in the same domed building that Micah suggested he would be. Getting his attention away from Brax was what proved to be difficult.

"Wow," Lucy said to Micah. "Some friendships don't fade with time, do they?"

Lucy and Micah watched as Brax and Alderic sat side by side, laughing and talking animatedly. It was nice to see Brax so happy, but the idea of Alderic being there still confused Lucy.

Why had there been no record of him after all this? Why did he hide from them?

Micah cleared his throat, getting Alderic and Brax's attention.

"Ah, Lumen," Brax announced. Then she looked at Alderic. "Lumen."

The duo broke into a fit of giggles again.

"Sorry, sorry," Brax said, seeing the annoyance on

Micah's face.

"I take it conversations went well?" Micah asked, the hope apparent in his voice.

"Yes," Alderic said with a smile, but then his face turned serious. "We understand what is at stake, and we are prepared to fight alongside you."

Relief flooded Lucy.

"The South.... It was..." Lucy tried to tell them, but the words died on her lips.

"It was the worst thing I have ever seen in all my life," Brax said for her, a hushed solemnity in her words.

Lucy could only nod. "Our Denoran armies are split. Some soldiers are supporting Sloan, and I'm not sure if King Tralont has enough soldiers to triumph in battle."

"Our people will unite and fight together," Alderic replied with ferocity.

"I know some warriors who have a soft spot for the freedom of females and children," Brax said with a wink.

"And with your power, Miss Baum," Alderic said to her, "we know you will lead us to victory."

"My power?" Lucy repeated. Then a new question came to her mind. "Alderic, you have been here in The Elderwood for a very long time... what do you know about the magic inside of me?"

It hadn't occurred to her to ask before that moment.

"It was dormant for as long as I can remember," he said with a slight smile. "It woke up the very first time you crossed through the portal."

Lucy's heart jumped.

"You should have seen how it would sulk around when you were gone," he chuckled. "It waited around for you all the time. Then when the time was right, it left with you." There was a glint in his eye, as though he knew something she did not.

"Where did it come from?" Lucy asked, desperate for answers. "Please, tell me. Help me understand."

"How about I show you instead?"

The magic inside Lucy sprang from her hands and twirled around her in a dance.

Alderic barked a laugh. "Oh, so now you come to say hello."

"What is happening?" Micah whispered to Brax.

"You're about to find out," Alderic replied. "Follow your magic, Lucy. It seems to want to show you for itself."

THE EMERALD green mist zoomed in and out of tree branches, joyously floating along a trail to another part of The Elderwood.

Where are you going?

The other times they were in The Elderwood, her magic didn't appear. Lucy had assumed it was simply because she didn't need it here when she was safe, but perhaps it was something else.

Keeping up with the trail, the footsteps of Micah, Brax, and Alderic lumbered behind her. What did Alderic know that he hadn't told her yet?

Taking a sharp turn, the magic stopped at the entrance to the dark forest. Lucy took a giant step back, cautiously watching as her magic bounced up and down.

"I figured it'd take you here," Alderic said.

"Isn't it unsafe?" Micah asked, catching up to Lucy and putting a hand on her shoulder, as if to stop her from following the magic into the dark woods.

Lucy had no intention of entering such a terrifying space, but realistically speaking, if her magic went in, then so would she.

"No," Alderic scoffed. "It's not unsafe at all. Why would you say that?" He looked at the three of them as though they were insane.

"Hmm, maybe because it's a forest of black trees with blood-red leaves?" Micah said.

"Maybe it's the shadows that crawl over the forest that don't seem to touch anywhere else?" Brax supplied with sarcasm.

Lucy's heart warmed seeing the two friends so seamlessly banter.

"Oh, right," Alderic said, wide eyed. "It'd probably help to take the glamor off." He waved his hands in the air and said an ancient Fae spell.

As if the world around them was melting, the forest scenery began to change. The dark shadowy sky swirled with color, the black and deep brown tree trunks turned hazy, and the red leaves rippled in and out like a stream of water. Ever so slowly, their view before them changed.

The shadows disappeared, revealing a brilliant forest, surrounded by trees of gold and silver, the bright yellow sun shining down on them. White flowers of all kinds covered the grassy plains in between the towering trees.

"What is this place?" Lucy asked in awe, watching as

the soft breeze caught in the branches of the illuminated trees. "Why was it hidden?"

"This is the reason this realm exists," he said earnestly. "The most sacred place among all Fae."

Brax's wide eyes stared unblinking as she walked through the entrance and into the grandeur of the forest. "Is this... it cannot be." She looked back at Alderic in wonderment. "The gold and silver trees. The endless fields of white flowers. Is this...?"

Alderic smiled as if reading her mind. "It is."

"It's *what* exactly?" Micah asked, frustrated that he was clearly missing something.

"The true name of our realm is Porvanai," Alderic said solemnly. "The resting place of the gods."

Lucy's head spun at the declaration.

Porvanai was layered deeply within Fae religion... so deeply some considered it myth.

"Is anyone going to explain this to me?" Micah asked, breaking the silence.

Brax walked deeper into the shimmering forest and Lucy's eyes followed her magic as it sprung along with joy, twirling itself around the glittering trees.

"All Fae come from the gods," Alderic explained. "Gods are the only truly immortal beings on this plane of existence; even Fae lives will expire." He lifted his hand to the miraculous trees before them. "This is where the gods come when they are ready to rest. They do not die, but they can retire in peace, here forever."

"Are they asleep?" Micah asked.

"Some, not all," Alderic replied. "Most keep to themselves and remain here in their forest—we call it Thrin-uin. Others roam around when they get curious."

"Like my magic?" Lucy asked, her voice nearly a whisper.

"Yes, like yours," Alderic laughed. "In all my time in Porvanai, I have never seen a god reach out to another the way this one did to you. I truly believe it belongs with you somehow."

"A god cannot belong to another," Lucy said.

"No, it cannot," Brax agreed.

"Maybe it was just looking for a little adventure," Micah suggested. "It can't die, right?"

"Correct," Alderic said.

"Then when all is said and done, it will return here," Micah said, as though it was obvious.

Alderic, Brax, and Lucy slowly turned to look at him.

"You know, Micah," Brax said slowly. "I think that's the most intelligent thing you've ever said."

"Do you know who it is? Whose power this came from?" Lucy asked.

"No," he shook his head. "No one knows, and I don't think we will ever have a way of finding out. But that doesn't matter anymore, because it's you now. It's your power—and so far you've done everyone proud." He winked.

But Lucy couldn't agree. She thought of Abe. Of her father. Tristan and her brothers.

"Even them," Alderic whispered to her, as though reading her mind.

Her emerald magic came bounding back toward her,

shimmering with knowledge that Lucy was finally starting to understand.

"Now you see why it is so important we keep the realm safe," Alderic stated fervently. "You are not just a guardian of an ancient forest. You are the Guardian to the Gods."

Micah inhaled deeply and stood up straight, as though he was taking in the enormity of his task.

"I will go to Vytyr," Brax told Micah. "Alderic gave me Sanni's old potions to travel there. It won't take me long."

"Thank you... You'll know where to find me," Micah said in reply.

Lucy's hope fell.

She had already promised herself she would never leave him again, but she had to. There was no way for him to leave the property safely until Alderic broke that curse. But she had to go back, she couldn't leave her mother unprotected at the estate. And she wouldn't be leaving him forever.

Not in that sense.

The panicked look in her eyes softened as Micah met her gaze, nodding gently. Letting her know he understood.

"I will continue to train," Micah said to the group. "Do you think Quillan would be interested in giving me some lessons on this thing?" He lifted the axe in his hand.

"I am sure of it," Alderic said proudly. "I will have all the advisors prepare our soldiers."

"What will you be doing?" Brax asked.

"I will be in my study, finding a way to break this horrid curse I've caused." Alderic's face crumbled in dismay.

"I must return to my family," Lucy said softly. "My brother is trying to get the king to listen, but I need to make sure my mother is safe at the estate. She will probably need help with the extra Fae there."

Alderic, Brax, Micah, and Lucy stood shoulder to shoulder in determination, looking into Thrinuin, knowing they wouldn't hide from this fight. Then, they looked at one another closely, realizing that this may be the last time they'd all be in the same place together.

"Then it is settled," Brax said, clapping a hand to the back of Alderic's shoulder. "We prepare for battle."

TWENTY-SEVEN

MICAH

"Are you sure this is going to work?" Micah asked Quillan as he stood next to Brax in the open space of the lawn outside of the cabin.

"I am certain," Quillan replied, stoic focus and determination set in his brow at all times. "Move the axe as I've shown you and enter that space where your magic resides."

"What do you mean *enter the space*? The magic is just... in there somewhere." Micah imagined his magic just swimming through his veins, only occasionally willing to show up.

The faint sigh from Quillan put a sparkle of amusement in Brax's eye, but thankfully, for once, she kept quiet.

"It isn't fair for you two to keep telling me to *use my intent* and *find the space where my magic resides* when I've had magic for such an infinitesimal amount of time compared to you. I haven't had it for centuries. I haven't had it all my life, learning to grow with it. I've had it for months. That's it."

He didn't mean to snap, but he was drained.

He was losing his patience.

He was just so fucking tired.

A softness came over Quillan then, and he walked up to Micah slowly, his large palms out in a peace offering.

"You're right," Quillan replied. "You haven't had the time nor the training. You don't know our histories and you don't know the nuances to your magic yet."

Micah sighed. It was rare that someone saw and acknowledged the difficulties he was facing.

"But none of that matters." Quillan's harsh words came out like a whip and ended Micah's moment of relief. "Today, or tomorrow, or the next day, an unrelenting, powerful Fae will come here prepared to take your magic."

Quillan took a step closer to Micah, and Micah took a small step back, not used to seeing Quillan so hostile.

"He will come here and kill anyone in his way to get *your* alchemy." Another step toward Micah. "Your Lucy. Her family. Brax. Me. My entire village." A powerful glint in his golden eyes brought forth the predatory power Micah recalled from Quillan's form as the shadow beast. "You would leave the gods without a resting place? You are willing to risk all of that simply because this is *hard?*"

"Of course not," Micah bit back, trying his best to stand his ground. "I'm just saying I don't know how."

"Then find it within you to figure out how," he said fiercely. "Lives rely on your dedication to this cause."

That was it. That was the problem... Everyone relied

on Micah to do this the right way, but he was given nothing in return. No training. No support. No fucking option to even take the job. He was just there in a destiny he did not want, or at least one he had not intended.

He wanted to fight back. He wanted to yell at the Fae in front of him that he would do anything to protect those people, all of them, but he didn't know how his magic worked. He didn't know if he could do it.

"I know," Micah said, running a hand through his hair. "I just..." The words got stuck in his throat. Was this the future that he wanted? "Can you help me?" He asked faintly.

"Lumen," Brax groaned. "We've been trying to help you utilize your magic, you buffoon," she spat at him, throwing her hands up in frustration.

"No—" he tried to explain, but Quillan cut him off.

"Guardian," Quillan said quietly to him, his deep voice a near rumble. "You are a protector, are you not?" He closed his eyes and sniffed the air, his head bobbing slightly as if he was savoring the scent.

Micah didn't miss the feline way his neck curved into the movement.

"Yes," was all Micah could say.

"A protector in this life, as well as your life before," he said, opening his golden eyes just inches from Micah.

Micah nodded, remembering his position in the police department. Remembering the lives he tried to improve. It felt like a lifetime ago.

"Close your eyes," Quillan instructed.

Micah looked at him doubtfully. He felt like a fool closing his eyes in front of these people, but then again since he found out magic existed, he fell in love with a beautiful Fae woman, he found magic of his own, and now was speaking to a man who could turn into a fucking cat, he decided the rest of his life was sure to be equally strange.

Quillan just gave him a look as if to say *"really?"*

He sighed and closed his eyes.

A moment later, Micah felt Quillan lean closer to him, standing a breath away. Micah tried to steady his breathing as Quillan's strong hands weighed down on his shoulders.

"There is a power inside of you that has nothing to do with your magic," Quillan said to him quietly. "It is a place that speaks to who you are as a person. Your generosity. Your patience. Your intuition. It is everything that makes you who you are."

Micah took a deep breath, searching for that place within him.

"Your magic does not come from your mind," Quillan said, softly tapping a finger to Micah's temple. "It's deeper than that. It is a well that lies within all Fae; and you, Micah, even though you don't feel as though you were Fae before this... you were. No mortal could have taken on the magic from Alderic. No mortal could have pulled magic from thin air to save his friends."

Micah thought about that. It had been something that had bothered him this whole time... How he went from a mortal man to a magical Fae in the stretch of one moment. But perhaps something Quillan was saying was true. It did make sense. How could anyone just be empty of magic one moment and filled with it the next?

"Your Fae heritage is more than the blood within your veins," Quillan's voice rumbled. "It is in the loyalty your family had for our people. It is in the sacrifice your family made to keep a life changing secret."

Micah's heart sank at the thought: the reality of that sacrifice. His throat tightened.

His grandad.

His mom.

Now him.

Was their family cursed to live this life alone? The responsibility of an entire realm in his unprepared hands?

"There's more that burdens you," Quillan said as if in realization, squeezing his shoulders. "Speak, Guardian."

But Micah wasn't sure he could say it. Could he voice that he hated that his entire family had this obligation to shoulder?

Part of him wanted to say he never wanted the job, but was that true? The tightness in his throat seemed to make a blockade the size of his fist.

The very thought of leaving here...leaving his position as guardian... It made him uneasy.

It was no longer about what he left behind in his life before this. Giving up this role would mean giving up every bit of the magic, the good and the bad.

It'd mean no more cabin.

No more Brax.

No more Lucy.

Even if things weren't perfect between them, there was still so much they had yet to figure out. Once all of this was behind them, maybe they'd have a real shot...

But more than that, he wanted to learn more about the magic and his family. He was tired of the secrets and lies and wanted the truth—the whole truth. Maybe spending time with Alderic would answer more of his questions. Maybe this role didn't have to be as isolating as it was for his family before him.

Micah cleared his throat. "When I first was... *appointed* to this job, I was still deep in my grief. I don't think I was ready for it. For any of this."

Micah opened his eyes, nervous to see Quillan upset at his admission, but instead, he remained stoic. No judgment upon his face.

Micah glanced at Brax standing over his shoulder. She nodded at him, giving him the strength to continue.

"I was mad when I found out about the curse; about all of the ways my family had to sacrifice their wants for this cause. But the more I am involved, the more I understand." Micah took a deep breath in. "I want to be here. I think, somehow, I was always made for this. Not because of my grandad or my mom, not because of the cabin I've always visited, but because I am a protector. I've always wanted to ease the pain of others and bring justice to those who deserve it. I want to do the job the right way."

Quillan squeezed his shoulder and took a step back, dropping his hands. "You are the Guardian." He lifted a fist to his chest, held it over his heart, then bowed his head. When he looked at Micah again, there was a smile on his face. "I think you've found where your magic lies."

"What do you mean?" Micah asked, confused as always. "I only said that I'd keep trying."

"Yes."

Micah waited for him to continue, but Quillan just stood there silently. All knowing.

It's awfully fucking annoying always being the only person in the room not knowing what the fuck is going on.

Brax smiled and walked up to Micah, reading his annoyance.

"I know you've heard me talk about magic and intent, but I don't think you've ever allowed yourself to accept your magic," she said. "You've just kind of went along with it."

"I've accepted it," Micah responded in defense. "I've been here this whole time, haven't I?"

"You've been here because you weren't given any other choice," she said with a wistful smile on her face. "But listen to what you just said. You said you wanted to be here. That you were made for this. Do you truly believe that?" Her eyes remained on Micah's face, searching for answers he perhaps could not say aloud.

Micah's breathing hitched, just in the slightest. He had said that, hadn't he... And did he mean it? Did he mean all of it?

He squeezed his eyes shut and looked deep within himself.

Even without Brax. Without Lucy. Without his grandad and mom. Would he choose this? Would he choose to stand guard over a mystical realm and take over the magic that was hidden deep within his veins all this time? Would he stand against injustice and fight for what was right?

The answer was yes. To all of it, always. That is who he was.

The Guardian.

"Yes," Micah said, and as he spoke, a flare of red magic came crashing out of his chest and swirled around his body.

It felt like a crackling fire and a raging wind, then suddenly a warmth grew deep inside of him.

His magic, buried deep, nestled near his heart.

It was there all along.

"You found it," Quillan said, a statement, not a question.

Micah nodded, amazement filling him. He looked at his hands as they held his red swirling magic, the axe nowhere near him.

It was him doing this.

Him.

Not the axe. Not The Elderwood.

The magic was his.

"Then let your training commence."

"Stop doing that," Micah grunted as Brax hit him in the side for the fifth time.

"Then stop leaving it open," Brax snarled. She spun and kicked at his side again, and Micah blocked her foot with the handle of the axe.

This had been going on for damn near an hour and Micah was spent. First the training with Quillan, then combat practice with Brax.

He stood up straight to prepare for another

onslaught of Brax's Vytyrian fighting tactics, but instead, she kicked him in the side again.

"Damn it, Brax, will you knock that off?" Micah yelled, clasping his side in his hands.

"No," she said as she swung at him, managing a blow to his shoulder.

Hit after hit, she never stopped coming for him. He could barely block half of them, let alone manage to get a hit back at her.

Micah fell to the ground in a heap and threw his axe down next to him. Lifting two empty hands up to the air, he shouted, "That's it! I need a break!"

"You don't get a break. Pick up your weapon," Brax demanded. She stood over him, panting from exertion. There was an intensity in her eyes that Micah didn't understand.

"No," he said calmly. "I'm taking a break." He leaned forward to stand, placing his axe on the ground to steady him.

"There are no breaks in war," she said as she kicked him backwards, his body hitting the grass with a thud. "Pick up your axe and continue."

"No." Micah looked at her through a veil of simmering frustration.

Brax lifted her foot again to kick him, but Micah's magic responded first, grabbing onto Brax by her ankle and flipping her feet over head, and onto the ground.

"Yes, finally," she said with violence dancing in her eyes. "Again."

"No, Brax," he said louder. "I'm done. What's gotten into you?"

"We aren't done until you can beat me," she said, preparing to advance on him again.

"Then I guess you can beat my fucking ass all afternoon because I'm done fighting," he said through gritted teeth.

"You aren't done!" Brax cried, nearly shrieking with frustration. Her eyes were wild and her nostrils flared as her breaths heaved. She bobbed on her toes and yelled at him again. "Get up!"

He said nothing.

"Get up!" Brax screamed, taking a step closer to him. "Get up!"

But Micah heard it... the crack in her voice at the command.

"Why?" Micah asked her quietly.

Brax opened her mouth to reply, but no words came out. She looked away quickly and took a step back.

Micah got up and walked over to her.

She picked up her fists and got into another fighting stance, her breathing uneven and her feet heavy on the ground.

"What's going on Brax?" His voice was a near whisper in effort to keep her calm, approaching her slowly as he would a wild animal.

Her stance didn't falter, but a lone tear escaped her eye and fell down her cheek. "Because you need to be ready."

"We're doing that, Brax. We're getting ready." He brushed a tear off her cheek with his finger. "What's this about?"

"No. Not *we*. You." She shoved him back, then wiped

the back of her arm across her face, erasing any sign of tears. "Now fight!"

He grabbed her fists lightly in his hands and brought them together to his chest, holding her there. Her hands were shaking and she was panting for breath, her gaze darting everywhere but to him.

"Tell me what this is about and I'll do anything you say," Micah told her earnestly. "This isn't about you wanting to whoop my ass, so what is it?"

Her hands quaked under his. He had never seen her look so shaken. Slowly, her eyes rose to meet his. More tears welled there, not yet cascading down her beautiful bronze cheeks.

"We need to do everything we can to prepare you," she said quietly. "I've seen…" She bit her lip, trying to find the words. "I've seen what Sloan has done to people… to good people." Her eyes darted across his face, taking in his features as though she was memorizing them in case she never saw them again. "But I've never fought alongside someone I've loved. You are my best friend, and I can't let anything happen to you."

"You're my best friend, too," he told her.

That was the most important thing at that moment. Not that they would fight together. Not that they would train and prepare for battle. What mattered was that they were friends who loved one another—because that was the only thing worth fighting for.

Love.

"You're the only real friend I've ever had," she whispered.

"You know, that makes sense," Micah said lightly,

releasing her hands and holding her arms. "You aren't very nice."

Brax snorted in laughter, and Micah smiled back at her, pulling her in for a hug. He held her there as she sniffled, her body slowly relaxing into his.

"I know this is scary," Micah told her, resting his chin on the top of her head. "It's never easy risking things so close to us... but we know this is the right thing to do. We will fight, and we will win, because there is no other option here." He gave her a gentle squeeze and let her go, pulling her away from him to look at her. "We can do this."

Brax nodded, her eyes still full of worry.

"This calls for a fire," Micah announced.

"And a beer," Brax finished for him.

He smiled, recalling the times over the last few months that Brax would pull him out of his dreary moods with a fire and a beer. While she ran inside to grab the drinks, he picked up his axe and went to light the fire.

Without Brax around, he wanted to try something else with his magic. He lifted his hand and commanded his magic to arrange the firewood in just the right way. Then he held onto his axe in one hand and the matches in another.

"Light," he told the match, and instantly it burst into flame. He had no idea how this power actually worked, but he felt it there within him now. Ready to be used.

As Brax returned, they sat on the tree stumps and looked out into the fading sky above them; the sunset turning the world into hues of orange and pink.

Brax still looked completely broken, and it lit a fire of resilience in Micah's soul. He would do anything for his friends, even if it meant training until he was more sweat than man. He hated seeing Brax like this.

"Come here," he said, lifting his arm for her to come closer.

She scooted toward him and leaned her head against his shoulder silently. "You're a good person, Micah. And I'm better for knowing you."

"I feel the same about you. Thanks for always being here to help me."

"You're welcome. Now make sure you don't die, you overgrown radish."

CHAPTER
TWENTY-EIGHT
LUCY

Lucy's magic had been quiet since the return from The Elderwood. She wasn't sure if it felt at peace from visiting its previous home or uneasy at the battle to come—probably both.

That was one thing she was learning each day, you could feel many conflicting emotions at once, and they don't always make sense together. Lucy felt happiness and terror; love and fear; hope and despair.

Sitting in the garden, she closed her eyes as the sun warmed her face and the scent of the flowers filled her with calm. Another set of opposites, peace and trepidation.

She kept going over what would happen next in her mind. Soon Sloan would arrive looking for Jasper. They would give him Jasper as a trade for Tristan, and ensure the safety of her brothers... but it would just allow him to become stronger.

Unfortunately, there really wasn't any other way. She

needed her family safe and *together* in order to take down Sloan.

A group of children ran through the garden, surprising Lucy and pulling a smile to her lips.

"Stop running, you hooligans!" The violet haired Fae called, chasing after them. When she turned and saw Lucy sitting alone, she stopped to apologize. "I'm so sorry. I'll go get them and tell them to stop."

"Please, don't." Lucy reached her arm out to get her attention. "Really, it's fine." She smiled as she watched the kids running after one another, playing a game of sorts. "It has been a long time since we've seen happiness in this garden, and I welcome it entirely. Let kids be kids while they can."

She nodded, her violet hair falling from her fraying hair tie. "I'm Ruthani," she said with a wave. "I'm sorry my hair is such a mess right now." She tried to flatten it closer to her scalp.

"Stop apologizing," Lucy told her, a sharpness in her tone she didn't intend. "You were imprisoned with your family and are fleeing for safety. Do you really think I care about how your hair looks? Your hair is beautiful."

"Thank you. My mother used to hate that I would color it such bright colors, but my father always loved it. She ran her hands through it again. "Sure wish I could tame it now, though."

"Come here," Lucy said, pointing to the bench beside her. "I'll help you get it out of your face, so it's easier to chase those rascals." She tried to add more lightness to her tone, but it was hard. Why did this young female think Lucy cared about how she looked in the midst of civil unrest?

She sat hesitantly, and Lucy turned her head to braid her hair into an elegant crown.

"You aren't quite what I expected," Ruthani told her, her gaze still on her siblings playing in the mud.

"And what is it you expected?" Lucy asked, her fingers moving at lightning speed as she braided.

"You were betrothed to Lord Sloan, were you not?"

Lucy straightened her spine and took a deep breath, considering her response. "I was."

"And it was your choice?" Ruthani continued.

Lucy clenched her teeth. "It was." She put the last section of hair into a stronger tie, then dropped her hands.

Ruthani turned to look at Lucy, eyes full of scrutiny. "Then what happened?"

Lucy considered telling her a half-truth—considered making the answer easier to hear, more palatable for a stranger.

But Lucy never was one to water herself down for someone else.

"I agreed to a business deal so that Sloan could help me catch the Fae who murdered my father," Lucy told her with fire in her eyes.

Ruthani didn't balk for a moment.

"And when I found out that he was the Fae responsible for so much death and destruction, I turned my plans on him instead. So yes. He was my betrothed, and now he's the target of my wrath."

"Good." Ruthani smiled as she looked back to her

siblings, her entire demeanor changing. She was no longer sitting as though she was nervous and on edge.

"That was not the response I expected from you," Lucy admitted to Ruthani, regarding her carefully.

Turning her head back to Lucy, Ruthani's eyes were fixed, full of bold determination. "I needed to be sure you were someone we could follow."

"Follow?"

"Brax told us you could be trusted, but I needed to be sure. We will not walk in the footsteps of some love-sick female, but perhaps we can follow a female who straightens the crowns of others." She smiled as she lifted her eyes to her braided crown of hair.

"Who is this *we* you speak of?" Lucy asked, noting the significance of her words.

"The Fae here are scared," Ruthani told her, "but we are not weak." Then she stood and turned to Lucy. "Thank you for the weapon, it came in use," she said, offering the amethyst dagger back to her. Brax must have given it to her for protection during their time in the South.

"Keep it," Lucy murmured, still thrown by the conversation. "Use it to keep you and your siblings safe."

Ruthani nodded, sheathing it. "And thanks for the hairstyle," she said with a wink as she walked away.

Lucy stood and watched in awe as Ruthani gathered her siblings. The interaction left her heavy with emotions she couldn't describe.

Seeing Ruthani with her family opened up feelings within Lucy that she had been trying to avoid. The people who mattered most to her were on the front lines of this conflict, and worse, they were all spread out; no unified front.

Hugh and Gregory were in the South, no doubt captured alongside Tristan, Wes was desperately trying to get the royals of Central Denora to believe his claims, her mother was trying to run the business and keep Jasper in line, and her father was... dead.

Each time she thought it, it was as though an arrow shot through her heart again and again.

When will the grief ease? She wondered. *Will I always fall to my knees in despair at the memory of his death?*

There had to be a way to defeat Sloan, but how?

There was nothing left to do but keep going, and if they all died tomorrow, at least she could say she went down fighting. Looking up to the bright blue sky, Lucy squeezed her eyes shut and pleaded that they all made it out alive.

"I believe you've just been played, sister," Wes said. Her eyes shot open to see her brother sitting on a nearby bench.

"How long have you been there?" Lucy asked, incredulous. She was certain he was not there a moment ago.

"The entire time," he said with a wink. "It's not my fault you aren't very observant." He stood and walked toward her.

"Wesley Baum, I daresay you are keeping secrets. When I see father in the afterlife, I am going to give him a piece of my mind for giving you, of all people, the ability to sneak up on others," Lucy said with a scowl. "As if you weren't already nosey enough."

"Stop complaining," Wes said, chuckling. "You're just

annoyed that Ruthani played you like a fiddle." He pretended to play a violin and did a little jig in the middle of the garden.

"Why would she do that?" Lucy asked him, still reeling from the strange interaction.

"Ruthani is strong. She reminds me of you and Brax; determined to do the right thing. I think she was sizing you up."

"Well, I—"

But before she could finish her sentence, an alarm blared all throughout the estate. The deep reverberations of the siren vibrated Lucy's bones.

Someone's coming.

"Get the females and children back inside to safety," Wes told her, seriously. "I will identify who comes."

Lucy took off in a flash, ensuring the protection of those who needed it most. Then she went to collect Jasper.

If Lord Sloan was here for an exchange, then he would get one.

And she would get Tristan back.

"MOVE your feet before I remove them for you," Lucy threatened, dragging Jasper through the manor to the front foyer entryway.

Anita had helped settle the Fae guests and put Milton in charge of keeping them safe and quiet during the trade. No one wanted Sloan to find out that they had secretly taken his prisoners right from under his nose.

Wes positioned himself at the door, and Anita stood at the ready, her magic steadily gathering. They looked perfectly poised and calm, the complete opposite of how Lucy felt.

Lucy's heart hammered in her chest. She was so thankful her younger brothers were away and somewhere safe. There could be no more mistakes, no more risks to their family. This final trade would bring them all back together.

Pulling Jasper to a wrought-iron chair in the grand entryway, Lucy tied him securely, ensuring his captivity.

"You don't understand," Jasper gasped, looking at the door in sheer panic. "If he takes me, he will kill me!"

"That wasn't the tune you were singing to Brax the other day," Wes said.

"It's true! You can't hand me over!" Jasper pleaded. "I will do anything. Anything!"

"Will you change your ways and help us thwart Sloan?" Lucy asked pointedly.

Jasper recoiled in disdain. "No, absolutely not. I'm desperate, not an idiot."

Lucy rolled her eyes.

"But anything but that!"

"Silence," Lucy commanded, sending a silencing spell over him once again.

"You'd think subservience to us would have been preferred," Anita said to no one in particular.

Lucy looked at the grand front entrance as her fingers trembled with nerves.

What if Sloan takes Jasper but doesn't return Tristan?

What if Jasper's magic allows Sloan to become too powerful?

What if there's no stopping him after this?

She had to shake the thoughts out of her mind. Dwelling over the what if's would do nothing to help her here. The only option was to keep going, even if every thought pained her. She couldn't go back and change time even if she wanted to... and she did. Desperately.

The soft folding and unfolding of Anita's arms shifted her attention to her family beside her. Wes stood directly next to Lucy, prepared to receive their brother and bring him to safety. Anita was a bit further down the hall, guarding Jasper for their barter.

She replayed the plan in her head over and over again. They would each prove their side of the bargaining chip, they would send Jasper over to Sloan, Wes would get Tristan and hurry him off to safety, and then they'd close the doors to Sloan and his soldiers as they figure out their next steps.

All that mattered right now was Tristan and her brothers and getting them home safely.

Her entire body was on edge as they waited in silence.

"Are we sure we are ready for this?" Lucy asked her family. Patience was never a virtue that took kindly to Lucy.

They looked at one another, worry heavy in their stance.

"There's no other choice." Wes turned to the door. "He's here."

With his shoulders back and a steadfast expression

on his face, Wes opened the doors to Lord Sloan and a small squad of soldiers as they approached the entrance.

"Ah, what a warm welcome," Sloan called out with false sincerity. "I see we are ready for the big event." He rubbed his hands together selfishly.

"Show us Tristan," Wes demanded, staying clear of Sloan and his soldiers.

"Do you doubt my word?" Sloan asked facetiously. "Tsk, tsk. I am the only Fae of honor here."

"Honor?" Lucy spat in disgust. "Your plans to murder the king and hurt anyone who gets in your way is the opposite of such titles."

Sloan just smiled at her as though he was seeing her for the first time. "My dear. How I've missed you."

"Tristan." Wes demanded.

"Yes, yes," Sloan replied, waving to his soldiers. "Bring the boy forward."

The group of a dozen males in navy uniforms parted as a soldier escorted Tristan to the front of the crowd. His eyes were wide with fear, but he was otherwise intact.

Anita drew in a quiet gasp as Lucy held her breath.

He was there. He was there and he was unhurt.

Thank you, she said to the stars.

Wes walked back and grabbed Jasper by the collar. "Here. Give us our brother, take your prize and leave." He shoved Jasper at Sloan's feet.

Sloan looked at Jasper, flummoxed.

Jasper fell to his side and pushed himself away from Sloan by his feet, his hands still tied.

"I believe there has been a misunderstanding," Sloan

said seriously, the forced civility now gone. His ice-blue eyes met Lucy's with anger and disdain.

"And what is that?" Lucy asked. "You want a trade. Take him, then give me back my brother."

Sloan broke into a low laugh, the sound like gravel in his throat. "I do not want that sniveling coward. Keep him. Kill him. I don't care."

"What? You don't mean that," Lucy said, taking a step forward.

As though he was talking to a petulant child, he rolled his eyes and sent a bolt of magic straight to Jasper's chest—killing him instantly.

"I do," Sloan replied, a sinister smile creeping over his face. Taking another step toward Lucy, he continued. "I do want a trade... but I want something worthwhile. I want a magic that compares to no others."

Lucy couldn't breathe.

How did she not see this before?

"I want *you*, my beloved."

"What? No." Wes nearly shouted the words. "Absolutely not. That was not the deal."

"It most certainly *was* the deal," Sloan replied, keeping his cruel eyes locked on Lucy.

"She's not coming with you," Wes snarled.

"Oh, she will," he hissed. "That magic will be mine, and then we will go have a little chat with that mortal you're so fond of, hmm? Or perhaps I can do that *after* I kill your brothers."

Micah.

"I will give you the time to think it over," Lord Sloan replied, casually looking at Anita. "I've got three of your sons," he called to her. "Three sons for the price of one daughter? Well. That must be worth it, don't you think? I'll even let everyone in the manor live."

With a sneer, he turned on his boot and walked back through the entrance.

"Wait," Lucy called weakly.

Sloan paused without turning.

"No," Anita commanded. Throwing a silencing bubble over Lucy, so she could not continue. "You cannot have her."

"I'll be back," Sloan replied, continuing his walk.

Lucy watched as the soldiers carried Tristan away, his face scrunched in concern.

She wanted to yell at them to wait. To come back.

She wanted to scream that Laurent Sloan could have her if he freed her brothers. If he left her loved ones alone.

But the words didn't come as each of the soldiers left through the door and Anita rebuilt the wards around their home.

Tristan was gone again, and Hugh's and Gregory's lives were added to the barter.

The entire Baum family line rested in her fate.

And she would give herself over to her enemy if it meant saving the ones she loved.

TWENTY-NINE

"You are out of your mind," Wes snarled at Lucy as she stood before him in his office.

"I am of perfectly sound mind," she replied, but the passion was gone from her words.

"You will not give yourself, and your magic, to some monster who wants to take over Denora!" Wes shouted at her.

He paced before the fireplace, trying to calm his mind.

This can't be happening.

"I will not live to see my family die because of my inaction," she scowled back at him.

"Lucella. You must hear what you are saying." Wes stood before her and put his hands on her shoulders, bending down to enter her line of vision. "If his alchemy is as strong as it was before, then you will not be able to overpower him. He will bend you to his will and command your magic. He will be unstoppable. Do you understand that?" The desperation in his voice was clear, but it had no effect on Lucy.

As he looked into her eyes, he saw her surrender and it terrified him.

It didn't matter what anyone told her, she would trade her life for the life of her brothers. It didn't matter that it would make things worse. It didn't matter that it would allow Sloan to become more powerful.

"Before you make any drastic decisions, please go check on the others. I need to make sure Mother is okay," Wes requested as he pinched the bridge of his nose and spun away from her.

Sighing, Lucy walked to the door, then paused. "If the roles were reversed, you would sacrifice yourself for us."

"And you'd try to stop me, too," he replied dejectedly. He turned to look at her, their sorrowful eyes meeting the hard truth.

No matter the decision, everyone in their family would be hurt by the outcome.

I will find a way to fix this, he swore.

As Lucy left the room, Wes closed his eyes and called upon his father's magic. A brilliance went through him, a levity cleansing him of his worry.

He had only used this magic a few times, each time utilizing it to travel without being heard. However, when he used that magic, his family always seemed to be shocked at his arrival. Knowing his father, there had to be more to it. Letting the ethereal light pass through his body, he let go of any reservations holding him back.

There was no time to learn this magic slowly. There was no time for hesitation.

"If you're listening, Father," Wes said to the room around him, "I'm ready to harness the rest of your magic. Help me help our family."

Wes stood in the center of the room with his eyes closed and arms open wide, feeling the radiant light covering him from head to toe until a weightlessness encompassed him. Opening his eyes, he looked down at his body, astounded at what he saw.

"You sure love a play on words, don't you, old man?" Wes said with a breathless laugh. Taking a deep breath, he welcomed more of the light in, watching as his skin glimmered like stars around the room. The effect was nearly blinding.

Lucy had his shadows, and Wes always thought that was the more remarkable magic. However, Wes had the opposite, and he had never truly understood what it meant until now. Sure, he could create light and have a lightness to his feet, but as he looked down at where his hand should be, he realized what else this magic allowed. Wes could bend the light, making him disappear from view.

"I believe it's time to put this magic to the test," he said to himself, excitedly. He left his study and turned down the hall to find his mother.

At the first intersecting corridor, he walked past Bernard and Milton.

"Are you going to leave?" Milton asked Bernard, scanning the hallway for prying eyes. He looked directly at Wes, but didn't even acknowledge him.

Poor lads, Wes thought. *They don't see me coming.*

Wes never enjoyed listening in on other people's conversations, but he'd be lying to say it hadn't come in handy more than once.

"I would never leave Madame Baum and these children," Bernard replied, horrified at the thought.

"Nor I," Milton replied. "Then we will remain and carry on until our last dying breath."

Their words were hushed, and the enormity of their loyalty almost made Wes take pause and thank them. However, Wes was on a mission, and there was so little time left.

Passing through the hallway, Wes found Anita in the library, poring over books with different stones illustrated in them.

"If you're going to stand around, you may as well help me search for an answer," Anita said suddenly.

Wes dropped his magic and looked at his mother in surprise. "How did you know I was here?"

"It's your father's magic," she replied with a sad smile. "When we were in the garden, I thought I felt the presence of your father because of the story I was telling. I didn't put it together until later that I just felt his magic within you."

"Nothing gets past you, does it, Mother?" Wes asked in admiration.

"Sloan's declaration certainly did," she whispered, turning her gaze back to the open books before her. "There must be a way to stop him with alchemy. He is not invincible."

She huffed as she flipped page after page, searching desperately for an answer.

"Mother," Wes said, in realization. "I think you're right... and I think I have a way to get help." He grabbed Anita's hand and stilled her progress. "I need you to keep Lucy busy. Don't let her leave. Give her things to do to keep her feeling important and useful. The moment she thinks all is lost, she will arrive on Sloan's doorstep without our knowledge."

Anita vehemently nodded, knowing Lucy's stubborn streak better than anyone.

"Lucy is not to be trusted," Wes replied. "I will be back as soon as I can."

"Where are you going?" Anita asked, concern etching in the fine lines of her face.

"To gather our allies."

ARRIVING at the Lumen property took more time than Wes initially wanted, but he knew Lucy would come here to say goodbye before she turned herself over to Sloan.

Micah needed to hear the truth before Lucy tried to spin it in her favor.

"Lumen!" Wes yelled, beckoning him as soon as the cabin was in his eyesight.

Micah ran outside in a spurt of speed that surprised Wes.

Hmm, seems he's found his magic.

"What's wrong? Where's Lucy? Is she okay?" Micah asked in a hurry, searching over Wes's shoulder for Lucy.

Wes clasped Micah's shoulder, reassuring him. "Lucy is fine."

Micah's shoulders dropped in relief as Wes watched him. The way his tension fell knowing Lucy was safe.

"Micah, you love her, don't you?" Wes asked, seeing it clearly for the first time.

"More than anything," Micah replied as though it were obvious.

"And you would do whatever it takes to keep her safe from harm?"

Micah tensed again. "What happened?"

"Where is Brax? She may as well hear this at the same time." Wes said, looking through the trees in search of the warrior who made his blood heat, and not always in a bad way.

"I'm right behind you, you putrid turnip."

A flare of fire surged through his body at seeing Brax, but more than anything he was simply happy he didn't have to say this more than once.

"Say it," Micah urged.

Wes nodded, seeing the determination set in Micah's stare. "There is no way to sugarcoat this. Sloan came for the trade, but he didn't want Jasper. He wants Lucy."

"Well, he can't have her," Micah growled.

"Correct, but Sloan made an offer she couldn't refuse. The safety of our entire family for her and her magic."

The color dropped from Micah's face. He knew as much as Wes did that Lucy would put the life of those she loved before her own.

"No..."

"Yes," Wes replied. "She's more powerful than all of

us, so we have to work together without her knowing. We must figure out how to stop her from making the biggest mistake of her life."

"We'll just tell her to wait. That there's gotta be another way. She has to see that Sloan having all that magic is only a recipe for trouble." Micah paced on the uneven grass lawn before him, running his hand through his hair.

"She won't listen," Wes countered, then asked the question he was praying would change the course of their upcoming battle. "Have you learned more of your alchemy? Can you take him down?"

"He has been practicing," Brax answered for him.

"No," Micah replied, cutting Brax off. "I'm not strong enough. I won't make enough of a difference."

Wes feared that answer, but it wouldn't change their next steps. "Will you fight with us? I have a plan, but it will only work if everyone is on board. And Lucy can never know."

"I would do anything for her," Micah promised.

"Then listen carefully," he said, looking from Micah to Brax. "There are many moving parts here, and yours can't falter."

By the time Wes returned to the Baum estate, it was almost dark.

I think I've had enough of single days turning my entire life upside down, he thought to himself.

Just that morning he was prepared to get his brother

back and fight the good fight against Sloan with Lucy by his side, and now he was at risk of either losing Lucy or losing his three brothers.

Neither option was acceptable.

However, this time he wouldn't sit back and watch as life passed him by, the way he did when his father died. The moment Wes took charge of the family business, his life turned upside down then, too. It seemed so trivial now that he thought about it. He was so upset about having to take over and make the decisions for his family just days ago, and now he was traveling through realms and making secret plans to take down a maniacal tyrant.

Hurrying to the library, he found his mother poring over piles of books on a variety of subjects. She had "Stones and Rock Formations" open on one side and "The Myth of Porvanai" on the other.

"Any luck?" Wes asked.

Anita just slumped back in her seat despondently. Her hair was a mess, as though she was pulling at the edges as she searched. With a wave of her hand, her smudged make-up was perfected and her hair back in place.

"Where's Lucy?" He asked, tension rolling through his muscles.

"Don't worry, she's still here," Anita replied. "I guilted her into doing some housework. I told her I needed things done before I was left alone without any children to care for me."

"Mother!" Wes scolded with a shocked smile. "You did not."

"Of course I did," she said, waving her hand at her

son. "I needed to keep her busy while we figure out an answer to this. I will not be losing *any* of my children."

The words were a challenge that Wes was happy to take on.

"I agree. I have a plan, and you probably won't like it, but I need your help."

THIRTY

MICAH

Micah swung his axe through the air, slicing at such speed and strength, he could easily take down multiple Fae attackers at once. Now that he had found where his magic resided within him, it was almost difficult to keep the power at bay. His magic was dormant for so long it seemed to flare with strength and purpose—a purpose he had been seeking for a very long time.

He could feel it coursing through his veins, zooming through his lungs, lacing every muscle—he was pure Fae magic and strength, and he was happy to wield it.

If only it was enough to stop Sloan.

He swung the axe again, roaring through the movement, pulling his magic along with him as he created a devastating blow with each swipe.

Micah would do nearly anything to keep his mind from his reality at the moment. As soon as Wes left, Brax got her supplies and hurried off to do as Wes requested. Micah went the other direction and traveled into The

Elderwood to tell Quillan and Alderic of the new plan. Unfortunately, the entire timeline had moved up dramatically, and they asked for time to discuss before they gave their answer.

That didn't matter to Micah, though. He barely heard their request as he rushed back to the portal to return home. He would travel to Denora to protect Lucy using his newfound strength. She would be protected by her family and those who loved her. He was halfway across the property to the other portal when the truth hit him.

I can't leave.

Stopping in his tracks in the middle of the forest, Micah fell to his knees in anguish. The love of his life needed him to fight for her, and instead he was stuck on the sidelines, unable to make a difference at all.

He screamed, allowing all the pent up anger and frustration to spill out of him. It didn't matter how many times he chopped wood or ran through the forest, the resentment still thrived inside of him.

Fucking curse.

He walked back to the cabin and began to head inside when the portal to The Elderwood rippled with light. Changing course, Micah went to greet Quillan, and was shocked to see who was with him. Alderic stepped out and smiled, looking around the new realm. According to what Quillan had told him, Alderic had never left his realm before.

"Hello, Micah," Alderic greeted him as more warriors came through behind him.

"Have they agreed to band with Denora?" Micah asked, hope coating every word.

"Yes," he replied grimly. "Quillan is checking their vitals here in this new realm, ensuring they will be at their peak performance." His footing slipped, and he grabbed Micah's arm.

"Are you okay?" Micah held his arm and guided him to the tree stumps around the fireplace.

"I'll be fine," Alderic reassured him. "It has been a long time since I've visited a mortal realm. The air is different, and as you know, time moves differently here."

"Why are you here? You could have sent Quillan, or requested my presence back in Porvanai?" Micah couldn't understand why Alderic had come, especially if it wasn't necessarily safe for him.

"Because there is much we need to discuss."

"I'm not sure how much time the Baums have until Sloan comes to collect his bounty," Micah told him. "Lucy will do it. She will give herself over to that asshole if she thinks she's protecting her family. We can't let her."

The rage he felt tensed through his body, but Alderic just sat there smiling at him.

"What?" Micah asked.

"You're in love," Alderic stated, but it wasn't a question.

Micah nodded, then he recalled the words Alderic told him when Lucy came to The Elderwood. "How did you know before? You hadn't met her for more than a few minutes, and you knew exactly what to say to me... how did you do that? Is that part of your magic?"

"No," Alderic chuckled. "I had five sons. I've seen the

signs of love in young males before." He sat, lost deep in thought.

"What happened to your family?" Micah asked him.

"Our family," Alderic corrected him with a smile. "They did what most do. They grew old, created families of their own, and died."

"Weren't they Fae?" Micah remembered Lucy saying the lifespan of the Fae was much longer than mortals.

"Yes and no," Alderic said vaguely. "Unfortunately, there isn't time to talk about that just yet. Shall we save that story for another day? I'd like to share more about our family with you."

There was no arguing that—they were running out of time. He nodded and sighed, looking at the warriors as Quillan prepared them.

"Good, good," Alderic said, wringing his hands. He looked around the group cautiously, his eyes darting from Fae to Fae, hesitant to speak what was on his mind.

He stood and Micah watched as he approached Quillan and the other warriors.

"Quillan, I know you are aware of the risks we take in joining this cause, and I just want to say thank you for your devotion to our people and to the fight against evil." Alderic placed his hand over his chest and bowed.

Quillan bowed in response.

Micah watched carefully, reading Alderic's body language. Nervous smiles. Fidgety hands. Shaky breath.

Something bad is coming, he realized.

His heart fell.

He followed Alderic. "You said they are here to fight.

All of them? The soldiers from The Elderwood—from Porvanai—will be there to guide us?"

Quillan gave a resolute nod, and brought his spear down beside him with a great, agreeable thump.

"Actually," Alderic began, his voice trailing off.

No.

Micah knew what that meant. He knew this was the face of someone preparing to declare devastating news. He'd seen it before in his dad's eyes when he was told his mom had died.

"To break the curse, we must cut off all connection to the portal," Alderic said finally, as though he had to rush to say it before he lost his nerve.

"Cut it off, how?" Quillan asked, his usual emotionless face full of worry.

"Cut it *down*, to be frank," he said with a sad chuckle.

Quillan took a step back, but Micah only inched closer. He needed to hear it, he needed to hear the words.

"You're telling me," Micah said on a hushed breath, "that the only way to end the curse is to close off the portal? Forever?"

He couldn't even fathom it. This beautiful realm that he had just been introduced to? The family he found there? The *answers* he found there?

"Yes," Alderic said softly.

"If we close the portal, what would that mean for each of its inhabitants?" Quillan asked, trying to understand.

"The gods would be safe within Thrinuin, but I am not sure how Lucy's magic would return when her life comes full circle... As for the rest of the villagers," Alderic said, looking at Quillan. "They would be safe within the realm as they've always been. We will continue to live and to thrive."

"But we would never see you again," Micah said flatly.

"No, you would not." Alderic said sadly.

Lucy would never be able to use the wood again, either. Would their family business still thrive? Would everything Corvus built be gone forever? Everything Lucy fought for, all for nothing?

It can't be all for nothing...

"Wait," Micah said, sensing more about the issue at hand. "How would the warriors return after they've helped us?"

"That is the bigger problem." Alderic's eyes glanced to Quillan with devastation, and then to Micah with apology. "If you break this curse, you will be able to go to Denora and fight against this immoral Fae... but then we cannot accompany you. Anyone who leaves could never return home."

The words came like a punch to the gut; the wind knocked out of Micah at the realization.

"So either I fight... or you fight?" Micah asked sullenly.

"That is how it seems," Quillan replied. His mouth opened as he said more, but Micah heard nothing.

The blood rushing through his ears drowned out everything else around him.

Either I'm trapped here or they're trapped there.

"I need... I need time to think," Micah replied, leaving

the Fae in the center of the yard as he walked deeper into the tree line.

His feet pounded into the uneven terrain, following a dull path into the woods.

He couldn't believe that this was what it all came down to. If he accepted the end of the curse, Denora wouldn't have the allies it needed to take down Sloan. Lucy would be hurt over losing access to The Elderwood, but she'd understand... But would Micah's presence be enough for her? Would she even be able to look him in the eye if they lost the battle? Would there *be* an after if they lost at all?

But if he kept the curse, then he wouldn't be there with Lucy. He wouldn't be able to wield his alchemy against Sloan to help Denora gain victory. What if something happened to her and he never saw her again? Could he even live with himself for remaining at the property while the battle raged on?

Before he knew it, he was standing in front of the tree house yet again. As always, his feet brought him to a place of comfort... but nothing could comfort him now.

Why couldn't he have it all?

Why couldn't he break the curse, keep his allies, and help Lucy fight this fucking prick? Why was his life a never ending list of sacrifice?

Squeezing his hands, he realized he had never put his axe down.

This place was full of magic and secrets that he had never asked for. Grabbing the broken rungs of the tree house ladder, he climbed the gnarled tree until he was standing in the teetering tree house.

If I had to pick, I'd pick ending this curse. I could come and go as I please. I could fight alongside Lucy. I could make my own path in life...

But he knew he would never leave her defenseless.

He squeezed the axe until his knuckles turned white and heaved it up above his head and let it come crashing down on the tree house. Again and again, he swung the axe as it sliced the wood into chunks, letting the pieces rain down below him.

Boom.

Into the wall, collapsing a corner.

Boom.

Into the base, creating a man-sized hole.

Boom.

Another swing into the wall across from him.

If he couldn't chop down the fucking Elderwood tree, he'd chop this down.

He heaved his axe above his head once more, but then the entire structure began to sway. This way and that, the tree house rocked back and forth, causing Micah to lose his footing and grab for the walls to steady him. Realizing he didn't quite think this through, he jumped down from the hole he cracked open in the side of the tree house and landed on the ground.

Taking a few steps back, he watched as it shuddered once, twice, and then crashed to the ground in a heap.

Decades of memories reduced to a pile of warped scrap wood.

He leaned against the trunk of a nearby tree and knocked his head into the bark over and over.

Get a grip, Lumen.

He wanted to say that he had grown more than this over the past year—that he had learned and matured, but really, he was still the same lost little boy who missed his family.

So he did the only thing he could think of... he walked back to the house to speak to the only other Lumen left.

THE KITCHEN WAS quiet as he walked in, Alderic and Quillan waiting for him with bated breath.

He wasn't sure who would be disappointed or thrilled by his decision, but he knew not everyone would be happy.

As he opened his mouth to speak, Alderic stood up first and stopped him. "Micah, can we talk before you share your decision? I want you to hear a little more before you feel as though you are rushed into anything."

Micah took a seat. Part of him was relieved to not have to make the choice yet. However, another part of him anxiously awaited the moment when his decision was final—just so he could move on.

"Do you know anything about my magic?" Alderic asked Micah.

Micah shook his head no.

A weak smile spread over Alderic's lips, revealing the young Fae he once was. He brought his hands up before them and twirled his fingers, revealing a shimmering mist that formed a small hole. Sticking his hand through it, it disappeared.

A look of confusion crested over Micah's face as he

tried to understand what happened. A tap on his shoulder made Micah turn around in shock. Alderic's hand was floating midair, poking out from another hole in the air.

"Portal magic," Alderic explained proudly. "Each Fae has their general powers, but some Fae hold extra magic... special to them. This was always mine." He removed his hand from the hole and closed the small portal he created. "When I was young, I didn't under-stand my magic. I didn't realize that with my eager want for adventure, I was creating portals to other realms that didn't want to be found."

"You created the portal?" Micah asked in awe.

"Yes, that one among many, I'm afraid," he said apologetically. "By the time I realized what I was capable of, I'd opened dozens of portals from our realm to others. Some portals I was able to close, as they were too dangerous for our realm. However, others I loved too much to let go."

"Like The Elderwood," Micah offered.

"Yes," Alderic said. "Sanni and I went there often, enjoying the beautiful trees and the magnificent biolu-minescence at night. It was more than anyone could have ever dreamed, and I'd dream of it often." He looked down at his hands, taking a deep breath to find the words. "After I'd crafted my first bow, I was wonder-struck by its unique capabilities. When I thought of the ways we could use this new material, it was all too easy to return. How could I pass up the opportunity to strengthen Denora's defenses? How could I pass up the honor to give Denora such power?"

"What about the people there?" Micah asked.

Quillan answered this time. "We didn't let him know we could see him. He came and sat under the cover of our trees and never took more than he needed. It was why we felt the urge to trust him."

"It was Sanni's doing, really," Alderic laughed at the memory. "She was there singing and dancing as I collected the wood I needed, and she caught the eye of some of the children there. She sat in the shade, with her eyes closed, softly humming, when a small boy named Quill came up to her and asked her to sing the song again."

Quillan smiled. "We all loved Sanni." He put a hand over his heart and bowed in remembrance.

"She loved you all, too," Alderic said with a satisfied smile. "After that, Quillan's parents came to us and removed the glamor on the realm, allowing us to see the villagers. After a time, they showed us Thrinuin and made us promise to keep the realm safe from harm." His brows set in a determined line as he recalled each moment. "Sanni and I worked together to take my portal magic and place it in an amulet with her alchemy, so only those with the key could enter the portal."

"Lucy's amulet," Micah said in a whisper.

"Sanni and I kept it safe, using it sparingly, until we decided our time had come to finish our lives with our friends." He pulled a chain from around his neck where a simple gold ring hung. "When our children were well established at the small cabin, we left them, making them promise to keep the secret. Making them promise to keep the land safe." His hand clutched over his chest, his eyes furrowing with distress.

"Are you okay?" Micah asked, standing to approach him.

"I'm fine," Alderic said, waving him off. "It is just... with the realization of the curse I'd planted on my family... it breaks my heart to know I've caused anyone pain, especially the ones I love so dearly."

Micah sat back down slowly when a question came to him. "If only those with the amulet could enter, how was Lucy able to come and go freely without it?"

A twinkle came to Alderic's eye as he answered. "The gods granted her special magic. They found her worthy of the knowledge of Porvanai and granted her something unique."

"If we close the portal, everything changes," Micah said sadly.

"Yes, you're right. It does."Alderic leaned forward in the kitchen chair, making Micah really look at him. "Just remember, with the portal closed, there is no more need for a guardian."

"Yes, but with the portal closed, then that god inside of Lucy never gets to go home. Lucy's family business will be gone forever. And I..." He almost couldn't say the words. "I finally found a family who understands me... I'm not ready to let it go."

"Are you sure, son?" Alderic asked him carefully.

"I'm sure. The warriors can still go and fight against Sloan to stop him. Lucy will be protected, and I will be here when it is all over."

Quillan's eyes softened at his answer, sadness filling them.

"If that is your choice," Alderic said, pain lacing his words.

"I'd do anything to be there for Lucy, but it's not me who she needs. Besides, sometimes doing the right thing means doing the hard thing."

Alderic nodded, and the three Fae walked back outside to meet with the warriors. "Micah, can you go grab your axe for me? I want to explain the alchemy to our warriors."

With a nod, Micah jogged off to the broken down tree house, regretting his outburst now that he was left with nothing to comfort him.

At his return, a few of the warriors had walked back through the portal, leaving their numbers from closer to thirty warriors down to near a dozen.

"Are they getting the rest of the fighters?" Micah asked, handing Alderic his axe.

"Not quite," Alderic said with a resolute smile. Then, as Micah, Quillan, and the other soldiers stood in the grass, Alderic swung the axe and chopped the tree cleanly in half.

THIRTY-ONE

LUCY

Leaving was the only option.

Lucy had gone through the different possibilities for hours, but each of them ended with unacceptable results.

You made a promise, she scolded herself. *You told Micah you'd stop running.*

Squeezing her eyes shut on her bed, she tried again to see a different path out of this mess. She didn't want to run. Every time she had done so in the past, it left her with an unfavorable outcome.

But this was different... This was life or death, and as she analyzed every avenue, it always came down to her or her family. In Lucy's mind, there was no acceptable reality in which she survived and her family did not, which made her decision easier.

Her life was not more important than theirs, and she would do whatever it took to keep them safe. Alive.

The truth was, she wasn't sure if she could survive another death in her family. Her father's murder rocked her to her very core, and the idea that she would have to experience more Farewell Ceremonies due to her inaction was unimaginable.

This is the only way.

She sat in the center of her bedchambers, staring at the brick walls and trying to gather the right words to make Wes and her mother understand her choice. With the estate staff gone, Anita had been giving her chores to do throughout the house, clearly to just keep her busy. Lucy could have ignored them, but instead, she worked through them as she solidified her plan. Besides, knowing she was going to be putting her mother in even more pain once she left made her uneasy. It was best to keep her mind off of it.

Life with Sloan would be difficult, to say the least. The idea of having to join him for dinners and live under the same roof as him made her ill, but being near him would allow her to keep fighting against his tyrannical power. It would keep her family safe as she smuggled out messages to her family about his awful plans. She could bring him down from the inside and make her way back to her family.

Unless…

Unless he found a way to overpower her completely. Then he would force her to bend to his every whim.

She sighed, knowing the likelihood of a happy ending for her was slim—but there was still a chance. There was a chance she could get to Sloan, outsmart him, keep her family safe, and find her happily ever after with Micah once and for all.

Even if she failed, she had to try. Her sacrifice would

give her family more time to gather allies and prepare the king for Sloan's attack. And maybe, in the grand scheme of things, that's all that her family really needed: time.

If only they would see it the same way. It didn't matter how many times Lucy went through it—there was no way her family would let her surrender to Sloan. Instead, she would have to leave in the dead of night, when no one would expect it.

Old habits die hard, huh?

Closing her eyes, she took a deep breath in and out. She didn't want to do this, but she had no other choice. Opening her eyes and holding on to the little bit of courage she had left, she left her bedchambers and headed to the study.

Anita sat at the couch and Wes was in the wing-back chair at the desk.

"Ah, Lucy," Wes called to her. "I'm glad you're here. It's time for us to talk." The tenor of his tone told Lucy he was likely awake half the night, his voice raw and tired.

"I know what you're going to say," Lucy began, but Anita stood and held her hand up.

"We know you plan on leaving us when we least expect it," Anita told her.

Lucy froze.

"Probably in the middle of the night, and then we won't even get the chance to say goodbye," Wes replied with a sigh.

"How... What?" Lucy asked, astonished.

"Lucy. This is what you do. You aren't nearly as

unpredictable as you'd like to think," Wes replied, stone faced.

"Darling," Anita said, trying to soften the mood. "We know we cannot control you, so we would like to help make this as smooth of a transition as possible." Her eyes gleamed with tears as she spoke, apparently hating the words and hating that Lucy would be sent away with that monster. "So, please, let us take you there. We can say goodbye to you and greet your brothers in tandem, hmm?"

Lucy couldn't believe it... they were letting her leave. Part of her rejoiced, knowing she could have the closure she so desperately craved... but another part of her was suspicious of their acceptance. Maybe they believed in her ability to thwart Sloan on her own? Maybe they agreed that the betterment of the family was more important. Either way, she was getting what she wanted.

"Thank you," Lucy said vehemently. "This is what I want. Thank you for finally listening to me and accepting that I am old enough to make my own decisions."

Wes bowed his head, his steepled fingers touching his lips deep in thought. "I'm thinking we should go to him on our terms... not his. Let us have the day together, and then we will collect our brothers at dusk."

Lucy's heart raced with anticipation... Soon she would save her family.

THE DAY WENT by in a blur as Lucy kept her impending departure on the forefront of her mind. She walked in the gardens with her mother and took in the vibrant colors and scents that she would no longer have in the cold of the North. She drank amartium with Wes, dug through their father's favorite weapons, and shot them into the sky in fits of laughter.

She thought about going to visit Micah one last time, but she couldn't do it. There was no assurance she would actually follow through with what she needed to do if she fell into his arms once more. Again, she was breaking her promise to herself to never leave him. Unfortunately, keeping him safe would always be priority, whether he understood it or not.

Instead, she wrote letters to explain herself to all of those who mattered to her most in all the realms: her mother, all six of her brothers, and Micah.

She saved his for last because she had no idea how to put into words the enormity of her feelings for him. How do you tell someone they changed your destiny? How could she ever find the words to say that the stars are brighter because of his existence? That the moon has new meaning and the rustle of the leaves in the trees will always call his name? That her heart will belong to him and him alone for the rest of time?

The letter she wrote didn't carry the immensity that was her love, but it told him enough all the same.

She piled the letters neatly on her bed. They weren't goodbye letters, and she told them so. She would find a way back to her family, one way or another. Even if they were no longer in this home, even if it wasn't for centuries—she would make it back and reunite with them when the time was right.

When Sloan was no more.

"It's time," Wes told her as he buttoned a fine suit jacket.

Anita walked into the room behind him, holding a bundle of small vials.

"What is that for?" Lucy asked.

"Wes made arrangements for us to have the traveling powder for our use in case of emergencies," she explained, her beautiful dress a shimmering gray. "In case we are in need of a swift exit."

Lucy's eyebrows furrowed, but she nodded in agreement. Lord Sloan may be pleased to have Lucy in his grip once again, but it didn't mean he would make it easy for her family to leave.

Taking the vials from her mother, she placed them on the coffee table before her. With a wave of her hand, the bottles multiplied. Instead of just five, there were ten, then one hundred, then more, as the vials fell off the table.

"Lucy! What in the realms are you doing?" Anita yelped, backing away from the enormous pile of traveling powder.

Ensuring your safety, she thought to herself.

With those vials, they would always have a means of escape. Lucy wouldn't be there to whisk them away in the midst of trouble, but with the potion, they would have the power to do it themselves so she could see them again.

And that was where true freedom was found—in the power to make your own decisions about your future.

That wasn't exactly what was happening with Lucy, for it was not her choice to be imprisoned with Sloan. However, it was still her choice to save her family, and it made each moment of impending suffering worth every bit.

"This way, if you need more while I'm gone, you have it," Lucy smiled at her mother gently. Anita returned the gesture, but it barely met her eyes. Instead, a line of worry etched between her brows.

Wes checked the time and hurriedly took Lucy and Anita's hands. "Let's go. Bring us to Hugh's house, first. There's something I need to get."

With a gentle squeeze of her fingers around the family members who would stand by her side as she ensured the safety of all Baums, she took a deep breath and brought them to the South.

In a blink of an eye, they were standing in the middle of her brother Hugh's kitchen, the room dark and musty since his absence.

Wes and Anita dropped Lucy's hands and instantly began scouring the room. For what, Lucy was unsure.

Wes took off down the hall. Anita opened the kitchen cabinets, rummaging for something and cursing each time she closed a door and opened a new one.

But what was most curious of all was their clothing.

Wes was not in the fancy suit jacket he left in and her mother was undoubtedly not in a gorgeous glittering gown.

Why in the realms are they in fighting leathers?

Lucy watched as Anita wore a fitted long sleeve tunic under a leather vest with worn leather pants. Her hair was woven into an ornate bun at the top of her head and secured with pins—a far cry from her usual elegant updos with flowers and barrettes.

"Mother?" Lucy asked, forcing calm into her voice.

"Yes, dear," she replied, still searching through the cabinets.

"Why are you dressed this way?"

"It was a glamor, darling," she replied calmly, as though they were speaking of the weather. "I am looking for Hugh's fentyr-salt. Do you know where he keeps it?"

"Why are you looking for salt?" Lucy asked, her face contorted in confusion. "What is Wes doing? Why are we here and not with Sloan getting my brothers back?" The last words out of her mouth were more of a shout than a question, but she had had enough. "This is not the time for silly games!"

"You're right," Wes said breathlessly as he approached the room from the hall behind her. He stood before her in deep brown leather, clad from neck to toe. "We are not in the business of fooling around when our family is in need, and we don't intend on starting today. That is why you will not be going over to Sloan just yet, Luce."

"What?" Panic rose within her and her stomach roiled with unease. "What do you mean? I have to go there! We have to save them!"

Anita put her hands on Lucy's shoulders, calming her. "And we will." She handed her a pair of leather pants and helped her take her dress off. "But if you really think we were going to let you go so easily, then you, too, are foolish, my warrior of light."

"We have a plan," Wes announced, opening the over-sized canvas bag he dragged through the house. Thrusting his hands inside, he pulled out weapon after weapon, expertly made by the Baum Bowyers themselves.

Lucy watched as she quickly dressed herself, too confused to defy.

"Sloan expects us to fight for you, and if we tried alone, we would likely fail. But what he doesn't expect is the rest of the Fae who will fight for Denora. And that, dear sister, is a fight we will surely win."

He handed Lucy a bow with a quiver full of arrows, each engraved with what she thought was their family crest. In fact, it was the Lumen family crest all along.

Micah.

Her heart ached for the one she loved.

Was there a chance that they could win this? That there was a way to both save her brothers and be free of Sloan forever?

She looked at Wes with the most pride she had ever felt. He planned all of this? How had she missed it?

"There is a benefit to being light on your feet," he winked at her. "But now we must hurry. It is about to start."

"What is about to start?" Lucy asked, but no sooner did the words leave her mouth as she heard it.

An explosion rocked the ground beneath her feet.

Wes smiled grimly.

"War."

RUNNING through the streets of the South reminded her of her last visit. However, instead of the females and children penned in magical cages, they were freed. Instead of the uncertainty and confusion of what she saw clouding her judgement, her mind was clear. And instead of the fires blazing from the homes of the innocent, Lord Sloan's fleet of wagons was burning to a crisp.

Wes had explained as they made their way across town they had allies placed around the South, ready to fight against Sloan. A few were insurgents in Sloan's military forces, and others were from Denora's military, sent by Duke Renfro himself.

Lucy couldn't believe that he convinced the most arrogant Fae in all of Denora to side with him, but then again, Sloan was threatening to take that spot, and clearly Renfro couldn't let that happen. What would his poor ego do?

Her mind reeled at her new situation. She wasn't about to surrender herself to Sloan. She would not let her brothers die at his hands.

They were going to fight, and for the first time in days, she felt like they really had a chance.

THIRTY-TWO

WES

Adrenaline vibrated through Wes's body as he watched the battle unfold. Nearly everything was going according to plan.

To his right, Denoran soldiers provided by Renfro were actively fighting Sloan's. A loud clang of metal rang through his ears as swords met and great blasting lights of magical defenses lit the dusky landscape. The roar of battle cries sounded through the South, and he watched on from afar as he sent his petition for success to the stars peeking their way through the clouds above.

To his left, his mother stood at the forest line, digging deep into her remarkable power over nature. She looked like a completely different person in her leather pants and vest. In fact, Wes wasn't sure he had ever seen his mother in pants before. Within the length of a breath, she changed into her raven form and flew into the forest, leaving Wes and Lucy with the rest of the battle.

"Where did she go?" Lucy asked, shouting over the ever present sound of clashing. She tightened her quiver closer to her body as she gripped her bow in her other hand, strumming her fingers down the bow—a nervous habit Wes had watched Lucy do for years.

"She has her own plans," Wes said, not sure where his mother went. He knew it was important, and he trusted her implicitly—there was no time to question it.

However, Lucy was one he did *not* trust.

Turning, he held her tight in his arms and bent down to look her directly in the eye. "I need you to make a vow to me, Lucella."

The color in her face drained.

Vows were made between two Fae only in the most desperate of situations. They were looked down upon by the elders for their violent consequences. Once a vow was made, it could not be undone. Ever. If a vow was broken, the Fae would not just die, but terrible torment would spread over both Fae and their families.

"You must not give yourself willingly to Sloan. This is bigger than you and me; bigger than our family. We are all here to fight for the livelihood of Denora—for the future of all our realm. Do you understand that?"

He looked into her eyes, urging her to see the truth; begging for her to comply and promise she would not make any dumb moves while the battle unfolded.

She opened her mouth to speak, but Wes cut her off again.

"If I believe that you are out there trying to sacrifice yourself for our brothers, I will not be focused on the battle before me. Mother will always be looking over her shoulder for you. I will be scanning the crowds, praying you are still with us. We cannot afford to lose our footing in the fear that you aren't keeping your word."

The words were harsh, but Wes did not have the time to tiptoe around it. He knew this conversation was pertinent, and he also knew that if he had tried to have it earlier, Lucy would have just left. She would have transported herself right to Sloan's feet, knowing her family was safe at home.

But they weren't safe now, and they needed her to fight.

Battle magic raged behind them as the fight crept closer and closer to their position. Renfro's soldiers were formidable, and with their support, they would surely take Sloan down.

Lucy glared at her brother, her eyes turning a bright green. He recognized it as the steadfast sign that her magic was ready to pounce.

Wes smiled, knowing he had her then. Shoving his hand in front of him, he spoke the solemn words he had never dared to speak before.

"With this vow, I am tied to you. Under the guidance of the stars and the blood of the gods, I will keep this promise, or face the wrath of the unknown."

Lucy shoved her hand in his and repeated the words. Then she added, "I will not sacrifice myself for my family."

A pang of worry shot right through Wes, but before he could amend a single word, she ripped her hand from his and they were met with a flash of white light, sealing the vow between them.

"You better not sacrifice yourself at all, Lucella," Wes growled at her, pointing his finger in her direction.

Lucy just smirked as the green glow of her eyes grew. With a soft jump, she was floating midair, her hair raging in a wind that circled only her. "Don't worry brother," her ethereal voice sounded. "I have no intention of letting Sloan win today."

He watched as she joined in the fray, shooting arrow after arrow into Sloan's soldiers. They never saw her coming and each of her victims dropped to the ground with a thud. With each kill, she summoned her arrows back to her, allowing for a never-ending supply.

Wes would have laughed at her brilliance, but he had other tasks that required his attention. Even after the soldiers began their attack on her from high in the sky, he knew Lucy was more than capable of taking care of herself.

Summoning his lightness, Wes sprinted to Town Square. With his invisibility magic pressed tightly around him, he remained undetected as he took stock of their progress.

The soldiers were deep in the thrall of battle. Very few green uniformed bodies of Denora covered the ground. However, it seemed as though more and more navy blue soldiers of the North were finding their way to the battlefield. But how?

Renfro had said his spies gave him the numbers, and he built this team accordingly. He even brought extra soldiers to make the slaughter more prominent—how were they so outnumbered?

Where are you? Wes thought to himself, scanning the crowd for Sloan.

There was no way he was actively fighting, not with this many of his soldiers doing the work for him... but he had to be close by to give his commands.

Wes bypassed the small tents used by the soldiers. Sloan was calling himself *King*—there was no way he would encamp with anyone below him. No. His ego had inflated an impressive amount, which meant that wherever he was, it must be fit for a king.

And indeed it was.

At the very back of Town Square, Wes saw it at once. The old meeting place for government affairs was transformed into a castle of ice, the frozen crystals glistening in the light.

Renfro didn't mention this, he cursed. *Sloan must have warded this with his alchemy so enemy spy masters didn't pick it up from above.*

A delicate flicker of candlelight in a window was enough proof that someone remained inside the building, and Wes would bet any amount of riches that it was Sloan, biding his time until he struck.

Just then, a raven came and landed beside him. With a rustle of its feathers, it transformed back into Anita, her eyes wide with the chaos of violence surrounding them.

In that moment, Wes was thankful that Anita was the only one who could see him when he was using his father's gifted magic.

"I'm sorry I've been gone so long. I tried to send the word out to as many as I could." Her voice was raspy and her eyes were wild as she took in the clash of swords and the screams of injury as Fae battled Fae.

"Who did you tell?" Wes asked her quietly, trying to think of any who he had missed. He lifted some of the magic, allowing himself to be seen.

"You'll see if they accept the call," she said with a fierce look of determination in her eyes.

That would have to do for Wes, because they could use all the help they could get.

"I will go to the forest line and begin my line of offense," she said.

"Don't block every path in," Wes reminded her. "We are still counting on the warriors from The Elderwood..." His voice trailed off, concern filling him. They should have already been there.

Anita nodded and took off in her bird form as Wes turned back to face the castle of ice.

He still had a few tricks left, so he rushed to get in place before more of his surprises arrived.

CHAPTER

THIRTY-THREE

MICAH

"What did you do?" Micah asked Alderic, breathless.

His mind spun with the repercussions of Alderic's action... The Elderwood portal—it was gone.

It happened in what felt like slow motion, but Micah couldn't stop him. Alderic took the axe and the light for the portal lit up as though he was going to step through it—but Alderic didn't enter the portal. Instead, he swung the axe with all of his might and chopped the tree down, using his magic to ease it down as it fell.

"I did what I should have done centuries ago, Micah." Alderic's eyes were wide, looking at Micah with such love and sorrow. "No one should be held prisoner to the past."

"But I wasn't a prisoner," Micah begged, dropping to his knees on the hard, uneven ground next to the tree. "I chose this. I chose to stay." His voice wobbled on every word. The guilt threatened to consume him. "You..." His eyes darted to the warriors standing by, Quillan in the lead. "You're stranded here. You can never make it home again."

Quillan's gaze remained stoic as he replied. "We are here to serve the Guardian."

"How am I a guardian if I have nothing to guard?" Micah spat the words. "This isn't right." He shook his head, looking over to Alderic, panic and dread filling his every thought. "Fix it, fix it now."

With a forced smile, he shook his head. "I cannot. But what I can do is offer you a chance to live your life once again. A chance to *really* live."

Alderic lifted the axe to hand it back to Micah, and as he did it, he stumbled. Micah reached out to steady him.

"What's wrong?" The alarm in Micah's mind was blaring. The portal was closed. There was no way for Alderic, Quillan, or the other warriors to make it home again. There was no wood for Lucy to use in her family business. There was no way her magic would ever rest in Thrinuin again. He felt his world spinning.

"I am very old," Alderic said with a weak laugh. "Porvanai gave me a way to live without aging, and that will have stopped now that I have left."

Horror struck Micah. "So, you're going to die?"

"Eventually, yes," Alderic said with a soft smile. "But not until you return victorious. Not until we have the time you need to find peace with your life as a Lumen."

The words were a gentle embrace on his heart, knowing he could have both of the things he wanted above all else... A connection to his family, with both Alderic and his father, now that he was able to leave.

And Lucy.

He could have Lucy. He could leave this place and be there for her.

"I don't know what to say," Micah said to him, realizing the sacrifice Alderic made on his behalf. Then he looked at the warriors, knowing they would have no way to return to their loved ones. "I don't know what to say to any of you." His words turned to a whisper.

"There is nothing to say, Guardian." Quillan stepped forward as he spoke. "You are still our Guardian, fighting for the life of those who matter. Fighting for the innocent in the face of evil. Our allegiance to you knows no bounds; no realm can stop us from following you."

Micah's heart lifted in hope and Alderic smiled at him, all knowing.

"It started with your amulet," Micah said in hushed tones.

"Then with your alchemy," Alderic said proudly.

Micah looked at the Fae before him, and for once, he counted himself as one of them. He was a Fae with powers that could make a difference in the fight against evil.

A red ball of magic grew in his hands and determination set in his brow. Feeling the immense power coursing through him, he gripped his axe tight in his fist.

"Now, let's follow our allegiance to all Fae and take this motherfucker down."

THIRTY-FOUR

LUCY

The surge of magic running through Lucy was overwhelming. Her ability to strike her opponent directly in their heart from high in the sky only added to the adrenaline guiding her.

From her view, she could see the devastating battle raging on below her. Fires spread from the soldiers' tent village, the smoke creating a billowing haze that amplified the blinding light of battle magic. The slaughter of Fae life made her ill, knowing Sloan was at fault for all of this death. She tried to push more of her magic into taking down her enemy, but there were too many, and they were too widespread.

Lucy called to her Original magic and sent commands of all kinds.

"Stop," she called, but only a few of the soldiers closest to her were affected.

"Freeze," she demanded, but those who submitted to her power thawed quickly in the pressure of battle.

"Cease," she stated, hoping some would drop dead of their own accord.

Alas, nothing worked.

Nevertheless, Lucy pressed on, knowing moving forward was the only way to end this. And yet, the worst part of it all was not the exhausting fighting, nor was it the dread that seized her each time she thought about losing any more of her family. The worst part was that Lucy realized it was still the calm before the storm.

She hated to say it, but Sloan was brilliant. The decision to take over and become king had not been made in the midst of a cup of ale on some arbitrary night. No, he had been playing this long game for centuries. It made sense to her now that she saw his tactics up close.

He first made others fear him, murdering hundreds in the name of loyalty to Denora. For that, he earned the title '*Lord Slain*'.

Next, he added mystery to his repertoire. He lived alone in the castle with limited waitstaff and allowed himself to become nothing more than fable and myth, letting the people of Denora twist their own tales about him.

Then he worked carefully, slowly biding his time. He watched people... He took hold of what the Fae really wanted and needed in Denora, and he made them promises. Promises of more wealth and better opportunities for jobs. He promised them better quality food and support for the poor. He promised them a better Denora, and by doing so, he created loyal supporters who would follow him to the ends of time.

Until, finally, he tied it all with a beautiful bow, and

showed them his true colors. He was not in the South to make the realm better. He was there for total domination, and his followers, so blinded by his lies, would never turn their backs on him.

That was why they were down there, right then, fighting for his charming words and insincere promises.

Lucy watched as the battle grew more violent. More Fae, from both sides, were left broken and bloodied on the ash covered ground. As each moment passed, more and more of Sloan's soldiers made their way through the crowd, meeting the Denoran soldiers in a clash of brute force.

Where are they coming from? Lucy asked, searching the ground from the sky for an answer.

She scanned high and low, looking for something that felt amiss. Further into town, Lucy saw the Fae male prisoners, still in their magical cages, unable to escape and fight with the rest of Denora. Biting her lip, she continued to survey the land, pondering how she would free those innocent Fae.

At the edge of the square, the soldiers erected a small tent village for their lodgings. Lucy would not have thought anything more of it, but something caught her eye. It wasn't more than a small shimmer at the corner of a tent, but with the dreariness of the battleground, it was unmistakably out of place. Taking a closer look, she knew she was right.

A ward.

Sloan's alchemy powered his magic to unprecedented levels, even holding the ability to subdue Lucy. However, she was still housing the incredible powers of an Original. Using that form of her magic drained her if she used too much, but there was no better time to use it than while fighting for the lives of the innocent.

Holding her hand out toward the shimmering space, she sent her magic to release the spell. "Reveal yourself," she announced. Emerald magic soared like a shooting star through the sky and landed directly on the canvas. With a crackle, the air around it vibrated, breaking apart the charm. Piece by piece, like a distorted puzzle, the ward dissolved before her.

Lucy's lips curved into a well-deserved smile, knowing that not all of Sloan's tricks would be impregnable. But as she watched it disappear, she could barely breathe.

Once the facade had worn away, she saw that there weren't tents at the edge of Town Square as she first thought.

It was all an illusion.

Instead stood four multi-level structures, large enough to hold hundreds of Fae.

Her heart plummeted through her body as she watched the Fae soldiers in Sloan's command pour from the building. An officer stood at each of the enormous structure entrances, dispatching waves of soldiers to fight.

Quickly sending her magic to investigate, she found only one structure had been emptied, and another had just begun to join in the battle. But that meant Sloan still had two more buildings full of rested soldiers in reserve to dispense at any given moment.

He outnumbers us ten to one, Lucy realized, devastation filling her entire being.

She forced herself to breathe, squeezing the bow in her hands and tightening her quiver closer to her body.

Even with the immensity of her realization, she had no time to dwell over it, for just then, the trees in the forest began to shake, creating a creaking rumble that spread through the clamor of battle. First, it was just a minor quake, but then the colossal trees in the forest were swaying as though they were nothing but grass in the wind.

Lucy searched through the chaos for her mother, praying she would find her in time to protect her.

Flashes of her father's last moments came to her. Corvus falling to the ground, his body still and his eyes lifeless.

She refused to let her mother incur that same fate.

Close to the edge of the forest, Lucy found Anita forming vines that lashed out to enemy soldiers. The vines twirled and snapped in the air like tentacles with a mind of their own. Anita stood strong, her feet planted firmly on the ground as her arms twisted and directed them, grasping the leg of one Fae Northerner and flinging him into the dirt at top speed. Fae after Fae, Anita battled as fiercely as the military trained soldiers, defending her realm and her family.

Lucy would have watched on in admiration if it weren't for the wavering trees that traveled closer and closer to Anita's position.

In a single breath, Lucy appeared at her mother's side, yelling for her attention. "Something is coming!"

Throwing her hands high into the air, Lucy summoned a protection ward around them just as whatever was making its way through the forest appeared through the tree line.

First, hundreds of birds came soaring through—eagles, hawks, ravens, even little sparrows. Then, deer and elk rammed their antlers through the brush and right into the gut of an oncoming Northern soldier. Lucy and Anita stood close to one another as the birds dove away from her barrier at the last minute.

"I know," Anita replied over the rumble of stampeding animals, a smile blooming over her face. She looked at Lucy with a wicked gleam in her eye. "I invited them."

"You *what?*" Lucy said, her head jerking back to look at her mother in bewilderment.

"I told the woodland creatures that we needed help before Sloan destroyed all the good Fae left in the realm." Anita stayed focused on the animals pouring out from the trees, a curl to her lips showing her delight. "They said they'd discuss it and get back to me. Looks like they've come to their senses." She nodded to herself in approval, her hair still perfect in its sleek bun.

"And how are a bunch of sparrows going to help us?" Lucy asked in disbelief. She considered asking her how she could communicate with them, but decided against it. They had much bigger things to overcome and that could wait until after.

Because there *would* be an after.

"Don't underestimate the little ones," Anita told her disapprovingly, tightening the leather vest around her waist and then moving to tighten Lucy's around her shoulders. "When cast together, they create a mighty force to be reckoned with. Look!" Anita pointed to a small flock of birds just as they all attacked a singular Fae soldier, pecking at his eyes and shredding his skin.

"I never expected such violence from a tweeting song bird," Lucy said with a shudder.

Anita turned and looked back into the forest line as though she was anticipating something—or someone.

"What are you looking for?"

She sighed. "I asked more to come, but I guess some of them had no intention of helping us."

"What other creatures did you speak with?" Lucy asked, taking stock of the animals before her and coming up blank.

Then, a low growl sounded from behind her, making the hair on the back of her neck stand on end.

She spun in a flurry and raised her bow and arrow to the enormous wolven before her, pushing her mother behind her. One by one, an entire pack slowly made their way out of the dark forest, their glowing eyes locked on Lucy and her bow.

This was not Lucy's first interaction with the wolven, though it was the first time she had strong enough magic that she no longer feared for her life. They probably smelled the blood of the battle and made their way over to feast on whatever was left.

Lucy drew her arrow back, targeting the alpha that stood front and center. They would not hurt her or her mother today. Lucy took a deep breath to release the arrow, but Anita put her hand on her arm to stop her.

"No, Lucy! They are here to help!" Anita's smile reached from ear to ear.

"Excuse me?" Lucy said to her mother, thinking she must have heard her wrong.

"Thank you for coming," Anita said, speaking to the wolven instead, slipping out from behind Lucy with her hands clasped in gentle greeting. She took a few steps forward and the wolven stayed where they were, their hackles raised in warning. "The Fae in blue, with a mountain or snowflake on their shoulder," she continued, pointing to her shoulder as she spoke. She cleared her throat. "Ahem... eat *them.*"

The alpha barked a response, then led the pack of thirty wolven onto the battlefield. It was almost laughable seeing the mature wolven, which stood as tall as a grown Fae, grip the soldiers in their maws and shake them like rag dolls. One by one, they took out Fae enemy soldiers, and our Denoran army backed away slowly to allow them room.

"It's working," Lucy proclaimed in hushed amazement. Her eyes were wide in shock, seeing the Denoran soldiers steal the advantage once again.

That was until a fresh wave of soldiers came charging through the battlefield straight for the wolven. But this time, it wasn't just any soldiers...

The tusked Kerroz guards from the North.

Lucy remembered seeing them guard Sloan's castle, but she never thought they'd choose to fight in a battle that had nothing to do with their realm... Unless Sloan promised them more?

They came running at top speed, shifting into their

forms in their stride. Their bodies grew to double (and some triple) their size. Short, dark fur covered their bodies as they ran on four legs, like an enormous bull. Their two jagged tusks jutted out from their mouths as they grew two incredibly sharp horns atop their heads. They were designed for destruction, and that was what they brought.

Colliding with the wolven, they thrust their horns and tusks into the wolven's soft flesh, wounding them. Over and over, the creatures fought, racing toward the other's death.

"It's as though each time we get a handle on this, Sloan has something else up his damned sleeve!" Lucy fumed, her nails biting into her palms. "I need to get back into the air to help," she told her mother, looking into her beautiful eyes and praying she would see her again. "Be careful." Her heart ached to swoop her into her arms and deliver her back to the Baum estate where she would be safe, but she knew what it felt to be caged, and she would never do that to someone else.

"I will. I've got my friends here to protect me. You go."

Lucy turned back to the battle, her magic spinning around her, eager to get back into the chaos. And into the chaos she went, doing her best to keep her vow to her brother and help end this war.

THE BATTLE RAGED ON, Fae on both sides falling at the hands of the other. The death and disorder throughout the South was more than enough to make anyone retch. The blood and viscera that covered the ground made her question more than once if it was Fae or animal.

It was likely both.

There has to be a way to stop them.

Picking up fallen swords, she blasted them into her enemies at top speed, refusing to slow. She found being in the air allowed her better sight for battle, but her magic was dimmed by the sheer numbers. Even with her magic, Sloan sent out wave after wave of soldiers, having seemingly endless numbers. Her magic had been working relentlessly, trying to do enough to stop Sloan and his army, but there were just too many and they were just too strong.

We need more Fae to stand and fight, she realized, her stomach dropping.

But who?

There was no one left.

Lucy screamed as she shoved another sword into the gut of a Northern soldier, the gurgle of blood coming from his lips making her insides putrefy at the death of more and more of her kind. She'd do anything to preserve Fae life, but her enemy called for violence, and violence is what it would get in return.

Another low rumble came from the forest, further north than before. This noise differed from the utter pandemonium that followed the woodland creatures.

No. This was like a whisper on the wind mixed with the promise of peril.

Lucy tried using her magic to stretch her sight into the far off trees, but she was spent. She could do nearly anything as an Original, but she couldn't do everything all at once.

Grunting in frustration, she pushed herself into the sky. Zooming toward the forest, she shot arrows at her adversaries down below. Arrows came shooting back at her, but she dodged them and returned fire, soaring higher, knowing it wasn't making enough of a difference.

I can sit here and aim arrows at these soldiers all damn day, but it will never be enough. There are too many of them!

When she got high enough, she threw a protection charm around her and searched the battleground for a way to win. Left and right, she squinted into the distance. The sun had set in the wake of their war and the dust and smoke made the air hazy and thick.

With another rumble, she kept her eyes on the tree line. An obscure fog covered them, but it was too far away from the battle to be smoke. It was a thick, dark mist coming from the forest. It shaded the greenery and twirled around the tree limbs as though it had a life of its own.

Like a rolling wave, more and more of it poured out of the forest, shrouded in magic.

Lucy's chest tightened in recognition. Before she could even take one moment to second guess herself, the mist shifted into a pack of shadow beasts.

At the center of them all, she saw the one thing that lit up her entire soul.

Micah, riding on the back of a shadow beast shifter, his axe raised high as he roared for the end of Sloan.

THIRTY-FIVE

MICAH

There were soldiers everywhere.

Micah wasn't sure what he had expected, but this amount of bloodshed wasn't something someone could just conjure in their mind.

Hundreds of bodies were strewn across the endless battlefield, and the clamor of war rang loudly in his ears. Swords clashed with swords, battle magic bursting from both sides. Through the hazy smoke, he saw the bodies of enormous beasts tearing each other into mangled, bloody messes.

"Get ready," Micah told Quillan as they rode into battle. Micah tried to oppose riding on the warrior's back, even in his shifted feline form, but Quillan just rolled his eyes and insisted it was the fastest way to get to where they were going, so he complied.

As they got to the first line of soldiers, Micah jumped off of the shifter's back and began slicing his axe through the air, cutting down the soldiers in blue.

Quillan and his group of shadow warriors fought in

their shifted beast form, using their shadows to their advantage. Before they left, Alderic gave each of them weapons adorned with jewels imbued with alchemy to enhance their strength and endurance. Once they shifted back to their Fae bodies, they would be well prepared with weapons at hand.

At least, as prepared as war allowed.

Micah swung his axe, striking down Fae after Fae. With each fallen soldier, his resolve hardened. Death was a terrible and heavy burden to cast upon anyone, but Sloan had given them no other option.

It's for the betterment of the realms, he told himself with every kill.

And he was right, because it wasn't just the realms of Denora and Joterra they had to fight for. They also had to fight for The Elderwood, and Vytyr, and every other innocent realm who would fall during Sloan's self-righteous crusade.

Micah saw firsthand how alchemy could be wielded to hurt others when mixed with magic, and he wasn't going to stand around and let innocent Fae—and mortals, for that matter—suffer by Sloan's hand. Not if he had anything to do about it.

Wiping his bloodied axe on the lifeless body on the ground beside him, he tightened his grip just as a heavy longsword came rushing down. Micah thrust his axe high to block it, kicking his attacker to the ground with a thud. One after another, the enemy pushed on, and Micah met them swing for swing with his axe.

He sent a silent thank you to Brax for her relentless initiative to prepare him. Though he wasn't sure if it would be enough. Each time he took down one Fae, another popped up. When the Northern soldiers caught wind of his skill, they surrounded him.

Micah's eyes raged wildly as he glanced between the enemy circling him, searching for a weak point so he could escape. There was none.

With two Fae behind him and four in front, the best he could do was to attempt a roll to the side to take out the left soldier's legs. Micah took a deep breath in, preparing himself for the inevitable hurt as they each lifted their swords. With a roar, Micah brandished his axe and hung on tight. He bent his knees, ready for their onslaught, and then suddenly, they all froze around him.

Literally.

A thin sheet of ice encased each soldier, rendering them unable to move, their faces contorted and wild.

"Micah?" He heard the faint question from the lips of the one person he yearned for above all others.

He turned, facing Lucy with a breathless stare. It was as if the battle around them had ceased, because there was nothing else in existence that could have pulled him from her irresistible gaze. Micah's heart bottomed out at the sight of her. He had been so worried she would be hurt or weakened, but she looked perfect. Utterly perfect. Not a single scratch on her.

With a sigh of relief, he swung his axe to knock off the head of the two Fae behind him, dropped his hand to his side, and wrapped his arm around her waist, pulling her in close to his body. Then, he kissed her, *really* kissed her, with the passion only a liberated man could feel.

Because, after all this time, he was finally free.

Free of the confines of the Lumen property.

Free of his burden of grief that tainted his view on life.

Free to finally be the man he chose to be; creating a life on his terms, and no one else's.

His body was enraptured, his focus on her lips and her skin and her smell as the rage of battle continued on all around them. Micah was lost to Lucy, mind, body, and soul, and there was nothing stopping the free fall of relief he felt as he held her in his hands.

Lucy grasped his face with one hand, pulling away slightly to get a better look at him. Her other hand still clutched her bow tightly as she spoke, her body tense with worry. "How are you here?"

"Alderic lifted the curse," Micah told her breathlessly.

He barely had time to register the flaming arrow, heading straight for them. He shot his hand out above them, but he knew his reaction was too late. However, instead of striking them, the arrow stopped midair, a ward encompassing them and protecting them.

His eyebrows shot up, and he looked at her in question. "Was that you?"

"I couldn't kiss you while we were unguarded, could I?" Lucy replied like it was the most obvious thing in the world.

I love her so much.

There was so much on his mind, but that was the loudest thought of all. After all of this, he could finally be with her.

She looked at him carefully. "The curse is really

gone?" Her words were a whispered plea over the clash of battle outside of their little bubble.

Micah lifted one side of his lips in a half-smile. As grateful as he was, there was still so much heaviness weighing on him.

"Yeah, but it's a long story. One I'd be happy to share when we win this." There was no room for *if*.

Lucy nodded and opened her mouth to speak as a barrage of arrows came crashing into their dome, sending a flicker of light over her freckles.

Green light shone from her eyes and an angry sneer spread across her face. "Hold that thought," Lucy told him. Then she dropped the protection spell and crafted a giant gust of wind to knock the surrounding Fae to the ground.

Micah's hair blew back with the onslaught as Lucy rose into the air, her green magic twisting and twirling around her menacingly.

"I should warn you," she called out to the Fae around them. "I don't take kindly to people trying to hurt those I love." She rotated in slow circles as she lifted into the air, her hair dancing around her. "And if you want to aim your fire-tipped arrows at us, well... I *love* to play with fire."

Micah looked on in awe as Lucy put her hand out before her and squeezed, summoning all the fire from the Fae's arrows. One by one, their flames went out, speeding directly into Lucy's palm. Controlling the fire, she let it roll over her fingers with a satisfied smirk.

The soldiers looked at her in horror.

Micah couldn't help but grin like an idiot in love. His

badass warrior was about to rain down an inferno and they had no idea what was coming.

"Micah," she called, her ethereal voice floating over the chaos. "I will find you when I'm done here." Then she glanced at him and gave him a wink, her confidence making him want her even more.

He shook his head with a smile and ran off in the other direction, finding his Elderwood companions and joining in the throes of battle.

EACH SWING of his axe came with more and more effort, not because he was physically tired, but because mentally he could not imagine how the fight would ever end. He was bloodied and bruised, and every Fae on the battlefield looked the same. But, the Denoran military were obviously struggling more.

Micah had personally eliminated dozens of the enemy, his axe successfully cutting them down one by one, but he seemed to be the only one. The soldiers who fought by his side couldn't kill a single Northerner without teaming up, as if they were weak—which Micah knew was not the case. They were military trained Fae; the best Denora had to offer.

Maybe I just have an edge because my magic is newer, he thought to himself. *Or maybe because I hadn't been out here this whole time.*

Either way, the disparity between sides threw him. There had to be a way to win this. Sloan hadn't even made his fucking appearance yet—and whatever line of defense he had waiting in his make-shift castle was sure to be worse than all of this fucking bullshit put together.

His mind drifted to Lucy as he fought, knowing he was fighting for something important—something worthy. Here and there he would get a glimpse of her magic or hear her battle cry as she unleashed her fury on her enemies, and each time it sent a wave of pride through his chest.

If anyone could take on Sloan, it was her.

With a whimper and a growl, a massive wolf tried to limp away from a cluster of attackers.

"Hey!" Micah cried, swinging his axe in their direction to give the wolf a chance to escape. A group of three Fae shifters turned to face him, their bodies that of a man, but their faces had tusks, like a boar.

Micah gulped.

"Why don't you leave the pup alone and fight me instead?" Micah sneered as he swung his axe in his hands, sticky blood coating his fingers. Three to one wasn't ideal, but if it gave that wolf a chance to live, then it was worth it.

Luckily, his Denoran counterparts came to help, brandishing their swords with a grit Micah admired. Even with the oppressive strength of the Northern soldiers, his brothers in green never stopped pushing forward. They would do anything for their realm, and Micah was proud to fight alongside them.

With a swing of his axe, he cut the chest of one shifter, leaving a trail of blood in his wake. The Denoran soldiers swung their swords at the other tusked Fae, but nothing happened. It was as though their weapons barely made contact. Again and again, they swung and hit the shifters, but the effect was minimal, as though their blades were dull.

The distraction got the best of Micah, letting one shifter get close enough to him to slice his arm before Micah lunged away. Another powerful swing of his axe and Micah sliced the shifter's head clean off, the sickening thump more satisfying than he initially imagined.

Down to two opponents, the soldiers took one and Micah took the other. Swiping left and right, Micah met the strength of the shifter's sword hit for hit, until finally, his axe slid across his enemy's soft underbelly, gutting him and relieving him of his entrails. Micah leaned on his hands on his knees to catch his breath, but that didn't last for long.

Somehow, the other shifter was still taking on three of the Denoran soldiers.

What the fuck? How do they call themselves soldiers if they can't win a battle of one against three?

Coming up from behind, Micah lodged his axe into the back of his unsuspecting enemy. He dropped to his knees with a thud. Micah gripped his axe with two hands and put one foot on the back of the shifter as he kicked the body away, dislodging the axe.

"How were you able to penetrate him so easily?" One soldier asked Micah, barely able to catch his breath.

"The better question is, how are you guys still standing at all after pretty much having no fucking effect on these guys? Do you need better swords or something?" Micah looked at them incredulously.

"We are the head of our unit," the other soldier

replied, "and that's why we are still alive." His voice was rough from battle. "These swords should slice through them like warm butter," he said, then demonstrated by taking the blade to his own hand, leaving a thin, precise cut. "There is nothing wrong with us—there is something wrong with *them*."

Micah searched the battlefield and took in exactly what the soldiers suggested. The Denoran Fae were blocking every hit they could manage, but never getting enough of a blow to take down a Northern soldier in return. It would take two or three men to just take down one, and by the way they were outnumbered, that was just not a feasible battle strategy.

So what made them different?

He picked up a sword from the tusked shifter he had slain and held it in his hand. The weight felt like a typical sword. He cut the back of the shifter's bare arm, watching as it dragged across his skin. It was a little dull, if he was being honest.

Then he rolled the brute over, getting on his knees to try to sense if there was some sort of spell making them impossible to harm. He placed his axe down and ran his hands over the shifter's jacket. Immediately, a tremendous force repelled against him, pushing him away. It was as if he could barely make contact with him at all.

"What?" Micah murmured, putting as much force as he could to touch the shifter.

"That's the same thing that happened to us," the soldier replied. "But when you fought them, you could touch them before. What's changed?"

Micah looked at the shifter, taking in his uniform.

How could he dismantle a spell he couldn't find? Was it something in his uniform? What changed?

He picked up his axe to lean on as he stood, and all at once, the repulsion stopped.

Pausing, he looked back down at the shifter and had an idea.

"Give me your sword," he told them.

One soldier handed it to him, and Micah raised it curiously in his hands. Dropping his axe, he swung the sword at the shifter.

Nothing.

Then, picking his axe up once more, he held it in one hand and wielded the sword in the other. Swinging the sword into the enemy one last time, the blade plunged into the shifter with a brutal squelch.

"The alchemy," he whispered. Sloan had somehow made his soldiers nearly indestructible with alchemical magic.

Searching the dead soldier on the ground, he found a trail of sapphires sewn into the shirt, acting as more than just decoration.

Plucking each one off with as much speed as he could muster, he explained it to the soldiers.

"Sloan is using alchemy with his magic. It is a sort of power imbued within a stone to change the form of magic." He worked quickly, popping each stone off and collecting them in his hands. "It's why you can't breach their uniforms—it isn't your weapons, it's their defense."

"Alchemy? I've never heard of such a thing!" A soldier retorted, scoffing at the idea of a new, strange kind of magic.

"You don't need to have heard of it for it to be true," Micah said with an annoyed huff. "Listen, I've got an idea, but I need one of you to be the guinea pig."

"You want us to be a pig?" The other soldier replied with disgust.

"No," Micah said with a sigh, forgetting some phrases didn't translate to Fae. "I need one of you to be willing to try it out first. We need to see if I'm right."

"And how would you know about this, anyway?"

Micah ignored the man as he held the gems in his hand and his axe in the other. With a focused determination, he called on his power to transform the gems into a slightly different kind of alchemy. He wanted the gems to hold courage and honor, something Sloan knew nothing about.

When he felt the magic transform, the sapphires no longer looked blue. They were purple.

"How did you do that?"

Micah again ignored them, but this time he gave one of them a gem. "Swallow it."

"Excuse me?" The soldiers stood and stared at Micah with wide eyes.

"You need the gem to be touching you at all times, but you can't risk dropping it in the middle of a scuffle. It won't work to put in a pocket or a shoe, so just swallow it already."

"What if you're wrong about this?"

"Then you shit out a gem if you survive the battle."

The beady eyes of the soldier reminded him of Jasper, but really, it was just the look of fear. Maybe that's what Jasper felt all that time—fear. Sure would explain a lot.

However, this soldier was nothing like Jasper, because he would do anything for the good of his realm, so he swallowed it in one forced gulp.

Micah threw him his sword, then directed him to the nearest opponent. "Now go take him down."

The soldier took a deep breath, clearly exhausted and not looking forward to the endless fight. With a curt nod, he strode over to his next opponent, refusing to let fear stop him.

Micah had to give it to them, this Denoran military was fierce. They could be on their very last breath, and they'd still swing their sword for the honor of Denora. And that's exactly what this soldier did.

Raising the sword with all of his might, he swung the blade and immediately decapitated the enemy soldier.

The other soldier gave a victorious shout, shoving his hands in the air. Then he marched toward Micah. "Give me one of those!"

Micah gave him one, then held the rest of the handful out for him to take. "Get as many of your soldiers as possible to swallow them. I'll make a couple more handfuls to try to even out this battle."

With a firm nod, the soldier ran off and Micah hurried to the other dead Northerners, optimism surging through him.

This was it. Micah couldn't believe it. This could change the tide of war. And to imagine, what if he never made it there? What if he stayed back instead?

He shuddered, not willing to consider the possibility of losing. Because losing this battle would mean losing Lucy.

Turning another Northern soldier over, the tusked shifter gasped and coughed out blood.

He wasn't dead.

Micah lurched back on his heels, clutching his axe in his hands.

"Sloan will decimate all of you," the shifter laughed, blood spurting from the sides of his mouth, trickling down his tusks. "Just wait for what he has in store for you."

Micah didn't want to hear another word. Instead, he stood, used his axe to cut off the front of the shifter's uniform jacket in order to collect the gems, and left him.

After collecting the final gemstones, he hoped he had enough for them to gain an advantage on the battlefield.

But the enemy must have realized, because as Micah passed out the final gems to the soldiers, Sloan appeared.

He walked out of his enormous castle with a crown so large it gleamed across the brutalized south. Two enormous beasts lurked behind him; creatures with feline bodies, but paws the size of polar bears. These massive cat-like creatures pawed their way from behind Sloan, trailing him wearing ornate collars.

Collars adorned with more gemstones.

More alchemy.

Shit.

At that moment, Lucy raced to meet Micah, both of them staring wide-eyed at the monster who was to blame for all of this—all the death and devastation.

Micah told her about the alchemical gemstones on the soldiers' uniforms, how he was able to give them a fighting chance. "I'm not sure it will be enough, but at least it gives them their edge back."

"We've lost so many on our side," Lucy said, bitter sadness in her voice. They looked around and saw the truth of it. Sloan's force outnumbered them to a terrifying amount.

"We need more," Micah said in agreement.

Then, at that moment, a roar filled the sky.

Not just a roar, but a terrifying screech of rage.

"What the fuck is that?" Micah asked Lucy, but from the pallor of her face, he knew she had no idea.

Lightning filled the sky, and a low rumble of thunder echoed through the airspace.

"Lightning?" Micah asked. "A storm's coming?"

"No," Lucy said, her voice hushed as the rest of the battlefield fell still, the silence jarring. "Look... that isn't lightning... It's fire."

"Fire in the sky?" Micah looked again, his eyes searching for what Lucy saw. "Then what was that thunder?"

The rumble sounded again, *whoosh, whoosh, whoosh,* like a ticking metronome, the rhythm keeping time.

Whoosh, whoosh, whoosh.

"That's not thunder," Lucy said, her eyes looking to him in complete fear.

Micah didn't know what to expect, but if it scared Lucy, then he knew it couldn't have been good. His eyes scanned for Sloan, trying to get a clue as to what they were in for, but he only ever got the back of his head as Sloan stood in front of a tent speaking to his advisors.

His eyes darted to the sky once more and a blast of fire filled the horizon.

Fae shrieked as they ducked, covering their bodies in protective charms. Some of the Northern Fae ran for cover, but Micah wouldn't move. He stood his ground, waiting to see what their next battle would be.

And then someone screamed.

"DRAGON!"

Breaching the flames, an enormous green dragon soared through the sky, roaring and blowing fire as a threat to all those below. Its scaled body the size of a semi-truck—its wingspan twice that. A glow lit up the column of the dragon's neck as another roar tumbled from its throat and the sky filled with more dragon fire.

Lucy pulled on Micah's arm in alarm, trying to get him to turn and run, but Micah held her off. "Wait." He looked around at all the Northern soldiers running for cover. His eyes flew back to Sloan, who was finally in clear view.

A smile curled over Micah's face as he looked at the unflappable Sloan, looking like he was about to piss himself.

"These dragons aren't here to support Sloan. They're here for us," Micah told Lucy, pointing to Sloan's look of utter terror.

Turning his head back to the sky, he watched as a horde of dragons entered the atmosphere above them and blasted their fire.

"You never told me you called in the dragons!" Micah hollered in celebration to Lucy.

"That's because I didn't!" Lucy replied, laughter in her voice.

When he looked over at her, she was smiling. Then she looked at Micah and pointed up to the sky.

There, riding on top of the dragon like she owned the damn thing, was Brax.

THIRTY-SIX

WES

Hiding behind an overly decorative display case of ancient weaponry was not how Wes anticipated he'd spend his time during a war, but there he was. He had been there for hours as the battle raged on, but it certainly gave him a better view of the inner workings of Sloan.

In fact, Wes started questioning Sloan's mental stability.

Sure, Sloan was of unsound mind if he truly thought he was going to kill numerous Fae and take over as king of Denora… but to have such an ornate castle made of ice in the humid south? And to have taken the time to decorate a make-shift hide out in the middle of war? It appeared he was teetering a line of diabolical genius and complete nutty insanity.

Regardless, Wes kept himself hidden as he dug for more information that could help them win. So far he had found out that Sloan had used illusion charms to distract us from their actual numbers, he had acquired an entire battalion of shifters from Kerroz, and had adorned each uniform with alchemical power.

That last one was the current topic of discussion, because Sloan was absolutely furious.

"What do you mean the stones aren't working?" Sloan had hissed at one of his military officers.

"Sir, one of the Fae fighting with the Baums figured it out and has been pulling them off the uniforms of our dead."

"What? Who is it?" The depth of his voice turned more sinister with each passing question.

"A tall Fae I've never seen before. He arrived with the shadow beasts."

Sloan's eye twitched and Wes wished he could have been present for when Sloan learned of their arrival. "The King" had been hiding in here for the entire battle so far.

I wonder if he will ever leave this ice hideout.

"I believe it is the lost Lumen, sir," his personal guard, Roger, told him.

"Lumen." The snarl from Sloan was vicious, but the pride in Wes's heart was cosmic.

Sloan roared as he stood, knocking over an ice sculpture of himself. Roger stood quietly, not even blinking at the outburst.

Damn, I wanted to knock that over myself.

Sloan shoved his hands in his hair, knocking off his ridiculous crown, and began ripping out the pale strands.

"My Lord!" One of his officers said to him, trying to stop his hysterics.

"I am your KING!" He bellowed, the maniacal rage breaking through his falsely calm demeanor.

Ah, yes. The real Sloan.

Sloan raised his hand to strike his officer when the entire castle shuddered. He lowered his hand slowly, looking at the icy roof of his castle.

"We need to get to the battle tent and discuss next steps," Sloan announced, his voice an eerie calm. He straightened his jacket, then his hair, and took the crown from Roger without another word.

Sloan had rushed out of his castle for the very first time with the murmur of their next fated plans. That's what Sloan kept calling them, "fated plans," as though the stars had anything to do with it. As though his evil was justified.

Wes would have killed him the fifth time he said the infuriating words, but the two great calynx that he had guarding him made things exceedingly more difficult. Thanks to his father's magic, the felines may not have been able to see him, nor could they hear him, but every once in a while their noses twitched with curiosity at the lingering scent they couldn't identify. He was thankful they followed Sloan, leaving Wes alone.

Without the calynx roaming around the make-shift castle, it made Wes's plans much more accommodating. He sped through the building, searching up and down for his brothers. In each cold, empty room lay nothing but darkness. There was no life in the castle at all; the grandeur was all for show. Sloan was alone with only his trusted lackey, Roger.

In no time at all, Wes finished his task and caught up

to Sloan, following him across the blood-ridden terrain. Keeping his father's magic close around him, he slunk into the battle tent. Sloan's body stood rigid as he met with the lead commander of his military. Wes stayed far enough away from the calynx so that he wouldn't get in their way, yet close enough to hear each and every word.

"Sir," the lead commander spoke, greeting him. "Our numbers are dwindling."

The majority of Sloan's soldiers were on the front lines now, and with Lumen's brilliant discovery of how to counter his alchemy, it seemed the Northern soldiers were finally going down.

"We still have the might of an exceptional militaristic force at our hands," Sloan waved him off. "How many more units do we have in our barracks?"

"All units in structures one through three have been dispatched. Structure four is on standby."

"Good. Prepare them." Sloan's words bit out at the commander, then he went to stand at the front of the tent, watching the battle unfold.

Following him out, Wes stood off to the side, down-wind of the calynx, but still keeping his eye on the beasts.

From his position, Wes could see Lucy and Micah find each other on the battlefield and a wave of relief surged through him. It wouldn't last long, but at least they were together, and as they stared daggers into Sloan, Wes knew they wouldn't be giving up anytime soon. He searched for his mother, not seeing her through the chaos.

Still, Wes smiled as he watched Sloan masquerade as

a male of calm and dignity and not as an immature Fae who just had a temper tantrum and ripped at his hair.

Then a low rumble filled the air, and a flash of light lit across the sky. Each Fae inside and outside the tent looked around in bewilderment—even the Fae in the middle of battle paused as another round of thunder made its way across the sky.

A scream sounded in the distance and Wes followed the noise, looking into the sky at what finally made its way through... a massive horde of dragons.

His stomach dropped at the sight of such amazing creatures, but when he saw the magnificent warrior perched upon on the front dragon's shoulders, a fire lit within him.

Brax. That remarkable, breathtaking female. If I make it out of here alive... but he stopped the thought.

The outcome of his task was all that mattered. Sloan must be stopped and his family must be safe. Whatever happened beyond that didn't matter anymore.

"Are those... dragons?" the commander asked.

"Of course they're dragons," he spat. "What else could they be?"

The commander bent low, touching the floor in a low, trembling bow. "What are the plans to take the dragons down, my king?"

Wes knew Sloan had no fucking clue, and that knowledge delighted him.

"Send in the units," Sloan ordered in a rough, low voice.

"How many would you like, Sir?"

"All of them."

"But—"

The commander didn't have the chance to finish his sentence, for Sloan turned and berated him, which gave Wes the time to slink away once again. Wes had learned enough about his plans to know that they were on the right track. Besides, his favorite surprise was about to happen and he needed a nice view to enjoy the show.

He sprinted across the battlefield, thankful for the slight pause between fighting so he could make it to Lucy and Micah in time.

Finding them was easy. They were, like everyone else, staring up in the sky, watching the dragons in awe.

"Are you ready for my big reveal?" Wes whispered in Lucy's ear, making her jump.

"Where did you come from? Where have you been?" Lucy asked him, torn between anger and relief.

"Where's Mother?" Wes asked, anxiously searching for her across the crowd.

A raven landed beside him and shifted, revealing Anita. "I'm here," she said with an exhausted grin. She grabbed his arm in reassurance, calming him as much as she could.

"Did you do it?" Wes asked eagerly.

"I did," she said, nodding, tears in her eyes. "I found them."

"My brothers?" Lucy asked breathlessly, pain lacing each word. "Where are they?"

"They are on the other end of this madness," Anita said with a relieved smile. "Sloan knew we would be focused on his castle and battlefront, so he has them staged blocks from here in a small hut with just a few soldiers, but they are quite formidable."

"You didn't fight them, did you?"

"I couldn't," Anita said, with the first hint of sadness. "The shifters would have been easy to take down, but I couldn't get past whatever alchemy magic Sloan had cast upon the hut."

"Okay, that means they are safe in the meantime." Wes said, nodding his head, the next steps of his plans coming together quickly.

"Wes," Micah said to him, clasping him on the shoulder. "It's great to see you, and while I don't want to take away from the moment, you said you had a big reveal. Did you call in the dragons?"

"Absolutely," he said with a devilish grin.

"Did you set it up for her?" Anita asked, anticipation clear on her face. Their mother was ready to bring down this monster as much as the rest of them.

"What are you two talking about?" Lucy asked, getting frustrated. "I know you've been doing all of this sneaky nonsense so that I wouldn't find out and try to stop you, but I'm here now, so just tell me what in the realms you two have planned."

Anita and Wes smiled at each other—two partners in this chaotic masterpiece.

"Let's just say that fentyr-salt is used for more than just cooking, my dear," Anita told her.

"Just keep your eyes on the castle and I'll tell you in a minute." He looked up to see Brax and the other Vytyrian warriors riding the massive dragons as they got into place. Once they were in formation, Wes shot up a spark of his magic, signaling her to begin.

On his cue, Brax led the warriors and their dragons to the castle made of ice and blasted it with fire. The soldiers on the battlefield broke out into cheers, whooping and clapping each other on the shoulder as they watched the dragons attack the castle.

Wes walked behind Anita and held his hands over her ears as his grin stretched across his face. "Here it comes."

An enormous blast erupted through the castle, then another and another as the bombs he had planted triggered. They watched as the crystal ice palace went from an enormous solid structure to shards of ice in a matter of moments.

They knew the empty castle would not end the war, but it was a figurehead for everything they fought against. Besides, seeing Sloan so pissed off was just the cherry on top.

"That was amazing!" Lucy shouted, cheering with the rest of the crowd.

The wind above them whooshed all around as a dragon's enormous wings beat right above their heads, landing on the ground so close to them that Wes could smell the smoke from the dragon's mouth.

He took a step back.

Brax ran over to them and Micah pulled her into a great hug, swinging her around like a little girl. "That was so fucking badass!" He yelled, a smile stretched across his face.

Trying to fight him off, Brax did her best not to smile,

but they all saw it in her eyes. She was happy, and she didn't really hate the attention from Micah. "Put me down, you roasted marshmallow."

"You know, that is the first food insult I've understood," Micah said with a laugh, planting a big slobbery kiss on her cheek as he placed her down.

She wiped it off with a sneer but greeted the others with an easy smile. Micah and Lucy just laughed as they fell into an easy embrace, watching the Fae cheering.

"So, this is what you'd rather do instead of freeing the rest of the males of the South?"

Everyone there turned to see Ruthani clad in oversized fighting leathers and holding a longsword.

"How did you get here?" Anita asked in astonishment.

"You left an entire arsenal of that traveling powder out in the open. What did you think we were going to do? Just sit around and twiddle our thumbs while we wait for your return? *If* you ever returned at all?" Ruthani spit out the words as though she was furious at them for leaving her, but the truth was just beyond that.

She was one of them. Ruthani, just like Wes, Lucy, Anita, and Micah, had been hurt by Sloan and craved revenge.

And she would get it.

"We?" Anita asked, looking behind Ruthani.

With a wave of her hand, Ruthani lifted her illusion. There behind her stood every female that was freed by Brax. "We left the children at home—war is not meant for the innocent."

"Where did you get all of this?" Wes asked, referring to the leathers and weapons.

"We went back to our homes to prepare," Ruthani said, her chin lifting in challenge. "We are going to free our families and then fight by your side."

Brax stepped forward and took Ruthani's hand in solidarity. "I would be honored to have you at my side."

Lucy took Ruthani's other hand resolutely.

Then Anita took Lucy's.

Brax lifted her lips in a devious grin and held out her hand to Anita, closing the loop.

The four females stood in a circle, embraced in a fierce determination and looking ardently into each other's eyes. Wes looked between the females curiously. They had so much in common—such ferocity behind their femininity.

"People really *do* need to stop underestimating women," Micah said to Wes quietly.

But the moment was cut short, because Sloan's furious voice echoed across the desolated battlefield.

"Will you sit by as these traitors work to hurt your king?!" He amplified his words with his magic. Northern soldiers roused as they listened to him speak. "I call upon the last of our line of defense." He roared, and the calynx roared in return. "End this today, and rejoice as we walk into a new era of Denora!"

A rumble sounded from the last structure, and soldiers began pouring out.

"Brax! Get the dragons there, now!" Wes called. "Ruthani, get to the males and free them. Anyone able to fight, send here. Anyone who needs medical attention, bring them to the estate. Mother, go with them."

Micah rushed over to give Ruthani a handful of alchemical gems to use. Then handed some to Anita, Wes, and Lucy. He gave the rest of them to Brax for her Vytyrians.

Brax ran to her dragon and jumped with such grace and speed that she was up in the air in seconds.

"Micah, I need you to fight with our soldiers. Can you do that?"

A swift nod, a fervent kiss to Lucy, and Micah was off to fight.

"Wes," Anita said quickly, trying to get a word in. "I have an idea. Let me stay."

"Mother, you have the choice to do whatever you desire," he said, looking at her curiously. "I am not in charge of you."

"No, but you are the head of this family, and I look to you."

"No. *You* are the head of this family, and we would be lost without you," Wes said, the words coming out so fast he didn't even have to think if they were true or not. Of course Anita was the head of the family—there was no other option. It didn't matter to him that she was female, she was strong and just and held the wisdom to guide them all. He shot her a half grin. "Now go do whatever diabolical plan you have in mind, and find me when you are done."

With a brightness in her eyes, she transformed and took off as a raven in the night, headed straight for Sloan.

Be careful, Mother, he pleaded.

Ruthani was off in the next moment, headed to the prisoners that were taken in the first battle that started this war.

All of this was for them.

"I'm going to Sloan," Lucy told Wes, her eyes shining a deep emerald green, her sneer trembling as her jaw clenched.

"Get lost in your magic," Wes told her, repeating the words their mother had told her.

"No," she said thoughtfully. "It is in my magic that I am found."

THIRTY-SEVEN

LUCY

I am found in my magic, Lucy had told him. She had never realized the truth within that. For so long she had let the magic ravage through her, being a vessel for another, long forgotten god. She failed to stop and allow the magic to be who she *is* as much as it was what she *had*.

She closed her eyes and took a deep breath, allowing the magic to flood into every part of her body; in every blood cell, every muscle fiber, every strand of her hair. Her magic filled her until she couldn't take any more, as though it would overflow from her very being. But the reality was, she could. She could summon more and more of her magic, and continue to fill herself with the immense well of power because the magic was not something separate from her.

It *was* her.

In that moment of acceptance, her magic burst from her, creating a display of power so extraordinary it knocked over the surrounding Fae.

She rose in the air, a calmness taking over for the first time since they had arrived. Scanning the chaos below, she searched for Sloan. This war could not continue without a king, and since he was finally out of hiding, it was time to take him down.

Before she could spot him, the dragons made it to the barracks. Fire rained down, trapping the soldiers inside in an enormous ball of flames. Shrieks of desperation sounded from the tower, but there was no more remorse for those who sided with Sloan. Not anymore.

The dragons worked together with fire and claw to bring the structure down to a smoldering rubble, then they turned and joined the carnage; the battle forging on.

With a satisfied grin, Lucy turned her eyes back to the swarm of bodies, searching for Sloan. Her magic did the searching for her, taking charge of soaring through the South, showing her everything in her mind. What was left of the castle was off to the right, the barracks burning to the left, and the battle tent where she saw Sloan when the dragons came lay in the middle. The only person there was a worried officer, his gaze darting left and right amidst the melee.

Her magic scanned the rest of the South. She saw as Ruthani freed the males kept captive, the female's magic overpowering Sloan's soldiers in record time.

The calynx, she thought. *Those should be easier to spot.*

Her search shot to the other side of the battle to find Sloan riding on top of one of the felines with a bow and quiver strapped to his body. However, he was not alone, for Roger and another three guards held a trio of male prisoners.

Tristan, Hugh, and Gregory.

They each had blindfolds over their eyes and gags in their mouths, their hands tied behind their backs with some magical charm.

Lucy blinked the sight away and instantly transported herself before them, refusing to waste any more time. Her magic pulsed through her body, ready to unleash utter terror on this monster, but she needed her brothers out of danger, so she contained it best she could.

The calynx snarled and came to a halt at her unexpected arrival.

Sloan's eyes widened, but only for a second. "You will let me go free or I will kill them," he roared, his words heavy with his demand. However, Lucy caught he way it wobbled at the end of his request—he was scared. With Roger at his side, he jumped down from the calynx and strode over to her, looking ruffled.

His hair was wild and the ridiculous crown sat askew atop his head. The ornate jacket he wore was ripped at the shoulder and hung off his frame.

Sloan's running, she realized with delight.

"You will let them go free or I will kill *you*," Lucy replied, the magic in her body knowing that was a promise she would die keeping.

Sloan began to laugh hysterically, the deranged smile contorting his face. "You think you can still stop me?" He took a step toward her, shucking off his jacket. "I don't need those jewels to know I can take you down. You know, I thought I loved you once," he said, the words quiet, as though he was lost deep in thought. "But I was wrong about you. Seems I was wrong about your magic as well." He got close to her and lifted his hand as though he was going to stroke her face with the gentle back of his fingers.

Her magic sent off a warning to back the fuck off and the blast knocked him back a step.

Sloan only laughed more.

Lucy looked at Roger in disbelief. "And you stand for this? You stand by his side after everything he's done?"

She wanted him to say he was wrong for following him. Lucy wanted to hear that he just got too deep into things and couldn't find a way out. Anything would have been better than what he said next.

"His only mistake was thinking he needed your family involved in his affairs." A darkness swept through Roger's features at the declaration.

Lucy sent a blast of magic straight for Roger at the same moment the three guards fell to the ground in a heap. She whipped her gaze to the side and saw why.

Wes!

He stood behind the guards with a bloodied knife in his hand. Wes used it to get the blindfolds off of his captured brothers, then he yelled for them to run.

"NO!" Sloan bellowed.

Lucy quickly created a shield and sent it over her brothers as Sloan's magic came raining down on them. She fell to her knees at the weight of his power, doing everything she could to keep her brothers safe.

Sloan screamed with rage as Roger remained unconscious on the floor next to him. Ripping a ring from his finger, he crushed it in his palm, amplifying his power over her.

Crying out, Lucy held on. She had to hold on. She would not let her brothers get hurt. She could never let Sloan take away someone she loved from her ever again.

But even as much as she wished for that to happen, his magic was just too strong. Her shields crumpled under the might of Sloan's alchemy and a blast of magic sent Lucy to the ground.

Her eyes darted to her brothers as she watched them run as fast as they possibly could, even in their weakened states. Gregory and Hugh were nearly to her, Tristan behind him with Wes pulling him along.

Lucy bit back a sob as she watched Tristan, broken and bloodied, run as swiftly as he could.

But it wasn't fast enough.

"Arrow!" Gregory choked out.

Lucy's gaze darted to Sloan, and she saw him release the arrow right for Tristan. Sloan threw his hand in the air, guiding it along with his alchemy. Lucy tried to stop it, but her magic was repelled once more.

The whizzing arrow flew straight for Tristan, and there was nothing anyone could do to stop it.

It shot through the sky and hit with a sickening thud.

Directly into Wes's back.

"No!" Lucy screamed, and her magic completely lost control. Her shadows poured out as grief overtook her like a ship lost at sea. She screamed as lightning shot from her body and flames burst from the palms of her hands.

She watched as Tristan fell to the ground and

crawled back to Wes, sobbing and clinging to him, begging him to rise.

Hugh and Gregory were speaking to Lucy, but none of their words were heard. A barrage of guilt weighed heavily on her, she felt as though she was being crushed.

It was her fault another member of her family died.

It was her fault they would be in mourning.

It was her fault she accepted the vow not to sacrifice herself.

But Wes was the one to pay.

She screamed. She roared. She wailed for her family that was being ripped apart by this bastard of a Fae who cared for no one and nothing.

Then, a woodsy smell of musk and linen curled around her and a warm arm embraced her midsection, pulling her back to reality.

"Shhh, sweetheart," Micah's voice was calm, steadying her. "Come back to me."

Her shadows receded and her flames burned out as she slumped back into his chest, his arm the only thing keeping her upright.

All the while, Sloan was laughing. However, with her billowing shadows, he didn't see the other Fae that had come along with Micah.

"I've been speaking to your pets," Anita said sweetly in her entrance. "They are not very pleased with their recent treatment from you. In fact, they said they are starving and you've been withholding food?" She was sitting on top of an actual calynx as though she was made for it.

The words were sweet and kind coming out of Anita's

mouth, but Lucy knew she was setting him up for destruction. She had perfected playing pretend in front of male Fae her entire life.

"Attack!" Sloan screamed at the calynx, desperation coloring his voice. "Attack!"

"Oh, dear. They no longer respond to your commands, I'm afraid." She pet the other calynx as it came padding next to her. "You see... they've had a change of heart." Anita said, the ruthlessness coming out at last.

Bursts of magic tore from Lucy's hands, striking Sloan one after another. She wouldn't let anyone else get hurt. She would end this now.

He shielded with a clear ward and glared at her through furrowed eyebrows, the sneer on his face only making Lucy push harder.

With another blast of magic, she spoke to him in between her onslaught of power. "Why are you hiding, Laurent?"

Lucy sent a blast of magic into his shield.

"Are you finally showing everyone who you really are?"

Another blast.

"A worthless..."

Blast!

"Spineless..."

Blast!

"Weak, piece of shit."

This time she braced for his return attack, and she was ready for it.

He burst from his shield and pushed his two hands

out in front of him, adorned with jewels and gems from the crown on his head and the rings on his fingers. She took stock of it all as she blocked his attack, knowing exactly what she'd be targeting next.

"You will not defeat me! I am more powerful than you! Than anyone!" Sloan shouted, the words only more of his carefully sculpted lies.

"No, Laurent," Lucy replied, sending a pulse of magic, freezing him in place. She walked up to him, her heart thundering in her chest. "You're a dick on a power trip," she smiled, taking every ring off his hands. "But that ends today."

Reaching for his crown, his magic burst through hers, throwing her backwards. He scrambled to his feet and shoved more magic at her. His alchemy being the one thing that Lucy couldn't overcome.

As Hugh, Gregory, Anita and Micah tried to come to her aid, Sloan sent more of his magic, sending them all to their knees.

"We need to get to Wes," Hugh said over the roar of magic.

They all looked at their fallen brother in desperation. He was not moving, but Tristan was still there by his side, whispering to him.

Pushing his magic into Lucy, Sloan forced her to bend as well. "You don't understand, *beloved*," he spit the word like it was poison on his tongue. "This is how this battle ends. With me on top, and you beneath me."

"I will never serve you," she rasped between clenched teeth, trying her best to stand.

He forced more magic into her, making her knees

buckle. "You will kneel to me!" Then, Sloan lifted a thick sword from its sheath, and held it up, more alchemical jewels glistening in the fire of battle.

The magic in her body surged, begging to be released, but Sloan's hold on her left her powerless. Even knowing she was going to fall at the end of his sword, she refused to look away. Lucy would look directly into the eyes of her enemy and seek revenge from the void beyond. She would die with strength in her heart and no fear in her eyes. Sloan would not take that from her.

With a scowl he pulled the sword back and paused in surprise, his eyes going wide as he looked past Lucy to the forest line beyond.

A puff of hot air blew past Lucy's neck as she watched the self-proclaimed King Laurent Sloan quite literally tremble in his boots.

"I'm going to walk over to Wesley Baum," Brax said as she walked toward them. "And if you so much as make a single fucking move to one of my friends, this dragon is going to turn you to dust. Do you understand?"

Brax walked past Lucy and her family, still forced to their knees by Sloan's magic, and sprinted directly to Wes, pulling him close to her and sending her healing magic into his body.

Lucy almost sobbed in relief… but even if Wes was healed, it wouldn't stop Sloan. She wasn't sure if Sloan's powers could rival dragon fire, but it was a challenge she'd be happy to take.

"Come on now, Laurent." Lucy forced her eyes to his. "I thought you said you were the most powerful of them all," she goaded him.

She assumed one of two things would happen. Either Laurent Sloan would move to kill her as she sacrificed herself in order to give Brax the time she needed to heal Wes, or this dragon was going to fry his ass. Even if the vow she had made promised Wes she wouldn't sacrifice herself for her family, he didn't take one thing into account... Sacrificing herself for her realm was more important than anything else, and with Wes's leadership, her people could stand a fighting chance. And Sloan could never have Micah.

Wes had to live, so she would risk her death.

Sloan's eyes lit with fury and he made a move toward her at the same moment the dragon kept his promise and took a deep inhale above Lucy, blowing a jet of dragon fire directly at Sloan's head.

Sloan dropped his magic on Lucy as he shielded himself from the fire. Amazingly, the fire bounced off of his shield and Sloan exclaimed in celebration as he was safe from the bite of the flames. And while he may not have been burnt to a crisp, at least Lucy and her family were free from his power.

She tried to see Brax and Wes through the blaze, but the only thing she could do was duck down and stay out of the angry dragon's way.

Long moments passed, and her panic rose within her.

Please, please let Wes be alright.

The fiery blaze ended, and Sloan stood, a deranged smile filling his face. "I am stronger than a dragon!" He took a few steps closer to them, then paused.

Brax stood on her right, and to her left, a warm hand landed on her shoulder.

Lucy held her breath.

"There are eight of us, two calynx, and a dragon. You're really sure you're going to get away this time?" Wes's voice was rough, as though the pain still lingered.

Lucy choked down a sob of relief.

Sloan kneeled from his place on the ground and howled with laughter.

While Sloan was distracted, Micah used his magic to grip the crown from his head and smash it into the ground. Using as much force as he could, Micah crushed the metal into a heap.

"You think *wrinkling* my gems will make them not work for me?" Sloan's mirthless laugh grew.

The sound of it put Lucy on edge.

They had missed something. What did they miss?

She shifted in place, studying him, watching for the tell.

Wes moved to Micah's side and pushed his light magic into the crumpled mess of metal and gems that was once Sloan's crown. His magic changed from heat to pure light, as bright as the sun, as the metal melted.

Sloan's eyes widened for only a fraction of a second, but it was enough of a clue for Lucy.

He's afraid of the stones being destroyed, obviously... but there's something else.

Wes brightened his magic even more, causing Micah to shade his eyes as the gems burst into shards.

Sloan went quiet. He stared them down, a haze of orange coating his blue eyes.

That was it.

That was what Lucy was waiting for.

"It seems you and I were of the same mind, lost Lumen," Sloan voiced, the words like gravel. "You can't destroy something you can't find." His laughter started once again.

"You swallowed alchemical gems?" Micah asked, a growl in his voice.

"No," Lucy answered for him. "Look at his eyes." She pointed to Sloan's once ice-blue eyes to call attention to the hints of orange. "He fused the jewels into him somehow…"

"It's amazing what a bit of crushing can do to a gem. If you do it with just the right pressure, it can still hold magic." He tore the chain from his neck. "I do not need these weak gems on my body. The power is inside of me, and *you* cannot get to it."

Wes turned to Lucy, his eyes wide with a plan.

Her eyes burned with tears, but she held them back, knowing it wasn't time for an emotional reception, no matter how happy she was to see him standing next her, alive.

"Lucella," he said to her, his eyes glancing from her to Sloan, erratically. "Do you remember the gifts Father bestowed upon us?"

"Yes?" She could not understand why he brought that up. Undoubtedly his light was useful to melt the stones, but how could they melt stones they could not see? And how would her shadows help her?

Suddenly, he disappeared from the space before her.

"Where did he go?" Sloan asked, a rumble of anger

breaking its way through his maniacal laughter from before.

Then a whisper filled her ear. "Father gave me his light," Wes said only to her. "And he gave you his darkness."

She tried to hold as still as possible as he whispered the words, trying not to give any hint as to where Wes was.

"We may not be able to thwart him alone, but together we can."

Lucy still didn't understand. How? How would she be able to help her family?

As though Wes could sense the tension in her body and the panic in her mind, he told her one final thing. "Protect our family, all of our people, from my light with your shadows, and let us end this once and for all. Let us get lost in the magic to find ourselves on the other side."

With a deep breath, Lucy called on all of her magic. She called on her Denoran magic that filled her veins from the moment she was born. She called on the magic from the god that resided within her, making her an Original. She called on the magic from her father that filled the void in her heart. As her breaths came quicker and quicker, she continued to call to her magic. She let it fill her, let it pour over her, let it seep from the broken crevices of her soul as she knew the endless magic would be the only thing to stop Sloan and his tirade for power.

With emerald green magic swirling around her, and black shadow magic flooding the ground around them, she thrust her hands high into the air and screamed. "Now!"

With as much force as she could, she covered each and every Fae fighting for them with her magic. Every Denoran soldier. Each Elderwood shifter and Vytyrian warrior. Every bird, deer, and wolven. Ruthani and her clan of females, along with the males they had freed. The dragons. Brax. Micah. Her family.

Everyone but Wes—because as she covered them in shadow, he became the sun. His magic kindled within him, burning brighter until Lucy was forced to cover her own eyes as well.

The power pulled at her, the light from Wes challenging her dark shadows as it tried to pry them away from the bodies she was protecting. She screamed through the effort, her body feeling as though it was being ripped into shreds. More and more heat poured over her skin as Wes bellowed through the exertion.

But none of that compared to Sloan's frantic shriek for Wes to stop. The desperate cry of pain rang through the South until there was nothing but a stunned silence filling the air. The heat subsided and Lucy released her magic, unable to hold on another moment.

She fell to a heap on the ground, too weak to hold herself up, the sound of beating wings as the dragons left the only thing filling her.

"Lucy!" Micah ran to her and scooped her up, cradling her in his arms.

"Wes," she croaked at the same time Brax screamed his name.

Lucy forced her eyes to open, searching for her brother, aching to know if his plan had worked.

Wes groaned in response, and a sob of relief left her throat, knowing her brother was alive.

Micah lifted her in his powerful arms and brought her to Wes, placing her down beside him.

Wes's skin was bright red and hot to the touch.

"What happened?" Anita asked, her voice shaking.

"Lucy protected you with Father's shadows as I used his light to burn the gems from within Sloan." Wes's voice was raspy.

"He's gone," Hugh said, shaken. "Literally, there is nothing left of him but dust."

"You cooked him?" Tristan asked.

Micah stood, slowly turning in a half circle as he looked out into the battlefield beyond. "No," he breathed. "He cooked *all* of them."

Silently, the group helped Wes and Lucy to their feet as they stared into the war zone that was once the center of Southern Denora. All that was left were charred remains, blood and gore, broken and dilapidated buildings, and... their Denoran soldiers. Wounded... but alive.

"We won."

THIRTY-EIGHT

MICAH

Micah watched as Lucy held her family. The reality was Hugh, Gregory, Tristan, and even Wes, were almost killed in battle. If she had lost them, Micah wasn't sure if she could have ever recovered... He knew firsthand how difficult grief was to overcome. He lost his mom and his grandad and it changed who he was at his core.

Lucy smiled brightly at her mother as they shed silent tears of relief, but the tears stopped as they looked around the rest of the battlefield. The war may be over, but the work was far from done.

"I will speak with our soldiers," Wes told them. "Mother, why don't you go see how Ruthani and her group are doing?"

"I'd like to go with you to speak to some of the soldiers," Tristan said softly. "Some of them were my friends on that battlefield." His voice sounded far away, as though he was stuck in a difficult memory.

"And we'd like to see how our male counterparts

from the South are," Hugh said, and Gregory nodded. "We will go with Mother."

Brax turned to Micah with a half smile. There was something about the sadness in her eyes that made him pause. She must have known about the sacrifices that were made to get him here. "I will say goodbye to my Vytyrians and see the dragons off. Then I'll check in on Quillan and see how they're doing. You can find us by the forest's edge when you are ready to return."

One more nod and they were gone, leaving only Micah and Lucy alone at last.

Staring into the smoldering battle grounds, Lucy took in a deep breath, her chest rising so very slowly. Micah watched her from the corner of his eye, not knowing if she was ready to talk about it all. He shifted his weight so he was closer to her, and waited.

He wouldn't push her into talking about any of this, not after she had just watched her family almost die. Not after she had used so much of her power.

The seconds felt like hours, but then he felt it. The tiny twirl of Lucy's smallest finger wrapped around his in a silent offering, looking for nearness without demanding it.

He extended his hand to her, and she eagerly clasped it, holding as if he might be swept away if she let go. The tremble in her body could have been from exhaustion or from the terror she faced, and Micah decided it could very well be both, so he took his other arm and wrapped it around her, curling her into him.

A soft sob left her chest as she pressed against him, and he heard her gasp and hold her breath, forcing herself to stop. Micah whispered into her ear, "You don't have to pretend with me. Let it out."

Her head tilted up, and she looked at him, her eyes rimmed with red and wet with tears. "I can't let them see me cry."

"You can," he told her. "They will not judge you for that, and if they do, then they are idiots."

"They are idiots," she sniffled. "That's the problem."

"I've never seen a problem you can't fix," he said playfully, trying to lighten the mood, but all it did was cast Lucy's face to the sky.

Her eyes brightened with the pale shade of green, and she spoke the words into existence. "Rain."

Clouds rolled in and rain fell from the sky, putting out the remaining fires and cleansing the ash and soot off the faces of those all around. Lucy and Micah washed their hands and faces off in the deluge and found each other once more.

"Very clever," Micah told her. The rain would hide her tears. "But I don't understand why you won't let anyone see you cry."

"Because if I am to be treated like an equal, then I must act like a male. Male Fae do not cry, and they definitely do not weep for the loss of an enemy." The voice cracked as she spoke.

"You're crying for Sloan?" Micah asked, his chest tense.

"Absolutely not," she scoffed. "The universe is better without him... It's the rest of his soldiers. It could have been Tristan." Her mouth shook as she tried to hold in more tears. "He didn't know he was making such an error in judgment, and I would guess that many others felt the same way. Many of them were probably tricked into this, lied to about Sloan's true intentions."

Micah's lips formed a thin line, the heaviness of those words both hurtful and true. "You probably aren't wrong."

"But our soldiers will not see that. Hugh and Gregory will not see that. Too many were killed by those same enemy soldiers. I cannot weep for them." Lucy said, her voice rising as the last words sliced through the air.

"Yeah, but Tristan might be the one who needs to see it," he told her calmly. "Because he did have friends out there. He was the one almost duped into that shit show... Acknowledging those things does not make you weak, it makes you compassionate."

Lucy didn't reply to that, but wouldn't look at Micah, either. She continued to wipe the tears from her eyes; her face hardening more and more by the second.

"Come on," Micah said, taking Lucy's hand and pulling her. "Let's get out of the rain and talk... There are a few things I need to tell you."

They spent the greater part of an hour talking about the curse and Alderic's actions. Lucy's lip wobbled when Micah told her The Elderwood was closed off forever, and her green magic that had been swirling around her since the battle began settled on her shoulder as though it understood the desolate news that it would not be returning home.

"I'm so sorry I caused your family business to end," Micah said, the words coming out painfully slow. Lucy did everything she could to make her way into her that business, and it nearly cost her everything. And now it was just gone? It was possible she'd never forgive him.

"Don't apologize for someone else's actions," Lucy told him firmly. "Besides, if I were there, I would have done the same thing."

"You would have cut off ties to the portal?" Micah asked her in disbelief.

"If it meant your freedom? Of course." Lucy tilted her head as she looked at him, as though she couldn't believe he didn't understand. "Micah, you are important. You deserve to have a choice in your future. You deserve to be able to make decisions about your path, and that curse gave you no ability to do that. Alderic gave you a gift, even if it is a very hard one to bear."

She grazed her thumb on his cheek, either wiping away more ash or consoling him. He wasn't sure, but the gesture comforted him, nonetheless.

"I've got to figure out a way to get these guys back," he told her, looking out at the shadow shifters that had fought by his side. Thankfully they all survived. Being able to move between solid form and shadow helped them to combat the enemy with ease.

Lucy nodded and stood, taking his hand and walking him over to Brax, Quillan, and the other shifters.

"Need a lift, Lumen? I can call those dragons back?" Brax told him, a teasing lilt to her words.

"Yeah, I think I'll pass. That shit was terrifying."

"Leave it to males to pale at the sight of a formidable beast," Brax said, sheer joy on her lips.

"Your Vytyrian warriors sure looked badass up

there," Micah chuckled. "Make sure you send our thanks."

Brax laughed and sat next to Quillan. "And you, Quill. Make sure you tell Alderic we thank him," Brax said as her gaze met with Micah's. "For everything."

Yeah, she knows.

"Don't call me Quill," Quillan replied dryly.

"I'll tell him," Micah told her, an unspoken conversation passed between them, one of appreciation and love for his best friend.

Then he looked at Lucy and every bit of his heart felt like it would shatter because he knew she wouldn't be coming with him, and he would be a selfish prick if he asked. She needed to be with her family, and he understood. But right now, he was responsible for The Elderwood warriors, and he needed to find a way to help them.

"It's time to go home," he said, looking at Lucy, and he wished she would go with him.

THIRTY-NINE

LUCY

The aftermath of war was utterly indescribable. Lucy couldn't get her mind to turn off the memories as she lay in her bedchambers in the Baum manor. All the dresses in her wardrobe somehow reminded her of Sloan, so she opted for a soft tunic and a pair of deep navy leggings. No matter how comfortable she tried to make herself, she couldn't stop seeing the devastation of war when she closed her eyes.

There was so much joy, having ended a tyrannical ruler, his control, his power... yet, there was such sorrow as well. Each of the soldiers had lost brethren on the front lines. Animals lay dead after sacrificing their lives for the lives of Fae. Even the pack of wolven was reduced to only a handful of survivors, but according to Anita, they were proud to have fought against evil and hoped this would bring more respect for their kind in the future.

The dragons were long gone. Brax had explained that she recruited Vytyrian warriors to the cause, then traveled to Kerroz. As soon as she told them the Fae needed help, they were happy to step in. Apparently they weren't always dragons, but actually shifters. They had kept their identities hidden, as is their tradition.

It all felt surreal. The oddest part of walking through the South was not the awestruck citizens bowing down to her. It was not the strange way the soldiers had considered her and her group, largely formed of females. It was that the only dead were from their side, and all of the enemy soldiers were obliterated—truly, dust in the wind.

It took days for the Fae to work together to remove the remnants of a violent war. The buildings were reformed, the bodies sent off to sea, and families were reunited.

Even her family was gifted that.

She squeezed her eyes shut tighter as she sat up, trying to shake the painful memories away. Lucy didn't know how to describe the way Anita cried as she held her three sons in her arms after they were released from captivity. Or the sound that escaped her throat as Wes stood before her, after being nearly killed with an arrow.

Even more difficult was the eerie silence on the battlefield after Wes finally killed Sloan.

Wrapping her mind around *that* fact was almost impossible. It was done. The war was over, the evil was defeated, and her people were safe... so why did everything still feel so uneasy?

A knock on her door pulled her from her troubled thoughts. "Come in," she called.

Tristan walked in, his hair longer than the last time

they were in Baum manor together, but the light from his eyes was still missing. "Hey Luce," he murmured.

Lucy patted the bed next to her in invitation. They sat in companionable silence, but her mind was anything but quiet. She couldn't believe he had almost been killed.

"I almost lost you," she whispered to him, tears escaping from her hazel eyes.

He took her hand in his. "From the sound of it, we almost lost you, too."

Closing her eyes, she forced deep breaths, trying to keep her emotions down.

"Why are you locked up here, Luce?" Tristan finally asked her. "Mother said she's trying not to pry, not to push you away, but I told her this is the time to barge in. She didn't want to hear it."

"And that's why you're here? Prying?" Lucy asked, the energy gone from her usual witty remarks.

"Yes." Tristan turned to face her on the bed. "And to ask what happened with you and Lumen."

"With Micah? Nothing." She turned away from him and stood up in a hurry, walking to the other side of the room. "The battle was over and it was time for all of us to return home. I came to my home, and he went to his."

Lucy's words came out more clipped than she had intended, but avoiding that part of the battle aftermath had been the hardest.

"It's time to go home," Micah had told her. Then he took his Elderwood warriors and left with them, saying he needed to see if he could figure out how to get them back to their realm.

She wasn't sure why she thought he'd come home

with her... Denora wasn't his home. And Joterra wasn't hers... so who were they kidding, really?

"Ah, so that's what it is," Tristan said, a small smile making its way over his face as he glanced at her from across the room.

"What *what* is?" Lucy snapped, turning to face him from her spot near the door.

"Why all the arguing?" Wes said, stepping into her benchambers.

"No one invited you in here," Lucy told him, frustrated by the brothers who couldn't seem to stay out of her personal life.

"Luce is upset because Micah went home and didn't invite her." Tristan's curt response made Lucy cast magic to the flower vase on the side table, knocking it into his lap and spilling water all over his trousers.

He only laughed.

"Lucy, since when do you need an invitation of any kind to do what you want?" Wes asked, a twinkle in his eye.

She crossed her arms in front of her. "What do you expect me to do? Leave my family after we are finally together again? All to chase after some male?"

Tristan stood from the bed and walked up to her. "That's all he is, huh?"

Lucy turned her face away from him, but Wes was there by her side, gently taking her chin in his hand. The look in his eye was so much like their father's and all she felt at that moment was grief.

She pushed his hand away and turned from them both.

"The threat to us is gone, Lucy," Wes said. "The boys will come back from Lord Klimek in a fortnight, and they are absolutely oblivious to the danger we faced. Hugh and Gregory are here, spending time with Mother before they must get back, and Hugh will soon be with Lisette. That beautiful baby that will be born any day now and bring even more joy to our family. Mother is fine," he said, breaking out into a chuckle. "I mean, really, did you see her out there?"

He tried to get her to respond. To laugh, to smile, anything—but Lucy refused. Because even if everyone was safe, how long would it last? How long would it be until something else tried to tear their family apart?

"Luce," Tristan said. "Look at me. I'm fine."

Her eyes shot to his, and she refused to pretend she wasn't mad. "But you weren't fine. And you didn't tell us until it was too fucking late. Until you did some bone-headed thing and left our family without a second thought."

"Well, it seems like bonehead, split-second decisions run in the family then," Tristan teased, not letting her words hurt him.

He was talking about her decision to leave Denora to go to The Elderwood on her own to prove to her family she was worthy of more than being shipped off to an arranged marriage. It truly felt like a lifetime ago, and in a way, it was. Lucy was not the same person she was when all of this started. She changed more and more with each passing day.

"Yes, we can all agree you two are the boneheads of the family," Wes said, slinging an arm around each of their necks, bringing them in close. "But can we also agree that life here needs to change?"

Lucy stilled under his words. Pulling away, she turned to him, looking into his eyes. "What do you mean?"

He smiled and jerked his head toward the door. "Come on," he said, letting them go and walking out of the room. "We've got a meeting we can't miss."

WALKING INTO THE STUDY, Lucy wasn't entirely sure what to expect. However, when she saw a formal meeting underway, she felt oddly underdressed.

Anita stood to the side silently, respectfully greeting their guests, looking as beautiful as ever in a deep violet dress.

The chairs were arranged for an official assembly, and when she saw who was in attendance, her heart thrummed wildly in her chest. King Tralont sat in the study, Duke Renfro by his side. Across from them sat... Ruthani? And to her shock, it was Brax beside her.

There was another seat in the row, and Lucy stayed back, waiting for Wes to sit, but instead, he remained standing.

"Go sit," Lucy whispered to him eagerly, not wanting to offend the King.

"The seat is yours, Lucella," her mother said. Then she walked over to her father's old desk and sat as head of the house.

Lucy's mouth went dry. Was her mother purposefully disrespecting King Tralont?

Wes simply took her hand and led her to the seat, then stood back with a wink as she stared on in awe.

What the fuck is happening?

"Miss Lucella," Duke Renfro spoke at last.

"Duke Renfro, King Tralont," she said with a bow of her head in return.

"It appears we have some business to discuss," King Tralont said, boredom in his tone as though he would rather be anywhere else. His gaze kept trailing to Anita as she sat at the large desk.

"I have informed our king of the transgressions of Lord Sloan," Duke Renfro shared. "He has been stripped of all titles and has forfeited the right to the Northern Territory."

"Well, that's good, since he's dead and can no longer claim it," Brax said sarcastically.

Lucy was all for putting people in their place, but the *king*? She almost choked on her tongue.

"Quite," was all Tralont replied.

Duke Renfro continued on. "I have also shared with King Tralont your valor during battle. Without your courage and bravery, our realm would have suffered greatly. We'd also like to thank the mortal that joined you in battle, but we did not think traveling to Joterra was the best decision at this time."

"He is not *only* mortal," Lucy said before she realized she had said it.

"Lucy is right," Wes continued. "He is Alderic Lumen's ancestor, and a great and powerful Fae."

"He is... both Fae *and* mortal?" Tralont asked, curiously. "I have never heard such a thing."

"Perhaps if you would have listened to my son the first time then you would be more privy to the happenings of your people," Anita said sharply.

Oh my stars, Lucy panicked. *The king is going to sentence all of us to death for our disrespect.*

"Perhaps you're right," he replied.

Lucy nearly fell out of her chair.

Ruthani was the only other person in the room looking as surprised as Lucy felt.

Brax sat back lazily without a care. Tristan and Wes stood with secretive smiles on their faces. And Anita sat like a queen, fearing nothing and no one.

"As I said, there is business to attend to," Tralont continued, "if we can get on with it without any more outbursts?"

Lucy just nodded her head as Anita stared on, stone faced.

"Ahem," the king went on. "To begin with, Duke Renfro will relinquish his command of the military immediately."

Lucy felt a pit in her stomach.

He is going to punish him because he helped us?

"You can't do that," Wes said, standing up for him.

The king shot him a glare that would have brought Corvus Baum to his knees. "You will let me finish speaking. I will let you know when I am in need of your input."

Wes's lips formed a tight line as he took a step back, obeying his king.

"Renfro will relinquish his command and take on the position of Lord of the Northern Territory."

Duke Renfro's jaw dropped slightly. "My King? Are you sure?"

"Why are there still people speaking?" The king complained as he looked to the ceiling, his hand on his head. "Master Wesley Baum will take over Renfro's position as the leader of our Denoran military."

It was Wes's turn to stare slack jawed at the king.

"Do either of you have objections?"

They shook their heads "no" in reply, and the king broke his first small smile.

"As for the females of the room," the king said, uncertainty in his voice. "It is unheard of for a group of females, such as yourselves, to have created such a powerful force. If I am not mistaken, it was you four at the front lines of this battle? Freeing our prisoners from the South? Using almighty power to stop Sloan? Speaking with the wolven to fight on our side. And..." he looked at each of them sitting there, Ruthani, Lucy, Anita, and then stopped on Brax. "Riding on dragons?"

"You're damn right," Brax said with a devilish grin on her face.

King Tralont broke into a hearty chuckle.

Lucy assumed this was the most Tralont showed amusement.

"Well, it seems as though we owe you our gratitude," the king said.

"You owe us more than that," Anita spoke.

Lucy wondered when her heart would stop pounding so loudly in her ears so that she could hear people speak. Because there was no way in all the realms that her mother just said what she thought she said.

"Excuse me?" Tralont replied, taken aback.

"The reason Lord Sloan had so many followers is because Denoran traditions are horridly out of date," Anita said, then she stood from her seat and stepped in front of the desk. "Sloan offered freedoms to females so that they may become equal to their male counterparts. He considered more support to the needy so that the poverty lines between us may not be so steep. He was a tyrannical maniac, but he had original ideas that we should not ignore."

Something within Lucy loosened in that moment. She had been so convinced that she was so blind to have followed Sloan for so long that she really doubted how it started. Knowing her mother also thought that his preliminary views of Denora were meaningful gave such relief to Lucy.

"How dare you share in your support of the male who tried to overthrow the crown!" Tralont stood, fully offended by Anita's response.

Lucy got up and stood next to her mother, then Brax and Ruthani followed suit. Wes and Tristan stayed back, allowing them to speak for themselves. They didn't need any males rushing in to save the day.

"We are not looking to overthrow you, King Tralont," Lucy said carefully. "We are looking for a seat at the table."

"Why? Denoran tradition has not changed for a millennia!"

"Exactly. Which means it's out of date and needs to catch up with the rest of existence," Brax snapped.

"We are not looking for more than others. We are looking for our equal share." Anita's shoulders straightened as she spoke, her regal posture making her every bit of a leader Lucy would be proud to follow.

"We want to pick our own jobs," Lucy said. "And not just in typical female positions."

"We want to pick our own partners," Ruthani shared. "No more arranged marriages."

"And we want to elect our own heads of house," Wes said, finally. "Anita Baum is the most qualified person for this position in our home, and I guarantee other houses feel the same about their female leadership."

"And you must provide to those who have less than others," Brax said, pointing to Tralont. "No more of this nonsense where the poor Fae have to suffer in silence as the rich Fae stuff their faces with gray poupon."

"What in the realms is gray poupon?" Tristan asked Wes under his breath, but all Wes could do was laugh.

Duke Renfro stood, trying to calm people to their chairs again. Once everyone sat, he spoke. "Correct me if I am wrong, but what I am hearing is that you are insistent that we improve our rights for females and that we need to provide a better quality of life for the most needy of our population?"

All four females replied at once. "Yes."

Renfro shot a small smile to each of them, then he turned back to the king. "King Tralont? These seem like reasonable requests, do they not?"

The king let out a gruff, noncommittal noise.

"I'm sure if these formidable Fae could stand against any enemy to the throne and fight for the people of Denora, then they only have the best intentions in mind, do they not?"

The king let out another gruff noise, but it seemed more like assent.

"Very well," Duke Renfro said, turning away from the king and smiling at the Fae in the room. "We will get that started and look forward to updating you on our progress."

He gave them a quiet wink, then led the king to the door, leaving the Baum estate.

Lucy stood frozen in place as the room erupted in celebration. She couldn't believe any of what just transpired had actually occurred. Did her mother really talk back to the King of Denora? Did Wes really just get the position of commander of their military?

"What's wrong, Baum?" Brax said to her, punching her shoulder to break her of her shock.

"I can't believe that just happened."

"Personally, I can't believe you're still here."

"And where should I be?"

"Lucella Baum," Anita said over the celebration. "If you don't get your behind to Micah Lumen this instant, I'm going to ask Brax to feed you to a dragon." She smiled and laughed with pure joy.

"You want me to leave?" Lucy asked, unsure how to decipher her words.

The cheering stopped and Anita walked over to her daughter. Cupping her face gently, Anita looked deeply into Lucy's eyes. "I want you to follow your heart. And there's only one place you can find it."

"But this is my home," Lucy replied, her panic growing once again.

"Home isn't a place," Brax told her, and Anita dropped her hands. "It's so much more than that. It's where you find solace after a long, hard day. It's where you feel safe when everything else feels too hard. It's where your heart resides."

Each of her brothers gave her an encouraging nod, and Ruthani just smiled.

Brax grinned at her. "Go home, Lucy."

Home.

CHAPTER

FORTY

MICAH

The warriors from The Elderwood had no interest in staying in Micah's cabin, so they worked together to cut down a few trees and build temporary homes in the center of the wooded property. They told Micah they preferred to be among the trees and valued their privacy.

Micah couldn't blame them. He made for shit company as he moped around the cabin, missing Lucy. Alderic traveled between the cabin and the camp where the warriors lived, giving Quillan and his shifters more attention. As much as he wanted to connect with Alderic, they needed Alderic more. Whereas Micah had gained more than he could have ever imagined, the warriors had only lost.

Micah wasn't sure what to do.

Should he go home and visit his dad?

Should he wait around and see if Brax was going to come back and check on him?

Would Lucy ever return?

And who was he now that he wasn't the Guardian? It had taken him so much time to finally come to terms with who he was in that role, and now it was just gone? Another path ripped away from him?

He played these same thoughts over and over in his head and never came up with an answer. His desire to see his dad surpassed all else, but he couldn't take the risk of venturing beyond the property and potentially losing the opportunity to connect with either Brax or Lucy.

So, instead, he stayed. He told himself that after a month or two, if nothing changed, he would give the cabin over to the warriors and take up his dad's offer to go live with him and Lori. They had an overly rambunctious dog named Zero, but otherwise, they were good people. People who loved him. Although he couldn't say they really knew him anymore.

He had been pacing around his bedroom in the cabin, unwilling to go back downstairs and face reality. He was tired of looking out the window and not seeing the visitors he craved. He was tired of looking at his phone and knowing he should pick it up and fucking call his dad. He was tired of laying in bed, staring at the ceiling doing jack shit.

It felt insane to go from fighting in a full-blown war to coming home to peace and quiet. It was too damn jarring.

His gaze caught on a glinting red jewel in the corner of his room. He cringed when he saw the axe that saved dozens unceremoniously shoved away.

A weapon that special shouldn't be mixed in with my

dirty socks, he thought to himself. Then an idea came to him.

He stormed downstairs, grabbed a can of nails and some pieces of wood and put his mind to work, doing what he did best and pushing the pain away.

BY THE TIME he was done, he had created a beautiful two-piece wall anchor to display his axe. The wood needed to be prepped and stained, but so far, he was pretty happy with how it turned out.

"Since when are you the woodworker?"

Micah spun to find Lucy sitting on a cut down tree trunk next to the fire pit. His heart raced as he took her in. She wore a light, comfortable shirt and tight navy leggings, accentuating her curves even more. Her hair was loose, and she was playing with the ends as if she was contemplating putting it back into its customary braid. A shy smile played on her lips.

"Well, I figured I had all this wood around to put to good use," he replied.

They just looked at one another, smiling until Micah couldn't take it anymore.

"Is this visit for business or pleasure?" He asked, knowing one of those answers could cleave his heart in two.

"Perhaps both," she teased as she stood up. Slowly, they walked toward one another.

Micah sighed as he took her in. There was pain and

hurt there in her eyes, but she was the one who needed to let him in. He couldn't force himself into her life again if that wasn't what she wanted or needed.

She paused a few steps away from him, her freckles on her perfect face dancing in shadows from the canopy of leaves above them.

"If you are here for a social visit, does that mean you are here to see me?" Micah asked, realizing he sounded juvenile but not giving one fuck. He was done playing games, and he just needed to know where they stood.

She nodded.

"Is this you saying goodbye to me again?" He asked, his throat bobbing at the terrifying possibility.

She shook her head no.

"Do you plan on staying for a while?" He asked, his mouth dry.

Lucy shook her head once more.

His heart fell, his mind raced, his soul shattered.

I should have known this was coming.

He closed his eyes and dropped his head, trying to think of what to say next. She placed her hand on his and he wasn't sure if it felt like ecstasy or torture.

"I don't think a while will be long enough," she whispered.

Micah's gaze darted to hers, his eyes wide in wait.

"I was thinking more along the lines of *forever*, if that was okay with you."

Before she could finish her last word, Micah pulled her to him, his lips finding hers in a wild rush of kisses.

Forever?

His hands cradled her face as he kissed every freckle, the tip of her nose, the curve of her lip, the line of her jaw down her neck.

She giggled as her hands gripped his shirt and pulled him closer to her. "Hold on," she whispered, and then they were in his room.

He pulled off her shirt and began kissing every inch of her body that he could reach. Behind her ear. The divot in her neck, then across her clavicle. He went lower, cupping her breasts and taking each pink tip between his lips, listening to her moan his name. He got halfway down her body before he paused, resting his forehead on her stomach.

Holding her close, his fingers pressed down on her soft curves. "You mean it?"

"Promise me forever, Micah." Her words were breathless and full of burning devotion.

Her hazel eyes searing into his was his complete undoing.

Bringing his lips to hers, they were a clash of lips and tongue and heated desire. She pulled his shirt over his head and he tore at her leggings, destroying them so he could feast on every bit of her flesh, and he did. Her hips bucked, his tongue wandered, and she screamed his name like he was the only thing she would ever need again.

When she was warm and ready, he kissed her once more and sank down into her, making her gasp. Their desperate pace slowed as they stared at one another, and Micah committed the moment to memory.

"I promise."

Giggling and feeding each other bits of cheese, Micah and Lucy sat head to head at the corner of the kitchen table. She pulled on a pair of leggings she had stored in his drawers months ago, and one of his clean shirts. He loved the way she looked in that shirt in his kitchen, so happy and carefree. Leaning in, he kissed her again, never wanting it to end.

"Sorry to interrupt," Alderic said from the doorway. Chuckling, he made his way across the kitchen to the fridge as Lucy pulled away, blushing. "You two lovebirds have been busy today and I've tried to leave the house to you, but an old Fae gets hungry sometimes."

"I'm sorry," Lucy said, blushing. "I never meant to keep anyone away." She stood, flattened her shirt and walked over to Alderic, smiling. "It is so great to see you again."

"Same to you, Lucy," he said sincerely. "I knew you'd be back," he said, then shot an *I told you so* look to Micah. "What took you so long?"

"It's a long story," she said sheepishly. "I wanted to say thank you, and I'm sorry." Lucy wrapped her arms around her midsection. "I know your sacrifice was immense, but I thank you for freeing Micah." Lucy placed her hand out, landing on his arm—but when her skin connected with his, she jumped back with a yelp.

"What's wrong? Are you okay?" Both Alderic and Micah ran to her, thrown by the strange outburst.

Her eyes widened, and she nodded vigorously. "Yes. Yes, I'm fine." Then she shot her gaze to Alderic, asking,

"Where are your soldiers? Call them over to the portal immediately."

"What?" Alderic asked. "I don't understand. The portal is gone, Lucy. There is nothing left there for us."

"Trust me," she said with a smile that reached ear to ear.

Alderic merely nodded and left the room, his eyes furrowed in confusion.

"What's going on, Lu?" Micah asked her.

"Come on, I'll show you," she said, pulling him out the door.

Lucy marched outside directly to the tree stump where the portal once stood. The fallen tree was still on the ground, too large to remove on his own. Micah didn't have it in him to ask the warriors to move it so soon.

A rustle of tree leaves and hurried footsteps followed in their wake, Alderic gathering his brethren as quickly as possible.

"Miss Lucy," Quillan said to her.

"First, let me say thank you to each of you," Lucy said seriously. "Your sacrifice gave my people the upper hand in the war, and if it weren't for you, I truly believe we would have lost many more Fae lives. You all fought valiantly, and you will be honored for many years to come."

Each warrior picked up their staff and slammed it to the ground in unison—their typical way of communication.

"Thank you," Quillan said, stepping forward. "But why are we gathered around the broken portal? There is nothing left for us here."

"You're right," she replied with a crooked smile. "There is nothing left here for you, but there was something left for *me*."

She picked up her right hand and held it out to them, showing her palm glowing a bright green light.

"What?" Micah asked, shocked. Then his eyes darted to the tree, and there at the middle of the fallen tree trunk, the same symbol began to glow, first green, then white.

He looked back at Lucy's hand and watched as the emerald green mist soared from her palm and wound around her body, then the felled tree.

"It's time for you to go home," Lucy said with a grateful smile.

"Can that even be possible?" One of the warriors asked.

"Anything seems to be possible with this one," Alderic said in awe.

"Will we be able to go visit them?" Micah asked her, hope lifting in his chest.

She shook her head. "I'm not sure, but I don't think so. This feels like a one-way trip." Her magic poured out of her in earnest, a green shimmering mist twirling like a tornado. "But I would hurry if I were you, because someone here is awfully excited."

Micah looked at Alderic and Quillan, words not coming to him. He wasn't ready to say goodbye—they barely had time together.

As if Alderic could read his mind, he nodded and clasped Micah on the shoulder. "I will stay if you ask me to." His voice was quiet and full of love.

Micah considered it. Having Alderic would bridge that gap between his life and his mom's. It would help him understand his magic. It would mean everything.

But this was not Alderic's home, and there were so many others who relied on him that needed him more.

"You have done so much for me. I just ask if you find a way back, come visit." Micah said, taking in a deep breath of air. "Until then... Thank you."

They met in a warm embrace and Micah knew it would be the last time he ever saw anyone from The Elderwood ever again.

"Goodbye," Alderic told him. "You have made the Lumen legacy something to be proud of."

Quillan smiled and clasped him on the shoulder. "You are a worthy man to know."

Then, the warriors and Alderic stood before the broken tree, and Lucy's magic came out in a rush, surrounding them. The immensity of its light grew and grew until it became too bright. Micah covered his eyes with his hand, trying to see, until suddenly, a flash of light so bright forced Micah onto the ground.

When he opened his eyes and stood, the men were gone and Lucy's green mist had vanished.

"What happened? Did it work?" Micah asked.

Lucy smiled and nodded. "They are gone, back to The Elderwood." Then she lifted her hand and looked down at her right palm. It was clear, no sign of the sigil anywhere. "My magic is gone, too."

Micah's smile dropped. "What do you mean? Are you okay?" He held her hand in his and looked it over, analyzing her face, trying to ensure she was safe.

"Yes," she laughed. "I don't feel it anymore inside of me, but I can tell…" she closed her eyes. "It's happy. It's home." Then she took his face in her hands and kissed him gently. "And so am I."

EPILOGUE

ANITA

Anita sat at the desk that was now hers. The entire study belonged to her now, in fact, as head of house. She sat in the same wingback chair her husband once sat in, and looked around the room. While there were things she was excited to change, like more windows for better light, and she was definitely going to burn Jasper's desk, there were other things she was excited to keep, like the oversized fireplace that really had no place in a room this size or the comfortable couches her family now sat in when they gathered.

That in of itself was the biggest change through this entire ordeal... Her family was once so separated by linear expectations. Tradition always expected the eldest sons to take over the family business. Then, the eldest daughter was promised to a formidable Fae. Over time, the youngest children would follow in the elder's footsteps... There was really no room for true conversation. There wasn't time to talk about wants and desires, and there was certainly no space for talking over fears.

But now that had all changed.

Her family sat in this room countless times, working together and listening to one another.

The only thing that could have made it perfect was if Corvus was there to see it all.

Over the past months, she liked to think he was around, watching her, sending his love from the great beyond. But more than anything, she missed talking to him. She had taken to writing him notes; it made her feel that he was closer. And every time she felt overwhelming joy or pain, or if it was just a slow, rainy day, she did just that.

Dearest Corvus,

Life has a funny way of leading you to be exactly where you are meant to be... While I wish it were you here by my side, I know that you live on through our children. I see it in their shining eyes when they are up to something devious. I see it in their smiles when they are overcome with joy. I see it in their immense power that you have shared with them, creating some of the toughest Fae to ever walk the realm.

It has been quite interesting to see the landscape of Denora change—in both our connections to one another and the way our government is run.

Lord Renfro has expanded his reach from the North to the rest of Denora, uniting us as one strong realm once again. He has also opened the gates to our business as we oversee the mining of ore from the North. We are using it to improve our weaponry as we no longer have access to The Elderwood.

Hugh and Gregory are working hard in the South. They

work closely with me and assist me here in Central Denora when I am needed in the North. Hugh and Lisette are doing wonderfully and our grandchild is a magnificent delight.

Wes has taken a liking to his new position as commander of the military. The king offered him the title of Duke Baum, but he respectfully declined, saying he'd rather be hands-on with his soldiers. Your gifts to him have helped him find who he really is and what he truly wants in this life. I have never seen him happier. Although, I suspect his additional time with that hilarious Brax has something to do with it. Can you believe she called him a moldy corn cob last week?

Tristan has been here at the house with me much more lately. He spends so much time with Henry and Simon, it really is a blessing. Tristan has taken a liking to art and has been seeing a counselor for his trauma during the war. It has been a hard road for him, and we are so proud of his progress.

Henry and Simon have found an interest in farming and have been taking their lessons straight to the fields, though their tutors seem to despise it.

To be quite frank, my favorite part of this "changed Denora" are these new roles the king has allowed Denorans. So many Fae are following their heart, and there is much joy in the kingdom.

Lucy has followed her heart, as well. You were right about her all along. She is so much more—our warrior of light.

You know, I laughed when you gave Wes your light and Lucy your shadows. Initially, I thought your magic had made a mistake. I thought the light would go to Lucy for her namesake and the shadows to Wes for his never ending brooding, but I see now that you made no errors. You gave Lucy the shadows to show her not to be afraid of the dark sides of her and light to Wesley to allow him to shine brighter than the sun.

You have always guided our family, and I know you will continue to do so. In the meantime, I will lead our family with the love and compassion you've always shared with me, with as much of your stubbornness as I can muster. Our love has always been a choice, and I would choose it again and again.

Thank you for giving our love wings to fly and to follow our family across the realms. You are always with us and will forever have my heart. There is no force that can ever separate us, and you will be mine for all time.

Your dearest love,

Anita

"Are you almost ready, Madame?" Bernard asked her from the doorway. He gave her a polite smile as he straightened his ornate uniform he only ever took out for formal occasions.

"Absolutely," Anita said. "Just one more moment."

P.S.

Lucy picked violet flowers for her wedding in remembrance of you. They are stunning, just like her. You would be so proud. I'm sorry the two of you didn't have more time together, but we feel you with us today on her wedding day. Send a butterfly her way.

And with that, Anita Baum sealed her letter to her deceased husband, straightened her magnificent flowing gown, and walked to the garden where Lucy was to marry Micah, and they would live side by side in an equal partnership because their love was a choice, too. And in those choices, they would always choose to try to understand, they would always choose to forgive, and they would always choose to love.

EPILOGUE

LUCY

Pull. *Slide. Sand.*

The same movements that once brought her peace in a time of turmoil now gave her peace in a time of complete and utter joy. She sat under the great shade of the trees in their yard as she looked back on the past decade of her life. Her father would be gone for ten years that week and it was causing many difficult memories to reappear.

Memories of her father's death.

Flashbacks to the icy male who tried to take everything away from her.

But also the reassuring comfort of the male who gave her life once again.

"Abe! Get back over here!" Micah yelled from the line of trees, chasing after a barefoot little boy in overalls.

Abe cackled as he sped away from his father, sprinting directly to the tree house Micah made him on his 3rd birthday. "You can't get me, dad!" His sweet voice called out.

Lucy laughed as Micah tripped over a branch and caught himself at the last minute. "Man, is it me or has he gotten faster?"

"It's those Fae genetics." Lucy winked at her husband, and he reached down and gave her a kiss. She would never get tired of those kisses.

"I'm trying to get his shoes on," Micah said, holding up a pair of gym shoes and a pair of socks. "I swear, hanging out with Brax and he's become more feral than ever."

"Abe!" Lucy called to him in singsong. "Mommy wants to hear another story!"

Micah gave her a look that said *that's not going to work*, but Lucy just raised her eyebrows and waited him out. She knew exactly what Abe loved most, and it was telling anyone within earshot his favorite stories.

Slowly, little footsteps made their way to Lucy, and when she turned she saw Abe, all of six years old, holding up a stick and brandishing it like a sword.

"Daddy and Uncle Wes once battled alongside a dragon, Mommy! Did you know that?"

She feigned shock. "I did not! Why don't you sit down and tell me all about it." She patted the seat next to her on the long wooden bench.

"Yeah! Auntie Brax came in on a DRAGON and then it was all like *rooooarrrr*!!! Then Daddy fought with his axe like *swing swing*, and then Uncle Wes used his flashlight powers and melted the bad guys brains!" As he told the story, Lucy casually put on his socks and laced his shoes, tying them tight.

"And I was just there to cheer them on, huh?" Lucy

said, jokingly. She always loved listening to her child, a perfect little mesh of Fae and mortal upbringing. He believed in magic, but only saw bits and pieces in their lives. Abe traveled with them back and forth between realms and they were waiting to see if his mortal or Fae genetics were stronger before they decided to follow any educational pathways.

Lucy was perfectly happy if Abe wound up with no magic. She loved him more than words could describe, and she was proud of the life she and Micah had built.

"No, Mommy," Abe said, like she was crazy. "You were there as their protector. That's what you do, Momma. You keep us all safe." He smiled and his toothless grin made her smile in return.

"And where did you hear that story?" Lucy asked, surprise filling her.

"That's the story Daddy and Uncle Wes tell me all the time!" Abe proclaimed. "You should see when we get Uncle Tristan to play, too. He always picks to play you and he grabs the blankets to make the shadows." Abe jumped off the bench and zoomed around the yard with his arms outstretched, pretending to carry a blanket over his shoulders.

She bit her bottom lip, and her eyebrows furrowed, trying to keep in the tears.

Micah sat down next to her. "I always invite you to play, you know." He nudged her shoulder with his.

"That's what you tell him?" She looked at her husband with tears brimming in her eyes.

"You can cry around me," he said, wiping away a tear that escaped. "And yes, that is how the story goes. I think

Hugh was the one to tell it first, and it's been his favorite story ever since."

"Well you don't need to exaggerate," Lucy said with a huff of laughter, wiping the wetness from her cheeks.

Micah grabbed her chin and turned it toward him slowly. "There is no exaggeration, Lu. You are our protector. You always will be." Then he kissed her softly, only to be interrupted by Abe jumping into their lap to separate them, pulling on Micah's hand and demanding more play time.

Micah gave her a quick peck and followed Abe into the forest, talking of dragons, and shadow shifters, and the most beautiful place they could ever travel.

The leaves overhead ruffled in the breeze and the sun shone brightly as they danced. Lucy closed her eyes as she listened to the joyous laughter from her son and gratitude filled her from head to toe.

Tonight is a full moon, she thought to herself with a giggle.

So many years ago she was stranded in Joterra, waiting for a full moon so she could recharge her amulet and rush back to her home. She never thought her life would be filled with so much love, all thanks to a dying amulet, a quarter moon, and the man who stole her heart.

Acknowledgments

We made it.

It has been a little over two years, and the end is finally here. We dove right into The Lumen Legacy and have experienced it all together. Well, all of us, and Lucy, of course.

We've traveled to Joterra, to fawn over our broody and reliable Micah. We've journeyed through to The Elderwood and fell in love with the most beautiful landscape. We've explored all over Denora, from the cold icy North to the exhilarating South. We've battled at the Baum estate and have come out on top. We've met Fae and mortals. We've flown on dragons and rode on shadow shifters. We've solved mysteries and gained alchemy. We've done it all... together.

It's mind blowing to know that I came up with an idea on a whim, and what was supposed to be a free short story has turned into a complete trilogy with a spin-off short story. (If you haven't read <u>The Bowyer's Baker</u> yet, check out my website!)

Through it all, I have had the most amazing support system imaginable. My husband has always cheered me on, encouraging me to follow my dreams, and helping with the logistics to make it happen. He even named the first book! Hubby, I wouldn't be where I am today without you and your love, and it means more to me than I could ever put into words.

Mom, you've been my number one proofreader and supporter, making sure I tie it all up with a nice little bow, and I appreciate all of your time and dedication you've given to me and my series over the years. Not to mention always being my biggest fan and helping me land amazing experiences because of it!

Kids. I am finally done, and yes, I will play jungle animals with you now.

To my friends... You have all pushed me to keep going and I love you for it. From my coworkers asking me why they still see me at work, or friends asking me when the next book is ready, I appreciate your constant support. You've made me feel seen throughout this entire journey, and that is a wild thing. When people introduce me to others and say "and she's an author!" it never fails to make my heart swell with pride.

My writing friends—there are so many of you! Elayna, you've never wavered on your support. Lisa, you always encourage me to keep going. Jess, you read my whole series in a week simply because I needed another set of eyes, I will NEVER forget that! Becca, I love connecting over this journey. Nisha, Daniela, Lisette, Cassandra—The list can truly go on forever, because this industry is a group of amazing individuals who lift each other up. I will forever be grateful for the amazing community I've found in all of you.

To my readers: We made it! Sometimes it felt like the finish line would never come, yet here we are. I hope you are proud of Lucy and the growth she's made. I hope you found a part of yourself somewhere in this book. We all get lost sometimes, but that doesn't mean we stop trying. I hope you see throughout all of these characters: Lucy, Micah, Wes, Anita, Brax—even Ruthani and Tristan—it is okay to be lost sometimes. In relationships, occupations, friendships, families... The world is big and scary, but you don't need to do it alone. Remember to lean on those who love you.

And when you're feeling spicy, call someone a moldy vegetable and see if that helps.

XO SA

ALSO BY S.A. HEIDEN

ABOUT THE AUTHOR

S.A. Heiden has always lived in her own fictitious world with her nose in a book. She thrives off of coffee, fantasy and wine and indulged in all three as she wrote her first of many books for you!

When she isn't writing, she's hanging with her family and her dog, Penny.

Keep an eye out for more books to come! Make sure to stay in touch on her website www.saheiden.com, join her newsletter, and follow her on Facebook, Instagram, and Goodreads!